GARDEN COTTAGE

GARDEN COTTAGE

A Mackinac Island Women's Fiction Novel

with Romance

By

Carrie Fancett Pagels

Hearts Overcoming Press

Cover Illustration by

Lorna Bricco

This book is a work of fiction. Places, names, characters and incidents are either products of the author's imagination or used fictitiously.

ISBN Number: 979-8-9928267-5-3

Hearts Overcoming Press

United States of America

Dedicated To:

Lorelai Ember Byrnes

My wonderful little energetic granddaughter who inspires me!

&

In Memory Of:

Rebecca Tellez

A beautiful soul, and a wonderful reader/reviewer who blessed me so much!

Endorsements
for the Mackinac Cottages series

Butterfly Cottage
This lovely novel, centered on three generations of women as they face a summer of change, will resonate with readers long after the last page is turned.
~~Suzanne Woods Fisher, bestselling author of *On a Summer Tide*

Lilac Cottage
Mystery, romance, inspiration plus deeply nuanced characters you will love, and enchanting Mackinac Island—Carrie Fancett Pagels delivers all these and more in her fascinating new book, "Lilac Cottage." Plan your life so you can read it straight through!
~~Kay Moser, Aspiring Women series

Tandem Cottage
In this gripping story, author Carrie Fancett Pagels brings heartfelt emotions, hope, faith, and trust. The story captured me from the beginning and I couldn't stop reading. Everyday people with unique experiences. A great read that touches the heart and soul.
~~Melissa Henderson, Award-winning author

Garden Cottage
Warmth, humor, and a touch of mystery captivate, in this novel that blends an empty nest and some slightly achy joints with the reminder that life isn't over at sixty. As Carrie Fancett Pagels takes readers on a Mackinac Island summer escape, she invites us to discover that new beginnings can be had for every age. At times hilarious, entangled, and mysterious, *Garden Cottage* was just the story I needed to read.
~~Naomi Musch, Award-winning author

Main Characters List

Paula Ecker

Terrance "Terry" Ecker, Paula's deceased husband

Jeremy Ecker, Paula's son, rising college senior

His girlfriend Mia, recent college graduate

Claire Ecker, Paula's daughter

Clark Jeffries, Jr., Claire's longtime friend

Jackie Lasley, Paula's aunt

Victor Lasley, Paula's uncle, deceased

Frank Cadotte, Jackie's fiancé

Gennaro Di Imperiali

Lucia, Gennaro's deceased wife

Leo Di Imperiali, Gennaro's son

Ivan Zudika, PA & Dr. Tiffany Morton – Claire's co-workers in Montana

Prologue

Mackinac Island, Michigan 2025

Seated outside Joann's Fudge Shop, Paula gasped as a glob of peanut butter and chocolate ice cream dripped from her cone onto her yellow cotton summer dress. "Oh no!" Horrified, she grabbed a paper napkin and dabbed at the mess—making it worse.

Her daughter, beside her, poured bottled water onto another napkin and then handed it to Paula. "Here, Mom, let me grab a Shout wipe." Claire, a nurse practitioner, unzipped and dug through her crossbody bag.

"Thanks." Paula's cheeks flushed as she swiped the second napkin on her chest. "Good thing that you're coneless today."

"Coneless is not a word, Mom."

"Should be."

A deep chuckle carried from nearby and she cringed, afraid to look up. Seated across from them, in the cavernous hallway between Joann's and the next shop, sat a handsome man with thick black wavy hair.

How embarrassing, even though he cast her a look of good humor and not a mocking one.

"You are on vacation, *cara signora*. It's all good." His strong features softened as he waved his broad hand in a half-circle. "And you're enjoying the best ice cream on this island." He raised his own cone to his full pink lips. Attired in a European-style close-fitting casual suit, maybe in his late thirties, the stranger didn't have a single spot on his own clothing. Which kind of burned her.

She resisted the urge to scowl.

"Here, Mom." Her beautiful girl opened the stain removal square and passed it to her.

"Thanks, sweetie." But she was self-conscious about dabbing at the dark brown splotch on her new dress.

Claire raised a copy of Paula's book on grief. "Actually, she's not a fudgie; she's an author who did a book signing today."

She cringed. Could this possibly get any worse? She hated having anyone call attention to her—a trait originating in her childhood tragedy. She'd loved meeting Island Bookstore customers, though, who were all very gracious, and she'd signed a lot of copies. Hopefully someone would be blessed by what she'd written.

"Oh, yes, I know." He took a bite of his cone. Again, no drips.

She hadn't seen the fellow at the signing, but that didn't mean he'd not been there. Someone that striking she'd have noticed, though. "You've read my book?" She only had the one. A full-time librarian and widow of five years, she had no desire to repeat the writing process again. But the venture had been therapeutic.

"*Sì.*" He finished his cone as a dark cloud seemed to cover his features. "*Grazie mille* for writing that book." He rose and pressed his hand to his immaculate chest. "Thanks so much." He gave an almost imperceptible bow and then turned in his glossy expensive-looking leather shoes and headed out the corridor to the street.

Claire took the two napkins and the stain-removal wipe and tossed them in the nearby trash can. "That was interesting." Her teasing tone suggested she wanted to say more.

Paula pulled her lips in. "Yeah. I wonder what his story is." Had he lost his mother and Paula reminded him of her? "It was weird having someone recognize me."

"Your picture is on the back cover, Mom." Claire sighed, like she used to do as a teenager.

"Just a headshot."

"Come on, stop worrying about the poor gorgeous man and let's go soak that dress."

So her daughter thought he was handsome, too. "I wonder if he's a tourist, like he'd accused me of being. I mean, not that it's bad to be a tourist, but . . ." Her family had lived there for generations, even though Paula resided elsewhere.

"Nope." Claire's emphatic monosyllable surprised her. "He's got that rich businessman vibe."

Regardless of his situation, Paula longed to know more about the young man's story—and why he'd been so grateful. If she ran into him again, she'd definitely ask him.

No, she wouldn't. Not after making a mess of herself in public.

Still, he'd piqued her curiosity.

Chapter One

Yorktown, Virginia, March 2026

Unwelcome realization walloped Paula as she eased her vehicle into her driveway—she was alone. Truly alone as she returned from the rehab center. An empty house greeted her, empty nest with her kids gone. Was this how the rest of her life would be—no one there to welcome her home? No one to share time with her?

Whose fault is that? The doctor had to reschedule her surgery and it had messed with plans for her son, Jeremy, to fly home during spring break to help. But this was also her own fault in being here without help and choosing to opt for rehab admission post-op. If she'd not insisted that Jeremy stay at college, then she'd have had help and could have come home.

As Paula tentatively stepped from her car with her "new" knee, the eerie *caw, caw, caw* of a crow carried from a nearby Southern pine tree. She'd leave the CR-V in the driveway for now, closer to the back door. At least the cicadas didn't buzz in the backyard—a sound she'd always hated. She leaned on her cane as she retrieved her bag from the trunk.

A text pinged to her phone and she set the bag down and checked the message. Claire asked if she'd gotten home. Paula crinkled her nose. Her daughter had sounded so relieved, the previous month, that her brother would be there for the surgery—said she'd been overwhelmed by her workload and was grateful her younger brother could help. But when she'd learned Paula had been on her own and in rehab afterwards, Claire had a fit. If Claire knew that Paula had just driven herself home from rehab, she'd have a complete meltdown. When her friend had to cancel her help, Paula skipped her morning pain meds and drove the short distance home.

She texted Claire that she was home and then grabbed her bag and closed the trunk. She slowly turned. No one sat at the greige aluminum table in the backyard nor at a chair by the smaller black picnic set on the deck.

Memories of a backyard full of teenagers, Claire's friends, for her sixteenth birthday, flooded her memory. Fifty people celebrated while she and her son, Jeremy, had watched. Then eleven years old, Jeremy had served Costco cake on pink and purple plates. Her husband, Terry, had failed to put in to get time off for the big event. That had been in 2016, four years before he'd passed. She sniffed as she opened the gate and then carefully walked three steps toward the deck.

"Welcome home!" her neighbor, Bud, called out from his side of the fence. Although in his eighties, he and his wife kept active by dancing, hiking, and traveling to see grandkids.

"Thanks! I'm glad to be back." It felt like it had been months, even though she'd only stayed a week at the rehab facility. Because she was alone—with no help. Not like Bud, who had scads of kids, grandkids, and other family in the area.

"You call us if you need anything, okay?" Bud waved goodbye.

"Will do."

Comforted by her neighbor's words, she turned the backdoor key and took a tentative step inside the hallway. Dead quiet assaulted her ears. Everyone gone. Their beloved Westie had died when Jeremy left for college three years earlier—so no joyful barks to greet her. The noise at the rehab center, a kind of ebb and flow of daily activities had been annoying—something she had no control over, but this silence portended her future.

Alone.

Oh, for heaven's sakes, this pity party needed to end.

Paula and Terry had discussed what an empty nest might be like, but she'd never imagined that she'd be the only one in the nest and that her fledglings would soar over a thousand miles away. At Christmastime, she'd gotten a little taste of the empties when Jeremy came home from the University of Michigan for only one week. He'd claimed he needed to get back to Ann Arbor and his duties there, but it felt more like he'd grown ten-foot wings and wanted to use them. At least her boy had come. Claire remained in Montana because she was a new hire and they were understaffed. That was logical, but to Paula it reminded her how Terry would always use his busy job as an excuse, including during holidays.

Lord, don't let my daughter prioritize her career over life with her future family.

Paula rolled her small suitcase into the dining room and headed to the kitchen. Now to make herself a mugful of tea, just the way she preferred.

A text sounded on her phone, again. She pulled her phone from her pocket. *Jeremy.*

> Hope you got home OK. Big news! Job here in MI for summer. Call you after class.

Her heart fell. She moved to the dining room and pulled out her highbacked chair with the sturdy arms, which she needed to help lift herself back up. *Jeremy not coming home. Claire in Montana.* But this was how life was supposed to be—the birds were supposed to fly away from the nest. Still, it hurt.

Her phone rang. The last twenty calls she'd taken had been from groups wanting her to volunteer for events. She'd had to explain she was in rehab for surgery.

Please, God, don't let it be someone wanting me to do something for them. She glanced at the number, one from the 906 area code in the Upper Peninsula, but not one in her contacts—hopefully nothing was wrong with Aunt Jackie. "Hello?"

"Oh, I'm glad you answered. Could you do me a favor and ask Jacqueline to bring me over some of those pecan rolls she makes?" The crackly unidentified voice marked the caller as a longtime smoker.

Paula cringed at the odd call. "Who is this?"

"Jacqueline's neighbor."

"My Aunt Jackie's neighbor?" She smooshed her eyes shut. "Mrs. Parsons?" She could picture the elderly woman peering out her side window at them.

"That's what I just said." *Definitely on crank mode, by that ornery tone.* "Your aunt's not answering her phone."

"You do realize I live in Virginia and not on Mackinac Island, right? Over a thousand miles away."

"Oh. Right. But I thought you could ask her." Edna Parsons voice softened—but only slightly.

Paula shook her head. "Why not go knock on her door?"

"I did!" The woman practically shrieked her response, and Paula pulled the phone away from her ear. "I hammered on that door until someone walking by yelled at me to knock it off!"

Paula frowned as she brought the phone closer. Aunt Jackie had expressed some concerns about her neighbor recently acting "weird," but this seemed well beyond odd. Did the elderly woman have dementia? But why wouldn't her aunt answer? "How long since you've seen her, Mrs. Parsons?"

"Who? Seen who?"

Oh no—had the woman already forgotten? "How long since you've laid eyes on my Aunt Jackie?"

"It's been about two weeks since she kicked me out of her backyard. I thought she'd be over that by now."

Not touching that issue. Paula exhaled a sharp breath. "I am just out of rehab for knee replacement surgery and walked in the house when you called."

"I can't believe Jacqueline has cut me off like that. I think kids call it 'ghosting' you, but she's not a ghost." She mumbled something unintelligible.

Mrs. Parsons made no inquiry as to how Paula was doing—no questions, no concern. "All right then, thanks for calling. Bye now." Paula ended the call. How had Edna Parsons even gotten her number?

She'd call Aunt Jackie later, but right now, she needed to get some ice on that knee and get it elevated in the recliner. Who knew that packing up her belongings and coming home would wear her out this easily?

God knew. And He'd have to take care of her now.

No one else was here to help.

Bozeman, Montana

Claire jabbed the security code onto the raised numbers of Ivan's house lock and then shoved open the elaborately carved modern teal door. Poor Pup was standing by the back French doors, shaking.

"I'm coming, baby! Your daddy got delayed and couldn't get home last night." She'd done a ton of favors for her friend and workmate, who was maybe, might be, kind of her secret boyfriend. But this was her favorite thing to do for Ivan, because she loved this little pup so much.

As soon as she opened the levered knob, Pup burst into the backyard and soon did his business. "Poor little buddy. Glad I could stop and help you out, boy." Her phone buzzed again. She'd had several messages from work but no time to check them. She had to get back in her car and to the hospital.

Within minutes, she'd left Ivan's home, slammed the door to her Outback and zipped out onto the highway. *More buzzes. Ack!* She'd check them when she got on the elevator. She could hardly wait to see Ivan. He had something important he wanted to ask her. Her heartbeat ticked upward. Those stolen kisses and embraces were becoming more frequent. But with him having lost his wife only a year earlier, she'd kept things in the friend zone.

Friend zone.

That's what she and Clark Jeffries had tried to do. She frowned as she increased her speed and moved into the fast lane. She and Clark were combustible. She didn't want a high-octane relationship. She'd always dreamed of having the best friend she fell in love with and married. Seeing Clark was like playing with fire. It had been that way since that first kiss. Her face flushed in remembrance.

She and Ivan had taken things slowly, very slowly. They were friends, and she helped him with Pup whenever he had to be out of town or work late. Work relationships on the neurosurgery floor were prohibited, and they'd been super careful there. Lately though, he'd begun placing an arm around her shoulders or touching her hand just a little too long, and staff had begun to notice. Dr. Shepherd, in particular, had been casting warning glances at them.

Buzz, buzz, buzz. Oh my gosh.

It was fifteen minutes after her shift began when she parked in the already-full lot. Quickly she scanned the phone—none from Mom; thank God she arrived home yesterday from rehab and today was fine. She ran across the parking lot to the hospital and hurried inside the employee entrance and down the hallway. The elevator doors opened. *No one.* Needed to check her messages.

Girl where are you??? Call me!!!

She frowned at the text from Pam, the head RN on the neurosurgery floor. She opened the text from Kylie.

OMG call me B4 u come up

Her eyes widened. What was going on? The elevator stopped on the second floor, and the pediatrics head, Dr. Cross, strode inside.

She offered him a tentative smile. "Good morning, Dr. Cross."

"Is it?" He raised his thick silvery eyebrows. "You tell me."

She bit her tongue. She didn't know the man well but that was an awfully strange thing to say. She and Cross were about the same height, and at eye level, so she faced forward and averted her gaze.

When the elevator stopped at the pediatrics floor, Cross left the elevator, calling back to her, "Guess I'll see you down here later." A smug expression flitted over his lined face.

What? Why? What did he possibly mean? Was she being moved to pediatrics? She knew Dr. Tiffany Morton was concerned about Ivan and her, but yikes, that would be drastic.

She exhaled hard and pressed the Close Door button. No point in calling anyone on her floor, because she was almost there.

As the door opened, the scent of something sweet wafted toward her. Across the hallway, as she exited the elevator, she caught a glimpse of the Neurosurgical Director's secretary, Ann, in the open doorway. When Ann locked eyes on her, Claire's smile slipped from her face at the woman's hard stare and pursed lips.

What was that? Ann usually reminded her of her mother—all efficiency, cool, calm, collected, and kind, but never cranky. *Maybe Ann is having a bad day.*

Claire turned to the left and headed toward the heavy double doors, which normally were shut tight. Today, however, they were propped open and streamers hung down. Through them, she spied many staff members clustered around the nurses' station. She pushed the streamers aside and headed in, just as Kylie, her face a mask of shock, rushed toward her.

Claire paused as her friend reached her and grasped her arms, her horrified expression a wild contrast to the background noise of laughter and cheerful conversation.

"I tried to reach you!"

"What's going on?" Claire peered around Kylie's shoulder as Ivan leaned in to kiss Dr. Morton full on the lips.

Claire's mouth dropped open and if her chin could have dropped off, it would have bounced a gazillion times on the terrazzo floor. Ivan. Her Ivan. *Not my Ivan.*

"Girl, he really led you on. Everyone's talking about it!"

Her face heated all the way down her neck. *This is worse than being dumped—okay not dumped since we were never an official twosome—because I'll be pitied on this floor.* Obviously everyone knew about her friendship with Ivan and clearly they thought she'd expected more, given all the texts from that day. Humiliation City on the Neurosurgical Ward. "When did this happen?"

"They got hitched at the conference in Boulder."

The one she was supposed to be at, but Ivan had charmed her into letting him take her slot, offering for her to take his spot at the next conference in North Carolina, closer to her home in Virginia.

And he'd gotten her to watch his dog.

What a fool I am.

"We better go over there and congratulate them." Kylie released her arms, swiveled, and motioned for Claire to follow.

A multi-tiered white cake, in wedding cake style, had about a third sliced out from it. Was she still Dr. Morton, or had she taken Ivan's name, Zudika? Tiffany wiped white frosting from her new husband's handsome face. And there was part of the problem. The PA had such stellar drop-dead good looks that he could sweep any lady off her feet.

She couldn't say Ivan took advantage of her, because their relationship hadn't been that intimate. But he'd led her on a merry chase.

But could he say the same of her?

"Hi, Claire! Come have some cake. We're celebrating Dr. Morton and Ivan's nuptials!" The charge nurse, Debbie, infused her invitation with snarky glee—for surely she'd be spreading gossip all over the floor, if not the entire hospital, once everyone went back to work.

Dr. Morton rotated toward her, away from Ivan, who averted his gaze. *Wow, he looks like he's searching for sand to put his head in.*

Tiffany raised one well-manicured finger toward Claire. "Dr. Shepherd wants to speak with you."

Their director needed to see her? She wanted to ask about what, but when Ivan lifted his head, his sheepish face spoke volumes. Were they going to fire her? *No way.*

"Sure thing."

"Now." Dr. Morton's tone could have sliced that cake in half.

The crew gathered around the station quieted.

Kylie's eyes widened.

Claire turned on her heel. No one was going to can her—they had no grounds. The pediatrician's words repeated in her mind. If they tried to send her to a different department, no way was she going. She'd worked long and hard. Dr. Cross wasn't going to be her new boss.

Tears threatened.

I will not cry. This is not my fault. Those two have likely been having a thing going for over a year, and Claire had just been Ivan's pawn in making Tiffany interested in him.

Everything shuffled and clicked and fell into place. This had been Ivan's plan all along. *Wow.*

She pushed aside the brightly colored streamers and headed to the director's office. "Hi, Ann. Dr. Morton said that Dr. Shepherd wanted to see me."

"Yes." Lips compressed, she rolled her chair back from her desk and stood, straightening her skirt. She went to the door to the director's personal office and rapped on it, then entered.

Ann didn't immediately come out.

If she resigned, Claire needed to go immediately to Human Resources. If there was any chance Dr. Shepherd intended to terminate her contract, then she needed to get a leg up. Maybe she should tell him immediately that she was quitting.

Ann emerged. "He said to go on in."

Claire nodded and then, head high, shoulders back, she strode into the director's office. "Good morning." She kept her voice bright.

To her surprise, he was smiling. Maybe she was wrong. "Good morning. Lots of excitement around here." A flicker of annoyance crossed his strong features. "And I've got a great opportunity for you."

"Coming here and working as a neurosurgical nurse, and then a nurse practitioner, has been an awesome opportunity." She'd finished her nurse practitioner certification requirements at this hospital.

He blinked and raised his salt-and-pepper eyebrows, looking a little surprised.

She wasn't giving up without some pushback. "In fact, those great ratings I've gotten from the team and my supervisors and from my patients have really convinced me that I've been in the right place."

Until now.

"I, um, that's wonderful that you feel that way." He rubbed his square chin. "But have you ever considered working with children?"

Oh no. There was no child neurosurgical program at this hospital. "Not particularly. Plus, we don't have that subspecialty here." She blinked at him and smiled, waiting for the proverbial other shoe to drop.

"Well, we do have a stellar pediatric unit here."

She sat there, hands in her lap. She was not moving to the pediatric unit. Sweat broke out under her collar and on her hands.

When she said nothing, he cleared his throat. "We're moving you to the pediatric floor."

"Why?" That single word had slipped out before she could stop it.

"Dr. Morton, as you know, is our premier neurosurgeon."

"She sure is, and Dr. Tiffany Morton has given me wonderful reviews."

He nodded and then steepled his hands in front of him. "I have to keep her happy. And I want to retain you on staff. After you take a day off, following this sudden wedding, pediatrics it is."

"No." She stood. No two weeks' notice required—they weren't keeping her on the neurosurgery floor. "I resign. Effective immediately."

"This isn't your fault, you know," his words came out low.

She raised her eyebrows. "Yes, I do." In spite, Tiffany Morton got rid of Claire and left the unit shorthanded while their director went along with it.

She spun on her heel and headed out to see the HR rep. The next phase of her career that she'd been considering was coming sooner than she'd planned.

Chapter Two

Bozeman, Montana

Did all of Claire's belongings actually fit inside only one large suitcase and an overnight bag? *Really?* Yes, really. She swiped sweat from her forehead as she zipped her cases shut. Had she even lived in this place? Claire surveyed the studio apartment one last time. This had been a fully furnished apartment intended for a visiting nurse, which she'd been when she'd first arrived. Even the linens belonged to the owner of the place. She'd texted her landlord and given her notice. She'd emptied the fridge—not much there and her landlord said to leave anything in the fridge and cupboard that hadn't expired and that she and her elderly husband would finish the rest.

The cleaning weekly fee had already been paid.

Surreal. Surreal that she'd just quit her job. Surreal that Ivan had gotten married. And surreal that she, her two bags, and her Outback would soon be on the road. That Subaru had sure come in handy out here for off-roading.

She placed her apartment keys on the kitchen counter.

What about Pup?

Guilt grabbed her tight. That dog would be left alone. Ivan was so lazy with that dog that the vets in town had listed Pup as Claire's dog. "Pup Ecker" was on his official records. Which meant that sort of, technically, he was maybe hers. She'd walked him regularly. She'd taken Pup on hiking trails. She'd brought him to every single vet appointment in the past year. She fed him. She stayed with him when Ivan was out of town—which had been a lot.

He'd not even named his pet. Claire had even gotten Pup's dog license, required in Bozeman, in her name—as was the Rabies certification. How could she abandon what was essentially her pet?

Mom sure missed their beloved Westie. Claire wouldn't be taking Pup to Virginia, where everything reminded her of Dad. Earlier, when Claire had called Mom and suggested that she could come help, she'd not shared that she'd quit. Instead, Claire had told her that she could take a break and come check on her. Mom, of course, insisted that she was going to be fine and didn't need help.

Claire brought her bags to the car, put them in the trunk, and headed out.

As she neared Ivan's place, no vehicles were in the driveway. Even though the huge home had a double garage, he'd often left his Mercedes convertible in the driveway, unless it was nighttime. There shouldn't be anyone there since he was at work. PA Ivan Zudika would no doubt be moving in with Dr. Morton, who detested any kind of animal. She'd send Pup to the kill shelter. Claire parked and headed to the front door, where she tentatively entered the keycode. What if those two were inside? She cringed, but then she opened the door.

No sound of voices.

"Pup!" she called out and the dog charged toward her.

She bent to pet him, as he wagged his tail like a crazed fan at a University of Michigan football game. "Calm down."

She needed the dog food, his water and food bowls, and his heartworm and tick pills. She'd paid for all of those anyway. "Anyone home?" She called out.

Thank God, no one responded.

She grabbed Pup's leash, his harness and all his other things, and shoved them inside one of Ivan's big garbage bags.

"Come on, Pup. We're going on an adventure." He followed her outside and leapt into the back of her car, like he'd done a hundred times before.

Soon, they were heading east. As they departed the area, she cast a longing look at all the gorgeous mountains that ringed the city. She'd miss the mountains. Miss her colleagues.

Her phone rang. Clark Jeffries was calling. *Really? Now?* He'd barely been in touch this winter, after their New Year's Eve call. She'd reached him that night while working on the floor, as a favor for Ivan, but Clark had been at a party. He'd seemed distracted. Things had been strained between them since she'd left for Montana, but this winter . . .

She took it on the car's Bluetooth speaker. "Hey there!"

"Hi. Glad I reached you." Clark sounded breathless.

"Same number since 2020." Snark infused her voice.

Road noise was all she heard, as she awaited his response.

"Yeah, I know." He sounded bummed.

No apology, no explanation, but hadn't she been swamped with work and also mooning over Ivan? "FYI, Clark, I quit my job and I'm headed east."

"What? Really? Where to?" It sounded like he was shuffling papers.

"Mackinac," she blurted out. "My great-aunt just asked me to come watch her cottage while she's in rehab." Thank God her great-aunt Jackie welcomed her there, and Claire could regroup before Mom arrived.

"Seriously?"

"Yeah, she said my timing was right in the nick of time, because she was going to get someone to house sit." In the nick of time—that's how she'd felt about Clark. He'd saved her in the nick of time when she'd been so depressed about her father's death. But then their relationship got too intense for her.

"Um," Clark coughed, "have you talked with anyone else on the island?"

She stiffened at his formal tone. "No, why?"

"I'll catch you up when you get back, eh?"

Pup barked.

"Is that a dog?"

"No, I have a new neurological disorder where I have a dog barking tic, ya big goof!" Claire laughed. Pup barked in agreement.

"When did you get a dog?"

"Um, it's a long story. I'll catch up with you when I get back."

"Sure. Let's take her running when you get here."

"Pup is a he and I'd love that."

"You would?" He didn't sound sure.

"Yes." And if she was honest, she loved him. *Period.* But she hadn't been able to deal with all that meant. She exhaled a sharp breath. "Could you do me a favor, Clark?"

"Sure. Anything."

She knew he meant it. "Gosh, I hate to ask," especially since he'd not spoken with her in months, "but I don't have reservations or anything for tonight. Any chance you could put your computer skills to good use and get me a hotel about halfway home?"

"Home?"

"Oh, I meant Mackinac." She gave a curt laugh. "It's always felt like home."

"Sure. I'll get you reservations and call you back."

"Thanks! You're the best."

"No, you're the best."

"You are."

"Nope!"

"We're both the best then."

"That doesn't make sense, Claire."

"It does for us."

"Yeah, that's kinda true."

Clark was right. They'd known each other almost all their lives. If she'd put her career on hold, if she'd not run off to Montana, then she might be Mrs. Clark Jeffries right now. But she hadn't. She'd worked so hard to find a specialty spot. But Clark hadn't agreed to try a remote work situation, either, so she wouldn't accept all the blame. Last summer, when she'd been at the Mackinac Medical Retreat on the island, they'd rekindled their romance. But neither one of them was willing to budge. The two of them, always butting heads, even when they'd been in love. She'd seen how that had worked with Mom and Dad. It hadn't. That's why Ivan had seemed so attractive, so compatible in the workplace. But that hadn't been a real friendship. Ivan's interest was transactional.

She switched on the radio, not wanting to dwell on these thoughts. She adjusted the sound higher, as a woman's voice came on.

"Psychopaths, or sociopaths, come from all walks of life. But they have a number of things in common. One element is narcissism—making sure their own needs are being met. Doesn't matter if it's at the expense of the other person. Early on in a relationship, they'll keep asking for favors that are small. If you meet those, then they'll ask for more and then even more. Masters of discerning what their prey needs, victims won't even see it coming—"

She turned the broadcast off. Claire's neck tightened. That had been Ivan. *Always needed something.* She shook off the foreboding that she'd just dodged a bullet.

Yorktown, Virginia

When Paula woke, after a good night's sleep in her own bed, her stomach growled. That made her think of Mrs. Parsons' strange call the previous day and her food request. Something wasn't right. Come to think of it, Aunt Jackie hadn't spoken with Paula since before the move to rehab. She'd not wanted to worry her aunt about the surgery but had finally shared with her about the date, and that she'd be in rehab after. But Jackie had not contacted her.

She rolled over slowly and grabbed her phone from her bedside table and then called Jackie's cellphone.

On the fourth ring, Jackie answered. "How's my favorite niece?"

What a relief that her precious aunt had answered the call. "Your only niece!"

"True. How're you doing? Are you still in rehab?" It sounded like there were people laughing in the background.

"No, I just returned home yesterday. What's my favorite aunt been up to?"

Jackie had been more like a mom. But with Jackie only twelve years older than herself, she sometimes felt like a sister.

Background sounds carrying through on Jackie's phone were strangely familiar.

Recognition clicked and turned—rehab facility noises.

"Well, I hate to tell you but I've also been in rehab."

"What?!" Her voice emerged as an almost-shriek. No wonder the sounds on the phone were familiar. "What happened? Why didn't anyone tell me?"

"You had your own recovery going on. Claire and Jeremy and I discussed it, and we agreed no sharing until you got home."

"So, my kids colluded with you?"

"Yup."

What happened?"

"Fell and broke my femur."

"Oh my gosh. That must've been painful." She stretched her left leg, her new knee complaining. That was difficult surgery but not like she'd heard about broken femurs.

"It was horrible at first."

"Oh no. I wasn't there for you. I'm so sorry."

"No worries. Jeremy came up with some pals and that Mia girl whose folks run the bike-and-scooter place on the island."

"Oh, yeah, and I know her and the place. You and I may be needing those rental scooters this summer."

Jackie laughed. "Not renting from that tightwad dad of hers but Mia is a good kid."

"Yeah." Paula had met her on the island. "Jeremy hadn't said she was at school with him."

"Ah, kids, ya never know what they're gettin' up to."

"True." Jeremy had always been super open with her. They'd had an extraordinarily close relationship—until this past year when he'd become more withdrawn.

"Don't worry about me. My friends have pulled out all the stops to help."

"Oh my gosh, I'm so relieved." She swapped the phone to her other hand.

"How about you, Paula? Have you gotten support?"

Paula's neighbors had checked on her as had several friends. "Oh yes. And you'll not believe who I got my first call from as soon as I got home—Mrs. Parsons."

Her aunt's loud exhale carried over the phone. "I think she's gone off her rocker. Her daughter is out of the country, so she can't help. The few people who tolerate her rudeness—I can't call them pals because they aren't—can't get her to go to the mainland to the doctors to get checked."

Aunt Jackie had been tolerant of her cranky neighbor for years. "Wow. She seemed fine last summer, but yesterday she was out of it."

"How did she get your number?"

"No idea." From outside Paula's window, a jet's sound carried—a common occurrence from military aircraft in Hampton Roads. Her knee spasmed, as if reminding her how she'd once parachuted from aircrafts. Most of her fellow Army Airborne vets also had knee replacements.

"Oh. Oh no." Jackie groaned.

"What?"

"I just remembered that she has a spare key to my cottage, which I gave her many years ago, for emergencies. And I have a list of numbers on my board—including yours."

"She didn't say anything about going into your place, though. I think she would've mentioned that you weren't home."

"I dunno. She's been getting pretty strange. Ends up sitting in my backyard instead of her own. Was showing up at breakfast expecting for me to cook for her—like she was one of my guests."

"Wow. That's kinda scary."

"Yup. I've got . . . a pal who will check on the house." Her tone of voice sounded strange, but maybe something was going on there. "She'll make sure the garden shed is latched, too.

"Good idea." This week, Paula intended to fertilize her own flowers, which were beginning to pop up all over since she'd been gone.

"Speaking of the cottage, Paula-baby, I have a favor to ask."

"What is it?"

"You know how you always enjoy coming up for a couple of weeks in July?"

Aunt Jackie operated a B&B on Mackinac Island, a quaint Edwardian cottage that looked like you were stepping right into the past. The place had been in Paula's family for generations, and her uncle, Jackie's husband, along with Paula, had inherited it. "Of course. You know I love coming up."

"And I always love having you."

"Thanks. But it would just be me this year if that still works out for you. What's your favor?"

"I'm not going back to the island."

"What? No way." Her aunt loved running the B&B—but suffering a thighbone fracture was serious business with a long recovery. "Not ever, or just this season?"

"Not sure. But I have . . . a friend who'll call my usual guests to inform them that we can't host them this year."

"Wow." Paula tried to wrap her mind around the cottage being off-limits to summer guests. "I bet that's a bitter pill to swallow, as Uncle Victor would have said." Victor was her mother's younger brother, and only in his early twenties when he and Jackie took Paula in to raise.

"Yup. He would have." Jackie sniffed. "We've got friends, the Parkers with their large resort, and they've held spots for my guests, and have given them a significant discount."

"That's really nice of them." The Parkers' place wasn't far from the cottage.

"I wondered if you might consider coming up for the whole summer?"

Paula rapped the fingers on her free hand on the glass-topped table. "The entire summer?" Probably out of the question with her job.

"I know you'll have physical therapy for a while."

"You, too. But I was told I'd have exercises I could do at home."

"Yup, same here, but I'm getting lots of PT during rehab. We'll both be two gimpies for now."

"But we'll get better."

"We will." Her aunt laughed. "And then we'll do something fun, like celebrate your sixtieth birthday in big style!"

She cringed. Sixty was . . . old. But with starting a family a little later in life, and this knee surgery, she felt more like ninety. "How about we celebrate it as fifty plus ten?"

"Sure thing. But listen—I hate to say this, but your husband, God rest his soul, left you and the kids in very good shape. Have you thought about early retirement?"

Every . . . single . . . day . . . since he'd died. But she hadn't wanted to tell anyone that. "They have a great replacement for me at the library. At least that's what I've heard. Someone with a new Library Science Degree who's looking for a permanent position." Like her own.

"You could come up and check on your poor old auntie. And do all the fun things you usually do—just for longer."

"Aw, guilt and a promise in one sentence! That's why you've been a great mother to me."

Jackie exhaled a sharp breath. "I wish your mom and dad—"

"It's all right. I know."

They were both silent for a moment.

"Love you, Aunt Jackie."

"You gonna come up and stay at the cottage this summer, then?"

"Let me pray about it."

"Give it to the Lord and He'll guide you."

"As long as He moves me to do what you want? Ha!" How many times had Aunt Jackie pushed Paula to do something, and she'd prayed on it and had been led to do just as had been suggested?

"You said it—not me." Jackie did air kiss sounds. "Kisses and talk with you soon."

"A whole summer on the island?" As silly as it made her librarian heart feel, Paula did the kisses back. "But you won't be there."

"But you'll have company."

Paula stiffened. "Huh?"

"Haven't they told you?"

"Told me what?" *Who? What?*

"Uh oh, gotta go, my handsome physical therapist is here. Bye!" Paula got out of bed, her left knee complaining loudly as she stood. It was still much better than it had been before surgery.

Who hadn't told Paula what? Her stomach growled loudly as she made her way down the hallway. Surprisingly, she was doing okay—not a ton of pain.

As she pulled the coffee creamer from the fridge, she froze. This one was Jeremy's favorite. And he was working on the island.

Would her sweet son get to stay with her after all? But who was "they"?

Hadn't "they" told her? The only "theys" she could imagine were Jeremy and Claire. But had she meant Jeremy and his pal, Mia? No. Her folks lived on the island so she wouldn't need a place.

She snapped her fingers. Jeremy's buddy, Leo. He must want to stay there, too.

Paula couldn't help grinning as she grabbed her mug and then pushed the start button on her coffee maker, which she'd set up the night before.

Time to start thinking about what she'd pack.

I'm heading home. At least it felt like that to Paula—Mackinac Island and the Upper Peninsula had that kind of effect on her. She'd pack her essential clothes. Her meds and health products took up their own small case.

Am I certifiably crazy? Driving over a thousand miles by herself with a knee that even within a month would have barely recovered.

At least that wasn't her right leg. The surgeon had said because it was her left leg, she could drive, even longer distances, after two weeks.

That would be one week from now. She pressed her hands to her face, which was hot. She'd have to ask the library for the summer off, but she'd already been told she could have a few months if she needed it. Was this a need or a want?

As Paula wrote out her packing list, she couldn't help thinking about that nice young man she'd run into the previous summer. Maybe she'd see him again.

Mackinac Island, April 2026

If Gennaro accomplished anything this summer, it would be to speak with Paula Ecker if he had the good fortune to run into the author again. His face flushed recalling their last meeting, even as he stepped outside into the crisp breeze blowing off the Straits of Mackinac. He'd not embarrass himself like he'd done the previous time he'd seen the woman who'd written the book that had saved his life. Still, he'd be on the watch for her. And how silly was he, stepping out of the resort's toasty atrium into the chilly weather?

"Hi, Mr. Di Imperiali!" Alyssa Parker, the wife of Carter Parker, whose family owned the resort where Gennaro worked, waved at him from the circle in front of the entrance.

"*Buongiorno*!"

Carter, a young widower, had met Alyssa when she'd worked as a nanny for him. He struggled to secure toddler, Kelsey, in her stroller. Alyssa's son, Sammy, pushed his stepfather aside and bent by the little girl, who was about the same age as Gennaro's second youngest granddaughter. Whatever the boy had said worked, because Kelsey beamed up at her stepbrother and then climbed into the stroller. Sammy proceeded to push the fancy stroller while his flummoxed parents looked on and then moved to keep up with their kids.

Gennaro grinned as the little family exited down the drive.

Kelsey turned and called out, "Bye!" in a sweet little voice.

"Bye-bye!" he called back. A twinge of remorse hit him then. If he'd remained in Rome, he could have seen most of his family members much more easily.

With a small shiver, he returned inside to the glass-enclosed atrium.

Maria Parker emerged from a nearby office. "I can't believe you've been back from Italy for over a week already."

He patted his belly, still surprised even after all these years, when his hand met a firm abdomen. "I enjoyed all my family members' cooking during my break."

The resort owner moved closer. "Did you visit your *ristorante*?"

"Ah, yes." His face heated. "My eldest girl still hasn't removed my name from the sign."

"Probably a good move—name recognition and all that."

"Right." He rubbed his chin. "But I want her own name to get well-deserved recognition of its own."

Maria placed her warm hand on his arm. "Gennaro, have you given any thought to what we asked you, in Switzerland?"

He swallowed. "You and Parker have been very kind in . . . I may say, harboring me?" He raised his eyebrows.

"You make it sound like you're a criminal."

He quirked his lips to the side. "Some foodies say it's criminal that I've gone missing."

"That's all voluntary—so not illegal."

"Sometimes I feel like I'm letting everyone down."

"All those accolades and Michelin stars!" Maria removed her hand. "But this is a guilt-free zone, like Hamp and I have always said. And Parker and Jaycie, too. I'm so glad you went to them in Switzerland after . . ."

"I am, too." He pressed a hand to his heart, feeling the buttons on his white starched shirt.

"On a better topic. Did you get to see everyone while you were in Europe?"

He laughed. "Impossible. My daughter and her family will come over to Sault Ste. Marie, Ontario, this summer, from Toronto. And my brothers are talking about making a trip to the States."

Maria shook her head. "Didn't you say they'd never do that?"

He laughed. "Sometimes they need a break from all those Di Imperiali estate chores."

"Your family certainly passed on the gardening gene to you. I'm excited to see what you grow out back this summer."

"My Italian ancestors loved their vast gardens." It was what had supported them and made the Di Imperiali name famous in their region—that and being descendants of nobility. But along with being the former chef of a world-famous restaurant in Rome, he also didn't need people knowing about his family's aristocratic history. "And of course, I had to help with planting and harvest."

"I enjoyed those peppers you grew last year—we harvested a lot in the fall. Gianni even had me put some into a casserole at Thanksgiving." She laughed.

Someone who understood him well was Gianni Franchetti. He and his wife, Kareen, who was Maria's mother-in-law, were insanely wealthy and well-connected but they tried to keep all of that under wraps to lead a normal life. Not that Gennaro was in Gianni's league, including in the older man's very tall stature, but Gianni understood the toll fame and wealth could take.

"Thank you again for those products you shipped over to us this winter." Maria's beautiful smile widened. "What a blessing that your family has all those fields full of olives and grapes and tomatoes."

"You are very welcome. I'm looking forward to growing some heritage seeds I brought back from the Di Imperiali gardens."

Sorrow crept over Maria's pretty face. "My own little gardens in Texas were a balm to my soul after my husband died. I wish I had some of our seeds left. I'd plant them."

He nodded. "There's something about seeing new life come from the soil—and the reminder of family."

"Yes. Seeing life go on, even if it's just some jalapeño pepper plants or squash."

"I won't be planting those." He shook his head.

"Before I forget, that book you shared has finally made its way to me. My husband sometimes wonders if I really have gotten over the loss of my sister and my husband." She pressed a hand to her chest. "They both died too young."

"The book on grief?" Mrs. Ecker's book had saved his life. "You know I first got it from Parker, right?"

"No. I didn't realize that." She tilted her head. "Did you want me to give it back to him?"

He waved his hands back and forth. "No. Please don't."

"No?"

His chest heated up to his jaw. "Parker gifted that to me in Switzerland after I first arrived there."

"Oh."

"Yes, and I intend to finally get it signed by the author this summer." A strange niggling of hope moved in him. Mrs. Paula Ecker's words had given him so much hope after his wife had died. He'd been surprised to find her so lovely—her book headshot didn't do her justice.

"Is she coming back to the island? I got to know her a little when she was speaking at the Lilac Cottage medical retreat. Such a sweet lady." Maria laughed. "Hamp has known Paula for a long time, but she's usually busy with family when she's here on the island at her aunt's B&B."

"Her aunt's got a place?"

"Yes, Garden Cottage—not far from here."

His face heated again. "Ah, that explains why the bookstore staff said she spends a few weeks each summer at a bed and breakfast." He'd thought she simply rented as a tourist.

"I don't want to burst your bubble, but her aunt, Jackie Lasley, is in rehab and her inn is closed." Maria flipped her palms over. "We're getting Jackie's guests here—she referred them to us."

"Maybe that wonderful author will come here anyway?" He shrugged. There was always hope.

And if she did, he wasn't going to let her slip away this time. He'd get that autograph and get to know her better—if that was even possible. Not only was her book a godsend, but his impression of her, besides her beauty, was that she was good-natured and warm.

"Hamp might know. My husband keeps track of a lot of islanders. But he's said nothing about Paula coming to take care of her aunt's place. It would be a shame for it to go empty if Jackie stays on the mainland for further treatment."

"Yes." And it would be a shame if Mrs. Ecker didn't come to Mackinac, as he'd wished.

Hope did spring eternal, though. And he wouldn't quash his hope in finally sharing with her what her words had done for him. For his family.

Maybe not this year, though.

He could wait. It had been years already. And finally, his heart was healing from the loss of his one true love.

Thanks to Paula Ecker.

E grazie a Dio. And thanks to God.

Chapter Three

Mackinac Island, Michigan, Late April

If dread, anticipation, hopefulness, and glittery love could be made into a feelings bomb, then Claire had one fully prepared for her first meeting with Clark. With a friendship lasting most of their lives, Claire right now had no idea where she stood with Clark. Yes, he'd gotten her a hotel room and yes, he'd texted her to make sure she was safe on her trip. But since she'd arrived . . . nothing. Granted it had been a long drive and she'd spent a lot of time with Aunt Jackie on the mainland at the rehab center. Today, though, she'd track Clark down and see him in person.

She petted Ivan's dog. "Sorry, Pup, I'll let you out but you can't come with me this morning."

The pooch jumped off the bed and headed to the door. When she opened it, he went down the hallway. She followed him down the stairs, spying her reflection in the beveled mirror of her aunt's antique coatrack. Strange to think generations of her family had viewed themselves in that same mirror.

She let the dog out and then donned her lined raincoat. With a slight drizzle going outside the cottage, she grabbed her mini umbrella, which was imprinted with cats and dogs dancing on a rainy background. That umbrella always made her smile. Mom had a funny sense of humor and often bought her and Jeremy gifts with a definite pun intended.

She opened the door and Pup trotted back inside. She grabbed a nearby towel and rubbed him down. "I'll see you later, Buddy."

She headed out the back door and into the garden and cringed. There was a time when Mom could have gotten down on her knees and worked in this garden, but those days were probably past. A twinge of guilt shot through her.

Time to start helping with the weeding and prep work as soon as it warmed up. This was still very early.

Claire headed out the gate, making sure she'd securely latched it. With clouds threatening overhead, she clutched her umbrella in her left hand. Maybe this wasn't such a great idea. Still, here on Mackinac Island, the weather could change in a heartbeat. There could be a looming thunder burst and then the sun would blaze and cumulous clouds would roll in. At least there were no predictions of sleet or a stray snow flurry today.

In under ten minutes, she made the turn for Clark's office. What would she say? Through large windows on the streetside, she viewed many people gathered inside the building. She could keep going and fuel up on caffeine at Lucky Bean.

A sudden breeze whipped cold rain droplets onto her, the gust encouraging her to head into Clark's office building. It was toasty in there, so she partially unzipped her coat.

Inside, a silver-haired couple spoke with her dear friend, who stood at the counter. The sweet-faced lady waved a cream envelope high. "Oh! We can't forget!"

Clark gaped, as a look of dread and shock crossed his face.

"We're so sorry we're late with this, Clark!" The man clapped his hands. "We definitely want to be there to celebrate your big day with you."

Clark raised his hands, not accepting the envelope. His dark eyes locked on hers.

The man, sporting a gray fedora, pointed at Claire. "That must be your beautiful bride-to-be, Brooke. And even wearing a Montana T-shirt, like your new location."

A sudden urge to flee hit Claire, but she stood frozen there.

Bride-to-be? Clark was still getting married? To someone named Brooke?

"I'm not . . ." Claire started.

Clark shook his head. "We're not."

The couple glanced between the two of them. "Oh. Sorry."

"I'll come back later, Clark." Claire turned on her heel, her face flushed up to her hairline. She exited the doors like someone or something was chasing her, and she ran across the street just as a cloud burst open. She'd not even had time to open her umbrella or rezip her coat, and now she stood on the corner, drenched—like someone had tossed her into a cold plunge tub. She began to laugh. A kind of crazy laugh, as the late April tourists ducked into the few open shops to keep dry. She managed to get her umbrella raised, but it was pointless. Humming "Singing in the Rain," she continued down the sidewalk to the coffee shop. She and Mom loved watching that old movie. She resisted the urge to go dance in the street, like in the movie. She knew what horses left in the road and wasn't getting anything on her new running shoes.

The rain continued pelting but at least she had a little protection. Some comfort—*not*—as her hair dripped down on her sodden "I love Bozeman Montana" imprinted T-shirt, a gift from Ivan. She was suddenly tempted to google him and see what he and Tiffany were up to. She got under the awning, closed her umbrella, and ducked inside. She hung the umbrella on a nearby stand and then got in the back of the short line.

As she waited, she checked Ivan's Instagram account. The beaming PA and the MD stood clifftop at one of Claire's fave places to hike. Both had thumbs up. She scrolled down through Ivan's Instagram. He'd never posted any pics of him with her when they'd done their hikes. Claire had taken pictures, though. Tiffany was definitely not an outdoorsy type of woman. So, he'd converted his new wife, then. *Humph.*

Claire moved up in line. She needed to sit with a nice hot latte and a muffin and try to process what had just happened back there. *No subscription to the Mackinac Island Town Crier, so I didn't read Clark's engagement announcement.* On the other hand, since the newspaper took a hiatus during the winter months, maybe the engagement had never been posted. Numbness crept into her soul. Why had no one told her? And why wouldn't he accept that RSVP envelope?

"What would you like?" The cashier, a twenty-something, dark-haired man with flashing dark eyes, waited for her answer.

She'd like a second chance. She'd like to have told Clark about how she really felt. She'd like to have not been so emotionally constipated that she couldn't deal with her desires to be more than a friend. But she stood there, soaked from head to toe and squeaked out, "Latte."

"Name?"

"Clark." *No, why did I say that?*

"We'll call your name when it's ready."

Mouth agape, she wanted to correct what she'd said. So much correction was needed in her life. In her course of action. *Too late.*

Claire turned and found almost every seat taken. She quickly headed to an open stool at the counter facing Market Street.

She sat and began to replay the tape in her head. The older gentleman thinking he was late getting their RSVP back—that must mean the wedding was . . . Was it imminent?

Dread added more chill to her sodden clothes, and she shivered. Two seats opened beside her at the counter, as two teens, dressed in matching dark hoodies, left—tossing their empty cups in the trash as they went.

Two thirtyish women with reddish hair and fair skin, maybe sisters, slid in at the counter. The taller one rolled her eyes. "I still can't believe she canceled the wedding—after everyone made their reservations and all that."

"At least we're getting a nice vacay, and now we don't have to wear bridesmaid dresses."

The redheaded strangers both laughed.

"Clark!" one of the baristas called out.

Claire stood, and the two women shot her a weird look. She retrieved her drink. But when she got to her spot, one of them had set a backpack on her seat.

"Do you mind moving that?" Claire didn't care if the woman minded, she just wanted it off her stool.

The stranger glared at her.

Bizarre, but there were lots of weirdos out in the world.

The woman snatched the backpack away and set it right beside Claire's chair, so she had to step over it to get in. This was not worth it. But there was a principle involved here, too. She took her spot again and sipped her latte. *Delicious.*

Outside, the rain had slowed to a pitter patter. Carriages filled only halfway with tourists rolled by, and dockporters who'd ducked out of the rain were now again delivering luggage to hotels.

"She looks like her, Sis." the second redhead hissed to the first.

From the corner of Claire's eye, she caught the woman beside her shaking her head.

"I'm using my refund from the bridesmaid's gown to take us out to dinner at Winchester's tonight."

"Great! Afterward we can drink away my refund over at the Mustang."

The two laughed and pretended to toast glasses.

"Clark did us a favor by bailing on our cousin."

Claire stiffened. Clark? Her Clark? Not her Clark—someone else's.

"Oh no. Wrong. I don't know where you got your info about him bailing." The woman beside Claire pulled her phone from her pocket and began punching at the screen. "Here's the reason." She held the phone toward her sister.

Claire couldn't resist stealing a glance. A gorgeous blond lumberjack of a man with bulging biceps held a trophy aloft, a dazzling flirtatious smile on his face.

"That's her new honey."

"No way."

"Yes, way. Met him at this local lumberjack show on the mainland, and he invited her out to Montana where he competes and does a bigger show."

"A lumberjack?"

"Yup."

"Not a computer geek?"

Claire's jaw must be bouncing off the floor. Couldn't be. Had to be. Was it? If so, she wanted to shout at these two that some computer geeks were even more amazing than any hunky lumberjack could be. Blinking hard, she rose, her hands shaking as she clutched her latte.

She stepped over the woman's backpack, fighting the urge to ask them if they were talking about Clark and his fiancé, Brooke.

Not doing it.

Swallowing hard, she went to the coat rack and grabbed her umbrella.

Lord, I hope they're right.

Really? She hoped that Clark had lost his chance at happiness with Brooke?

If she was going to be honest with herself, then yes.

Yes, yes, yes.

The door swung in. Clark gaped at her and then looked past her at the redheads.

Aggravation sketched a dark look over Clark's even features as he took Claire by the elbow and guided her out of the café.

That old familiar sensation raced through her. Her heartbeat accelerating. Her breaths becoming harder to make. That desire to clutch him by his Oxford shirt and pull him to her and kiss him right there.

But she wasn't afraid now. She wasn't so young she didn't understand herself and could control herself. And reining in those impulses didn't mean she had to flee from them.

"Claire. I need to tell you something."

She raised her hand and shoved it at him, in the universal gesture to stop. "Don't want to hear it."

At least not right now.

She pushed past him on the sidewalk and jogged off on the sidewalks toward home.

Home?

Since Dad had died, Yorktown didn't feel like home anymore.

But Mackinac did.

Mackinaw City, Early May

With its elegant white columns and colonial front façade, Aunt Jackie's facility looked more like a resort than a rehab center. The tasteful, if minimalist, sign out front announced this as the place—as had Paula's GPS, or she'd have missed the building altogether. She parked her car, suddenly mindful that until she'd returned home, she'd only have access to her vehicle when she left Mackinac Island. A strange sensation, but she knew that once she got on the island she'd quickly adjust to the "no cars" rule and be happily walking around town and hopefully biking around the over eight-mile perimeter. *If my knee cooperates.*

She got out of her hybrid CR-V and used her fob to lock the Honda. There'd be no trouble identifying her vehicle in the storage lot. She'd indulged herself and had the car custom painted in Lake Huron turquoise blue after her husband had died. He'd have teased her unmercifully about that choice. Not that he'd have been around enough to see it—not in the last decade of their marriage. Still, she missed him and what they'd had and all that they could have been. She'd held out hope that when he retired, he'd give all his attention to her—like he had to his hospital work. When he'd announced that he'd probably not stop working at Riverside until he dropped dead on a shift, she'd had no inkling that his prophetic words would come twenty years earlier than he'd joked about. Except to her it had been no joke. It was clear he'd intended to never actually retire. That pain had hurt worse than when she'd come down hard on a parachute landing, during her military career, and had first injured her knee.

That whirring sound in her ears reminded her that her blood pressure was getting wonky. She drew in a few deep breaths and then shook the tension from her shoulders. She had business to accomplish. First up was how and when Aunt Jackie wanted to be moved back home.

Inside the well-lit building, a gleaming tall, white, curved counter was staffed by several women attired in business wear. Name badges announced the two forty-something brunette women as Holly and Toni.

"Hi. I'm here to see my aunt, Jaqueline Lasley." Paula smiled at each woman. The one on the left, Holly, raised her eyebrows while the one on the right, Toni, laughed and said, "This must be Jackie's big day. She's already got two visitors back there."

"Toni, I think we can let Jackie have three guests. Her boyfriend was here earlier with the other two."

"Boyfriend?" Paula repeated dumbly. "News to me."

"Oopsy." Holly cringed.

"The cat's out of the bag now." Toni stood. "Can I have your driver's license please?"

Paula pulled her Virginia DMV license from her wallet and passed it to the receptionist. "How long has my aunt had a sweetie?"

The two women exchanged a quick glance, and Toni shrugged. "They're in the back in the atrium."

"Let me show you." Holly stood and adjusted her button-up shirt. The matching light blue pants had an adorable rippled edge on the bottom. Paula needed to take a little more care with her own appearance.

Right now she looked like the bedraggled traveler that she was. Old jeans, a loose U.S. Army Airborne T-shirt, and scuffed New Balance tennies composed her travel outfit. She trailed behind the younger woman down the spacious and immaculately clean hallway. Thankfully, the lighting wasn't those awful fluorescent things that she'd had at her rehab center in Virginia. Instead, there were wall sconces, recessed overhead lights, and table lamps atop console tables on each side of the wide terrazzo-floored hall.

As they neared a corridor, beyond which the hall opened into a larger room, Paula recognized voices. Her heartbeat stuttered upward. Jackie was laughing. And someone else she knew said, "I can't believe how great you're doing."

"Claire!" Paula stopped in her tracks. She knew Claire said she wanted to take a break, but it sounded like she wanted to do more of a caregiver visit with her. Paula was having none of that.

Holly continued on as Paula stood there, gaping.

"You should see how I've got both the garden shed and my little hangout in the backyard all fixed up."

Either she was having an auditory hallucination, or that definitely was her daughter's voice. She tried to wrap her mind around the situation. Claire loved her job in Montana. She did a lot of outings with a fellow medical professional there and hinted they might take a trip together.

What would Claire be doing there? And why wouldn't she have told Paula?

When Mom walked in, Claire opened her arms. "Surprise!" She should have told Mom that she was already there. Dad, if he were alive, would have had a meltdown if he'd known she'd quit. Mom wouldn't. But Claire was still trying to regroup before she shared her humiliation with her mother. "Since you said you didn't require my services, I came to help Aunt Jackie." That was the truth—but not the entire truth.

Mom blinked, like she did when she didn't know what to say.

"You look great, by the way. How are you feeling?"

"Amazingly well, considering." Mom gave Aunt Jackie a big hug and kiss, and then kissed Jeremy and her.

Claire grasped her mom's arms. "Since I'm here, I'll help you with your PT."

"Super. I've got appointments made, but I'll need to exercise at home, too." Mom hugged her and then turned toward Aunt Jackie.

"Look at you, Jackie! No wheelchair." Mom made a little rock-and-roll motion with her arms.

Her great-aunt beamed. "I just finished a physical therapy session, and these two helped me get into the chair from the walker."

"We'll help you get back up, too," Jeremy offered.

"That was so sweet of your sister to pick you up in Ann Arbor and bring you up North." Aunt Jackie rocked slightly in her chair.

Where was Jeremy's car? He'd told Claire that he'd bought one in January. When Claire had asked him, he claimed he didn't need it up there and that a pal was storing it for him. "I was happy to bring my bro up here."

Aunt Jackie beamed at Jeremy. "Great that you got that job on Mackinac Island for the summer. That's a good friend who recommended you for it."

"Yeah, Leo's a good pal." Jeremy grinned.

Leo struck Claire as a huge flirt. He'd chatted her up like she was potential date material. Maybe it was because Leo was Italian. Maybe most Italian men were like that. When she and Dad had visited Rome together, the young men were much more attentive to her than in the States—despite her father being with her.

Jeremy leaned in toward their great-aunt. "I wish you were gonna be there with us. Maybe later this summer?"

"We'll see. I really want to move back to the old farm in St. Ignace."

Mom squeezed Aunt Jackie's hand. "We'll do whatever we can to check on that, but aren't there still tenants on the mainland?"

"Until a week ago." Auntie's lips compressed into a line.

Mom gestured to Claire and Jeremy. "Where are you two staying right now?"

Jeremy shoved his hands in his pockets. "I move into the workers' quarters tomorrow."

"I've been staying in Aunt Jackie's cottage, getting it set up for your arrival. I've packed up a lot of her personal items and put them in the big storage closet."

"No worries about previous guests showing up, Paula. I've sent letters to all the folks who your beautiful daughter couldn't reach by phone or email."

"Great. That's important." Mom, despite being almost sixty, had few lines and an ivory complexion. She'd driven two days to get there, and she still looked great. Hopefully Claire got her mom's skin genes.

"It's exciting that you'll have your wonderful daughter here while she takes a nice well-deserved vacation. I'm sure glad I get to see all of you."

Mom nodded slowly. "She could use one by the sounds of things at that Montana hospital."

"Yeah," Jeremy agreed.

Guilt swatted at Claire's chest in a staccato beat. This was no short-term vacay, and little bro knew it.

"I had Claire take the garden room with that nice extra space."

The garden room overlooked the backyard and had a large first bedroom, with two full beds as you entered, and then you went through another door to enter a room with three walls of oversized screened windows. When the windows were opened, it gave the effect of sleeping on a screened porch—which it once was. This had always been Claire's favorite set of rooms, and when they were younger, she and Jeremy shared them. Thankfully, he had his own space now.

"It's always been very comfortable. Thank you."

Mom squeezed Auntie's shoulder. "Thanks for offering me your room, Jackie. I'm not sure I'm up to those stairs just yet."

Another twinge of guilt pinched Claire's conscience. She should have gone home despite Mom's resistance. Ivan's abrupt betrayal had put her brain on fried mode. And then there was that little bit about finding out about Clark's canceled marriage. That one she still couldn't wrap her mind around. Thank God he'd not shown up at Garden Cottage since she'd arrived.

"Claire can handle those old stairs just fine, and Jeremy, too." Auntie pointed at each of them.

Jeremy nodded. "Yup."

"It's going to be wonderful." Jackie grinned. "Makes me want to get better soon so I can come visit you all at the cottage. And I've got news."

Jackie raised her left hand to show Mom the engagement ring that she'd displayed for Jeremy and Claire earlier.

Mom gaped. "Wow."

"I want to have my fiancé come meet the kids. You already know him, Paula-girl."

"I do?" Mom lifted Auntie's hand and admired the ring. "Congrats on your engagement, and this person definitely has good taste in rings—and in fiancé!" She leaned in to kiss Auntie again.

"It's Frank Cadotte, the pharmacist."

Mom's jaw dropped again. "I just read about his work for the tribe and all the volunteering he does."

"His family has a long history up here at the Straits—especially in the Soo and on Mackinac Island."

"Didn't you and my mom go to school with him?" A flicker of pain skittered over Mom's face. She rarely spoke of her parents, who'd been killed by a teen driver while they were walking to their car after a homecoming game at the school where they both taught. That was in lower Michigan when Mom was really little and her biological uncle and his wife, Aunt Jackie, had raised her. Auntie Jackie had been like a grandmother to Claire and Jeremy.

"Frank and I were in the same class." Auntie fiddled with her new ring. "I always thought he was cute." She grinned.

"Apparently you still do." Mom gave Auntie a squeeze and then stood.

Mom was being so understanding. That was worse than if she'd acted like other parents and gave her the evil eye and yelled at her—scold Claire for not telling her what was going on.

It wasn't Mom's fault that Dad was gone. It had never been her fault.

This current situation was the first time she'd realized, though, that Mom was on her side no matter what. She didn't have to perform or achieve to get her approval. She may have been "a daddy's girl," but it was Mom who'd demonstrated unconditional love—just like she was doing right now.

She turned away and swiped at her eyes. She'd tell Mom everything. *Soon.*

Chapter Four

Jackie's fluttering eyelids revealed her fatigue. Paula gestured toward her kids. "Can you two help Aunt Jackie back to her room, or should we grab someone on staff?"

Claire rose and pushed back her long chocolate-brown hair. "They told us to come get them when Auntie got tired." She headed off, her stride all-business, which was her take-charge medical professional walk.

A bittersweet memory of Terrance walking that same way after he'd made PA resurfaced, bringing moisture to Paula's eyes.

"When will you be back?" Jackie patted her chair's armrest.

Paula swiped at a tear. "Next week, and I'll go over everything you want me to look at in the house."

"We can chat on the phone, too."

"Of course, like we already do."

"Just let me know when you'll be here, eh, because Frank has a habit of coming almost every day except Sunday. He's very involved with his church."

"Sure thing, but Frank can always run and get doughnuts if he gets bored with our conversations." Paula laughed. "That place next door is a powerful magnet for anyone who visits here."

"They've got great bacon doughnuts." Jeremy stood and stretched his long legs.

"Bacon, eh?" Jackie laughed. "Bring me one of those sometime."

"I'll go get it right now." Jeremy ambled off.

Paula couldn't believe her son was there and would also be on the island. She called after him, "Me, too."

He turned his shaggy head and gave her a thumbs up.

"He needs a haircut." Paula sighed.

"He said he was waiting for you to pay for the barber."

Paula raised her eyebrows. "Seriously?"

"Kids. Well, he's not a kid anymore but while they are still in school, they kind of are."

"Except me."

"You pulled a doozy. Enlisting in the Army." Jackie shook her head. "But if you hadn't, then you'd not have those two beautiful kids."

"And you'd have no grandkids," Paula blurted.

Jackie's eyes danced in mischief. "You mean great-niece and nephew?"

She shook her head. "Look, you and Uncle Victor raised me. These are your grandchildren, like I've said before."

Jackie tapped her fingers to her head. "I know that in here, but I don't want to do anything to take away from your parents' memory."

Paula raised her hands. "Okay, I'm not gonna fight with you about it."

"Victor and I did call you 'our girl' in case you didn't know."

Paula made a smart-aleck face. "And I called you two 'my parents' behind your back, so there!"

"I know. I'm pretty sure everyone in town said something to us about it at one point or another, eh?"

When she'd first arrived in St. Ignace, Paula had been almost mute. She spoke, but rarely. It wasn't until she began to see her aunt and uncle as her new parents that she'd settled down. "They had me for only eight years, and you've had me for over fifty!"

"We'll see those two again. The older I get, the more I can sense them waiting right beyond the horizon."

"Don't be getting any ideas, Jackie." Paula drew her eyebrows together. "Your fiancé, Frank, won't be happy with you leaving for heaven, and neither will I. Lord willing, not any time soon."

Claire returned with a thick-set woman with gray hair pulled back in a ponytail—her nametag "Helen" dotted with stars. Jeremy trailed in after them with two small bags held aloft and jogged over and handed one to her. He turned to offer one to Jackie.

"Jeremy, thank you. Can you please put mine in my rollator basket?"

"Sure thing."

"Are you ready, Mrs. Lasley?" The staff member looked at the walker and then turned and looked around. "Or do you want a wheelchair?"

"Walker, but I'll be stiff at first, so be patient with me." Jackie's firm voice brooked no argument.

The woman saluted. "Aye, aye, skipper." Then she situated the walker by Jackie, and she and Jeremy helped her up.

Her aunt wobbled a bit but stood, clutching the walker for dear life. "I think I sat too long."

"I'll set a timer next visit, okay?" Claire slid her arms around Jackie's waist. "You feel ready to take a step?"

Her girl looked perfectly at ease in this role. Pride swelled in Paula's heart.

Jackie nodded. "Getting old is for the birds, eh?"

Helen cupped her hand around her ear. "This little birdy heard you got a rock on my day off."

Claire moved out of the way as Helen moved closer.

Jackie frowned. "A rock?" She focused her efforts ahead of her as she used her rollator to move a step forward.

"That big diamond on your left hand." Helen pointed.

The diamond in that ring looked over a carat and was surrounded by smaller stones. Obviously, Frank meant business. Had those two dated each other before Jackie met her uncle?

Her aunt blew out a hard breath. "I am soon to be Mrs. Frank Cadotte."

"Congratulations. We gotta get you done with all your rehab so you can walk down the aisle without this old thing." Helen clapped her hands.

"We will." Claire's determined expression conveyed that she intended to help make that happen. She was so much like her dad had been.

"Afraid I'm not going to be much help." Paula shook her head. "Not with still rehabbing my own recent knee replacement."

"Mom, we'll get you walking and biking around Mackinac in no time." Jeremy called over his shoulder as the four moved away.

As they walked away, Paula's heart did a funny flip. Her summer had just gotten busier. And she was fine with that. Strange how if she'd been in Yorktown, she'd have been around more people at work when she returned, and yet she was sure she'd have felt lonely this summer. She had friends in the community and at church, too. Judy and Bobbie had been a great help. But of all the acquaintances from the numerous organizations that she volunteered for, none bothered to even text her or call, much less visit her at the rehab center. That stung.

She needed her family. Was that such a crime? A memory washed over her.

Paula clutched Uncle Victor's hand as he walked her into the church. In the front, two coffins, holding her parents' bodies, were each draped in a blanket of sweet-smelling white flowers. Her new aunt Jackie, her uncle's young wife, walked behind them. Earlier, Jackie had whispered that at least Paula didn't have to look at what had happened.

Each step seemed like a long, long time. They had to sit near the front. She'd have to stare at those boxes. Grandma and Grandpa turned to look at them, their eyes red and faces wet with tears. On the other side of the aisle, her parents' friends and fellow schoolteachers looked just as sad as Paula felt.

Her young Uncle Victor slid into the pew, and Paula followed. When they sat, Jackie wrapped her arm around her. "You're not alone. We're with you. God is with you. We're your family, and we all love you."

She'd glanced up at the pretty twenty-two-year-old, who she barely knew. Yet she loved her. She was family, too, now.

When Paula began to cry, her uncle lifted her onto his lap, and Aunt Jackie slid closer and held her hand. From her purse, Grandma pulled Squidgie, a little bear that she'd crocheted for Paula, and handed it to her. Grandpa passed a cleaned, ironed, white handkerchief to her.

She wasn't alone.

Paula shook her head slightly. She wasn't alone now, either. And she had a bacon doughnut to prove it.

She chuckled. What other new things would make her laugh this summer? And what would give her concern—like why had Claire decided to take leave?

Alarm bells in Claire's head alerted her, *Better tell Mom now about dog status at the cottage or regret it later!* She should have thought about that before she stole Ivan's dog. Rescued Pup, not stolen—she wasn't a thief but a knight in shining armor or a princess freeing him or whatever! Still, even though Aunt Jackie gave her the okay, Claire should ask permission. She touched her mom's shoulder. "I hope you won't be mad at me for what I'm gonna . . ." she caught herself, "tell you. I need a favor."

Mom swiveled and raised her eyebrows. "Like I shouldn't be mad when you failed to tell me you were vacationing up here?"

Before her words could form her response, Jeremy chortled. "Vacationing? Mom, she's here for the summer."

When Mom stopped walking, Claire did, too.

"I intended to ask you about it, but then I finally, uh . . ." she swallowed hard, "I finally got an opportunity to take some extended time off." Quitting one's job was absolutely a permanent thing, though.

"What about your apartment?"

Claire didn't want to lie.

"Isn't that just a park-n-go kind of place?" Jeremy frowned.

"You get what you pay for, and that studio wasn't much." Claire made a face of disgust.

"Why didn't you just fly here? That's a long drive in your SUV." Jeremy pretended to be steering a wheel.

She gave him the stink eye and resisted asking about his own car again. She'd shared way too much with her brother, who was obviously still as immature as she remembered. "But I got to see all that great scenery." And she had no intention of returning to Montana.

"Won't your friend miss you?" Mom began to walk again, and Claire followed suit. "The PA with the dog you've been watching?"

"About that dog." Claire chewed her lip. "Pup has come with me." Instead of to a shelter, like Tiffany would have demanded of Ivan.

At least she'd not told Jeremy the whole truth about the dog.

"What kinda dude doesn't even name his dog and calls him 'Pup' anyway?" Jeremy snorted.

"I took him with me, Mom, because I knew Ivan would neglect him once I left."

Again, Mom stopped walking, and she grabbed Claire's arm. "Please tell me you took that dog with permission."

With God's permission and conviction by the Holy Spirit. "Yes."

"Whew! So, where is he?" Mom gave her a knowing look. "That dog is already at the cottage, isn't he?"

"Ha! What're you gonna do, Mom?" Jeremy poked their mother. "You know you love dogs."

Mom sighed. "All right, but I insist he be given a proper name. I'm not calling him 'Pup,' that's for sure."

"I'll name him." Jeremy pretended to toss a basketball through a hoop. "How about Hooper?"

"No!" both Claire and Mom chimed together.

Jeremy mimed crumpling paper and flinging it over his shoulder. "Mom gets to name him because it's her rule."

"I'll be the queen of the cottage." Mom raised her hand as if pretending to wave a scepter.

As they reached the parking lot, Mom tipped her head back and laughed.

"What's so funny?"

"If your dog is anything like ours was, then he'll be king of the house."

"Yeah, he's like that. A lot of energy, too."

"Rex means king in Latin," Jeremy informed them.

Mom raised her eyebrows. "Then Rex it is."

As long as Mom let Ivan's poor dog stay with them, then Claire didn't mind her naming Ivan's pet. *No, Rex is my pet now, and he never really was a pet to that man.*

Mom flinched.

"You okay?" Claire moved closer.

Mom bent and then rubbed her knee. "I'll be better once I get in the car."

But would she be? Knee replacement surgery was a major undertaking. Mom still had lots of physical therapy ahead.

Claire hadn't been there for her mom, but she would be now.

Fully present. "Mom, I want to see your PT schedule and exercise regimen. I'm gonna help you with all that."

Paula fastened her seatbelt and started the car while Jeremy grabbed his suitcase from Claire's car. *Seriously?* Claire was going to help her with her PT exercises and get her to her appointments on the mainland? In less than a month, Paula's life had taken a seismic shift—and she was thrilled.

Her son returned shortly and hoisted his huge suitcase and backpack into the trunk and shut it. He set his computer in the rear seat and then slid into the passenger's seat and buckled up.

Claire wasn't telling them everything, Paula was certain of that fact. But she didn't want to pick Jeremy's brain—not too much, anyway. But Jeremy was acting odd, too. He seemed a lot happier than he had at Christmastime. Maybe with the surgery behind her and Jackie doing well, he was relieved.

As they left the lot and she pulled out onto the busy street, she was reminded more of driving in York County than around Northern Michigan. "This is more traffic than I expected this early in the season."

"Yeah, Sis was surprised, too."

Paula pulled out into traffic. Was Claire's supposed "vacation" or "summer break" something more?

"Good thing Sis is a traveling nurse, or I bet that hospital wouldn't let her take extended leave like that."

She opened her mouth to correct him but then clamped it shut. Obviously, Jeremy didn't realize that Claire had switched from traveling nurse to permanent staff as a nurse practitioner this past year. "I think you're right. A permanent employee wouldn't be allowed that much time." She chewed her lower lip.

"Nope."

Full-time permanent staff didn't take summers off. That was a fact. She exhaled a sharp breath. Then again—wasn't that what Paula was doing? Might be time to change the subject. "How do you feel about working on the island this summer?"

There was a long pause, accompanied only by road noise.

He exhaled a hard breath. "It's great to be seeing my best friend all summer. Working with Leo should be good."

The way he said it almost sounded like there was another best friend—not Leo. But maybe she was reading too much into it. "You've got other friends you've made on the island, too, right, from our other trips?"

"Oh, yeah," that came out faster. "It's going to be a blessing to be here and have you and Sis and them all here."

Now she was quiet. What a lovely thing for her son to say. She reached across and squeezed his arm. "I'm sorry I never got up to see you at school this year, son."

"You had a few things going on, didn't you?" He gave a curt laugh.

She placed her hand back on the wheel, as a navy F-150 cut her off. "Ugh. That's definitely like driving in Hampton Roads."

"Yup. But you'll be on the island soon. Bikes, walking, and horses."

"Speaking of bikes, Aunt Jackie said Mia came up with you. We both wonder how such a nice girl could have such grumpy parents. Ack!"

"Mia is great—no thanks to them." He rubbed his face. "She's been very active in Wesley Society with me."

"That's wonderful."

"Hey, I should give you a heads-up about my employee housing." His voice dropped almost a register. "There's rumors they don't allow islanders to stay there."

She curled her lips. "We're not islanders." But even as the words left her mouth, Paula knew that wasn't exactly true. The Lasley family had been on Mackinac for over two hundred years. Aunt Jackie had married into the family, though, but Paula hadn't lived at Garden Cottage in almost forty years.

"If they find out our family owns Garden Cottage, then I may have to move in with you."

Paula raised her eyebrows. "And that's horrible how?"

Traffic ahead of her slowed to a crawl.

"Aw, come on, Mom. I didn't say it's horrible. I just wanted to be out on my own." His grumpy voice conveyed that to perfection.

She couldn't argue with that. "You're exactly right. But the thing is," she turned toward him, "you'll be on your own very soon. And you could be far away from me."

She focused back on the road, as the truck ahead of her began to move faster.

"Yup. If I get accepted into my top doctoral program, then I'll still be here in Michigan." He reclined his seat a bit.

"Oh, wow, I didn't know they'd accept undergrad graduates into the psychology doctoral program at U of M."

"Nope. They usually don't. But Wayne State has a great clinical psych program."

"Ah, but do you want to be in Detroit?"

"Lots of great profs there."

"That's really important."

"And rent is cheaper." Again, that lower register voice, as if there was something important he wasn't telling her. But her son had his own money, having inherited it from his dad, as had Claire.

She stopped at the light. *So many cars.* "This is wild—almost like being at home and driving down Highway 17 during rush hour."

"No rush-hour car traffic on the island, though, Mom."

That made her smile. When the light changed, she drove forward.

"Hey, Mom . . ." Jeremy waggled his hands as if changing course. "On a different topic—I'm glad Claire got away from that Ivan guy for a while."

"Yeah?" She wanted to say, 'Me, too,' but bit her tongue.

"The stuff she told me about him made me think he's a sociopath."

"Really?" She frowned and made her turn onto the road that led to the interstate.

"It's a vibe I got."

"I always say trust your gut. But in fairness to her pal, neither of us has met him."

"True. But given some stuff she's said, I have no desire to meet that jerky dude."

"Someone who she believes neglected his dog and let her take him out of state isn't exactly nice-guy material."

"Exactly."

Clark had been nice-guy material. But he'd put some demands on Claire that weren't so nice—like asking her to find work on Mackinac. "Well, Ivan won't be on the island."

"Yay!" He punched the air.

"You and I will make sure your sister has a great summer, won't we?"

Jeremy's phone sounded for a text message. He didn't answer her question but read the text and then typed something back.

"Who's that, honey?" She shouldn't be so nosy. He was a young adult, after all.

"Um, it's Mia. She got a break at work."

Her boy had never had a girlfriend before. Dates, yes, but no steady girlfriend. "Have you thought about asking her out? I mean, like dating her?"

As she approached the stoplight, it turned from yellow to red.

"Do you care if I take Mia out to dinner tonight?" There was the tiniest bit of challenge in his voice, that struck her as strangely defiant.

Truth be told, she'd been waiting for this change since Terry had died. She and Jeremy had become super close once his dad passed away. On one level, she did mind a little bit not sharing dinner, but on another she was relieved that he was asserting his independence, and she'd just suggested the idea of a date. "Not as long as you get me settled at the cottage and bring me back takeout."

"All right then." Quick as a flash, he texted Mia back.

"Take her to Pink Pony and bring me back some whitefish."

His phone dinged again. "She's good with us going to dinner." The affection in his voice left absolutely no doubt how he felt about Mia.

How sweet. Her son was becoming a grown-up man. "I'm really happy for you. Maybe this will be the start of something special."

From the corner of her eye, she caught him turning to give her what looked like a hard stare. "Um, yeah, Mom, I think so."

What was that about?

Chapter Five

Mackinac Island

What a joy to be in the backyard of Garden Cottage, again, and able to start her garden. Her friend Debbie Nabozny, in St. Ignace, had instructed the garden center to send Paula some fabulous vegetable seedlings—the same kind that had worked for Deb and Dan at their Bayview home. A kind drayman had delivered them earlier that morning, and Claire had carried them to the back for her. She still had to plan out the garden, but these would be a great start. The garden gate creaked open just as Paula set her seedlings in a row on the rectangular picnic table in the backyard. She swiveled to see Edna Parsons, attired in a fluffy pale blue robe over what looked like pink bunny pajamas, and leopard print slippers.

"Mrs. Parsons?"

The woman scowled at her. "Ya know gardens are a waste of time, don'tcha?"

Paula straightened. "Is there something you need?" Neighbors didn't normally come walking into someone's backyard uninvited.

"There's grocery stores on the island." She punched at the air as if punctuating her point.

Nodding, Paula moved between the table and the neighbor. Maybe if Edna couldn't see the seedlings, then she'd get off this topic.

"You'll spend way more of your social security money on all those gardening things than it costs for Doud's to bring some good old veg to the island."

Obviously, the physical blocking technique didn't work. "My aunt Jackie said to tell you hello." She forced a smile.

"She told me you were over there harassing her at the rehab center, when I called." An odd smile crept across the woman's face.

There was no way Jackie would have said that. "You're right. I never should have gone over there and tickled her until she cried." Yes, Paula was being silly, but this woman wasn't responding to rational questions.

Edna Parsons gaped at her. "Tickled her? Why, that's just cruel!" She turned on her heel and left the yard.

Thank God for small mercies. The woman positively put her teeth on edge.

As was his custom on his walks, Gennaro's first stop was the beautiful Edwardian cottage near Arch Rock, surrounded by different flowers each season. Many years ago, his wife, Lucia, had captured the beauty, and the poignant essence of enduring charm that this place effused. She'd sat across the street and sketched the place while he'd taken dozens of pictures—until the neighbor, a cantankerous older woman whose small rambler was in disrepair, had charged across the street and shooed them off.

The Edwardian cottage had been the only house that his beloved had ever painted. When he'd asked why that specific place, she'd just shrug. When he'd learned the cottage was a B&B and they could come back and stay, Lucia had waved off his suggestion. She'd had the painting framed with a simple light wood, also unlike anything she normally created. Then she'd hung it in her walk-in closet. He'd not seen the painting again until after she'd died and his daughters were clearing out her belongings.

He'd never understood what the cottage had represented to her. But when he'd returned to the island to work for the Parkers, that cottage had been the first place he'd walked to on his morning rounds. Often, when he strolled past, the neighbor would be sitting on her porch step dressed in her robe, smoking cigarettes. Today, the older woman stood by the stoop of the Edwardian, touching a concrete angel statue that stood atop the squared stacked stairway. It looked like she was trying to lift the statue.

There'd been lights on at the house in the few weeks since he'd arrived, but he'd never seen anyone there. Today a young, dark-haired woman emerged through the front door and onto the stoop. "What are you doing?" Her loud voice carried. No matter—the older woman had no business trying to remove the ornamental figurine.

Another woman appeared, her wavy hair streaming over the shoulders of her short-sleeved blue floral dress. "Mrs. Parsons stop that at once!"

"Shut your trap, Paula!"

The lovely Mrs. Paula Ecker lived here? Why had he never seen her there before? The woman who'd saved his life lived in the cottage that his wife had spent half of their Mackinac Island visit painting?

The author was here. This time, he'd have her sign his book. He'd speak with her without running off. He'd find out her next book signing and he'd go in this time.

Was it possible his wife, Lucia, sensed something about this place?

Nonsense. Coincidence.

As he pulled his cap lower, head down, he walked on, his heartbeat stronger than it should be with such simple exertion. He headed into town. He wanted to stop at the bike-rental place to learn if they could reserve a group of bikes for when his family arrived later in the summer. He walked on past the park and then past Doud's, and a pizza place before he crossed the street to the bike-and-scooter rental.

His son Leo's close friend from the University of Michigan, Mia, was there working for her parents. Bike rentals were busy, with a fair number of tourists in line, even this early in the season. The heavyset girl bent over a tandem bike, adjusting the seat upward. The sun peeked out from behind the clouds and filtered through her long tunic top, worn over pants. Of the few times he'd seen the college girl with Leo and Jeremy in Ann Arbor, he'd never realized she was pregnant, not overweight. Jeremy was a good kid, shy, not fast with the girls like Gennaro suspected his once-shy Leo now was. Leo spoke of Mia "hanging out" with him and Jeremy a lot. What did that hanging out look like?

Was Leo the father?

He rubbed his hand over his face. This was going to be an uncomfortable conversation with his son. This wasn't something that he could send in a text nor a phone call. He'd need to meet with Leo soon.

Although tempted to call and tell Aunt Jackie about the crazy neighbor's latest stunt, Paula would just inquire about a few basic gardening questions. She settled at the kitchen island and called Jackie's cellphone.

"Good morning, my sweet Paula."

"Hi, Jackie. How are you?" Paula took a sip of her strong Columbia supreme bold brew.

"Fantastic. Frank is here and brought croissants—chocolate-filled ones."

"Yummy. I'm making scrambled eggs once I've had my caffeine."

Jackie laughed. "I bet you didn't call to ask about breakfast menus."

"Nope. I had a garden question." And a whole lot of questions about Edna, but that could wait—nothing Jackie could do right now.

"Yeah? Ask away."

"Last time you got the soil tested was . . . when?"

"Um, never."

"Never?"

"We used to have a 'recipe' if you want to call it that, for keeping the garden soil good. That lasagna method, I think."

"Okay. I read about that, and some friends do that."

"My garden guy has had to help me out the past couple of years. But he's moved to the mainland—too expensive to live on the island."

"So, you never had the soil tested? This book I have recommends doing that every few years."

"Remember, I haven't done much in the way of vegetables back there in a while, eh."

Not since her uncle died. "Right. I think I might do it."

"May have to go to the cooperative agency on the mainland."

"They have mail-order kits, too."

"Wish I could help you out, kiddo."

"This was helpful. And enjoy your croissants!"

Another female voice sounded in the background. "Will do. Oh, the nurse is here. Talk to you later."

"Bye." Next time she'd bring up about the neighbor. First, though, she'd call the police and ask what one did when neighbors tried to haul off yard ornaments and fixtures.

After breakfast, Paula headed out to the cottage's huge backyard. She'd love to fill much of it with more vegetables like Debbie had sent—despite her knee's complaints and Edna's warnings. Most of her friends back in Virginia were gardening and bragging about the payoff— with a bountiful harvest over the summer. Granted, most of those friends were retired, unlike her. But she did have this summer entirely free. One thing she remembered about her youth—vegetable gardens took some planning before any hard labor. Grandma Lasley's garden book in the parlor bookcase was well beyond Paula's capabilities. *Time to see if the bookstore has something more basic.* She ought to get her summer resident's library card soon, too, for books she didn't want or need to own.

Paula pulled her sunglasses on, adjusted her "Librarians of Virginia" fanny pack, and headed out to the Island Bookstore. As she walked up the street, two seagulls swooped down nearby onto the verdant grass and squawked at her. She chuckled. A cute pair. Were they a couple or just pals? She'd read that seagulls mated for life.

As she made her way farther into the town area, she took a right turn past Marquette Park, by Doud's Market, and went up a block and turned left by the old Frenchman's cottage. Market Street was her favorite road on the island. A ferry sounded its horn, and she grinned. After several more blocks, she turned left again to get back onto the main street.

She passed the fudge shop. Last summer she'd been in that nearby corridor when she'd run into that intriguing stranger. She remembered his dancing dark eyes and his gentle laugh when he pointed out the enjoyment of her ice cream cone—which had dripped profusely onto the bodice of her dress. The chocolate stain had never come out, nor had she forgotten that memory. She'd not run into the man again while they were on the island. She was old enough to have a son in his late thirties, which was about how old the guy had seemed. Why was she dwelling on this person anyway?

Hadn't curiosity killed the cat? Nope, she wasn't one for all those old adages. She wanted to know how her book had benefited him and what had happened in his life that had made her grief book a blessing to him. Who had he lost? Maybe his dear mother or grandparent.

When Paula reached her destination, she strode through the atrium and up to the entrance to her favorite island store. Why wouldn't it be? Books everywhere and fantastic owners and staff. *Like a home away from home.* She adored being surrounded by books. This establishment also hosted authors all summer long for book signings. Paula hadn't signed up for any this year because she'd not written anything more. She also wasn't sure that people would keep buying her grief book.

As she entered, she didn't see Tamara, the manager. Neither did she spot Mary Jane, one of the owners, nor Jill, a long-time staffer. Instead, a young woman with a perfect ivory complexion and long, curly, pale blonde hair rang customers up at the register. A twinge of disappointment coursed through her. Change was inevitable, though. There often were new staff members each season. She went to the gardening section and perused the shelves.

Embarrassed at requiring the most elementary of gardening books, she tucked it under her arm. She slipped past a petite woman with short white hair who held a garden structures book with a beautiful pergola on the cover. Paula located the Mackinac Island novels section of the store and looked for her Yorktown friend's new novel. She picked it up and flipped to the back and read the blurb, which had her smiling.

She took her books to the register. Thankfully, there was no line right now.

The cashier, whose nametag announced her as "Angela," beamed at her. Not a common name for the Gen Z twenty-something she appeared to be, but the name suited her. Perfect white teeth shone behind her pale pink smile. She was gorgeous in a way that made Paula think of Old World style. Very ethereal looking.

"This is for you to take home." The blonde handed Paula a medium-weight book with a stark dark purple cover entitled *Sociopath or Charmer—How to Spot the Differences*.

Paula cringed. "Um, not my cup of tea."

"Oh, it's for your daughter to read."

"For Claire?"

"Yes."

How had her daughter beat her to the store already? Paula needed another cup of strong Columbian coffee before she tried to figure out that answer. "Did she already pay?"

"It's taken care of." The beautiful young woman held her hands parallel to her waist and then moved them apart.

Did this gal think she was a Jedi or something? What's with the crazy hand movements? If Jeremy was with her, he'd laugh at the cashier. "Okay. Thanks." If Tam or Mary Jane were there, she'd have checked with them to make sure.

Angela rang her up.

Curious about Claire's book, Paula flipped the paperback over. The summary indicated the nonfiction book thoroughly covered the differences between someone with a charming personality versus a sociopathic manipulator. Paula raised her eyebrows.

Claire had never fully explained the reasons why she and her ongoing summer crush, Clark Jeffries, hadn't taken their relationship any further. Paula had known the young man most of his life—no way was he a manipulator. Maybe Claire wanted some closure on her odd relationship with her colleague, Ivan. That guy, from what little she'd heard, had charmed her daughter completely—until recently.

Paula had been careful not to intrude too much on her daughter's privacy. But she'd ask a few questions about why she'd ordered this book.

Her skin prickled as she recalled Claire sharing that she'd brought Ivan on all her most remote back-country hiking trails.

Holy Ghost bumps? She rubbed her arms.

Who could resist huge begging-for-a-walk puppy dog eyes like Rex's? Not Claire. And she needed a good stroll. She'd been holed up in the den all morning, reading about medicinal essences for neurological conditions. If she kept this up, she'd need eyeglasses.

"Come on, Rexie. I'll take you on a nice walk up Market Street." She could really use a caramel frappe from Lucky Bean. Now there was a place that proved how valuable scents were—and tastes.

Claire located Rex's harness. No way was she taking a chance with a simple collar and leash—not after he'd made a break for it when Mom had him in the backyard. Rex cooperated as she fastened the clips on the vest. "Good boy."

She patted the dog's soft head. Did he even miss his owner at all? She sure didn't. Whenever she thought of Ivan, she felt disgust. Not just with him, though—with herself. *What's wrong with me that I even wasted time on such a strange pseudo-relationship?*

The handsome healthcare professional was a charmer, that was for sure—unlike Clark. With Clark Jeffries, what you saw was what you got. And all those people who claimed men were not talkers—they should meet her pal. Ivan had been more a listener. He asked thoughtful questions and gave complete attention. His concerns about her dad's death had dissipated quickly, though, and he'd switched the topic to her inheritance. At the time, he'd discussed what he'd gone through with his wife's estate and how hard that was. Maybe, though, he was trying to get her to share how much she'd received. Stupidly, she'd confided that Dad's insurance policy provided her with over a million. Her face heated at the recollection. Thankfully, she'd shared nothing about Dad's estranged family, the wealthy Eckers of Connecticut, when Ivan had asked if she might be related to them.

One of her friends on the floor, Kylie, said that Ivan lost interest in Claire when he'd learned what Dr. Morton's net worth was. How he'd gotten that info, no one knew. But Tiffany Morton was married. Ivan had dangled his friendship with Claire in front of Tiffany, who was unhappy in her marriage, and who was a very competitive woman.

She clipped the heavy lead, a shorter leash, onto Rex's harness and led him outside to the front yard. Horses' hooves and the jingle of bells marked a nearby carriage in the street—the sounds of Claire's youthful summers. Rex yipped a greeting to a passenger's white fluffball miniature poodle, which earned him a disapproving glance from the owner. The woman patted her pet and pulled the dog closer on her lap as the private carriage moved on.

"Yeah, if that was my pup, I'd protect him from the vicious likes of you, too." She laughed as she picked up her pace and led Rex onto the sidewalk.

Not as many families in the street this year, in comparison to when she'd come with her family—not her entire family, because Dad would usually stay and work. He'd use the excuse that he'd keep up the yard and take care of Mom's flowers. Back then, Mom made no attempt at growing vegetables, which were now her obsession. *Okay, not an obsession, but something she seems wrapped up in more than any other hobby.* Since Dad's death, and the Pandemic and all that entailed, Mom kept randomly trying to improve her gardening skills. Strange to see her bookish mom relying on instinct for planting, fertilizing, watering, and dealing with weeds. Claire's pals who were into that kind of thing watched YouTube videos, searched through TikTok, and bought tons of gardening books. Mom's interest seemed more emotional—like she was trying to get some comfort or healing from growing veggies.

"Claire Ecker?" Clark's deep voice still sent thrills through her but now was accompanied by irritation.

He had recently been headed for the altar with Brooke, his schoolteacher fiancé, so she ignored him.

"Claire!" he yelled, again.

Two teen boys on bicycles flew past, one raising his long thin arms overhead.

He jogged across toward her. "I . . ." He bent and petted the dog's head. "Who's this big guy?" He straightened and grinned, a tentative smile tugging at his lips.

"This is Rex—formerly known only as 'Pup' by his idiot of an owner." Wow, had she just blurted that out?

His dark eyebrows raised above his eyeglasses' frame. "I bet there's a story there."

She gave a curt laugh. "There is, but it's not very interesting."

He tilted his head. She resisted the urge to pull him into a hug—not out here on the sidewalk and maybe never again. And that hurt to the point of triggering a stomachache.

She winced.

"You okay?" He took a step closer and squeezed her hand.

No. What she wanted to do was pull him close and kiss him like there was no tomorrow. But that wasn't happening.

Never, ever, again. She did feel more than a little sick.

"Maybe you better sit down, Claire." Clark grasped her hand more firmly. "Come on over to my office and I'll get you some water."

Although she resisted, Rex pulled her, too, and Claire quickly crossed the street with them, as they avoided an oncoming dray, whose nonplussed driver paid no heed to them.

When they reached Clark's computer programming business, she pulled free. "Rex can't go inside, can he?"

Clark placed a broad hand on his chest. "My office, my rules. Thus, Rex is welcome."

"Any co-workers with dog allergies?"

"Nope. And even if there were, I'd tell them to go take a break." He grinned.

Gosh, how she'd missed that smile. Pain spread across her chest. She could have found a position somewhere here at the Straits. But there had been no neurosurgical floors with openings. And she'd prioritized her career over what they had.

Why? It seemed stupid now. *Too late.*

A breeze wafted the heady fragrance of lilacs her way. "Clark, don't those smell amazing?" She stepped closer to the light purplish-pink bush. Claire lifted a branch and inhaled. *Heavenly.*

When she swiveled toward her longtime friend, his lips had parted and his brows drew together.

"I can't smell them."

She stiffened, as fear shot through her spine. This was her fellow 'super nose' guy—her companion in all her island outings searching out the most fragrant flowers and wildflowers and avoider of all things stenchy. "What?"

"Covid." His simple statement of the word made her flinch.

Covid had killed her dad. Now Covid stole her dear buddy's sense of smell? That was their initial bonding element—back when they were young kids.

"We're gonna do something about that." She clenched her fists as she locked eyes on him. "We're gonna start you on an essential oil intervention that I've been tweaking for my patients."

"Nah, it's all right."

"No, no it's not. You've lost a gift."

He shrugged.

Was he accepting this loss because it also severed their connection? "Didn't you want to smell the beautiful flowers you and your bride would have had for your wedding?" She'd imagined that one day, maybe in her early thirties, that she and Clark would have had that wedding.

That was not to be.

"When were you going to tell me about it, Clark? Email me on your honeymoon?" She huffed a dry laugh.

"I'm sorry, I should have told you." His facial features slackened as he blinked at her. "I guess you didn't read the *Town Crier* out there."

"Nope, but I did see the most recent issue. I read that your bride will be teaching out west next year. I imagine that's why you were looking into coming to Montana." She crossed her arms.

Clark took two steps closer to her and raised a clump of lilacs. "I wish I could still smell these, but all I get is a vague sensation of something floral."

"I'm sorry." She touched his arm, feeling the muscles bunch beneath his oxford shirt. "But Clark, don't try to distract me. All winter you've hinted, texted, that you were coming out west, and now I learn why!"

"I wasn't coming to Montana because of her." His dark eyes were full of that look he got that always scared her a little. That look of a promise of so much more than she could handle until she got her training behind her.

"What do you mean?" That came out louder than Claire intended, and Rex barked. She bent and petted the dog, partly so that Clark couldn't see the multitude of emotions that surely showed on her face.

"She's got her own someone waiting out there for her." Clark's tone left no doubt that a man was waiting for his ex out west.

Must be the lumberjack that the two redheaded sisters at Lucky Bean were gossiping about.

"Hey, you two." Molly, Clark's cousin, stood at the building's door, waving at them. "Good to see you, Claire!"

In that instant, Claire couldn't have appreciated Molly more. And her longtime friend, the guy she cared way too much about that it scared her, wasn't getting married. Which meant . . .

Clark leaned in. "Let me think about your offer to rehab my sniffer." He tapped the side of his nose.

Claire nudged him. "You can be my guinea pig for the new treatment regimen I'm working on."

"Guinea pig? That's a new one. We've been a lot of things to each other, but I'm not sure that was one of them."

"Nope."

A sudden breeze stirred the lilac branches again and sent a shiver through her. Was she ready for him to be anything more than a guinea pig and pal?

He'd just gotten his heart broken. Her mind was reeling at finding first that he was engaged and now that he'd been jilted.

And a good friend would be there for him.

"How long are you staying on the island, Claire?"

A grin tugged at her lips. Wait till he learned that she intended to stay here—possibly permanently.

"It depends."

Chapter Six

Paula slipped into her gardening clogs and then trod across the backyard to start her morning work. In coastal Virginia, she'd go into her backyard before ten in the morning, to avoid the sauna bath that locals there called summer. She went inside the garden shed and grabbed her gloves, trowel, and shovel. Rex investigated the small wooden structure.

A faint barking carried from the street, and the dog ceased sniffing and raced toward the gate. The gate with a faulty latch. Cringing, Paula moved after the dog as quickly as her gimpy knee allowed. "Rex! Stop!"

With a thud, the metal latch gave way and Rex bounded out onto the front lawn, Paula in pursuit. "Rex! Pup! Come back here!"

A dark-haired man stood stock-still on the sidewalk as the dog charged toward him.

"Rex, stop!"

Attired in a blue T-shirt with khaki shorts and sporting a ballcap and dark sunglasses, the man's nonchalance surprised her. He bent, and the dog let out a single "woof" as if greeting an old friend. The stranger patted Rex on his head and looked up at her. "Mrs. Paula Ecker?"

It sounded like 'Powla,' the way he said it. As charming as his pronunciation of her name was, she stiffened.

Tall, dark, and handsome with a capital "H"—but the dad vibe he was giving off threw her.

"I met you last summer after your book signing. I'm Gennaro." He removed his sunglasses, revealing startlingly warm dark eyes.

Why did her heart give a sudden lurch? Must be because of the adrenaline after chasing Rex, plus all the work she had to do in the garden today. The gorgeous stranger looked different dressed in casual wear. "Yes, it's me. I remember you—and the ice cream fiasco." She'd certainly not tell him that she'd thought often of him and what her book might mean to him.

"You were enjoying yourself." He grinned.

"I'm sorry our new addition to the household got through the rusty bolt on the gate."

"No worries." He waved his broad hand. Rex licked it. "Hmm, maybe I didn't get all the dog bone dough off my hand after all."

"Dog bone dough? As in homemade dog bones?" She made a funny face.

"Sure."

"I tried that years ago and they all went bad in a few days." Paula cringed.

"Ah, there's a secret to making them last." He tapped the side of his nose.

"Like a chef's secret?"

Gennaro's lower jaw slacked as his mouth parted in an expression that she couldn't quite read. But just as quickly, he twitched his eyebrows and smiled. "Nothing secret, just good planning."

She really needed to get back to her garden instead of flirting—no, she wasn't flirting, they were only talking. As much as she longed to ask him about her book, right now didn't seem the correct time. "Speaking of good planning, I'd better get back to starting my garden before the sun gets too high."

He cocked his head to the side. "Looks like the garden is already doing fantastic." He waved toward the front of the cottage. "I see some very old lilacs, some newer roses, and look at those tulips."

She swiveled. "The flower gardens are in great shape, thanks to my aunt." She turned to grin at him.

His dark eyes showed genuine interest. But in her garden—or something else?

Her face heated.

"Are you putting in a salad garden in the back? Herbs?"

"Well, that and more."

From somewhere in the distance, a ferry horn sounded. How wonderful to hear that sound again—like part of a soundtrack that grounded her to this place.

"Well, I better get this rascal back." When Paula moved toward Rex, he circled behind the man's long tanned legs and hid.

"Come on now, Rex."

Gennaro pulled something from his pocket. "This weirdly shaped dog biscuit was a reject from my efforts this morning. Is it okay to give it to him?"

"Not until he gets his little doggy self in the backyard again." Paula scowled at the troublesome dog, who Claire had claimed was a perfectly well-behaved pet.

"Mom!"

She turned. Claire, holding a leash, jogged across the lawn toward them. Her beautiful girl.

Instead of running toward his new owner, Rex sat, tail wagging, gazing up at Gennaro.

"Oh no, it's the 'puppy eyes' thing." Paula shook her head.

"Who can resist puppy eyes, right?" The kind man bent and patted the dog's head again but didn't offer him the treat. "No cookie till Mama says so."

Paula pointed to Claire, as she reached them. "This is my daughter, Claire, and I guess she's this dog's mama, as you put it."

"Nice to meet you, Claire." He pressed his hand to his chest. "Your beautiful mother's book saved me in my worst hour." His face flushed.

"Glad to hear that." Claire glanced between the two of them before settling her gaze on Rex, who scooted behind their visitor.

"It's true, Mrs. Ecker. Your words helped me so many nights. The way you wrote about everything—the grief." His lips compressed hard and then relaxed. "I still can't believe you are here on Mackinac Island."

"Well, she is. All summer long." Claire's slightly mocking tone, infused with something else, made Paula's eyes widen.

Gennaro dropped his hand. "This is true?" His slight Italian accent was back in full force.

"Yes," Claire responded, not even allowing Paula to answer. "Mom is even putting in a garden so she can feed my brother and me since we're freeloaders here this summer."

The handsome man frowned. "You would never go hungry on my watch—but I think this is a jest."

"Yes." Paula crossed her arms. "She's kidding."

"Not joking about my bro and me being here, though."

"It's beautiful to have family here. I'm grateful my son is here."

"A son?" A muscle in Claire's pretty face jumped. She was plotting; Paula recognized that look. "How old is he?"

"Twenty-one."

Claire's pert nose crinkled ever so slightly. "My brother is twenty-one, too."

"Yes? Are you and he going to help grow the vegetables?"

Her daughter shrugged.

Gennaro cocked his head. "May I see this garden?"

"It's just a plan at this point." And one Paula really needed to get back to, instead of watching her daughter plot how to put her and this younger guy together.

Quick as a flash, Claire bent, grabbed the collar and hooked Rex's leash.

"May I offer your dog a treat now?" He pulled the homemade dog bone from his pocket and handed it to Claire, who sniffed the treat.

"Oh, wow, this smells great. Is that pumpkin, oat bran, coconut oil, maybe some basil, ginger, and I think oregano."

"Sì, sì, *molto bene*! Very good."

Paula headed away from them, toward the back garden, waving the two on. "Come on, stop sniffing stuff, daughter."

"I'm in the process of creating medicinal therapeutic oil sets for neurological conditions."

Surprised, Paula stopped and turned. "That's wonderful, Claire. You've been talking about this for a few years now." At one point, she'd indicated she'd use her inheritance from her dad to fund that project, but she'd not mentioned it lately.

"Very exciting." Gennaro patted Claire's shoulder in a paternal fashion, reminding her of how Terry used to do just that.

But Terry had thought it was odd for Claire and her pal Clark to have such wonderful olfactory senses. He'd poked fun of them for it, the few times he'd visited the island with the family. Lost in her own memories, Paula continued on to the back garden. Terry's idea of a family vacation was to impulsively take one of the kids on a huge, and expensive, jaunt—the swankier the better. Often, he'd not even included her in the invitation, much less the plans. Claire, who'd volunteered at her dad's hospital, had shared that Terry bragged about his destination vacations to his work pals.

That sad, twisted, broken feeling she'd had when her husband died now zoomed back, making her chest tighten. He'd never even told her that he'd received a large inheritance from his family—or that he'd come from a wealthy family in Connecticut, some siblings still alive. That came out after he'd died, during Covid. During the worst possible time. A pandemic that shifted everything.

Only Gennaro followed her into the yard. Not Claire nor her pup. "Your daughter said she needed an IV of caffeine."

"Oh my."

"I don't think she'll find that in your kitchen."

Paula nodded. "I'm guessing three cups of coffee will have to suffice."

"I used to live on very strong coffee." Gennaro rubbed the side of his face. "In Italy." The way he spoke, his constrained speech, felt like he was holding back. She was just getting to know this man, though, and she'd not push.

Paula gestured around the backyard. "This is our garden-to-be."

He raised his eyebrows. "I did not realize there were backyards this deep on the island. Not this close to downtown."

"This place has been in our family for over a hundred fifty years. Most families in town had huge gardens then."

"Makes sense, living on an island. Hard to get supplies in."

"My aunt and uncle maintained eight raised vegetable gardens as well as large in-ground plots around the border." But when Uncle Victor had passed, Jackie had cut way back. "All went fallow last year. She couldn't manage them."

"All this back here is a private family area—not for your aunt's B&B guests?"

"Yes."

"What a blessing."

And what a blessing was Paula Ecker, who'd practically saved his life. Her words, her inspiration, the scriptural encouragements in her grief book had brought Gennaro back from the depths. He could never thank her enough. Even his children wanted to meet her. And now, there she was.

Since he'd seen her after her book signing the previous year, he'd kept hoping he'd run into her on the island—but he hadn't. What a coward he'd been. He couldn't make himself go to the signing, for fear he'd gush at her and she'd assume he was a madman or a stalker, or both. Instead, he'd surprisingly met Paula and Claire, who he'd thought was her assistant, outside of Joann's Fudge, where all three of them were eating ice cream. At first, he'd not recognized her. The book headshot of her was quite awful. The real Paula Ecker had beautiful glowing skin, large expressive eyes, a very feminine form, and didn't wear the large spectacles like in the photo. And her musical voice—like that of an angel.

The backyard, though—not so heavenly.

Piles of dirt and massive bags of sanitized cow manure and mulch were strewn alongside raised gardens. The in-ground garden areas sprouted weeds. A tall wooden fence surrounded the massive area. "This is huge."

She laughed, that tinkling magical sound. "Which makes this a rather daunting project. But thankfully, my son and daughter can help me."

"I love gardening." Considering that his family owned some of the most fruitful farms in all of Italy, if not Europe, that was a bit of an understatement.

"Do you?"

"Absolutely. My family has . . . many gardens. It is a tradition where I live." And centuries of living from the land as well as providing for all the other families in the area. Olive groves for olive oil, fruit trees, tomatoes, and many grape varieties for wine.

"Well, I got a little overambitious, because all I really want is fresh produce for my family and guests." She swiveled toward him. "I forgot to ask you. What brings you here again this summer?"

"I live here during the season. I work for the Parker family's resort as one of their managers." Not as the premier chef of his own Michelin-starred restaurant in Rome. "And as I said, I sometimes am allowed to make some little treats in the kitchen."

"You're here year-round?"

"I was here most of this year until the winter. So I returned to Italy then."

She nodded slowly. "Well, it's quite a surprise to see you again. But I never did get that stain out." She shrugged.

"I am delighted to run into you again."

A smile tugged at her lips. "Would you like to hear what I'm putting in? Only other gardeners care about that stuff."

He pointed to the shadier areas. "I'm guessing your salad greens are going in over there."

"Yes, they'll appreciate a little shade. And I've got cherry tomatoes and Roma tomatoes here and two types of cucumbers next to them."

"For pickling and for eating?"

"Yes. I'm going to try some brined pickles and some refrigerator pickles."

"I can still remember the smell of my grandmother's kitchen filled with the scents of vinegar and dill as she canned her pickles."

"It's funny, I have trouble picturing an Italian grandmother doing that. I don't know why." Her cheeks turned pink.

"Ah, well, since she was a Michigander, of Czechoslovakian descent, try picturing that." He rubbed his cheek. "My maternal grandparents lived downstate."

"Oh."

His daughter would say he was 'oversharing' so he'd better cut this short. "Mrs. Ecker, it was a delight to see you, but I probably should be heading back to start my shift at the resort." He gave a quick bow.

"I enjoyed chatting with you, Gennaro. I love making new friends—especially young people like you, who are so full of energy."

Young? Full of energy? He blinked a few times. Some of that energy was her doing. And if he hadn't lost his wife and fought so hard to get healthy for his children, he'd certainly look his age and then some. Not knowing what to say, he offered a tight smile and departed.

He chuckled to himself.

I can be a new young friend—living in an old grandpa's body.

Claire and Rex hit Market Street just as three carriages full of tourists were heading past. Compared to the previous few years, during early season, these weren't packed too tightly. Not many kids, but then again, most weren't out of school yet. Plus, there were simply fewer kids in general.

That was sad. Friends her age weren't starting families. Between the high costs of childcare, the grandparents being far away or all the grandparents working, her pals could see they'd not get support for starting with kiddoes. And getting started with a career was important. At the hospital, almost all the workers having kids were in their thirties. Some older.

"Claire? Claire Ecker?" A female voice called out, and she turned.

Nearby stood beautiful dark-haired Rachel Welling, who owned Lilac Cottage and ran the medical retreat with her husband, Jack.

As Claire moved closer, she caught the dark circles under Rachel's eyes. Her messy dark bun looked like it might unclip itself at any moment.

"Hey, Rachel, how are you doing?"

"Hi there! Enjoying baby mama life for sure!"

Claire widened her eyes and blinked. "I couldn't believe it when I heard you were still going to run the medical retreat this summer even with a new baby."

"Ha! I have an almost retired oncologist and teacher who will do the heavy lifting, thank God. And Jack will pitch in when he's not changing diapers!"

"Oh, wow, so Dr. Austin and his wife Tamara are able to do that? That's great."

"Yes, but we're kinda scrambling to fill in some spots."

Claire cringed inwardly but hoped it didn't show on her face. She wasn't cool with being an afterthought. But that was pride speaking, and she knew it. "Hey, I can help but on one condition."

Rachel did a funny thing with her mouth. "Like what?"

"I don't have to wear my formal gown that I won last year!"

Chuckling, the other woman waved one hand downward. "Nah, Clark will want you to wear that when he's done groveling."

Eyebrows raising, Claire forced the air back in her lungs and gave a curt laugh. First she was an afterthought, and now she was a meany making everyone's fave computer nerd grovel?

Rex barked and began to pull, clearly done waiting for his walk to resume. *Saved by the dog.* "Oh, I gotta run, but email me, okay?"

"Um, sure." From the look on Rachel's face, maybe she understood she'd been kinda rude.

Inspiration hit her. "Listen, if I can speak about using scents, essential oil combinations, for treatment of secondary loss of olfactory sense, then I'm in."

"Yeah?" The color came back into the new mom's face. "I love that idea."

"Clark is my first patient." Claire waved. "See ya later."

Chapter Seven

Why did some mornings start out so . . . stinky? Paula jerked her head away from the plastic container she'd just opened. "Whew, who knew this fish emulsion could smell so bad?" It didn't help that the morning fog was thicker than usual and clung to the air for dear life, holding the fishy odor within.

The dog barked. He knew this stuff reeked—why hadn't she remembered? Uncle Victor used to make buckets of this stuff, and they'd both slop the cans as they marched out into the big garden. She turned and carefully measured out two tablespoons of the fishy liquid into the gallon bucket of water and then capped the emulsion container. Uncle Victor had done this initial prep work away from her. Still, those buckets had smelled bad—but she'd not minded, since she got to spend extra time with him in the fields. She could almost feel her rubber boots on her then-smallish feet. He'd give her a stick of Doublemint gum and tell her to chew it. Maybe that was to offset the smell.

Jeremy jogged into the backyard and stopped at the garden bench. He pointed at the bottle. "That's the stuff that's supposed to make everything grow better?" He pinched his nostrils. "That's stenchy, Mom."

"The things we gardeners do for the love of plants." She raised her interlaced hands, palms down, under her chin for a fake pose.

"Aw, Mom, don't do that." He made a facial expression of disgust. "Teenage girls doing selfies do that."

"What? Not old moms with young sons?"

He shook his head. "I'm getting breakfast, after I get that smell out of my nose."

"Make me something, too."

"Only if you wash the heck out of your hands when you come in." He frowned. "Spray room deodorizer on your clothes, too."

"Wow, you're such a, a, um—"

"Non-gardener?"

"Yeah, that." She hoisted the gallon of mixture off the table and headed for the vegetables planted at the back. If she started there, then the hardest part would be done first. 'Worst first', as her Grief Works support counselor had said.

She hummed as she poured out the emulsion mix onto the ground around the plants. *I'm happy. This makes me happy.* She'd not felt this good in a long time. Those slow walks in the morning with Rex, tending to this garden, having both of her children there, and making a new friend, had all combined to form a mixture of joyful living. She inhaled a deep breath, and then wished she hadn't, because the fishy stuff made her gag.

"You all right?" The deep male voice, carrying from behind her, startled Paula and she dropped the quarter-full plastic gallon container on the ground. Luckily, it didn't tip.

"Gennaro, what're you doing here?" That wasn't a warm welcome.

His handsome features tugged in regret.

"Sorry, you just startled me." She pressed her hand to her T-shirted chest, which proclaimed her a US Army Veteran in bold yellow letters on a fading navy background.

"I bring you something good." Gennaro lifted a basketful of lumpy somethings covered with a napkin. "Genuine artisanal breakfast bread from my region of Italy."

She blinked at him. "You had it flown in?"

He laughed. "I made it."

Her cheeks heated in embarrassment. Maybe she'd better watch it with her pain meds for her knee. *Flown in from Italy—sheesh!* "Oh, super. Thanks!"

He lifted the napkin. "See how nice they turned out?"

Rex bounded toward them and Paula had to prevent him from jumping up on her new friend. "Rex, stop." Luckily, the dog obeyed.

She smiled up at Gennaro. "Bring that in for Jeremy, please. He'll be thrilled."

"And you?" He tilted his head.

"I'll devour it. Maybe not till I've purged the fish emulsion from my hands, though." Paula cringed.

Again, he gave a deep laugh. "That's the smell of love. Love of the gardens. Nurturing the growth of what will produce and bring pleasure to the gardener."

He got it. He understood. Warmth spread through her, and she nodded. "You run in, and I'll be there in a minute."

Rex slumped down beside Gennaro, as if he still expected a treat.

"Can I help you after?"

She blinked at him. "I'm doing more emulsion."

"Sì. Yes, I understand. That smell brings me wonderful memories of my home, of our farm."

"You can tell me all about it over breakfast."

She'd love to talk with him about his family's farm. But this new friendship with this youngish man was veering into too much . . . more. Too much more of things in common, of interests, of seeing things the same way. This was what she'd always wanted with Terrance but hadn't had in their marriage. One reason they'd never had a real garden was because Terry was never home. And even if he had been, he had no interest in doing anything outside in the yard. Really, though, did Terry have much interest in anything she'd done?

"Are you all right?" Concern shone on his handsome face. "You look like you left me for a moment. I do that a lot, too—especially when I think of my wife."

She nodded. "Yes, I was thinking of my husband, Terry." This new friend understood her pain. Maybe that was enough. She'd made room in her heart for her pals in the grief group in Hampton. In fact, one of them was the brother of Gennaro's boss at the Parkers' Resort. She'd seen Carter Parker around the island and he'd greeted her warmly. The three of them shared something big. Something hard. Something life changing.

But they all had to go on. But were her kids ready, too?

Claire bounced down the back stairs as if she didn't have a care in the world. But her daughter was hiding something.

If she'd learned anything from her older mom friends about parenting adult kids, it had been to give them a ton of space.

And she'd tried, she'd really tried.

Rex ran to Claire and she patted his head. She waved at Mom's new pal. "Good morning, Gennaro."

"Buongiorno."

"Hey, I'm going for a walk, Mom. But I was going to leave Rex."

Mom gave her a thumbs-up. "No problem."

There had been a time when her mother would have asked where she was going. Had Claire gotten so old that she was past that? Mom had said it was good manners, not micromanagement, to explain one's whereabouts.

"Gonna grab a latte at Lucky Bean." That was only a tiny fib. She would go to the café, as an add-on, but not till after she'd seen Clark. She gestured to Mom and Gennaro. "Can I get you two something?"

Mom looked to Gennaro. "We've got Michigan cherry strong brewed this morning here."

The man patted his flat belly, almost as if he was expecting to pat a dad belly, which he didn't have. He blushed. "Sounds wonderful."

Rex circled Claire's legs. "Sorry, buddy. Should be back in an hour."

"See ya." Mom bent over her new tomato seedlings as Gennaro gave Claire a little wave and also examined the newest installment in the raised garden.

At least Mom wasn't as bad as the neighbor was about her plants. Mrs. Parsons had no one at her house anymore and actually named her flowers as if they were people. *Weird.*

Rex looked up with adoring eyes and wagged his tail as if to ask, 'Who are you to talk about people treating non-humans as babies?' *Yup, mea culpa.*

Claire bent and gave his head another good rub. "You're such a good baby, aren't you?"

"Rex, come help Grandma over here." Mom clapped her hands and Rex bounded over.

Seriously? Mom was calling herself Grandma and Rex was acting like she, not Claire, was his alpha? *Ugh.*

But who was she to point the finger? She'd just asked Mom to watch the dog for her, and Mom had taken care of Rex's feeding and had even washed him once since she'd been there.

Claire had let her mom, who was recovering from knee replacement, jump right into her caregiver role instead of vice versa.

That had to stop.

"Hey, Mom, I'm making dinner again tonight. In fact, while you're still in recovery mode, I'm gonna be chef around here."

"My own chef?" Mom glanced between her and Gennaro.

Was it her imagination, or was Gennaro gaping at her? But just as quickly, he blinked and his face assumed its normal look.

Whatever was going on there wasn't her business.

"I'm off to Doud's to get my ingredients for something wonderful for dinner." Something that wasn't a salad, a tuna sandwich, or a frozen dinner eaten by herself after work.

And for some crazy reason, that made tears well in her eyes.

It wasn't crazy to want home, to want family, and to enjoy the blessing of being with loved ones.

She marched out of the yard with purpose, just as the mist that clung to the island in morning lifted and sunlight cracked through.

Gennaro shoved a hand across his aching head as he reached his suite at the Parkers' resort. Would Leo stop by, like Gennaro had asked his son to do? What if his handsome boy had stolen his buddy's girlfriend and gotten her pregnant? How would Paula Ecker feel if this was the case? "I'm getting too old for this," Gennaro announced to no one, as he opened the heavy locked door and entered.

He kicked off his Italian leather loafers, a luxury item he'd never given up, even years after leaving his restaurants. The Parkers supplied him with a beautiful suite with an exit to a tiny garden—normally reserved for their extended family members. He'd been there long enough to replace the plain sofa with a cream-colored leather recliner. After a long day on his feet, he wanted to lie back.

In the minute kitchenette, where he'd soon feed his boy, he'd stocked the mini-fridge with his favorite cheeses and meats—goudas and hard parmesans and all manner of Italian delicacies and his favorite vegetables and fruit. All these years and he still had to be mindful of everything that went in his mouth. He grabbed a seltzer water from the fridge and then went to the couch and flopped down.

The staccato sound of hands pounding out a rhythm announced his son. Gennaro rose and went to the door and opened it. No matter what he might learn about Leo, this was still his baby. He pulled him in for a tight hug. "How's my boy?"

Leo patted his back hard. "I'm great. I'm as handsome as my dad, and all the girls at work love me." Leo stepped back and waggled his dark eyebrows. He'd gotten his mother's and Gennaro's best features and had even been asked to do a little modeling work—which his son had scoffed at.

"Come on in. That's something we need to talk about." He closed the door and locked it.

"Dad, I'm just joking."

"You better be." He didn't want to launch right into this, but he'd been stewing over Mia since he'd seen her. "Grab a drink and come sit down."

"Sure, but you seem upset. What gives?"

He sniffed. "I saw your university pal, Mia, the other day."

Leo swiveled from the mini fridge. "Ohhh." His features formed an expression of concern, but not of guilt.

"Yeah, ohhh, what's up with that?" He raised his eyebrows.

Leo shook his head as he opened the fridge door. “That’s not really my place to say.”

“You’re not the father?”

“What?” Leo’s outrage showed even more as he spun on his heel. “I can’t believe you think I’d steal my buddy’s girlfriend—or mess around with her. That’s so uncool. I’m not that kind of guy.”

Gennaro raised his palms. “Good, I didn’t think so.”

“It’s the quiet ones that surprise you.” Leo brought his Coke to the couch and the two of them sat down. “Jeremy hasn’t worked up the nerve to tell his mom yet.”

Why wouldn’t he tell dear Paula? “No?”

“Don’t you tell her!”

He waved his hands like a referee. “Okay, okay, but this is something his mother should know—so she can help them.”

“Yeah, those two have both been freaked out by the whole thing. The pastor at the Wesley Foundation has been counseling them, but it’s like neither one of them was registering mentally,” Leo tapped the side of his head, “that there’s a baby that’s coming at some point.”

“Sometime in the not-too-distant future, by the looks of her belly.”

Leo rolled his eyes upward. “She’s been wearing those caftan-type things, baggy shirts and stuff to hide it.”

“Do her parents know?”

“They didn’t even come to her graduation because the island had opened up for business and they didn’t want to miss out on making money.”

Sadness pulsed through him. “Poor girl.”

“They’re jerks.”

Gennaro nodded his agreement. “But she’s graduated from university already? That’s good.”

“Business major. She told her folks she has a position in the fall but she’d be here this summer.”

“What’s her position? Mom?” He shook his head.

“Yup. By then she’ll have a baby to deal with.”

He playfully slapped at him. “Don’t say it like that. They’re a blessing.”

“Pretty sure her folks won’t consider a baby a blessing, especially since it’ll be a shock to them.”

“Sorry to hear that. We should keep her and that baby in prayer.”

“Jeremy, too.” He crinkled his nose. “He’s been better since he’s been working on the wedding plans.”

“Probably should tell his mama before he’s saying his vows with the baby mama.” Paula shouldn’t be left in the dark.

"Yeah. Now, let's see what you're making me for dinner, Chef Gennaro." Leo laughed.

As much as his son protested keeping Gennaro's identity secret, he seemed to take special pleasure in it, at times, and liked to tweak him.

Soon, he'd prepared lemon butter linguine with shrimp and parmesan and fresh basil, served with a salad with light balsamic vinaigrette. He and Leo had eaten many of these little dinners together over the years since Lucia's death.

He watched as his boy ate, clearly savoring the meal. For the first time, it really struck him what it would mean when Leo graduated. Even though all his other children were gone and had their own families, it would especially hurt when his last one left.

Gennaro had been running. He'd been hiding—even from his own family.

"That was amazing, but I'd better get back to my lodgings." Leo made a silly face that he'd done since early childhood, when he was trying to get out of something. "Um, I hate to bail on you tomorrow for your doctor visit, but this really hot waitress from work agreed to go hiking through the middle of the island with me tomorrow."

"It's all right. Much better than learning you're about to be a daddy. I'm not ready for my baby to be a father."

"Not yet. I want to be thirty before that happens."

They exchanged hugs again, and then his son was gone. Wasn't this what he wanted, though? To be away from all the extended family in the village where he'd grown up? In Rome, where he'd built his career?

Things were shifting again. He could feel it in his spirit. Change was coming again. His back spasmed, reminding him of one of the reasons for transitioning from being a chef. At least he had good physicians here.

Going to a doctor appointment wasn't what Gennaro wanted for his one day off. But what was he to do? Tomorrow he'd drive to Petoskey for a checkup and hopefully keep all his kids from bugging him for at least another six months. As much as he'd wanted some space from his large intrusive family, he didn't want to drive by himself. At least Leo was going to enjoy the day.

Once, he'd been young and pursuing love. Then he'd found his wife. The love of his life. There'd never be anyone like her. He'd never remarry.

Why then, did Paula Ecker interest him so much?

She'd surprised him, that was why. The sober-looking librarian on the back cover of her grief book was surprisingly upbeat, with a wry sense of humor. Her words had saved him. Her sincere, heartfelt, serious, and faith-filled book had kept his heart beating even after he'd given up.

And she seemed to like him. *Not Chef Gennaro.* Not the celebrity everyone wanted to get close to. And not a sappy *romantismo* kind of thing. For goodness sake, the poor woman believed him to be much younger than herself. Which he wasn't. But he'd keep letting her think that.

It was humorous. He could run with that. He had no interest in finding a new love, nor did she. But with the quick friendship they'd formed, he'd need to keep things in check.

He should ask her to go with him to Petoskey. She could see her *zia* there, right? Her aunt Jackie.

He called Paula's number.

"Hello?"

He hesitated. "Mrs. Ecker, is that you?" He sounded like an idiot.

She laughed. "Who were you calling?"

"*Mi scusi*, of course it is you."

"I give you permission to call me Paula, my young friend, as I've said before."

He stifled a chuckle. "That is very kind of you, Paula, especially since your . . . young friend wonders if you'd like to go see your aunt tomorrow. I've got an appointment in Petoskey and I could drop you off."

He'd love to get to know her better. Time alone together in the car might help.

That made him smile.

Paula hit the reheat button on the microwave for her coffee as she considered Gennaro's request and narrowed her eyes. *Might not be a good idea to go with him.* "Yes," the word flew out of her mouth. "I mean, I think that's a day that works for my aunt. She gets a lot of visitors, and I had intended to go tomorrow, or the next day, anyway."

"Wonderful."

Had she really agreed to this?

"I will drive."

"Um, my sweet young man, when one asks someone to accompany them, that person asking normally does do the driving."

He chortled. "Haha!"

She loved his deep laugh. It reminded her a little of Terry's. There'd been a time when she and her husband had shared so much joy. "Touché!"

Jeremy brought his plate, which he'd cleaned off to the last bite, to the sink. "Is that Mr. Gennaro?" There was an edge in his voice, almost as if he was worried about something.

"Yes."

"Yes, touché, or 'yes' to your son? I think I hear him."

Paula grinned.

Jeremy ran his tongue over his upper lip, like he did when he was nervous. "Tell Mr. Gennaro that I said hi."

"I heard that." Gennaro's rich voice held warmth and good humor. "Tell Jeremy I said to sleep like a baby tonight."

Paula blinked. Was this some kind of strange Italian message? She'd gauge Jeremy's reaction when she told him.

Jeremy moved closer and grabbed the phone. "Sorry Leo can't go with you to your doctor appointment tomorrow but he finally got Emily to agree to go out with him."

Paula sighed and reached for the phone. Doctor appointment? It wasn't her place to ask, so she wouldn't.

"Oh? He was just there?" Jeremy turned his back to her. "Did Leo tell you himself?"

She tapped her toe while Jeremy paced the kitchen with her phone, continuing to listen to Gennaro, but saying nothing.

Finally, he returned to face her, his cheeks red.

What was that about?

"All right, giving the phone back to Mom now." Jeremy shoved the phone at her, his lips clamped tightly. Then he gave a curt wave and mouthed, "Going for a run," and left.

She lifted the phone to her ear. "Gosh, whatever you said to my son has got him all worked up."

There was a long pause. "He gave me permission to take you to Petoskey tomorrow."

"Permission?" She'd never gotten a chance to give him Gennaro's cryptic message about sleeping like a baby. Regardless, she had the next day to see if she could figure out what that was all about.

Chapter Eight

The following morning, Paula met Gennaro at the ferry docks, which were cloaked in mist. If it wasn't a trip for his medical appointment and for her to see her aunt, it would have almost felt romantic. What was she thinking? They were only pals.

"Good morning, Paula." He kissed both her cheeks, and she blinked at him

"Good morning." She touched her cheek. "Do Italians normally do that?"

He blushed. "Yes, for people we care about."

Not sure what to say, she nodded, and the two of them walked toward the pier.

When they got to the loading dock, the ticket checker pointed them to the Mackinaw City line, which was sparse. At the front were several families and behind them a few older couples with beat-up looking luggage.

Gennaro touched her shoulder. "Did you give Jeremy my message?" His handsome face, this close, did have more lines than she expected, and fatherly concern showed there.

She shrugged. "Didn't get the chance. He went to bed early. He headed out too early this morning."

His features relaxed, and she swore she heard him exhale a sigh.

She was just about to ask him what it was about, when a loud ferry horn from nearby left her ears ringing. Farther down the dock, one of the elderly women had tripped over her suitcase. Her silver-haired male companion tried to assist her up, without success.

"I'll go help." Gennaro hurried off toward them in a slow jog.

She watched, concerned about the other passengers but also observing that Gennaro couldn't run very fast. What was the doctor seeing him for today? In a moment, though, he'd helped the lady to standing. Their companions huddled around the woman who'd fallen.

Paula moved toward them as Gennaro rejoined her. "Is she okay?"

"Seems all right. Lost her footing when that horn sounded."

They boarded the ferry and soon were seated side by side on the long bench seat, the hum of the engines soothing.

"So quiet, isn't it?" Gennaro gestured around to the nearly empty lower deck of the ferry.

"It's nice. But sometimes things can be too quiet." She pressed her back against the vinyl upholstered bench. "I still can't believe both my children are here with me."

He turned toward her, his dark eyes serious. "Were you lonely with them gone?"

She tugged at her lightweight pink hoody's zipper. "I was expecting a totally different summer."

"How so?"

Paula glanced out the window at the water spraying up as the ferry cut through the deep blue water in the Straits of Mackinac. "I'd probably get sucked into doing tons of volunteer work—after my regular library job, for one thing."

"Why?" His full lips pulled downward. "Why do all that?"

"Ah." She flipped her hands over, palms upward, in her lap. "That's the way I've kept busy since losing my husband. I never thought I'd be a widow."

He nodded.

"I signed up for any and everything that would get me out the house—mainly when Jeremy went to college. Before that I helped with anything he needed. But he was only home a couple of years after his dad passed."

"So, once Jeremy was at university, then you became everyone's favorite volunteer?"

"Basically."

"I don't think you talk of this in your book." He stroked his strong jawline. "Of filling up time doing for others."

She flipped her hands back over. "No. I mainly talked about people pursuing activities that gave them fulfillment."

"And you thought those things would?"

"Yes."

Several rows ahead of them, a family occupied their entire row. A silver-haired man wrapped his arm around a woman with wavy short white hair, a teen with a Detroit Tigers cap worn backwards and a slightly younger youth were next, and at the end a couple who looked to be in their early forties leaned their heads together. Family was what mattered.

She swiveled to face him.

"But those volunteer activities didn't satisfy you?" He made a fist and circled it over his heart.

She leaned her head to the side. "I hate to admit it, but no."

"It's okay."

"Maybe I was fooling myself at first, that all that stuff at church and in the community and extra activities for my job would forge new connections and keep me from feeling lonely."

"But?" He shifted on the bench and locked gazes on her.

"I felt even more alone. Until Jeremy came home. Then it felt like normal life was back."

"You seem very close with your son. I have a great relationship with Leo, but he's gone kind of girl crazy in college."

She swiveled to look at him. "Gosh, Jeremy says Leo is very outgoing but he doesn't have a girlfriend."

Gennaro's handsome features tugged in surprise. "He's always talking about his busy social life and all the girls he takes out. He has had me a little worried."

"Really? Jeremy says lots of girls are interested in Leo, but he mostly stays to himself. He and Leo and some other friends go together in groups to different events."

"Why would my son act like he's a lady's man?"

"I don't know. What does Leo say about Jeremy?" She probably shouldn't have asked.

A strange look, like a fleeting deer in the spotlight, crossed his face. He placed his palms back on his legs. "Same thing. Friends going out together." He shrugged.

"I don't know why Leo would fabricate a busy social life. I think either Jeremy is fibbing or Leo is, but maybe at that age, who knows what they're thinking." She gave her head a tight shake.

A couple rows ahead of them, a toddler with huge dark eyes suddenly stood and turned to look at them. The boy waved. Gennaro waved back. "Seems just yesterday my boy was that age. And now he's a young man making his own decisions."

"Mine, too." Paula waved at the little fellow, too. "But things are really changing this past year. It's like I'm losing him."

"But he and my son are both graduating next year."

"Yes."

"And then they will likely be gone. We will both have to create what is our new normal for life."

She bit her lip and nodded, blinking back a rebellious tear.

Gennaro needed to soothe Paula. "I'm going to tell you a little truth about me, Paula." Not the whole truth—he was remaining incognito celebrity chef until someone outed him. And he sure wasn't going to tell her Jeremy's truth—he needed to tell his mom himself.

"What's that?" The pretty woman swiped at her eyes. If not for the stray tear, Paula would have looked adorable like that—clearly trying to be stoic.

"The opposite thing happened for me after my wife died." He patted his chest. "Definitely no volunteering. I wanted to be left alone. Not lonely. But away from lots of people—like all those people I had on my old job." Strange to think of it now as a job—then it had been a calling and an obsession.

"Oh?"

"I have a very large family in Italy. Many brothers and a sister." He quirked his mouth to the side. No need to disclose that he had five children and seven grandchildren. "Most of them lived near our villa."

"And these brothers and sister—were they intrusive?"

"Ha!" He tipped his head back and laughed. "Look in any dictionary and you will see their pictures by that word."

She smiled. "Oh my. So, what did they do after your wife died?"

"The love of my life, God rest her soul." Heat spread across his face, and he lowered his head.

She patted his hand in a motherly way. "I'm so sorry. She must have been a wonderful young woman."

He raised his head. His beautiful wife with her gray-streaked waves would have coughed at that description. She'd embraced becoming a *nonna* despite not spending much time with their grandkids. "Yes, she was very special. And my family didn't give me a minute's peace in getting over her. They all wanted to help in their own way."

The ferry cut through some choppy waves, and spray hit their window.

"I did get to spend some time with my maternal grandmother, before she passed away. She was a wonderful woman."

"That must have been hard after losing your wife."

"She was ready for heaven, she said." He needed to change this sad topic. "My mother was a U of M graduate like my son will be."

"Wow, really?"

"Scouts' honor." He did the American Boy Scouts sign. "I learned that one from my cousins. When we used to come to the states and visit at the farm, they'd teach me things. They helped me play baseball, and I taught them good soccer techniques."

The ferry hit a large wave, and Paula grabbed the end of her seat. "Oh my!"

Gennaro dug his feet into the floor and pushed his back against the seat. "Feels like it's getting a little rough."

"We're not guaranteed smooth sailing out here—just like in life. But we can trust God to provide."

"You're right." He pointed to the docks up ahead. "And I'm betting we can get safely to our port in just a few minutes. And I have a surprise for you in Mackinaw City."

Mackinaw City

What was Gennaro's surprise? Paula's nerves thrummed as they disembarked the ferry and rode the jostling tram to a parking lot.

"From here, we have to walk a couple of blocks to my car storage site."

"No problem. Is that your surprise?" She raised her eyebrows as he pointed toward the sidewalk.

"No, but it's related to it."

"Hmm. Please don't tell me you have a motorcycle."

He waved his hands back and forth in a crisscross motion. "No motorbikes for *nonno*."

She frowned, not sure she understood him. No motorcycle for now, 'no no' to motorbikes, or . . . what was Italian for grandfather? Surely not. But did Leo have a child tucked away somewhere?

A pair of seagulls swooped into the road, just as a van full of kids drove past.

"I love all these trees here." Gennaro pointed at the tall mature oaks on either side of the street. "We have different trees in Italy, where I grew up."

On the next block, he pointed to a fenced area, with parked cars and also a line of eight-deep garage bays.

"I've never noticed this place before."

"You probably never had need of it."

"No. We've always left our vehicles in storage in St. Ignace. And we know the people there."

At the gate, Gennaro passed the attendant a card.

The balding heavyset young man sported a thick blond moustache that reminded Paula of a caterpillar. "Come on through. I'll call for the bay to be opened."

The gate opened and she tried not to giggle as they stepped inside, and the gate was electronically closed again.

Security guards paced within the fenced perimeter.

"Wait right here and I will drive it back to you." Gennaro slow jogged off toward the back of the lot. He looked a little stiff today. Maybe that was from standing on his feet all day as one of the Parkers' managers. Maybe that was why he was going to the doctor today, to have his knees checked. She hadn't wanted to pry but maybe she'd ask him on the drive to Petoskey. She certainly wasn't the only person in the world with knee troubles and it was nothing to be ashamed of having.

Her phone pinged and she checked her messages. Claire wanted to know if she'd be home for dinner.

Would she? 'Probably,' she texted back.

'Will text you later.' She pushed the send function on the message.

Another message, this one from Aunt Jackie, said that her boyfriend Frank would also be there at the rehab center, but she looked forward to seeing her.

Hopefully that wouldn't be awkward. The pharmacist had always been very nice to Paula when she'd lived in St. Ignace. And if he made Jackie happy, then that was what mattered.

"That's a beaut, isn't it?" The gate guy did two thumbs up.

If she wasn't mistaken, the car that was pulling up was a classic Lamborghini. Someone had some very deep pockets. Terry had once pined for one but had given up the notion when he'd learned they'd cost the family several hundred thousand dollars.

The driver's window lowered.

Gennaro grinned at her like a schoolboy.

She shook her head. "I'm not getting in that."

"Come on. I won't race it. It's not a Formula One car!"

"Gennaro!" She wagged a finger at him. "Whose is this?"

"It's mine. It's old. Can't you see?" He gestured to include the entire car.

She lowered one eyebrow and frowned. "Other than the bird poo on it, this looks pretty pristine."

"The seagulls have covered up all the scratches then. Get in!"

She got in the passenger's side. "If this is old, then I'm ancient."

"I didn't say that—you did. Don't insult my friend."

She fastened her seatbelt. "Please don't show off in this."

He revved the motor and chuckled when she gave him her best librarian frown. He raised his hands from the leather-wrapped wheel. "I promise I won't speed. But I had to have this brought over from Italy because my son wants it when he graduates college. I promised it to him."

Maybe an old Lamborghini wasn't as valuable as a newer one. Paula had no idea. Jeremy would have googled the cost if he was with them. But he wasn't. And she sure wasn't going to pull out her phone to look.

Soon, they were on I-75.

"Thank you for driving within the limit. This does run very smoothly." She patted the dashboard.

"I'm going to miss taking this out on the road."

"You're still young. Why not get another sports car, maybe newer?"

"You are right, dear Paula—since I'm still in my youth." Gennaro suppressed a laugh as he tugged at his Polo shirt collar. "I may get a red convertible Mustang." That vehicle had been what he'd promised himself once he became a grandparent. Now he was that many times over and yet he'd not given up on this car, because it reminded him of Lucia. She'd loved this Lamborghini.

"I always wanted a convertible." She did a little drumbeat on the console. "A red Mustang one with white leather interior."

"Sì, sì. Like you cannot own when there are kids in the car."

"Yup."

"That's what I want, too. With white leather." He cast a quick glance at her.

"I had a car like that in my childhood. I loved that thing. My Barbie doll drove all over our house in that car."

He grinned, imagining little Paula doing so.

"But when . . ." Paula's voice hitched. "After my folks died, we never found it again."

Impulsively, he placed his hand on hers. "I'm so sorry. You said in your book they died tragically." As had his wife.

"Yes. After a homecoming game at the school where they taught."

"I know about homecoming. An American tradition at high schools in the fall. What happened?"

"A teenager, who'd been drinking, ran into them as they were walking to our car."

"Oh no." He squeezed her hand gently and then placed his hand back on the steering wheel. "Were you there, too?"

"No. Thank God I didn't have to witness that—like some of their friends did. I was a little too overactive and young to be at the homecoming, so my aunt and uncle babysat me."

"When did you find out?" She'd offered a few details in her book but omitted others.

Paula rubbed her eyes. "The next morning, when I got up, I went to the kitchen and instead of my mom and dad being there, my aunt was. It turned out my uncle had to go and identify my mom, who was his sister, and my father. And he took care of the things my grandparents weren't up to handling. He wasn't much older than Jeremy is now, around twenty-one then." She shook her head.

"Thank God you had them."

"Yes." She grabbed a tissue from her purse. "It's funny how something little—like that memory of the red Mustang—can trigger all these emotions. I remember how upset I was about not finding my doll's play car."

"But it was really about your parents being gone, wasn't it?" He'd lost Lucia's Gucci silk scarf, the one she'd worn when she'd died in his arms. And as much as he'd searched his belongings, he'd never found it. He'd even wondered if she didn't want him to locate that talisman and wanted him to move on.

"I'm sorry. I really didn't mean to get into such a maudlin topic." She wiped at her nose.

"It's all right." One day, he'd tell her about how Lucia had died.

Not today, though.

Not today.

Mackinac Island

Someone was fumbling with a key in the back door lock, shooting fear through Claire—especially after receiving those anonymously sent creepy books. No one should be at the door, but the noise continued. Jeremy was at work and Mom was visiting Aunt Jackie in rehab—no one else should have a key. Claire grabbed her phone and punched in 911 and grabbed a can of cooking spray from the counter. With those weird books being sent to her, she was taking no chances.

The door opened and Mrs. Parsons barged in, shoving an oversized Santa-faced Christmas mug at Claire, as she pointed the can of Pam at her.

"What are you doing?" Claire demanded, setting the spray down.

"What are you doing?" Mrs. Parsons shouted. The woman, who was about her great-aunt's age, seemed much older than Jackie.

"I'm standing in our kitchen watching you break into our house!" Claire huffed.

"I've got a key, you nitwit, so I'm not breaking in." Mrs. Parsons displayed the key and then tucked it into the pocket of her greatly oversized camo zip-up sweatshirt.

Claire crossed her arms. "What're you doing here?"

The neighbor shuffled in beat-up tan Crocs toward the coffee maker. "I'm out."

Watching in disbelief, Claire resisted the urge to call for her mother. Those locks were getting changed ASAP.

Mrs. Parsons filled her mug and took a sip. "Tastes great." She rotated slowly toward Claire and smiled.

"Mrs. Parsons, you can't just come into our cottage any time you want."

The smile fled and was replaced by a look of hurt and then anger. "But I didn't have any joe at home."

"You'll need to buy some then."

"Can you get it for me?"

"Sure." If that meant the woman went home, then sure she would. "I'll put it on your porch."

"Great then." Edna lifted the ugly mug as if toasting Claire. "I'm heading back home. Your place smells like dog." She waved her hand past her face.

Seriously? The woman had barged into their house, helped herself to coffee, and now was complaining about Rex?

When the weird neighbor left, she called her mother. No answer. *Ugh.* She left a message.

Claire put her tennis shoes on and then went out the back door. She locked both the doorknob and the deadbolt. *I gotta get out of here.* She grabbed her bike and rode off to Doud's. The overcast day leant a sullen feeling to the island, as if the whole place wanted to rest, but tourists were descending upon it. Of course, that was just her projecting her own feelings onto the weather.

Entering Doud's, she always experienced a feeling of warmth and familiarity—like getting a welcoming hug. As she entered the coffee aisle, her heart did a little flip-flop. A tall, slim, dark-haired man with khakis and a blue oxford shirt stood by the espresso selection. Suddenly all the angst over the neighbor dissipated.

Clark.

But when the guy turned toward her, there were no glasses on and a thick beard. The smile slipped from her face as someone tapped her on her shoulder and she startled.

"Claire Bear, whatcha doin' here?"

As she turned, Clark opened his arms for her and she stepped into his embrace, inhaling his piney fragrance that overrode the scent of coffee. "It's you."

"Well yeah, ya didn't think I was that hairy guy, did ya?" Clark's low teasing tone made her pull away.

She stepped back just as the stranger walked past, giving them the side eye.

"Nice outfit, dude," Clark told the guy, who just raised his bushy eyebrows and continued on.

They both laughed.

Clark pulled at his collar. "My blue is more vibrant than his though, right?"

"Everything about you is better than him." Claire patted his clean-shaven cheeks.

His phone buzzed and he silenced it. "I better get going. I've got a meeting soon, and we were out of coffee."

"Working man woes."

"Yup."

"I'm here for coffee for our neighbor."

"Why?"

"Edna Parsons has a key, Clark, and she came right into our kitchen this morning to help herself to our coffee!"

"No way."

"Way."

"Whoa."

"I'm asking mom to let me get the locks changed." She puffed out a breath of exasperation.

"Absolutely. Call John Hubel—he's the best. He's on the island regularly, too."

"Will do."

Clark paid for both bags of coffee and then handed her one. "I gotta run but let's do a bike ride tonight."

"Sure thing. And thanks for paying for the coffee."

Soon they parted, and she biked back to Garden Cottage. Funny how Mom was intent on making that backyard a true gardener's vegetable patch this summer. Her random efforts back home in Virginia had been pathetic. It was funny because Mom had grown up always having a garden, and she acted like through osmosis she should know what to do. Her tomato, squash and cucumber plants paid the price in a dreary death. At least she was now reading up on proper techniques and their plants here were looking good. It was good to see Mom getting off the gardening struggle bus.

When she reached the house, Claire set her bike aside, out front, and then carried the bag of Columbian coffee to Mrs. Parsons' door. As she approached the concrete stoop, she spied a pile of yanked-up white peonies.

But Edna has no peonies.

Claire swiveled to face their own front porch. The antique European white peonies that her great-grandmother had planted were gone. They'd been Aunt Jackie's pride and joy. Mom would be sick over this, too, and Claire's own gut was twisting.

She called the police. This was theft. This was malicious mischief possibly. Plus breaking and entering—no, not that because Mrs. Parsons had a key.

But this had to stop. She needed to ask island law enforcement what they could, or should, do. And she'd call Aunt Jackie to get her opinion on next steps.

Chapter Nine

Run, run, run, runaway girl! The old song refrain kept running through Paula's mind. She couldn't even remember who sang it back in the day. Del Shannon—one of Aunt Jackie's faves? And how had that refrain gone? Didn't matter—after enjoying so much time with Gennaro two days earlier, she'd defaulted to her usual stress reaction and wanted to run and hide.

She paced the small living room, reminded of how she'd run off to the military instead of putting her aunt and uncle, and herself, into debt for college. She'd been surprised to learn that her social security death benefits from her parents would end and not continue into college. The law had changed. She made her own plans. Sought out a recruiter. And off she went. Problem solved! But it hadn't been. Her aunt and uncle were hurt. Maybe even a little embarrassed—because they'd told friends she'd been accepted at the University of Michigan, and they were so proud of her.

But if she'd not enlisted, if she'd not met Terrance, then she'd not have her kids. She paused in front of a bookcase filled with a mix of novels and nonfiction books intermingling with framed photos of various family members.

She needed to be honest with herself. *Gennaro is making me want something more for myself—especially with my kids being adults now.* That was what was giving her the runaway drive. She needed to get out of the cottage. She grabbed her fanny pack and checked to make sure she had keys. The police had warned them to make sure the house was always locked, and John Hubel had changed out all the door locks for them the previous day.

She longed to see Arch Rock, one of her favorite places on the island and not very far from the cottage. She donned her shorts, T-shirt, and sneakers, determined to get on her bicycle.

As she stepped outside and secured the new deadbolt, Paula's knee gave a twinge of protest. Maybe riding a bike around the island this early in her recovery wasn't a great idea—especially not alone. But after all that lovely time spent with Gennaro, and what seemed like flirtatious behavior on his part, she wasn't going to invite him. She'd need to put a little space between them so the dear man didn't get any ideas. And as much as she'd love to ride with Claire, she'd gone to Doud's and was buying supplies so she could make them a nice dinner later. At least Jeremy had stopped by and pumped up the tires on all the bikes in the shed.

Simply the idea of doing this little ride cheered her up. She was getting her independence back. She carefully descended the steps to the backyard and headed to the shed. The sun shooting through the clouds should accelerate her tender plants' growth. She should locate Jackie's bottle of Neem oil and see if it needed replacing so she could keep the bugs off.

A pair of seagulls squawked at her as she opened the shed door. They acted like they were protecting the place from her. She located her bike and wheeled it outside. The two birds, now standing in the middle of the yard, stared at her.

The gate squeaked open. *Oh no, is that Edna?* She turned to see Gennaro.

He waved. "Hello, there. Sorry to startle you."

"It's all right, but I'm just heading off for a bike ride."

"I won't keep you then." Gennaro pressed a hand to his broad chest. "Where are you headed?"

She brushed back hair from her forehead. "Arch Rock. Not too far."

"Have a nice ride."

Nice that he didn't bug her about her bum knee and taking it easy. "Thanks." As much as she'd love to talk with him, the desire to finally do something on her own, under her own steam, pushed her across the yard with her twelve-speed bike. *Surely it was that and not from being on runaway mode.*

"I'll close the gate for you."

"Thanks." She rolled the bike across the backyard, avoiding her garden plots. "Thanks again for your help putting in some of these gardens."

"Happy to help. And thanks for coming with me to the mainland." He held the gate open and then closed it behind her as she went through.

She resisted the urge to make a comment about his fancy car, because he might take it the wrong way, since it was vintage.

She mounted the bike and headed down the carriage driveway in front of the house, to the street. Gosh, she'd not even asked him why he'd come by. On the other hand, he'd not texted her to ask about stopping.

She drove past a small group of walkers and then past a small carriage. When she recognized Pops Williams as the driver, she inclined her head toward him, afraid to lift her hand from the handle.

Take it slow and easy, she encouraged herself as she spied a large group of bicyclists ahead of her. Only a short ride to the rock.

All the riprap of rocks alongside the shore still startled her every time she saw it. Not like in the old days, but it was necessary. Two sailboats, one with periwinkle and white sails and the other with turquoise like her car, sailed in the distance.

A family group rode bikes immediately ahead of her. She recognized Carter Parker, who'd been in her grief group, riding with his toddler in the yellow bike trailer behind him. His new wife, Alyssa, and her son, Sammy, pedaled a tandem bike beside them. Paula didn't want to get too close. It was inevitable that she'd run into them at some point. But today, she wanted time to herself.

The island always did something to reset her spirit. She hung back a little, pedaling slower.

Lake Huron darkened to a deep indigo as clouds blocked the sun. The sounds of the waves, of children laughing and families chatting as they rode, lulled her into a comfort zone she'd not entered in a very long time. She should ride the whole way around the island. It would be amazing.

She could do it.

For now though, she spied beautiful Arch Rock, its limestone formation glistening overhead as the sun once again peeked out.

Paula pulled over to the side of the road and parked her bike. A chipmunk ran from the bike rack to the nearby brush, startling her.

How many times had she come to this place? Too many to count, but she'd always enjoyed it.

A man with thick white hair pointed to the numerous stairs that could take people up. "Honey, ya wanta walk up to the top, to celebrate our sixtieth?"

The tiny silver-haired woman beside him shoved her backpack at him. "No way, ya big galoot. Go by yourself if ya want!"

Paula's knee throbbed, just thinking about attempting that climb. As she stepped toward a nearby bench, she almost missed her step. What was going on? Fear shot through her.

"Ma'am? Are you all right?" A Boy Scout in uniform, probably one heading to the fort, stepped toward her, several other Scouts following him.

Embarrassed, she took the arm he offered her. "I need to sit for a minute."

Together, they took ten steps to the bench. At least biking over hadn't been an issue. Or was that what was causing her problem?

The pain in her leg made her wince. There would be some icing in her future.

"Is all right? Paula?" Gennaro's voice had taken on his Italian accent again. She looked up as he parked Claire's bike in the stand.

Now embarrassment mingled with relief and served up a platter of humble pie. Weird how it brought her back to her early military training, when someone was always having to bail her out. She shrugged. "I don't know what happened."

"Is this your wife, sir? She stumbled." The Scout shook Gennaro's hand.

His wife? She almost laughed. At least he'd not asked if she was Gennaro's mother.

"Sì, sì, let me help."

Had her friend just agreed that he was her spouse?

A panicked expression covered his face as he sat beside her. "You okay?"

The Scouts continued to stand there, while passersby gawked at them.

Gennaro turned toward the youths. "Is okay, I got this. Grazie mille. Thanks so much."

"You're welcome." The Scouts headed away, but her helper cast a quick glance back at Paula. She gave him a thumbs up.

"Your daughter came home just as I was leaving, and she offered her bike to me—said you shouldn't go alone but she had groceries to put away." Gennaro took her hand. "Paula, you're perspiring. Did you hurt anything?"

"My pride is shattered."

"Better that than your bones, dear friend." He squeezed her hand.

"I'm not sure what happened. I know as I was pulling in here, something felt a little off. I don't know what." She rubbed the side of her head.

"Maybe that?" Gennaro pointed to her bike. "Front tire is almost flat."

She gaped. "Jeremy just filled those."

He shrugged. "That may be, but it's flat."

"How am I getting home?" Her knee complaining and the tire flat, but at least her new buddy was there.

Gennaro pulled his phone out and called someone. "Maria? Hi there. I need a favor. Could the mini dray come pick up my friend and me? Her bike tire is flat. Arch Rock."

Whatever was being said on the other end caused Gennaro's eyes to widen. He stood and took a few steps away from the bench and turned his back to her. When he ended the call, he returned to the bench.

"Are they coming?"

"Yes, about twenty minutes. They'll put the bike on the back of the little dray."

"Great. But what was she asking you?"

He tipped his head back and then down. "My boss has me already married off to you, dear Paula."

"Like you just did—when you answered that Boy Scout that I was your wife?" She raised her eyebrows.

He raised his hands. "Sì, sì. Sorry, I got flustered seeing you there like that."

"Well, I appreciate you checking on me, and no problem."

"My son doesn't want me to be alone. Leo is always pushing me to date, but I tell him there is no one like his mama."

She nodded slowly. "My son used to say he didn't want me to remarry. His dad was never there for him, or rarely, and I think he likes having me to himself." She chewed her lower lip.

Jeremy had always liked having her attention—until recently.

"He'll be grown and off with his own family soon, though, dear Paula."

She frowned. "Why do you keep reminding me of that?"

From the crimson staining his tan cheeks, he looked like he'd been caught with his hand in the proverbial cookie jar. "It's on my mind, too, but Leo says he wants to wait maybe a decade to start a family."

"You'll still be young enough to be a wonderful grandpa." Recalling all the ointments he'd purchased on their trips and anti-inflammatories, she added, "And if you take care of your back and knee, you'll be fine."

What about her? She'd already had her knee replaced and would be sixty soon. If neither of her children had families for another decade, that would be a little tough.

"God has His own perfect plan for our families, dear Paula, and we don't get a lot of say on what our adult kids do." He shook his head.

"You're right." That fleeting feeling of gloom vanished. "Kind of like we have no control over exactly when a horse-drawn carriage, or in this case a mini-dray, will arrive."

"Yes." He gave a curt laugh and then sat beside her. "But now we can both rest our bad knees."

"What did your doctor tell you yesterday?"

"Same old thing. Keep my weight off and do my exercises—one of which is bicycling."

"I think for me maybe they'd rather I kept to a stationary bike for now."

He patted her leg. "Ask your physical therapist."

"She said I can go on a regular bike if my knee wasn't bothering me."

"How's your rehab going? You mentioned you'd been surprised at your quick progress."

She widened her eyes. "I've been astonished—until today."

He waved that thought away. "That tire is what got you."

Paula nodded. "I didn't wear any knee brace, though." On the trip, Gennaro had shared that he had to also see a foot doctor. "Do you wear your orthotics when you ride on the bike or does that make it kind of weird for pedaling? And how did you get those problems so young?"

His lips and eyebrows twitched as if he was going to say something, but then he blinked. "Oh, from standing too much on my old job."

"I can relate to that, from library work we're often standing at the counter. We even had a girl in her late twenties who ended up seeing a podiatrist for custom orthotics."

He nodded. "Say, wasn't that crazy traffic in Petoskey? So many people when we went."

It felt like he was changing the topic. "Good thing you allowed extra time." And she'd enjoyed the time they'd spent together. He'd told her about some of his wife's paintings and her various exhibitions. "Speaking about traffic, though, look at that line of bikes coming now." She pointed to a group of ten riders. With another small break behind them, another large group followed.

"Great family activity. We should get the boys to come with us on a night ride once you're up to it. And once you get a new inner tube for your bike."

"Or whatever else might be wrong with that old thing. I might get a new one."

He raised his eyebrows. "Get an Italian one—like mine and Leo's."

Her brain froze a moment, considering that he'd possibly imported those bikes plus his Lamborghini. His wife may have left them a hefty inheritance—not that it was any of her business. If it hadn't been for Terrance's parents leaving him so much, they'd not be as comfortable as they now were. Amazing that a family so toxic still wanted to include Terry as an heir—even more shocking that he'd told her his folks had died, like her parents had.

"I think a Bianchi Specialissima would suit you here on Mackinac Island. Classic styling for the road." He pulled his phone from his pocket and tapped at it. "Let me show you. It's beautiful and they sell them in the United States. Probably could get expedited shipment."

"Cool."

He grinned and handed her his phone, which showed a turquoise frame bike with numbers beneath it. For a moment, she wondered if the pricing was in Euros, but then she realized it was dollars. Almost five thousand. Before Terry had died, and then she'd realized the extent of his hidden money from his wealthy family, she'd simply have laughed. Now, though, if she wanted to, she could afford this. Her thrifty soul would never allow her that purchase, though. And her kids had been brought up to be frugal, so neither would they. Gennaro was from another world than hers. But why, then, did he work as a hotel manager?

Gennaro's happy expression slipped away when she didn't say anything. "These are like an investment—they hold their value. You could buy one now and in ten years you could sell it for the same amount."

"I don't even know if I'll be able to bike when I'm in my seventies." She crinkled her nose. "I mean, I hope so, but with already having one knee replacement, I wonder."

"You'll be all right." He touched her shoulder. "Plus, you'd have all those years to enjoy your bike."

It almost sounded like he was talking about something else.

Something that included him. And the way their conversations had been going recently, it reminded her more of her and Terry's complaints about getting old, not like speaking with a Millennial, like some of her work colleagues were.

"I think we'll fix this bike, and if it's unfixable then I'll get another comfort seat model from Walmart. And if they have a nice turquoise color like that Italian bike, I'll get that."

He touched the side of his nose. "I'll drive you there to get it."

"Sure thing." She flinched as her knee spasmed.

"We've got to get some ice on that soon."

She broke out in sweat and closed her eyes shut tight.

"You come to the resort. I'll send a carriage. My doctor says to alternate cold with heat. We'll put you in the hot tub at the resort."

She winked at him. "You got a deal, buster."

He laughed and pulled her into a side hug. "I'll be your buster any day, my dear Paula." And he kissed her on her forehead.

"I think I need one, don't you?"

"Yeah. Maybe not a buster, maybe something else."

Yes, something else—but with someone near my age.

Chapter Ten

Chirping, from outside her window, pulled Paula from her pain-medicated sleep. The cardinal's insistent sounds tweeted louder than usual. What was there to wake to? That same recurring horrible thought pushed its way into her consciousness. A breeze stirred the coverlet on her bed and caused a swishing sound at the windows. *I'm not in Virginia. I'm here at home.*

At her old home, at least, in what had been her grandparents' bedroom on Mackinac Island. And the birds were louder and more cheerful and easily heard through the open window, with its screen pulled firmly shut. Uncle Victor had taken care of the house for Grandma and later for her and Jackie.

Paula threw off her covers. Her knee protested. "I should have gone to Gennaro's and used the hot tub," she mumbled to herself. The ice had worked well, though, and she'd not wanted to mess with things. Still, the hot tub might have been good—if she'd not had to put on a swimsuit and have her almost sixty-year-old body on display. Nope, that would have been too embarrassing, plus it had occurred to her that her knee scar would be on full display, and it might not be a good idea to have a bunch of hot water on it. Gennaro had sounded understanding, but also disappointed—especially when she'd rejected his offer to come keep her company.

The reality was that right now she was not alone, and somehow things had defaulted back to the way things were when her kids had been at home. Jeremy was there—not off at college and not working away from home for the summer. Claire, too!

She sat up and slid her feet into her soft loafers. Once she got herself ready, she headed out of the room and toward the kitchen. Those wonderful kids of hers liked to get a hot breakfast when Mom was there, and she quickly got to work. She'd need another anti-inflammatory after this, but it would be worth it.

When Paula heard Leo's voice upstairs, too, she realized he must have crashed with Jeremy the night before. She added more food to the kitchen counter, turned the oven on, and then got down to business. When the oven cook timer went off twenty minutes later, footsteps hammered down the stairs. She raised her eyebrows. Some things never changed. She'd always been so surprised that her quiet and studious son could be so loud—as, obviously, was Leo.

Paula set a steaming plate of eggs, hash browns, bacon, sausage and hot biscuits in front of her son and his friend at the island. "I still can't believe you're here, son!" She'd been sure her summer would have been lonely at home. "I'm glad you could have breakfast with us, Leo."

Her son's friend, with curly dark hair and soulful brown eyes, seemed twitchy. "Grazie. Thank you for including me." A blush painted the young man's olive complexion.

"You're welcome."

"I'll pray, Mom." Jeremy bowed his head and so did Leo and Paula. "Lord, we thank You for this meal. We thank You for your goodness. And we especially thank You for friends. In Jesus's name, Amen."

"Grazie for the prayer, Jeremy. It's good we got to work together this summer."

"For sure." Jeremy swigged his coffee.

"And we got to hang out with Mia more." Leo's voice held an edge that Paula hadn't heard before.

Jeremy began to cough, choking on his coffee. Paula moved behind him and patted his back, but he kept coughing. Strangely, a slight smirk crept across Leo's face.

"Mia is friends with both of us, Mrs. Ecker." Leo whacked Jeremy on the back.

Her son, eyes wide, glared at his pal.

What was going on here? Some jealousy? Was handsome Leo poaching Jeremy's friend? Had Mia become more than a friend? She'd thought they'd finally started officially dating.

Jeremy pressed a napkin to his mouth.

"Mrs. Ecker, have you seen Mia this summer? She still works at her family's bike-and-scooter shop down by the docks."

Her son slapped his buddy hard on the arm, but Leo laughed.

Finally, Jeremy stopped coughing. Leo forked eggs into his mouth and then popped in a strip of bacon. Maybe he'd be the next one choking, if he continued to eat at that speed.

She eyed Jeremy's empty coffee mug. "You okay?"

"Yeah."

"Okay for refills on coffee?" Paula headed to the coffee pot.

"We both can use more, Mrs. Ecker, please."

"On it." She grabbed her own mug and the pot and carried them to the table. She set hers by her spot and then refilled each mug, earning a nervous smile from Jeremy and a head nod from Leo, whose mouth bulged as he chewed. She'd always fussed at her own son to not shove so much in there lest he choke, but his pal was an adult, so she had to let that reminder go.

Paula returned the coffee pot to its spot and prepared her own plate, putting about half the amount she'd loaded onto the guys' plates.

"I like this way more than my own attempts." Leo lifted his biscuit aloft. "Especially these with lots of jam on them."

"Thanks." Paula sipped her coffee. "This is a kind of cross between Northern lumberjack breakfasts and Southern biscuits."

"My aunt's and grandmother's, in Italy, were hard and dry. Of course, my dad's were perfect." He did a chef's kiss.

Paula frowned at the way Leo expressed that. "Why do you say that, Leo? Why, of course, were they perfect?"

"Um, well, my dad cooked for a living." He placed a finger by his lips. "He doesn't like to talk about that, so please don't say anything. He stopped cooking when my mom died."

Being a cook wasn't an embarrassing thing. Most jobs, though, didn't pay well. "Oh, well, I won't say anything." But he had a Lamborghini in storage. She'd intended to google the cost of one of those old cars but hadn't yet. Maybe Gennaro had been a chef, not a cook.

"My mother was a very famous artist in Rome, and my dad loved to cook for her."

"Your dad told me a little about her work." Maybe Leo's mom bought the Lamborghini. Not that it was any of Paula's business, anyway.

"My father would make American-style biscuits and gravy for us. And yes, they were always perfect. But my nonna's were awful."

Paula took a bite of her eggs, and the guys devoured more biscuits.

Jeremy lifted his biscuit. "Where we live, in Virginia, one of the neighbors showed my mom the right way to make this kind."

Claire, dressed in an oversized sleep shirt, trailed in, followed by Rex. "The only kind I do are from a Bisquick box."

"Ugh, even the canned ones from the grocery stores taste better than those." Jeremy scowled.

"You're missing out." Claire mussed Jeremy's hair.

Her son growled, but Leo laughed.

Claire headed toward the stove.

"There's a place for Bisquick mix in every kitchen pantry," Paula said. "But I have to agree—they don't make the yummiest biscuits."

"They do when you've worked a twelve-hour shift and haven't shopped in over a week." Claire turned and raised a spatula to punctuate her point.

Rex trotted right up to their visitor and plopped down by his feet. Leo bent and rubbed the dog's head. "You're a good boy, aren't you?"

"He's the best dog ever," Claire pronounced as she poured herself the last of the coffee in a huge Wolverines mug.

"He is," Paula agreed.

Jeremy eyed his sister. "Aren't you eating?"

She sipped her coffee, giving him the stink eye, then set the oversized cup down. "Whyyyy?" She drew the word out, with a grumpy tone.

Paula knew exactly why. She raised a hand. "There's plenty for all of us to have seconds even."

Jeremy crinkled his nose. "Good."

"Good," Claire grunted back at her brother.

Leo, who had efficiently cleared his plate, scooted back but then stopped. "Is okay if I get more myself?"

"Sure."

Claire clasped her drink. "We're pretty casual around here, Leo, so help yourself or Pipsqueak might scarf it all down."

"If I said I'd missed you while you were in Montana, then I take it back." Jeremy pushed back and rose, too.

As Leo filled his plate, Paula watched. His movements were similar to his father's. But his features were a little softer and smaller and his eyes lighter than Gennaro's.

"My dad got on a health kick after—"

"If my dad had got on one, then he might still be here!" Jeremy almost spat out his words.

Claire's eyebrows shot high.

"We don't know that." Paula had heard multiple explanations of why her husband had died when he did. Working in an ER during Covid and being over fifty certainly contributed. She resisted the urge to talk about God's timing. This wasn't the situation for that discussion again.

"I'd rather eat like this than have to eat how my dad does things now." Leo slid back into his seat. "At least he'll make me the good stuff if I specifically ask for it."

Claire pointed a hot-pink fingernail at him. "You know how to fill a plate! I better grab some before these two leave me nothing."

Again, Leo's face flushed. "I'm sorry. I overdid."

To Paula's surprise, Claire rounded the table, kissed their guest on top of his head and squeezed his shoulders. "Don't worry, kid, there's more left."

Leo's dark eyes widened in surprise.

"Ack! Claire, don't do that!" Jeremy picked his sister up by her waist and swirled her away from his friend.

"Whoa, when did you get so strong?"

"When you weren't looking and when you weren't home!"

"They aren't kids, Claire." Paula kept her voice as gentle as possible.

Leo raised his hand. "Is all right. My older sisters always do like that. Except they keep on kissing me all over my face until I make them stop!"

Sisters?

Claire laughed. "Do they really?"

"Sì."

How many kids did Gennaro have?

"You just gave me a great idea." Claire began making kissing noises at Jeremy, who ran to Paula like he was a little kid, again.

"Make her stop, Mom."

Claire filled her plate. "Worked for me! Thanks, Leo, for the great idea."

"Hey! Leave me some, why don'tcha?" Jeremy edged back over by Claire.

So Gennaro had at least three children. How old were these sisters? Even with a conservative estimate of a year between children, then one had to be at least twenty-three. Unless they were twins. So her new pal bumped from early to mid-forties, at least.

"Do you miss your sisters?" Paula knew she'd gone on a fishing expedition, but it was time.

"I'm lucky because since college, I get to see one who lives in Canada more." Leo finished off his biscuit.

"That's a big country." She waited till Leo swallowed and then asked, "Where does she live?"

"In Toronto with her family."

Family? That implied she had children. "Are you an uncle?" *Nosy, nosy, nosy.*

"Sì. I get to see my niece and nephew soon."

Niece and nephew. Gennaro's age was ratcheting up quickly. He was a grandpa of at least two. "That's great." She chewed her lower lip. She'd meant that he was older than he looked, not that Leo was an uncle.

"I'm glad my brother-in-law will cook for us. He's a barbecue king."

Claire set her plate on the table and sat down. "Ooh, I have wanted Mom to get a smoker and a new grill for out back. Unless it's going to mess with your garden ambience?"

“No smoker right now. You should’ve seen that bill for all the stuff we put into the garden.” Paula had been shocked by the total. Yes, she could afford it, but Uncle Victor had saved seeds, had a compost pile, and had friends who gave him loads of new topsoil each year.

“Mom, I’ll pay for it as long as you don’t mind a propane grill in your new garden.”

“Maybe your dad can come and grill for us.” She winked at Leo.

Leo frowned. “He doesn’t do any of that kind of thing.”

A cook who didn’t grill? Perhaps, after working in a kitchen all day, it was too much. But Leo had just shared that his dad cooked for the family. “Don’t Italians grill much?”

“Not like Americans do, with a gas grill in every backyard. More traditional style.” Leo tapped Jeremy. “Will you put a grill in your backyard? I’ll come see you if you do.”

“Aren’t you two going to be roommates this fall?” Jeremy had told her previously that they would be.

The color leached from her son’s face. “Um, no, I’ll have other, um, roommates.” He gave Leo a glare.

Claire glanced between the two of them. “Get on each other’s nerves too much this summer?”

Paula gaped at her daughter. “Claire, don’t be rude.”

Laughing, Claire sipped her coffee. “It’s great to be back annoying my little bro. Didn’t realize how much I missed it!”

Jeremy crinkled his nose in annoyance. “Maybe good and fun for you.”

She knew her daughter, and Claire wouldn’t let this go. Jeremy was an adult. If he and his buddy didn’t want to rent together, it was his business.

Why then, did this whole breakfast set her teeth on edge? Because something was up.

Of that Paula was sure and certain.

Claire ramped up the volume on her iPhone. “Goodbye Yesterday” by Elevation Rhythm played on YouTube as she danced around the kitchen and cleaned up from breakfast. The pulsing song was her new anthem. *Goodbye yesterday, for sure.*

Mom tapped her. “What’re you listening to?”

Rocking back and forth, Claire removed her ear bud. “Want to listen?”

Mom waved her away. “Nah, it just looked like you were really enjoying it.”

“It’s called ‘Goodbye Yesterday.’ I really love it.”

“Great title.”

“It is. How’s your knee feeling today?”

“Aw, even though it’s sore, I’m believing that I’m fit as a fiddle as my grandpa used to say—right in this old house. He’d say that even when he wasn’t fit as even any ancient fiddle. I sure miss him.”

“He’s even more fit up there.” Claire pointed heavenward. “And Dad is probably challenging him to a game of chess.”

Mom shook her head. “Checkers. That was Grandpa’s game.”

She couldn’t resist tweaking her mother. “Have you figured out what Gennaro’s game is?”

A sly grin stole over Mom’s face. “I’ll tell you my young friend’s favorite board game if you tell me Clark’s reason for texting you night and day.”

She was about to protest, when her phone pinged. Her mother glanced in that direction as Claire went to the phone. Clark had messaged her.

Her face heating, Claire turned away from her mother’s prying eyes and finished her cleanup.

“The only one you’re kidding is yourself, my dear daughter, if you think people don’t know about you two.”

Jaw dropping, about to protest, Claire swiveled around as hands raised, Mom backed out of the room.

What were Gennaro’s favorite board games? Did he even have any? And why was Paula asking herself these questions? Claire was being silly suggesting that they had something going on.

“Mom! Clark and I are walking Rex!” Claire’s voice carried from the hallway.

A sudden sadness that wasn’t quite grief, maybe a twinge, hit her. Why? She shook her shoulders. *Silly, silly, silly.* With Claire walking the dog then she had no excuse to walk the dog and hope that she’d run into Gennaro out on his morning walk. This was getting out of hand. Besides, she had lots of gardening to do. And she wanted to run over to the Island Bookstore and see if Tamara needed any more copies of her grief book. Probably not, but she’d check out some new Mackinac Island books while she was there.

She strode to the mirror. Needed a little more lipstick. She went to her dresser and grabbed her Revlon rose-colored Super Lustrous lipstick and applied some. This business of becoming a senior citizen was rough. At least most of her peers had a brood of grandchildren to distract them—not that she would ever pressure either of her kids to get married and produce little cuties for her to spoil. That was part of the problem with having her kids later. Then again, younger people were now delaying childbearing, too. But people her age generally had grandkids and some had great-grands. No point grieving over something she had no control over. Maybe one day there would be some grandkids.

At least she had Rex now. What a great dog. Perfect personality for their family. Just like Gennaro had the perfect personality for a man. *Good gravy, am I now comparing my new friend to the dog? Ack!* Paula shook her head at herself and then put the lipstick back in its spot.

She grabbed her keys and cellphone and headed out.

Edna Parsons stood on the edge of the property out front, a guilty look on her face. Paula raised her hand to wave at her, but the woman spun on her heel and returned to her own yard.

A police officer rode his bike up the street and stopped when he saw Paula and then dismounted. "Are you Mrs. Scott?"

"No."

"Is that her?" He pointed to Edna, who made an obscene gesture at the policeman before she hurried inside and slammed her door.

Paula forced her gaping mouth shut. "No, that's Mrs. Parsons. I can't believe she just did that. I'm sorry."

"That's her? She's getting worse and worse. We've had officers up here a half dozen times since March. I'm the newest guy, so it's my turn."

"My daughter called for advice, and they didn't say anything about it."

His pale complexion reddened. "I shouldn't have said anything."

Edna's door opened again. She cupped her hands around her mouth and yelled, "Old lady Scott messed with all my electronics, and you pigs aren't doin' anything about it!"

"Messed with her electronics?" Paula frowned.

"Says she hears people talking to her through her lights."

"Her lights?"

"Yup."

"I'm going to take another complaint from Mrs. Scott. Edna Parsons threatened to torch her house."

"Really?"

"Yup. And I'd advise you to be careful." He leaned in. "We're working with social services to get her evaluated. I mean, there's only so many times you can caution someone, right?"

She nodded.

The officer began to push his bicycle up the street but turned. "Oh, does your neighbor have children somewhere? Because she told us she doesn't have any."

"She has at least two, that I know of."

"Mrs. Parsons was adamant that she had no living family and had never had any kids."

"Oh, wow, that's not true."

He shook his head.

"I'll call my Aunt Jackie and see if she has a way to reach Mrs. Parsons' kids."

"We'd appreciate it if you could get us that information."

"Sure thing."

He continued toward the Scotts' cottage, two doors down.

Paula called Jackie and left a voice message. She walked on toward the downtown area. Today, puffy opalescent clouds bunched together overhead, looking almost unreal.

When she reached her destination and entered the store, Paula spied Tam standing at the register, speaking with someone. Tam's expression showed interest. "You know, that's a great idea. I think Paula's book should get some illustrations and be translated into as many languages as possible." Tam smiled.

As she rounded the corner, Gennaro came into view. Hands raised, he gestured as he spoke. "This book has helped so many people—myself included. And Mrs. Ecker also speaks at the medical retreat center here, too. I want to see her work reach more people."

"I agree." Tam's firm response warmed Paula's heart.

When she reached her young friend's side, she pinched his elbow. "Are you my new manager or what?"

"Or what." He laughed and then shocked her by leaning in to brush a kiss to her cheek.

Her face flamed.

He raised his hands. "*Scusa*! Sorry!" He touched his chest. "I'm so used to kissing my friends when I see them."

Tam's quirked lips prompted Paula to speak. "I see you've met my new young friend, Gennaro."

Was that disbelief or slight shock on her pal's pretty face? "Your young friend, eh?" She smirked at Gennaro, who nodded. Did he wink?

"I've been a regular here for the past few years." Gennaro waved around the store.

"You've certainly bought a lot of copies of Paula's book." Tam's accusing stare didn't seem to phase Gennaro.

"I've sent many to friends who needed her encouraging words—just like I did."

"Paula has a way of talking about grief that is real and addresses hard topics but is done in such a beautiful soft way." Tam's comments touched Paula's heart.

Gennaro nodded. "And relying on God's Word."

"I sure couldn't have gotten through without that," Paula agreed. Not just her husband's death but her parents' and uncle's deaths, too.

"You had way too much loss." Tamara, who knew all about Paula's past, spoke what she couldn't manage to say. Tam gently slapped the countertop. "Before I forget, we need more copies of your book. Mary Jane asked for another case."

"A case?" Paula repeated dumbly, surprised the owner wanted so many more.

Gennaro wandered away toward the children's section.

Tam leaned in. "Listen, he tells anyone who's in here while he's here, that if they need a book on grief, then yours is it. And he wants me to pitch you on the idea of making it a little more Mackinac themed."

She frowned. Were her sales primarily from her new pal? And was this a good idea? "Do you mean like a special edition?"

"Yes, with some simple illustrations. You could create a few different special editions if you put your mind to it."

Paula just blinked at her. She felt the presence of someone behind her and turned to see several customers lined up. "Sorry, Tam. Thanks. Let me get out of the way here."

"No problem." Her friend grinned, but the folks in line cast her some grumpy looks.

She headed toward where Gennaro was laughing at a kids' large board book. When she reached him, he lifted the brightly colored book and showed her the illustration of a dinosaur surfing around Round Island Lighthouse by the island. "I don't think you'll ever see this happening here."

"I agree."

He grinned. "I'm buying this for my grandson."

"Leo told me his sister has two children." Paula let that land and watched for Gennaro's reaction.

He blushed, making his handsome face even more appealing. "Ian will be five in a few weeks, and I'll get to see him for his birthday!"

This disclosure ratcheted Gennaro's age up into the late forties.

Still too young for her, even if a grandpa.

"That looks like a great choice."

He wrapped his fingers around her wrist. "You ought to meet my daughter and her family. They'd love to be introduced. They know how your book has helped me." He spoke so rapidly that his Italian accent slurred his words slightly.

"Um, I think your family wouldn't want some strange older lady coming to a family event. And a special one at that—a birthday."

He chuckled. "They like older people. Trust me. They really do. And they already asked me to bring you."

"Why?" She huffed a breath. "Honestly, I think that sounds really awkward."

He released her wrist. "Only if your walker or wheelchair aren't working well that day, for the park in Sault Ste. Marie, Ontario."

She raised her shoulders. "What wheelchair and walker?"

Gennaro shook a finger at her. "*Esattamente*. Exactly. You walk a dog for over a mile and ride over six miles on that stationary bicycle at PT. The only problem with them will be you won't look like what they think of as an older lady."

Old lady was what he means. "Depends on if my knee acts up that day and I limp. I could grab my cane. I named it Pinky because it's a rose-colored aluminum cane."

He clapped. "So it's settled. You will come. And Pinky is welcome, too."

"I'll bring my cane just to keep you in line."

Gennaro leaned back and gave a deep belly laugh that reminded her of her uncle Victor. Warmth spread through her. "Mrs. Paula Ecker, you intend to do me bodily harm if I am not behaving? I think maybe you are getting to know me better, and I see you have a naughty side."

She stood as straight as she could and made a poker face. "You, sir, are dealing with a librarian. I believe you forget yourself."

"Oh." He pursed his lips. "Yes, ma'am, I see you are a strict librarian if you bring Pinky with you."

She nodded. "That's right. Don't forget it."

"I won't. And may I buy you an ice cream so you can get some practice for the cake and ice cream at the party?"

"Practice?"

He made a show of feigning dripping ice cream falling onto his Polo shirt. Then he had the nerve to laugh again.

"And here I thought you were such a nice young man when I had that chocolate ice cream totally mess up my dress." She put her hands on her hips.

"I am only teasing you."

Paula opened her mouth to say something smart back, but all that came out was, "What board games do you like to play?"

Chapter Eleven

Scents of coffee laced with vanilla and mocha wafted out from Lucky Bean as the door opened again, and a group of teens dressed in denim shorts and matching blue T-shirts entered. Claire hunkered down at an outdoor two-person table, with her frappe, waiting for Clark. *Should I really ask him to come with me to see Aunt Jackie?* Maybe she should go on her own. With Mom's knee acting up and Jeremy busy working, their weekly visit to Petoskey was left to her.

As her friend half-jogged, half-walked up the sidewalk, warmth flooded Claire. How she'd missed Clark. No, he wasn't Mr. Charming or Mr. Smooth Guy, but neither was he 'Liar, Liar, Pants on Fire Fellow' either, even though his recent deception, lie by omission, made her think of that childhood taunt.

Clark handed Claire something in an Island Bookstore bag. "Mrs. Tomac asked me to bring this to you." He cringed. "But I don't think you're gonna like it."

"No?" Claire pulled a paperback glossy covered book with a mossy blackish background and turned it to read the cover. "*When Psychopaths Seek Prey.*"

Clark snorted. "Right? What did I tell you?"

She read the back cover blurb and scowled at him. "Did you buy this?"

He threw his hands up. "No way!"

"Then who did?"

"I have no idea, and Tamara Tomac didn't know either—one of the new workers held it there for you and didn't say who purchased the book." Clark rubbed his chin. "Could be from one of my ex-fiancé's pals—trying to scare you off."

She raised her eyebrows and widened her eyes at him. "Clark Jeffries, I have known you since we were little kids, and I know you're not a sociopath nor a psychopath."

He rubbed his nails against his chest and then blew on them. "I knew you were still fond of me. Not a psychopath nor a sociopath—what high praise!"

She reached out to swat him, but he backed away.

"I see you've got your drink. Let me grab mine." Clark jerked a thumb toward the café's interior.

When he left, she thumbed open the book and scanned the table of contents. Who knew that psychopaths could have so many aspects to them? One chapter title caught her attention—"Charm without Empathy." She flipped to it, immediately thinking of Ivan. He'd been such a charmer. More so at first. But there was always something "off" about the way he'd say or ask things. She scanned the first paragraph.

> Have you ever left a conversation with an absolutely charming person, who'd almost swept you off your feet, yet you felt like you'd missed out on something? Have you replayed a conversation with the charmer multiple times, only to discover that the person, while expressing much interest in your conversation, hadn't actually shown any empathy for your feelings about the topic? If so, you may have been dealing with a psychopath. Their conversational goals are about gaining something they want, as addressed in Chapter Four in this book. They'll all but dance on their heads to manipulate and ingratiate themselves, but in the midst of that, they will reflect empathy only if it's in their best interests to learn something more—to gain something they want.

Claire gave a hard exhalation of the breath she'd not realized she'd been holding. That paragraph could have totally been written about Ivan.

"You okay?" Clark set his cup down. "You look like you've seen a ghost."

"I was thinking about my . . . uh, friend out in Montana."

"The one who suddenly got married?"

"Yeah." She pushed her hair behind her ear. "I was reading a paragraph in that book, and it made me think about how I confided something to Ivan that I'd only shared with you and another close friend."

Clark frowned. "You mean about how you thought I was the greatest guy in the entire universe?"

She resisted the urge to roll her eyes. "No."

He touched her hand. "About your dad and what he did for you? About his crazy wealthy family?"

"Yeah." She clutched his fingers. "I was pretty lonely when I first went out to Montana, and Ivan had gone out of his way to make me feel welcome on the ward."

As she thought back on it, he'd especially do it when Tiffany was around. Trying to make her jealous, no doubt. At the time, Claire had assumed Tiffany was a very happily married neurosurgeon with no interest in their mundane lives.

"I don't know a lot about psychopaths. What did you read about sharing secrets?"

"Psychopaths only want to gain something from that kind of thing. They're not interested in your actual feelings or emotions behind the info."

"They must have to do a tricky dance step to get people to confide."

She gave a curt laugh. "I remember him telling me about his deceased wife. Some of what he said I could have found in old newspapers."

"Really? How?" Clark sipped his frappe.

"Oh, boy. I never told you this, but there was an investigation into her death and all kinds of stuff in the newspapers before I got out there."

Clark dipped his chin toward his chest before raising it again. "If you'd told me that, I'd have begged you to run from this guy."

She shrugged. "He was found not guilty of wrongdoing, but now I'm really second-guessing that. After I read that first book that someone sent me—"

"Again, it wasn't me."

"I believe you, but it's weird. Anyway, that first book about narcissistic charmers and the link with sociopaths had me thinking about him, too."

"Claire," he squeezed her hand. "Do you think this is more about you still being hung up on him?"

"No!" her voice came out louder than she'd intended, and she pulled her hand free. "No, no, and double times twenty no!"

A seagull nearby squawked as if agreeing with her.

He laughed and leaned back in his chair. "You haven't used that expression in a long time."

"Well, this situation called for it."

"Okay, back to what and how he learned about your father leaving you money—why did you disclose that?"

"Ack, he was sharing about how his wife had left him quite comfortable and how he could leave his job at the hospital but that he loved his work. And how some people at the hospital thought that since he had millions now—"

"He actually said, millions?"

"Yeah, and he acted like it was no big deal. In fact, he pointed out that most of the town people had to have millions to own any kind of property around there." She sipped her drink, which failed to deliver the cold comfort it usually gave.

"So you let your guard down?"

"Yes." She chewed her lower lip, trying to remember. "I'd told him earlier at work that my father had been a PA, too, but that he'd died."

Clark raised his shoulders. "Did he seem sympathetic?"

"You know, he kind of did. He encouraged me to share about him." But he'd said something that caught her off-guard. "Wait, we weren't initially talking about Dad. Earlier that day, I'd had to go down to HR to do some forms, including for life insurance. And Ivan had encouraged me to get the max—he said it didn't cost that much more, and it would help my loved ones if something happened to me."

"That's kind of creepy. Especially with him asking about your dad later. He didn't ask you about—"

"He did!" She knew exactly what Clark was going to ask. "He asked if my dad had been well-insured like I'd made sure that I was."

"Whoa."

"I'm thinking that now, but at the time, he'd made the whole thing very conversational." She rubbed her eyes. "But no genuine concern about my feelings about losing my father. It was more about him having taken care of us—of me. And later, when I had dinner at his house, when he was pointing out some of the beautiful and expensive artwork his wife had left for him, Ivan wormed the conversation around to how much my father had left me."

"And you told him." Clark shook his head.

"He was rich. He lived in a mansion with all kinds of expensive stuff and luxury cars. I thought my million and a half was pretty paltry compared to what he had."

"They always want more."

"That's actually one of the titles of a chapter in the book."

"Did it seem like he was possibly interested in you? Did he make you believe there could be something between you two?"

She didn't want to share that info.

"Ah, he did. But then, I'm gonna guess the doctor he married must have been loaded." Clark wrapped his hands around his drink.

"Yup. Her husband was an investment banker, and they had an amazing ranch with a mansion. And she brought money into the marriage."

A dray rolled past, the horses' harnesses jingling as they pulled a load of boxes to be delivered. The driver nodded in their direction.

Claire and Clark waved.

She pulled some lip balm from her purse and ran it over her dry lips. "Maybe I'm reading too much into things, though."

"Nah, you're right. I knew that guy was screwed up. What kind of dope lets someone take their dog?"

"A psychopath?"

"A sociopath?"

"A charming socio-psychopath?" She laughed. "At least I've saved Rex from a lifetime of being called 'Pup,' right?"

"Exactly." Clark drank the last of his frappe. "You might want to mail those books to his new wife."

"Ha! All she can see is that she got the prize. The 'hot' PA on the neuro floor, who all the staff loved."

"Some prize. What if he did kill his first wife? I mean, have you thought about whether he might off the neurosurgeon, too?"

Her jaw fell open, but no words came out.

What if?

What if Ivan had evil intentions toward Tiffany?

"I'm guessing you didn't invite me here to talk about psychopaths, though, did you?"

"Aw, no. I had a favor to ask."

"Fire away." He pretended to fire guns at her by pointing his index fingers toward her, thumbs up.

She winked at him and made the same gun hand gesture back at him. "Come with me to Petoskey to see my Aunt Jackie."

"I love Miss Jackie. She used to teach me in Sunday school. And we do, or rather did, her ad graphics for her B&B."

"Great. My brother is working, and Mom's knee is acting up. So. I'm picking up some of her meds in Petoskey and was going to have to visit my aunt on my own."

"When?"

"Uh, I was hoping on the noon ferry."

He pretended to choke. "All right. What's the point of owning a business and being your own boss if you can't play hooky?"

"I hoped you'd say that."

"Let me call my team and tell them where I'll be. And I'll have to take calls."

She raised her hand. "Fine by me. I understand."

"And let's stop by the Keyhole on the way back and give my cousin Aaron some grief."

"Sure thing. But you know he'll give it right back and add some more."

"I sure hope so."

How she'd missed this guy. Clark Jeffries was the best friend she'd ever had. And they could have had much more. But she'd not bent. She wouldn't find work in the area so he could stay on or near the island.

Then again, he'd been willing to move out west for Brooke. But not for Claire.

That was that.

Wasn't it?

She couldn't dwell on that. They'd work it out eventually. Right now, though, a concern that had been twirling in her mind popped up. "Hey, something's been bugging me a little."

"What's that?"

"My brother's friend Leo keeps talking about Mia, the girl whose nasty grandfather owned the bike-and-scooter place." She removed her frappe's top and swirled the remaining contents with her straw.

"Ha. Her equally nasty parents own it now."

"Yeah, well, my mom thinks Jeremy and Mia are dating. And Leo, his best buddy, keeps making weird cracks. The three of them hung out at school together along with some other pals."

"What's this weird thing Leo said lately?"

"Reminded us that Mia works there." Claire put the cover back on her drink and inserted the straw.

"She graduated U of M—summa cum laude. I was surprised to hear she was back for the summer."

"Jeremy told me she'd be going back to Ann Arbor at the end of the season. But he was really weird about how he said it—kinda twitchy. Like when he's lying."

"Wanta go down to the bike shop? Say hi to Mia?"

"Yeah. Enough talk about my weird thoughts on Ivan. Let's focus on my bro."

Clark feigned a movement to the left, then to the right, and pretended to throw a basketball shot. "The good old distraction technique."

"Yeah."

Paula sprayed Neem oil on her tomato, cucumber, and squash plants—amazed that they'd grown so quickly. She'd forgotten how the long days and the temperate weather on the island resulted in so much growth. Of course, it didn't hurt that they had access to all that natural fertilizer and compost. Her clay-based soil in Virginia looked nothing like this black dirt.

No need to water today, the good soaking they'd gotten the previous night took care of that chore. She moved to the carrot garden. She'd need to thin those sprouts soon, but not today. Her knee and back were almost done with any more gardening for the day.

The garden gate creaked open. "Hello, Paula!" Gennaro called out.

She turned to see him holding a large fern aloft.

"I brought you this for your front porch."

"It's beautiful."

"It was one Maria had been nursing along in the office. Her mother-in-law, Kareen, kept it well but Maria prefers herbs to plants."

"How did you get that thing here? It's huge." She moved toward him and touched the fronds.

"I rode one of those bikes with the trailer on the back. Come see." He waved for her to follow him.

They went to the front, where he'd parked the bike with what looked like a child-sized carrier in the back. "Do they have those at the resort?"

"It's Parker and Jaycie's for their little one. And Maria has already warned me that I must clean it out when I return it, so her grandbaby doesn't get dirty."

"It's amazing all the things you have to have for babies, isn't it?"

"Yes." He blinked. "I can't wait to see my daughter and grandchildren soon."

"That's lovely. I imagine they'll have to bring lots of stuff for the kiddies."

"Yes, they do. You should come with me to Sault Ste. Marie, Ontario, to see them when they come."

Something akin to a jolt of icicles froze her for a moment. What did this mean? Why meet his family?

"My daughter has been hearing about you for years. She's read your book, too."

The frozen ice thawed. They simply shared in a terrible grief experience. "Sure."

His smile could have lit up the front yard. "They will love you—I am certain."

"My friend, I am a senior citizen librarian and not someone most people get very excited about meeting. So, keep your expectations a little more down to earth, okay?"

He took her hand and kissed it, and she resisted the urge to pull away. This seemed a cultural gesture and nothing intimate. Still, why did it seem so?

"Gennaro, they will likely tolerate me because I am your pal, and nothing more. All right?" Still, she'd better be on her best behavior. And she did like kids—it was one of her favorite parts of her job, doing circle time.

"Okay, but I am very happy you will accompany me." He released her hand.

And for some reason, she was both happy, yet nervous, about her pledge to go with him.

What could go wrong?

"They'll be here in about a week."

"Great. But for now, help me get that fern up on the porch."

"It will look perfect where your neighbor removed that planter."

As if on cue, Edna Parsons' front door opened, and she peeked out at them, scowling.

"I don't know what else we can do for her. Social Services is supposedly trying to work with her family to take over guardianship, but that would require them going to court." If she knew her daughter like she thought she did, then her daughter would do nothing.

"Let's keep praying for her." Gennaro placed the large pot in the empty spot.

"That's a great idea. And the fern looks perfect there. Thanks, and thank Maria for me, too."

"I think let's pray she doesn't try to remove or damage anything else."

"Praying, yes, but Jeremy also installed a camera for me up front." She pointed.

"These days you need them. My wife's studio has had cameras for over twenty years. They're kept on continuously." He frowned.

She was taken a little aback by this information. "So her art studio is still open?"

"Sì. Same manager. He does an amazing job."

"But what about the art, since she's no longer creating?"

He swiped his hands on a handkerchief, reminding her of a much older man. Most younger guys didn't carry those. "We have so much still stored at the villa."

So he still owned a place in Rome.

"And they keep bringing out art from her back closets at the studio."

"Did she work constantly then?"

He exhaled a long breath. "I don't want to speak ill of the dead, but I don't think she had one day, since we were married, when she didn't work on something. All mediums. She was amazing. Oil, watercolor, clay—you name it, she did it."

"How did she do all that and keep up with her family?" She compressed her lips. Oh my, that slipped out before she could stop it.

He shrugged. "She didn't."

"Like Terry," she whispered.

"Your husband?"

"He worked all the time." Hearing Gennaro voice his wife's obsession with her art opened Paula's hurt over Terry's workaholism.

Gennaro hung his head. "But I did, too. I worked too much."

"But you stopped."

"If Lucia hadn't died, we'd both have won awards for most absent parents. But I have tried to be a better father now." He placed his hand over his heart.

"I'm sure you are. I see how you are with Leo."

He gave a curt laugh. "You know what is funny?"

"What?"

"He's the most misbehaved of my children. The most defiant. And spoiled."

"Leo is the baby—I think that's expected."

"We can't control what our adult kids do."

"I know. But when you meet my daughter, you will see that despite my wife and I not being available to her as much as we could have been, she's a wonderful parent herself."

"I look forward to meeting her and her family." And she really meant it.

Chapter Twelve

Thank you, Lord, that my little family is with me right now. This week like the previous, on his day off, Jeremy had spent the night at the cottage. Granted, he'd spent the prior evening playing games online with his buddies. Paula hadn't seen much of him until he came down to make popcorn, kiss her on the cheek, grab a pop, and head back upstairs. Birds chirping noisily outside her room urged her to get up and get going for the day.

She donned her robe and headed toward the kitchen. She couldn't wait to get her morning coffee. In Virginia, it had sometimes felt like the only thing that would make her morning worthwhile and certainly necessary before she'd headed out to the library. Here at the cottage, Aunt Jackie owned two tall Braun coffee makers with fourteen-cup capacity that she'd used when serving B&B guests their breakfast. During the week, Claire and Paula filled one only half-full. Claire had taken over coffee duty because she was particular about how she liked hers. And in the fridge, there'd be Paula's favorite coffee creamer, which thankfully Doud's kept in stock.

Paula padded into the kitchen in her fluffy purple slippers. When she spied Jeremy sitting at the island, she raised her eyebrows. "I take it your game ended before midnight."

"Yeah, the guys all have jobs that start early." He raised his coffee mug and took a long drink.

She headed to the cabinet and grabbed her US Army Airborne coffee mug, almost buzzing with the need for that caffeine jolt after taking extra meds for her sore knee.

"Um, Mom, there's no coffee left. Sorry."

Jaw dropping, she turned to catch her son's guilty look. "You didn't save me any?" Irritation bubbled up just as quickly as her thankful prayers had.

"There was hardly any in the pot. Just a short mugful."

"Really?" But he hadn't saved her any. *Not even a half cup. Ugh.* "Claire has gotten used to making a half carafe for the two of us." Still, she knew her brother was home but hadn't made enough for him. That was a whole separate can of worms as her uncle would have said. Claire and Jeremy were only recently getting along better.

"Do you want me to make another potful, Mom?"

Ugh. No, she wanted her own cup of coffee—that he was drinking right now. "I'll make it myself."

"Sorry. I wasn't sure if maybe you'd already had some."

"It's only eight in the morning, son." She made a quirky face at him.

He shrugged. "I know, but at home you're up by seven."

"We're not in Kansas, Toto." This wasn't the first time her son had finished off a pot of coffee before everyone had gotten some. And he always had an excuse.

She removed the coffee filter, tossed the grounds into the container they used to transport them to the garden, and then prepped the coffee maker for four servings. She turned the brew switch on and then headed toward the oversized refrigerator.

"Claire said to tell you that she's gone hiking to find some wildflowers that some botanist lady told her were in bloom. She packed a lunch."

That would explain the ice cube melting on the wood floor beside the refrigerator. She exhaled a hard breath as she bent and picked it up, then tossed it in the sink, and grabbed a paper towel. And of course, Jeremy hadn't noticed the melting cube at all when he'd gotten the creamer out.

She wiped up the water, tossed the paper towel, and retrieved the creamer from the fridge. Had she really thought about how much she missed her kids? Yes, she had, and she'd longed to have them around her.

Sometimes reality was a little harder than wishful thinking.

As the coffee brewed, she grabbed a small skillet. At least she could make herself that little scrambled eggs with peppers and goat cheese that she'd been planning. "Do you want to have those Mediterranean-style eggs that Gennaro suggested?" He'd said Mediterranean-style cooking was good for inflammation.

Another guilty look. "Sis said to tell you she'd used the last of the goat cheese on her sandwich and she'll pick some up later at Doud's."

She gaped at him. "Really?"

"Not my fault, Mom. Plus, she didn't know anything about what you had planned for breakfast. She wasn't with us when Gennaro suggested that."

Clamping her lips shut, again, Paula tried to will away the annoyance creeping into her head. Her own face must surely reflect the guilt she felt over her irritation with her kids right now.

Jeremy's phone pinged, and he glanced down at the message. "Claire says to save you some coffee because she forgot and only made the usual amount." He crinkled his nose. "She still thinks I'm like twelve and don't drink coffee—like I'm not a man now and not a kid. Or worse, she forgets I'm even here. Or worse yet—she doesn't care."

"Wow, don't go there. That's a very bad trail you ran down." She had to chuckle, though, because she was right on the path with him.

He raised his mug to his lips, but she saw his reddened cheeks.

"It took her a week to not make only five cups of coffee for herself, like she did in Montana."

He lowered his mug. "Yeah? She forgot about you, too?"

"Um, she didn't forget me—she was just in a habit." Definitely sounding like a mom making excuses.

"I make four cups for myself at college, but I bet I'd have remembered to make more for you." He jutted out his chin, looking more like his dad.

"What about if it was for me, you, and Claire? Would you have remembered?"

His lips pulled to the side. "Ah, I'm taking the fifth on that."

She laughed. "Like I thought."

"I'm used to making for you and me when we're at home, but not for her."

"Exactly what I was saying. We get into routines and then adjustable routines and we forget."

"Are you still gonna be mad at both of us?"

"Depends."

"On what?"

"I think you could make it up to me, for taking the last of the coffee."

"How?"

"Weed pulling." She placed her hand on her back, which wasn't hurting, just her knee throbbed. She bent over and feigned terrible pain. "Help your old mom out."

His chin dropped lower. "Not buying that, but I'll weed."

"Thanks. And my knee was really bothering me last night. Had to take a pain pill. Hence, I'm a tad grumpy this morning."

"A tad?" Jeremy raised his eyebrows. "It's just coffee."

She shook her head. "No. It's the life-giving effervescence of caffeine-infused goodness that will get me through my day."

The back door creaked open. Was Claire back already?

A shaggy dark head peaked in. "Did I hear something about caffeine?" Gennaro stepped in.

She'd told him the last time she'd seen him that it was best to come around to the back door, their private entrance.

"Good morning." She shoved her hand through her hair. She must look a mess.

"I was going to drop off some of that special goat's cheese that I told you about." He raised a bag.

"God bless you!" She could kiss him. She just might. It was the Italian thing, wasn't it?

But before she could do so, Jeremy jumped up and grabbed the bag from Gennaro. "You just saved my mom from a very grumpy morning."

"I think just seeing me," Gennaro made a comical voice, "might cheer her up." He pushed his chest out and pretended to walk like a rooster.

She couldn't help laughing.

"See?" He pointed to her.

"I'm getting a bath, Mom, while Claire isn't hogging that bathroom with the tub." Jeremy hurried off. Leaving his coffee mug at the counter. *Like usual.*

"Sorry if I intruded. When the door was open and I heard you two, I thought I'd check. I'm glad you were up, because the cheese needs refrigeration."

"Thanks so much. Can I get you some coffee?" She pointed to the coffee pot. "At least I've got some, now, to offer you." She made a grumpy face.

"So your kids, they finished off the last carafe?"

"Yup." She gestured to the stool at the counter. "Have a seat."

"Grazie."

She went to the cupboard and grabbed a U of M mug for her friend. "I really look forward to that one mugful of coffee I allow myself each morning. But I had to make more."

"The joys of parenthood. We love them, but they need to fly the coop. Then they fly the coop and we miss them, and then they keep coming back." He shrugged. "It's hard on someone like me because I like a routine."

She poured coffee into the two mugs. "I guess I do, too."

"Plus, you get used to doing things a certain way, and you don't have to communicate that to anyone. Then, suddenly, you have kids and grandkids who have to be told what is what. And even if you've told them, then . . ." He shook his head slowly. "But you can't stay mad, because you love them, right?"

"Right."

"I get it."

"You want creamer?"

"No, thanks."

She added hers and stirred with the teaspoon that Jeremy had left on the counter. "We're gonna need an espresso maker if you keep dropping in on us."

When she swiveled around, she caught him blinking hard.

"I don't mean to disrupt your household, Paula."

"Oh, no, no you aren't. And you brought me just what I needed to make up for Claire using the last of my own stash of American goat cheese." She slid the coffee mug in front of him. "Speaking of which, would you like to have some of those special eggs?"

"I have to get back to work soon."

"Aw." She shrugged. "I'll make them later then." She came around, set her mug on the counter, and slid into the seat beside him. "So tell me your secrets to managing life with your family." Maybe she'd learn more about him.

"Ha! This is one of the reasons I'm in the US working."

"Yeah?"

He swiveled slightly toward her. "My three brothers and their families live on the farms adjacent to my parents' property, which I now own. And they constantly come to their home for any little thing you can imagine." He tapped the counter. "And of course, my nephews and nieces expect Zio Gennaro to come visit, too, and preferably bring some of my cooking!"

"Your cooking?" Leo had mentioned his father's good cooking. "I mean, I know you said you enjoy it, but why would they think that?"

Face reddening, Gennaro cupped both of his large hands around his mug and practically inhaled his coffee.

"You must be really good for them to think that."

He set his coffee down and gave her a smug smile. "They must think so. And I can make a Bolognese sauce like no one else's."

"Ah. I'd like to try that sometime."

"Come to the Parkers' next weekend. I'm making a 'Pasta Fest' for their extended family."

"Now that's a huge family. I wonder if they steal the last mug of coffee on each other."

Gennaro raised his mug. "No doubt."

"Who all will be at this thing? And I didn't know the Parkers hosted private events."

"Just for their family. And yes, there are Carter Parker and his wife and two kids, Parker and his toddler, Gianni and his multitude of kids and grandkids and Kareen, and then there's Maria's kids and grandkids and Hamp. And probably some more." He shrugged.

She raised her eyebrows. "Wow. Do you feel comfortable cooking for such a huge crowd? I mean—I've helped with our church's suppers and it's tricky."

Conflicting emotions flitted over his handsome features—something like incredulity, pride, sadness, and finally settling on calm. "I know I can do it, and I'll have help."

"I could lend a hand if you need."

"Weren't you just telling me about how you did all that volunteer work to avoid being lonely?"

"Ha! And now that I'm not lonely I don't intend to distract myself like that. Plus," she wagged her index finger at him, "I'm not doing it to earn any kind of brownie points." Her faced heated at the implication.

He cocked his head to the side. "Don't you want to earn these brownie points with me?" He chuckled as he raised his mug to his lips.

She touched his upper arm, feeling the muscles there. "My friend, I am well past trying to earn brownie points with any man. And certainly not someone so young."

"So young, huh?" He laughed again. "Okay, so I accept your offer. No brownie points earned. And you just help this very young guy to serve a big family some pasta out of the goodness of your heart, right?"

"Right."

That was why she wanted to do it. Wasn't it? Simply to be nice?

He pointed to himself and to her. "You and me—we can watch and learn with that bunch of family members. Maybe they will make me not run from my brothers when I see them in September for my birthday."

"You're going back to Italy?"

"It's going to be wild. I'm flying back for a long weekend and returning."

"Tell them no Bolognese sauce while you are there!"

Confusion flitted over his face.

Paula leaned closer. "You said they expect you to make sauce for them."

"Ah!" His jaw fell open. "Sì. No sauces for that bunch while I am there."

"Just lots of birthday cake for you."

"*Spero che le candele non brucino la villa*!"

She understood candles and house, but what did non brucino mean? Villa was house. She'd look it up later.

Gennaro scooted back from the counter. "Grazie for your hospitality."

"You're welcome."

He pressed his hand to his cream-colored T-shirt. "I have to thank Claire and Jeremy for you making another carafe so I could have some of your delicious coffee."

She stood and slacked her hip, giving him the evil eye. "First of all, I would've offered you whatever coffee was left."

"Not if you'd already poured that last cup."

"I'd have made you another pot."

"So the same amount of extra work you had to already do."

She could see where this was heading. "Nope. Because I know you'd prefer to go back and have your espresso machine brew you your coffee the way you like it."

He wagged a finger at her like she'd done. "Uh uh, you don't know that."

"You said that espresso is the best and American coffee was basically wimpy."

He crossed his arms and nodded. "I did. But did I tell you about my awful daughters, who made Papà limit himself to only one cup of coffee a day?"

"Oh." No, he hadn't.

"They think for my health only one cup—like your doctor told you. You're right about kids being a pain sometimes."

"Even when they are right?"

"Especially when they are right."

"Ha! Wait until you meet my Antonia—she's always right."

What have I gotten myself into?

Claire stepped toward the taxi, where Clark awaited, wondering what she'd just gotten herself into. Am I really going up to The Woods restaurant with him so he can see if his sense of smell is improving, or is this a date? She'd certainly dressed like this was a date. A vibrant purple ruffled short-sleeved dress, her best dress sandals that were not for nurse practitioner's work, with their straps and high heels, and a silky lavender coverup.

Her buddy was attired in his usual work wear, khakis and a white shirt with tie, but he had a navy blazer draped over his arm. Her cheeks flushed. This was his typical uniform. Nothing special.

When she reached him, his features tugged in confusion. She was definitely sending mixed messages. "Thanks for the invite, Clark. I've been wanting to dress up a little and wear this new outfit."

"You look very nice. I should have told you The Woods isn't very dressy."

"I've never been there and I'm excited. But I'm even more excited to see if any of our scent challenges are improving your sniffer."

"I think it is. I noticed the roses, in the sun, outside my office today. I'm sure I smelled their scent."

Clark assisted her into the taxi. They sat across from another couple. The woman, like Claire, wore a summer dress and sandals while her husband wore business attire, like Clark. She felt less overdressed.

She tapped Clark's arm. "My mom is gonna meet Gennaro's daughter and her family when they come to see him over in the Canadian Soo."

"Really?" He raised his dark eyebrows. "Is there something going on between those two?"

"I don't know. Mom thinks it's because of her book. Gennaro is like a superfan and apparently his daughter is, too."

"I don't think there's such a thing as being a superfan of a grief book—that's kinda weird."

Claire elbowed him playfully. "Okay, okay, Mom says her book really helped Gennaro, and he tells everyone to read it. His daughter benefitted from reading it, too."

"So he's not introducing your mom to see if she can get along with his family?"

"We already know that Leo and I do not mesh." She scowled and leaned in. "That kid is too cocky, and I think he's a bad influence on Jeremy."

"All right then, don't hold back."

She elbowed him again, and he did it right back. Then a mini elbowing war commenced. She finally stopped when the guy across from them cleared his throat. The wife muttered something like, "Children, children."

When they arrived at the restaurant, Clark gestured for the other couple to disembark first. As soon as they got out, Clark gave her a quick light elbow in the side and then jumped out, laughing. But he did turn to assist her down.

"I won," he said, as she stepped out.

"Close your eyes." She pulled out a small scarf.

"What? Why?"

"I think you'll regret getting the last jab in, since you'll be walking around blindfolded for a bit."

"Aw, come on. I'm sorry." He raised his arms. "Go ahead and get the last mortal blow in before we commence the blind sniffing."

She stepped closer and gently poked him in the ribs. “There, now I’ve won. Now lean in so I can cover your eyes.”

When his face was close to hers, his eyes widened. He drew in a deep breath and pulled away. “I smelled your perfume. Something in it, anyway. Like lilies.”

She clapped. “Oh, wow, that’s great.”

He lifted her off the ground and spun her around as another carriage pulled up.

When he set her down, she poked him again. “You still have to wear the blindfold while I walk you around.”

“I’m not wearing that while we’re eating. No way, because the food here is great, even when I can’t smell it as well as I used to.”

“Maybe since you’re improving, it’ll go better tonight.”

As she tied the scarf around his eyes, she was sure he mumbled, “Every day with you makes things better.”

But she wasn’t touching that line for anything.

Chapter Thirteen

Why do I feel so nervous? Paula clutched her passport in her lap as though the blue booklet would fly away if she didn't. This trip to Canada she was making with Gennaro, to see his daughter and her family, was simply one friend supporting another. *Really.* Why should he have to make the trip into Ontario alone? Especially when Paula was free to accompany him? That's all it was.

Maybe it was because she'd learned the previous night that Gennaro's vintage Lamborghini may be worth over five hundred thousand dollars. A half million—that was half of the insurance money she'd received when Terry had died. Granted, she'd spent almost that much on paying off the mortgage and getting a multitude of home repairs done that Terry kept insisting they put off. Roof, windows, floors, bathroom remodels, foundation repair, trim wrapping, updated electrical—and the list went on.

Now, as they waited in a short line to go through the Canadian border crossing, she wondered what she'd been thinking. This was a bad idea. These probably weren't people who worried about house repair quotes—but when they could buy their next sports car.

"You okay, Paula?" She still loved the way Gennaro said her name as if there was an "owl" in the middle—Powla.

"I'm fine."

A deep chuckle rumbled from him. "My daughter and her family aren't going to eat you alive."

"You sure?"

He turned toward her and placed a warm hand on her wrist, his face serious. "That's my other daughter, the chef, who might do that."

She blinked at him. "The chef would eat me alive? Sounds grizzly."

He turned and slapped his hands lightly on the steering wheel of the Lamborghini "Maybe roast you would be more like it. You know—like they do these celebrities." He inclined his head toward his window.

The car in front of them moved forward, and they followed.

The agent leaned out of his covered security building. Cleanly shaven, with a pale complexion and light ash blond hair with light gray eyes, the agent's appearance was slightly ghostly. "Where are you folks from?"

"I'm a dual Italian and American citizen, and she is American." Gennaro passed his and Paula's passports to the agent.

The man examined the documents and nodded. "What brings you to our beautiful country?"

"My daughter and her family are meeting us at one of the parks here."

"Which one?"

Gennaro blinked and then blurted out the name.

"I take my kids there all the time. Have a good visit, folks."

"Thanks," Paula called out as Gennaro pulled forward.

"Can you get me directions to that place, Paula?"

"Bellevue Park? It's on Queen Street, a short distance." Paula read the GPS directions to Gennaro, and after a couple of miles, they arrived at the park. "When I was a kid, my aunt and uncle would bring me here."

"Not too far away, was it?"

"No, about an hour from St. Ignace." She chewed her lower lip. Uncle Victor had loved coming over there. He enjoyed hiking, picnics, and being by the water. "My uncle loved the outdoors."

"My daughter has learned to enjoy all that Canada, especially Ontario, has to offer. Her husband was a single guy for a long time before he met Antonia. He plans to take the family to every park in Ontario—if not all of Canada!" He laughed.

"That's quite a goal. Canada is a massive country." They pulled into the park, with its verdant lush grass and well-maintained and landscaped acreage.

Gennaro pulled into an open parking spot by a massive playground. He pulled a Dolce & Gabbana sunglass case from his pocket. "I better put these on."

The sky was overcast, loaded with thick clouds. "Not a lot of sun right now."

"This is best." He donned the glasses. "Oh, wow, I can see a lot better now with that little bit of prescription in there."

So they were eyeglasses and not just sunglasses. "Do you have any plain prescription glasses? I've never seen you wear any."

"I am having a little eye surgery soon. That will correct my vision." The way he said it, it sounded like he wasn't telling the whole story. "Look, there's my daughter's family."

He pointed to a silver-haired man in jeans and a T-shirt, who pushed a dark-haired boy on the swings. Nearby, a woman with a dark ponytail, attired in a bohemian long skirt and loose white tunic, pushed a little girl.

Paula hesitated. Maybe Gennaro needed a better prescription, or perhaps the other grandfather had come, too.

"Antonia!" Gennaro hurried toward the swing set.

The man turned; his face looked more youthful than she expected. "Gennaro!" The man grabbed the boy's swing and slowly lowered him to the ground as the young woman turned, too.

"Papà!"

Paula lingered by the vehicle, not wanting to interrupt the reunion. But hadn't her friend said he'd regularly visited with them? With the twenty-something mom staring in her direction, Paula slowly walked across the cushiony grass toward them.

Gennaro's daughter was beautiful, with high cheekbones and strong even features. Her eyes were a greenish color, like new ferns. Her whole face lit up when she saw her father.

"Look at you, Papà!" Antonia poked Gennaro's flat stomach. "You're so skinny!"

Gennaro patted his belly and nodded.

Antonia hugged her dad. "And where is my brother?"

"Leo is coming tonight to see you later. He had to work."

Paula drew closer, as the older man urged the two children toward Gennaro.

As she reached her friend, the silver-haired man said, "That's good you're keeping up your regimen, Gennaro."

Gennaro nodded, but embarrassment crept over his handsome face. "I take care of myself for my family, just like you do, Sean."

"Exactly. I'm down twenty pounds since I followed your advice." Sean tapped his Toronto Bluejays T-shirt over his belly.

"My husband is riding the exercise bike every night." Antonia jutted her chin out.

Up close, Sean looked about forty, but with prematurely gray hair. How did Gennaro feel about Antonia marrying a much older man? Maybe that wasn't an issue with him. Or maybe Gennaro would also find love with a much younger woman. That thought didn't sit well with her, but she was being ridiculous.

Gennaro swiveled toward her. "Paula, this is my daughter Antonia and her husband Sean."

"Nice to meet you." Paula held back a little and smiled at the couple.

"This is little Rosa who has us chasing her wherever we go." Sean pointed to the auburn-haired toddler who was circling around Paula and Gennaro.

Gennaro's granddaughter finally stopped and raised her arms. He lifted her and kissed her. She patted his face. "Boppa!"

Not to be outmaneuvered, the little boy wrapped his arms around Gennaro's waist. "We missed you, Boppa!"

"This is Ian, who started kindergarten this year and is doing very well. Aren't you?" Gennaro patted the boy's back.

Antonia beamed.

"You've got beautiful grandkids, Gennaro."

Sean grabbed Rosa as she tried to dodge past him. "What about you, Paula?"

Her heart ached to admit the truth. "I'm not blessed with any yet."

"Oh, but you will be one day soon. Jeremy is your son, right?" Antonia's silver chandelier-style earrings swayed as she looked between Paula and Gennaro.

Taken aback, Paula frowned. "Yes, Jeremy is my son. But . . ."

She caught Gennaro giving his daughter a tight shake of his head as he lifted Ian into his arms.

What's that all about?

"I hope one day I'll be a grandmother. I don't know when that might be."

"Jeremy is often with Leo when we talk with him on the phone." Sean set Rosa down. When the tyke ran, he surged after her.

"We're looking forward to meeting Jeremy tonight."

This was news to her, but she tried not to react. Her kids were growing up, and they sure didn't tell her all their activities. "I also have a daughter, Claire."

"The neurology nurse practitioner?" Antonia adjusted her right earring.

Heat surged up Paula's neck. Did they all know about her family? "Yes, she's taking a break right now and visiting with us on the island."

"We're trying to source some botanicals from our area for her—for her special medicinal oils she's creating."

Again, Paula tried to keep her facial expression neutral and nodded. Why was she being kept out of her own family's loop?

"Papà, you should put Ian down—your back could go out."

His back? Since when did Gennaro have a bad back?

"I'm fine." But Gennaro slowly lowered the child to the ground and kissed the top of his head.

Rosa struggled, and Sean set her down. She promptly ran to Gennaro.

"Oh no, you don't." Antonia took Rosa's hand. "Stay with Mama, and I'll swing you in just a minute.

"How is your knee?" Sean raised his own and kicked it slightly. "Mine has finally calmed down again."

Antonia waved at Gennaro from head to toe. "With all that weight gone, Papà's not limping at all anymore."

Who were these people talking about? Certainly not her young friend.

Except that maybe Gennaro wasn't so youthful. It seemed strange to see him with the glasses on. He must only need a mild prescription. And significant back and knee problems? That sounded more like . . . her.

Gennaro raised his palms. "No more of these health concerns. I'm doing great. No more picking on Boppa!"

The kids began chanting, "No more picking on Boppa," and circled him.

Gennaro's son-in-law raised his hands. "Well, that's that then."

A sudden realization made Paula's breath hitch. Terry had said those words when he'd last left the house alive.

Terry had packed his bag for his shift as Paula watched, hands on hips.

"Do you really have to take this extra shift? I'm concerned. Everyone's talking about the lack of ventilators at the hospital."

Her husband looked up, his expression grim. "Hon, I don't think those things are really gonna help anyone. In fact, the few patients I've had on them died more quickly."

Paula raised her hands to her mouth. When were the medical people in this country going to figure what was needed to stop this pandemic? "You're being careful, though?"

"As careful as anyone can be when we don't know what we're really dealing with."

"I wish you wouldn't take extra shifts. I wish you'd stay home. Think about us."

"Someone has to do this, honey. If everyone stayed home, who would take care of all the people with Covid?"

Terry had been taking extra shifts for years. Working extra hours. Now he simply had a full-blown excuse to do so, making himself seem even more virtuous. Was it simply to get away from his family? What if they lost him? How would the kids take it if they lost their dad to this horrible epidemic?

Her husband tucked the N-95 mask into his pocket. A cousin had mailed that single mask to them when they'd run out of them at Terry's hospital. "Well, that's that then."

Well, that's that then.

Suddenly, it seemed the little family had moved back to the swings, and she was standing there with her friend.

"Paula? You okay?"

"Oh, yeah, sorry." She swiped at the moisture on her cheek. "Just one of those memory flashes."

He took her hand in his. "Listen to me. You never have to say you're sorry about that—not to me not to anyone."

She nodded.

He didn't release her hand. "Do you know what triggered it?"

Again, she nodded.

He touched the side of his nose. "Now you know. Remember that. It will be a little easier next time, *capisce?*"

His granddaughter ran up to them. "Boppa, come on! Swing me high."

Hard to believe it was already time for him to drive his dear friend back across the bridge and into the United States. Gennaro and Paula continued walking across the verdant lawn to the parking lot, after saying their goodbyes to his daughter and her family. "I'm exhausted, Paula. Would you drive for Boppa?" Gennaro winked at her, but he half meant it.

"You do look exhausted, Boppa." She emphasized the last word and made an adorable little scowl. "But no way am I driving that thing." She pointed to his Lamborghini.

"But I'm really beat." He wiped his brow.

"No kidding. I was worn out simply watching you chase after those grandkids." Paula widened her eyes. "You really aren't in your late thirties or early forties, are you?"

He chuckled. "I never said I was."

"I know." She chewed on her lower lip.

A muscle spasmed in his back, and he pulled in a sharp breath. How would work be tomorrow if this was already starting?

"You okay?"

He rubbed the sore spot. He needed an ice pack pronto. "No more dancing around with my daughter and granddaughter for a while."

"You're not coming back tomorrow?"

"Thank God I have to work because I need a day away from Rosa before I can pull off grandpa duty." Just thinking about her sprints around the park made him tired.

She wagged a finger at him, looking very much like the librarian she was. "That's on you, buster, as my aunt would say."

He shrugged. "Who's Buster?"

Paula laughed. "The only Buster that I ever knew was our neighbor's dog."

He frowned. "We can't blame the pup for me being worn out."

"Nope."

He opened the passenger door for Paula. He'd noticed earlier that she'd had difficulty lifting her leg into the car. "Let me help you, okay?"

"No chance." But when she sat sideways to first get in, she just stared at her legs. "I'm not gonna be an invalid."

"No one said you were." He flinched as another muscle spasm stabbed his back.

"Are you all right?" She grasped his forearm, the warmth of her firm grip sending something good, something hopeful, through him.

"Sì, sì" But he had to take a couple more breaths before the pain passed.

Paula released her grip. "Why don't we pick up some pain ointment on the way back? I'm almost out, and you look like you could use some, too."

He couldn't help grinning. *This was quite the date.* Not a date, he reminded himself. They were friends. Pals. They weren't a couple, even though he had to admit he was floating that idea for the future.

Paula picked up her left leg to assist it into the car and then raised her right leg easily to join it. "We're quite the pair."

He chuckled. "Now you get it, don't you?"

"Yes. You're a young grandpa who is a little out of shape."

As he headed around the front of the car, he considered her words. Right now his back, his knees and feet hurt. *I'm not a young grandpa in my forties.*

Why did Paula want to believe that he was?

Maybe if she realized they were close to the same age, she wouldn't be so friendly with him. Maybe she'd kick this fledgling relationship to the curb.

He didn't want that. *Not at all.*

As he slipped behind the wheel, he resisted the urge to turn to her and say, "If you want to believe that, then that's on you." No Buster involved, though. Just a beautiful woman who'd one day find out exactly who he was.

Chapter Fourteen

Funny how it felt like someone had pumped Paula's heart full of kid love—Gennaro's grandkids were precious. Paula half waddled to the kitchen, her knee still stiff, recalling some of little Ian's antics on the monkey bars.

Claire stood by the coffeepot, Aunt Jackie's robe wrapped tightly around her. "Good morning, Mom."

"Good morning, my beautiful daughter."

Claire tapped the side of her head, where her drooping bun had slipped. "I'm looking spectacular, aren't I?"

"To me, you are." One day when her daughter had children, she'd understand how much that meant to have an adult child there with her. "You're a real blessing to me."

"I'm sure Jeremy is thrilled about sharing a bathroom with me, too, when he's here."

Paula huffed a breath. "I don't understand why one of you doesn't use the other bathroom up there when he stays."

"Because then that would have to be cleaned, too, Mom, and he figures I'll end up doing it—just like I had to do at home."

"You two are both adults."

"One of us is." Claire flipped her hand toward herself. "He's still on the parental dole."

Not only had Terry left insurance policies for each of the kids, but they'd unexpectedly inherited old money from his parents—who the kids had never met. Each had their own money. She wasn't going to touch her daughter's comment with a ten-foot pole, even though she longed to tell her that Jeremy paid his own way through college, unlike Claire.

"Sweetie, could you fix my coffee for me?" She sank onto the stool by the island and rubbed her knee. She'd not been the one chasing after kids, like Gennaro, but sitting too long had really stiffened up that new knee.

Concern flitted over her daughter's pretty features. "Sure thing. International French vanilla creamer?"

"Yup. You got your addiction from me."

"Is that what you call it?"

"Ha! You used to fill your mug a third full of that stuff."

"Not anymore." Claire poured the coffee and then added a tablespoon of creamer and stirred it. She brought her own mug and Paula's to the island.

"Thanks." Paula sipped the coffee, glad that Claire had brewed it on the strong setting.

"How'd everything go last night?" Claire opened the Tupperware box, filled with muffins that Jackie had made earlier that winter.

"Hand me a banana nut one, please, and then I'll tell you."

"Deal."

Paula accepted the treat and removed the paper wrapper. "Thanks." This was fun having her daughter here to talk with. How she'd missed these times.

"What was his daughter's family like?"

"Oh, Antonia's bunch is very athletic." Paula savored a bite of the moist banana and walnut muffin.

"How so?" Claire shifted on her seat.

"Those two kids were busy almost every minute that we were there. Throwing various balls, Ian kicking a soccer ball around, his granddaughter, Rosa, wanted someone to continuously swing her." She waved a half circle in front of her. "It was wild."

"But were they nice?"

"Oh my gosh, yes. So sweet. Polite. And can that son-in-law, Sean, ever cook." She frowned, thinking of how odd he'd acted toward Gennaro.

"Why are you frowning?" Claire peeled the wrapper off her muffin.

"Well, his son-in-law acted kind of . . ." She tapped on the counter. "A little weird toward Gennaro."

"How so?"

"Like he was afraid Gennaro would say something bad about his barbecue. He'd wait until Gennaro took a bite and he'd stand there, eyes wide, and face hopeful until Gennaro pronounced that it was good."

"A young guy looking for approval from his father-in-law?"

"Oh, no." She gave a curt laugh. "He's older. I'm pretty sure his daughter married a daddy figure. A silver fox though. Very handsome, maybe in his forties."

Claire straightened. "Really? Maybe he's seeking Gennaro's approval still. Guilty about having a young wife?"

"I don't know. It seemed more about the food being right. And when Gennaro approved, you'd think fireworks had gone off. Very strange."

"You mean like a chef approving an underling's work?" Claire pushed her mug around.

"Yes." Paula brought her hand down on the counter. "Exactly."

"Leo said one sister owns restaurants in Europe. What had Gennaro said about his past work?"

Paula scrunched her face. "He was a workaholic like your dad was." She clamped her lips tight. Claire was her father's daughter—she too, had been heading in the same direction.

Claire whooshed a sigh. "I think Dad had an addictive personality. He was addicted to work. Do you see that in Gennaro?"

Was her daughter admitting that Terry had any kind of defects and wasn't the perfect dad she'd insisted he was? "Not now. I don't see that trait, but Gennaro said he used to love his work a little too much."

Claire passed her a napkin. "Okay, but for the real dirt. Did his daughter like you? Is she nice?"

Paula averted her gaze. "Antonia is great. You should get your brother's opinion on her. He and Leo are supposed to go over there today for a visit."

"But was she someone you could get along with?"

"Why would that matter about her getting along with me?" Her voice came out more frustrated than she intended, so she softened her tone. "She understood quickly that we're only friends." Maybe because Paula had told her so a half dozen times.

"How was she with her dad?"

Paula tipped her head. *Bossy. And overly concerned about her dad.* Gennaro had overdone the chasing, though. When they'd stopped at the drugstore, the poor guy bought three types of pain creams. "Um, she fussed over him and seemed concerned about his health."

"Maybe because her mom died, ya think?"

"You don't act like that toward me." Again, Paula's words came out way more clipped than she meant them to. Claire had shocked her by not coming when she'd had the knee replacement. Paula gulped her coffee.

Her daughter's cheeks glowed red. "I should have come." It was as though she'd read Paula's mind. "I thought if I pretended there was nothing wrong with you, then nothing would happen to you."

Claire rose and came around and hugged Paula from behind.

She placed her hands over Claire's as her daughter hugged her neck. So that was it. The reason for her daughter's emotional distance. "Honey, I should have taken you to see that movie *Frozen*—even though you were a teenager then. Maybe that would have helped."

Claire kissed her cheek. "I'm sorry. I can't change how I acted. But I'm here now."

"And am I ever glad—you have no idea how happy this makes me."

A tap sounded at the back door just as Mom had headed off to take a shower. Claire hopped up. "I totally forgot about Clark coming by for our walk." She'd been too distracted by asking about Gennaro's daughter and her family. And a little emotionally sidetracked by revealing how she'd avoided facing Mom's surgery like an adult daughter should have done. *I'll make up for it.*

She'd better change clothes. Claire untied the robe's belt, which she'd put on to cover her cotton sleep T-shirt and lounge pants, and shuffled in her slippers to answer the door. When she opened it, Leo stood there. "Oh, it's you."

"*Ciao* to you, too, *bella*!" He looked her up and down. "Nice outfit." He stepped past her, inside.

She scowled at him. "What're you doing here?" Gennaro's handsome son acted like he was God's gift to women. She definitely wasn't a fan.

"Clark and I are walking Rex." Leo raised his hands and splayed his fingers, reminding her of some kind of Jedi move.

She crossed her hands over her chest. "No, you aren't. He's my dog."

He tipped his head back. "That's not what I heard. You stole him."

Wait till she got her hands on her little brother. "My name is on the vet's records in Montana as owner. That makes him my dog."

He shrugged. "If you say so. But we're still walking Rex." He whistled, and her dog charged down the hall toward him. Leo bent and rubbed the dog's fur, speaking to him in Italian.

This kid was a brat. How did he have such a nice dad?

From behind the screen door, Clark waved. "You ready, Claire?"

Leo straightened and turned toward her friend. "As you can see, she needs to change into proper clothing."

Clark opened the door. "Looks fine to me."

"Jeremy and I are walking Rex today."

"I don't think so." Clark ambled toward the annoying college boy.

"I thought you two were going over to Canada today." Claire crossed her arms.

"My girlfriend wants to see him, and she's off this morning." Leo kept rubbing Rex's fur, and of course her pet betrayed her by rolling over on his back for a tummy rub. "She loves dogs."

Clark shook his head. "He's not going with you."

"And my dog is not girlfriend bait." She was tempted to squish Leo's cheeks like she used to do with her brother when he irritated her.

Clark edged in alongside Leo. "Lose the robe, Claire, grab the leash, and put on your Crocs." He pointed to the pink clogs by the hallway bench.

Claire hung Aunt Jackie's robe on a hook, kicked her slippers under the bench, and slid into the Crocs. "Ready." She grabbed the leash and handed it to Clark, who bent and attached it to her dog's collar.

Leo rattled off something in rapid Italian. Her language skills were rusty, but it sounded like he called them peasants and something about a famous dancing chef.

Dancing chef? That rang a bell.

She and Dad had an amazing trip to Rome for her sixteenth birthday. Dad got reservations at a Michelin-star *ristorante* with a famous chef who danced after delivering a special entrée. She'd been shocked how such a heavyset man could move so lightly on his feet. The Dancing Chef had the darkest brown eyes she'd ever seen—like Mom's friend Gennaro. And he'd been rumored to be the descendant of Italian aristocrats who weren't too happy about him becoming a chef and restaurant owner.

Claire locked eyes on Leo, who was scowling. "Is your dad the Dancing Chef from Rome?"

Eyes widening, the young man straightened, stepped back and then raised his hands. "No. He's the manager at Parkers' Resort." He hurried past her, toward the stairs, and clambered up them.

Thou doth protesteth too much. But if Mom's Gennaro was that chef, then what had happened to him?

"What was that all about?" Clark attached the collar to Rex and patted him on the head.

That whole strange feeling she'd had about Gennaro and the stuff Mom said about him all converged. "I think Mom's friend might be hiding out on Mackinac Island." Kind of like she was.

"It's a great place to disappear from the radar."

"I agree. And we'd better disappear before Leo and Jeremy try to kidnap my dog."

The two of them headed out the front door. They walked to the corner, where two seagulls dive-bombed past them to grab someone's left-behind biscuit. They both laughed as Rex barked at the gulls. As they walked on, clouds clustered overhead, threatening another overcast day, but then the sun streaked through, highlighting the ripples on the sapphire waters in the bay.

"Guess what I'm going to do this afternoon?" Clark arched a dark eyebrow.

"Create some kind of new crypto currency—or possibly take over the entire internet world? Mwahahaha!" Claire elbowed him.

He pressed his free hand to his chest. "I am taking art classes this afternoon at the Watercolor Café."

"No way."

"Way." He shortened Rex's leash as a tall man, sporting a Yacht Club polo, passed by with a sleek greyhound.

"Is this art for pleasure or for your job?"

"Oof, I figure if I can't smell things like I used to be able to, then maybe I can at least do more visual things, like paint."

"We're gonna fix your sniffer, my friend. It's already improving, right?"

"Yup." He smiled down at her. "Did you get your kit all set?"

"Amazon shows the rest arriving today—the full array of essential oils that I've used at the hospital."

They continued walking, soon passing a fudge shop. Only a few tourists were on the sidewalks.

"So can you smell that any better?"

"It's weird. It's like I smell something. It's improving, but it's like my brain wants to identify that there is some kind of sweet sugary smell, but no, I couldn't say I can smell fudge."

"Do you remember when you wished you couldn't smell all the stuff common to Mackinac Island?" She immediately regretted her words.

"Yeah, every day. I feel like an idiot for ever having said that."

"I'm sorry."

"It was a good clue about my relationship when Brooke got upset—claimed I was pretending. And then she thought I was freaking out about getting married rather than that I couldn't smell."

"But you told her."

"Of course. But she acted like I was one of her students trying to get out of something."

"Wow. I'm sorry." She squeezed his shoulder.

A memory of Dad flashed into Claire's mind.

She'd been up late working on classwork, bummed that she could no longer attend classes in person. She'd left a cheese sandwich in the pan, on the stove. Suddenly she smelled char odor coming from the kitchen. She'd shoved back from the table and jogged to the stove. *Ruined snack.*

She'd just started making a sandwich again when Dad arrived home. Since the pandemic, he'd stopped hugging her, which kind of hurt, but was understandable.

"Hi, sweetie, how you doing?"

She was surprised he'd not fussed about the odor. "I guess you can tell what I just did."

He shook his head. "No, what?"

"Can't you smell the burnt sandwich?"

He'd sniffed the air. "Nope. But I see it." He pointed to where she'd tossed the sandwich in the side of the sink where the dish disposal was. "That's kind of weird."

Dad moved closer to the sink, set his insulated lunch bag down and leaned in. "I smell something really faint."

"It's pretty strong."

"Some of my Covid patients have lost their olfactory sense."

Alarm shot through her. Somehow, even then, it seemed like the Lord was preparing her for what was to come.

"I'm gonna sleep in the guest room downstairs tonight. Right after I wash my clothes."

"You okay, Claire bear?"

"Remembering about my dad losing his smell. And then, so fast, he was gone."

Clark squeezed her hand. "I'm sorry. I know you two were close."

They had been. Now, though, it felt like she'd frozen her mom out of her life to avoid being close to her and to not have to experience that horrible grief again. She swiped at her eyes, remembering the intense pain she'd felt during that time. Rex nudged her leg, and she bent to pet his soft head.

A dray piled high with Amazon boxes passed them in the street, drawing Claire back to the present. Were her oils on that dray? If she could keep helping people who'd lost their sense of smell to this horrible disease, then she'd be satisfied. She'd not been able to do anything for her father, but this she could do.

"What's your success rate with your regimen, Claire?"

"So far, over eighty-percent efficacy—especially with younger people."

"Am I young still?"

She wrinkled her nose. "We're everyday edging closer to thirty, so I don't know."

The door to the shop opened, and the scents of chocolate, vanilla, and caramel wafted out. Clark's brow crinkled. "I feel like I lost an important part of myself."

Already slim, her friend's clothes hung a bit on him. "It affects appetite, too. I can see you're still losing weight."

"Yeah."

She continued walking down the sidewalk, away from Joann's Fudge shop.

"Everybody says it's because the wedding was canceled. And I'm happy to let them think that."

It still stung to realize how close he'd come to marrying Brooke.

"Remember how we used to plan our wedding? Grand Hotel." She'd grown up with that iconic hotel as her dream wedding destination.

"That's out with the new owners." Clark's clipped tone reinforced his statement.

"Yeah, it wouldn't be the same." And even though she could afford it, it didn't have the same vibe now. "Mission Resort was another."

"Too many kids."

She swatted at him. "I thought you liked kids."

"Not at my wedding."

Rex barked.

Clark chuckled. "No dogs, either. Just grownup humans."

"Really? I can just imagine what your ex said about no kiddos. Being a schoolteacher, I imagine all her students would have been invited."

"My mom and dad agreed with me about no kids at the reception, but Brooke nixed that, too." He stopped in front of a T-shirt shop. "And I wanted a dress code, too, but she wanted casual. This was supposed to be a big formal event."

"Like we planned? We had everything all monogrammed, crystal goblets, the whole thing all with fresh flowers."

"Yes, but I wasn't marrying you."

No, he hadn't been. He'd almost marched down the aisle with Brooke.

She stopped, right in front of a dress shop, where the mannequins sported beautiful wedding garb. This island was known for its many weddings, but not so many purchased their gowns here. The door to the shop opened, and the girl from the bookstore exited, holding a gold-embossed bag.

"Hello there!" The young woman acted like Claire and Clark were her buddies.

"Hi." Unease crept through Claire.

Rex sat in front of the woman. She pulled a small dog biscuit from her pocket. "Speak, Rex."

The dog barked once and she gave him the treat. How did she know her dog's name?

"Turn." The woman swirled her hand in a circle, and to Claire's astonishment, her dog rotated completely around. She handed him another treat. "Good boy."

Why would her pet obey a complete stranger? She got what Mom called Holy Ghost bumps on her arms.

"Can you believe they finally got an actual wedding dress in that store?" The woman pointed to the window.

"I've never seen one there before." Clark rubbed the side of his face. His very handsome face. A face she'd loved for so long. And had missed so much.

Moisture filled her eyes and she blinked it back. The strangeness of this woman was affecting her.

"I have to get back to work." Giving a little wave, the blonde departed down the sidewalk, doing a little skip and hop as she went. *Definitely weird.*

Claire pointed. "Was that woman here this winter?"

"No. She showed up about the time you got here."

Claire didn't want to dwell on this oddness. *Different topic.* "Hey, would you mind if I did the Watercolor Café class with you? Do you think they have openings?"

"That would be great. I'll call them."

"Thanks."

"I'd thought about asking you to do the painting class with me, but I didn't want to . . ." he shrugged as he trailed off his words.

"Didn't want what?" She frowned.

Four bicyclists sped by in the road, the last one a teen raising his hands overhead. Good thing there weren't many carriages out right now.

He stopped walking and rotated toward her. "I'd never want you to think you were a rebound."

"A rebound?" She feigned outrage. "I'm the original. If anything, Brooke was the rebound."

And right there on the street, her old pal, her buddy, pulled her into his arms and kissed her so soundly that Rex began howling.

Definitely not the rebound.

Chapter Fifteen

A big baby—that's what Paula was for enlisting her daughter and new friend to come with her to the family farm in St. Ignace. Gennaro said he needed a prescription from St. Ignace, anyway. So it worked out. The three of them stood at the ferry dock, ready to check onto the boat to St. Ignace. With the short line, they were soon boarding.

"I'm going up top, Mom." Claire bounded up the stairs before Paula could reply.

Gennaro waved his hand back and forth. "Not for me. Fewer stairs down. My knee is acting up today."

"Sorry." Paula frowned. "It looked like you might be limping a little."

She and Gennaro went below and headed up the aisle toward the bow section.

Gennaro gestured for her to slide into the bench seat first. "I'm picking up something for my knee. It had been pretty good until I saw Antonia's kids last week."

She huffed a laugh. "You got more than a little wild in those games of chase."

"I know. And now I still pay for it." He winced as he sat.

"No games of chase for me for a while, if ever. I'm still doing my daily therapy exercises just to help me get around well."

"How much longer is your physical therapy?"

"They have released me to home exercises, so I guess I've graduated."

He gave her a high five.

"My aunt deserves a double high five, since she's finally able to be discharged."

"Jeremy said she was ready to be at home—but on the mainland. And he said she and her fiancé will decide where they want to live after they are married."

"I still can't believe she and Frank are engaged. But they are really sweet together."

"Some people surprise you." He tilted his head back, and then down. "Our kids, for instance."

"Oh, yeah?"

He tugged at his jacket cuffs, something she'd seen him do when he was nervous. "They don't tell us certain things, that's for sure."

Stiffness started in her shoulders. "When they're adults, they have the right to privacy."

Gennaro longed to tell his dear friend that her son would soon be a father. "There's privacy and then there is common sense. Sometimes they need parents to help them, but their pride gets in the way."

"I'm gonna differ on that. Maybe it's so overwhelming, they don't know where to start. And they want to decide that first." She frowned. "Maybe the control of taking an adult 'first step'?"

"Yes, but if they would only share with Mom . . . or Dad, then they'd get help in that first step." When he turned to face her, he suddenly felt like the over-fifty grandpa that he was—especially with his knee throbbing.

"Gennaro, what has happened that made you think about this?"

He'd promised his son not to say anything, and he kept his word. Never should have agreed to that, but he'd been so relieved that Leo hadn't stolen Jeremy's girl and gotten her pregnant. He forced a mask of serenity onto his face as he scrambled for a recovery. "My eldest daughter, Emanuela, set the precedent for me in withholding things. She'd been working at the restaurant, had been married about six months." He flipped his hands over. "But it wasn't until she fainted at work and another staff member caught her, that I learned dear Emanuela was expecting a child in few months."

"Wow."

"I felt like an idiot." He swiped at his forehead. He was sweating over almost revealing what Leo had said, but Paula wouldn't know that. "Emanuela knew I'd have made her stay off her feet more, and she was having none of that."

"So what happened?" She took his hand, and he gently squeezed her fingers.

"I told her I would always be her papà, and that while she was married and a grown-up, I was still entitled to my opinion."

"Ha! They don't want to hear our opinions, though, do they?"

"No. She said I could have my own ideas but to keep them to myself." Like he was keeping Jeremy's information to himself.

"That doesn't seem fair, but it's how it is these days, isn't it?"

"I can only imagine what my father would say if I told him he had to keep his thoughts private. He'd have a few choice words for me." *Quite a few Italian cuss words in there, no doubt.*

"It must be lovely still having your father. And being able to ask him his opinion on things."

He laughed, but then sadness chased his smile away. "It is. But he keeps sending me a two-word message."

"What's that?"

"Come home."

"To Italy?"

"Yes, to our family home. They're getting older."

Outside, light rain began to fall, obscuring the view.

"But I thought you visit often."

"I do. I'm there for months at a time."

"Ah, but they want you to stay there."

He couldn't imagine being that far away from this woman again. This sweet, beautiful lady he'd come to . . . yes, love. "Yes. He'd like me to make my home there, and transfer ownership of my villa in Rome to my daughter."

She blinked a few times.

What was she thinking? Would she come with him to Italy?

A villa in Rome? Not an apartment? When Paula had imagined Gennaro's poor wife dying, she'd pictured them in a small kitchen in an apartment. Even that would be very expensive in Rome. But a villa? A home in one of the most expensive places in the world? That and his fancy car put her younger pal in a world outside her orbit.

"My colleagues at work have been pushing me to come back to work soon and back home to Virginia, too. But it's like you were saying—adults must make their own decisions. I'm glad to help my Aunt Jackie make this transition. And I'm happy to be with my kids this summer." She chewed on her lower lip. She wasn't going to say that she didn't want to leave Gennaro, but it was true. She'd miss him. She really cared about him. And she loved him in her own special way.

Rain spattered the windows as outside the skies turned an ugly gray.

He released her hand. "When will you go back?"

"Not until Jeremy's done for the summer. Once he's settled into his new place."

"I was surprised Leo wasn't going to live with him." The way Gennaro said this, it was as if he was dropping a tasty morsel that she was supposed to swoop onto.

She could play this game. "Why do you think that is?"

When he blinked, she knew he was hiding something.

"Mom!"

Paula turned to spy a trail of passengers coming up the aisle, her daughter at the front, holding her dripping umbrella downward.

"Glad I had this umbrella. Scoot over Gennaro."

Paula and Gennaro moved in, and Claire sat down. "That sure happened fast."

Was Gennaro trying to tell her something about Claire? She had seemed to be hiding something. If it was about her job, Paula already guessed that she wasn't on vacation. She'd play the trump card.

She leaned in. "Claire, since you're not returning to Montana, have you thought about what you want to do next?" She smiled sweetly at her daughter, who looked shocked, and Gennaro who appeared surprised.

Claire resisted the urge to scowl. "Who told you?"

Mom placed two fingers on her eyes and then pointed toward her. "I have two eyes and a brain. I figured hospitals don't let new nurse practitioners take all summer off—not anywhere on this planet."

"Yeah, there's that." Claire coughed.

"Sweetie, I've been telling you to take a break. It's not like you have to work." Mom clamped her mouth shut, as if cutting off those words. When her mother had discovered that Dad's wealthy parents who they'd never had contact with had left him a substantial inheritance, she'd been shocked. Dad had implied his family had died before they'd met. Dad had only received notification shortly before his death. The trust funds transferred to Claire and Jeremy upon his death. Honestly, she'd been afraid to touch that money. Was Mom encouraging her to do so?

Gennaro narrowed his eyes and his brow furrowed. "What would you like to do?"

"I'm trying to develop my own line of pharmaceutical-grade essential oils that would be used for neurological interventions."

"Such as?"

"Onc example is to help Covid patients who've lost their sense of smell. There's good research showing the use of a specific scent protocol helps that return."

Mom leaned in. "And also it helps people with memory recall, right?"

"It can. There's promising new research with bedtime usage for patients at risk for cognitive decline."

"Sounds exciting." Gennaro pressed his hands together. "You and your mother should come to Italy sometime, to my family's estate, to see if we could grow some of the herbs or flowers you need."

"I may take you up on that." Claire bumped shoulders, just like she used to do with Dad and just like Dad, Gennaro bumped her back.

Something hopeful blossomed inside her—a wish for her mother to find happiness with this man.

"My family owns the largest orchards and vineyards in all of Italy."

Mom could never do a poker face, and her shocked expression and quick effort to compose herself spoke volumes. Was her intimidation by wealthy people something that had kept Dad from telling her about his own family—the Eckers of Connecticut, from old money? *Nah, that was because they were the most toxic people up there.* Dad had been right to keep them out of his life—and hers and Jeremy's. The one contact she'd had with her uncles had made her want to throw up. They were so rude and mean to her and her brother.

Claire nodded. "If I run into supply problems, I would like to talk with whoever is running those farms."

Gennaro's face reddened. "Oh, that would be my brothers. We aren't like those lords in England, with a bunch of estate managers and all that. My nephews chip in and will probably take over eventually. Me," he patted his chest, "I am no farmer, even though I like to garden—especially with your mother."

He patted Mom's hand, but when he tried to hold her hand, she pulled it free.

Yikes, staying out of that, whatever it is—or isn't.

All the way they walked to Claire's car, Paula listened as her daughter and Gennaro discussed what might be involved if she had to extract and import oils from Italy. Shocked by how much he knew, including about food exports, she realized how little she really knew about him and his background. They got Claire's vehicle from the lot and headed to the St. Ignace Pharmacy and parked.

"I'm going into the pharmacy with Gennaro, Mom."

"No sense in me going in and being tempted by those amazing Yooper bars they keep at the counter." Good thing Sayklly's

Confectionary didn't sell stock because she'd have invested the rest of Terry's life insurance proceeds in Yooper bars. The delicious chocolate bars, with a raised map of the Upper Peninsula on them, had been a huge hit at Claire's high school graduation party. This drug store and several other stores around St. Ignace carried the addictive treat. So she'd stay put.

Gennaro called over his shoulder as he got out, "We'll be right back."

Within minutes, Paula grew antsy. She got out of the car and stood facing the beautiful harbor across the street.

"Hello, stranger!"

Paula turned to spy her friend, Debbie Nabozny. Deb grinned as she walked from her parked car to where Paula stood. "Have you killed those seedlings yet? Or did they make it?"

"They're doing great! Thanks again." Paula pulled her into a hug. "How are you and Dan doing?"

"Great and our pups have been healthy all summer so far." Deb raised her hand and crossed her fingers. "Fingers crossed anyway. How about you? When are you coming for a barbecue at Bayview?"

"Soon as I get an invitation." She winked. She wasn't going to invite herself. Deb and Dan's rental kept fully booked through the summer.

"Let me check with Dan and I'll call you. Okay? Gotta get in there and pick up his meds before he refuses to take them." She laughed.

"Dan's not one to take anything." Just like her uncle had been. By the time Victor had figured out what was wrong with him, it was too late. He'd refused to see a doctor for his back. He'd gone to the chiropractor, finally, and the x-rays revealed part of the brutal truth—cancer, that dreaded evil disease, had settled in Uncle Victor's spine.

"You okay?" Deb squeezed her hand.

"Yeah." Paula waved her hand. "We're going by the farm today."

"Oh!" Deb's clipped voice held concern. "Have you been back there since, well . . ."

"Not since Victor passed."

"Oh." Again, that dread in her friend's voice. "Just be aware that it's not like it was."

"What do you mean?"

Deb's phone rang. "Oops, I gotta take this. Let's talk soon." She swiveled around and entered the pharmacy.

What were they walking into? Had the farm gotten that run down? How would Aunt Jackie live there if the previous tenants had left it a mess?

Soon, Claire and Gennaro returned, and they drove up to the family farm outside of town. The house's exterior looked well-maintained. "Someone painted."

"I think Aunt Jackie had that done last year." Claire turned the car off and unbuckled her seatbelt as Gennaro and Paula did the same.

"You go in first, Claire." Paula passed her daughter the house key. "I don't know what I'll do if they've trashed the place."

"Sure, Mom." Claire took the key and headed to the side door.

Gennaro came alongside her. "Come on, Paula, let's go look at that garden that you've told me about."

"Okay." They headed behind the house to the high wood privacy fence. At eight feet tall, it was meant to keep both people and critters out.

Gennaro swung the gate open. "What happened here?"

Paula followed him, gaping. "Nothing. That's what has apparently happened. Nothing whatsoever."

"Wasn't the fellow renting this place a landscaper?"

"He said he was." Hands on hips, she took in the mass of weeds and untamed jungle of plants. "Clearly he hasn't taken care of this garden."

"Much of this looks like, uh, volunteer plants—someone leaving the organic heirloom plants like those tomatoes, to reseed themselves." Gennaro bent and pulled up a vine of cherry tomatoes that was crawling on the ground.

Paula shook her head. "I thought my aunt was checking up on this place. This garden was my uncle's pride and joy." She swiped at raindrops that had somehow fallen on her face—but there were no clouds overhead anymore—the storm had moved off. Her cheeks heated.

"You are crying. I'm so sorry. This was a special place for you." Gennaro pulled her into his arms, and she didn't resist the comfort. She inhaled the peppermint on his breath and the piney scent of his aftershave. "In your book, you said this was a magical place for you because in the garden you and your uncle would spend hours working and talking." He patted her hair.

She nodded against his shoulder. But her uncle mostly did the gardening, and she did the talking. Lately, it felt like she'd forgotten everything he'd tried to teach her.

"You also said in your book that when your husband died—that's when you could cry for the loss of your uncle. That you had to be strong for your aunt when your uncle had passed away."

She sniffed. "Yes. And I was in shock. I couldn't believe it. The cancer moved so quickly."

"No one expects a man in his early fifties to die, *dolcezza mia*."

Had he just called her sweet? Paula searched her limited Italian but came up short.

"Paula, this is why I work so hard to take care of my health. I didn't want to leave my children alone—*né tutti i miei nipoti.*"

Paula pulled away. When she looked into his deep brown eyes, the caring she saw there almost took her breath away. She averted her gaze. "It's good that you want to keep yourself in shape for your family so you don't die early. I know they're concerned about you."

The way his daughter talked, you'd think he was an old man.

Gennaro took her arm and tucked it through his as they walked the perimeter of what had been the massive family garden. The place was as large as a football field, and her knee began to complain. When they'd finished the loop, Gennaro removed his arm from hers.

"All right, dear Paula, we can see this garden needs a complete overhaul." He made a large circular motion with his hands. "It's not how you and your uncle left it all those years ago."

"That's for sure."

"But your auntie won't be out in the garden so much, raising vegetables."

"Not this year at least."

"*Cara mia*, I'm not sure she and her fiancé would want to take this on."

In her mind's eye, she could see the place filled with a multitude of gorgeous vegetables, some of which Jackie used to freeze or can, and some Uncle Victor would take to market. But that was the past.

Claire jogged through the gate. Her smile slid off her face when she looked at the mangled garden. "Whoa, I guess the tenant's idea of being a landscaper sure doesn't jive with ours."

"Right," Paula and Gennaro chorused.

"But great news!" Claire threw her hands overhead. "The house is immaculate."

As her daughter dropped her arms to her sides, Paula gave her a long look. "Define immaculate." Teenaged Claire's idea of neat and clean hadn't been the same as Paula's.

Claire pressed her hands to her chest. "Mom, I'm a health care provider. This place could almost qualify for a bona fide care home—it's that clean."

Gennaro frowned. "You are kidding."

"My thoughts exactly."

"Come see." Claire turned and ran back toward the house.

Gennaro placed his hand over his heart. "I'm not running after her."

Laughing, Paula walked with her dear new friend up to the house. "So many wonderful memories in this place."

Gennaro opened the door for her, and she stepped into the kitchen.

Paula blinked. "Oh, I didn't realize Aunt Jackie had this remodeled."

"Maybe about a decade ago, by the looks of the granite color." Claire gestured around. "And the cabinet choices."

"This isn't the little country kitchen we made cookies in when I came to live here." But then she spied the yellow Formica-topped table. "Oh my gosh, it's still there. Our little yellow table that belonged to Grandma and Grandpa."

"Looks pretty good, too." Claire smiled. "Someone took care of it."

Gennaro ambled through to the living room. "This reminds me of my den at home in Italy."

Paula took in the cozy gathering of four overstuffed leather recliners gathered around the fireplace. "Those are newer, but they look comfy."

"Those could really work for Aunt Jackie."

"What about the downstairs bedroom?"

Claire exited the living room, and Paula followed.

Inside the small room, the brass bed shone. The two round rosewood bedside tables were topped by modern adjustable touch lights with USB ports for phone charging. "I got some lamps like that for me after you recommended that type, Claire, for after my surgery."

Gennaro joined them and pointed overhead. "Does the fanlight have a remote?"

"Sure." Claire picked up a small black remote from the matching dresser. "Closet has a few things in it. Looks like the tenants honored her request to leave this room unused."

Paula laughed. "The deadbolt lock on the door likely helped, too. Good thing the realtor unlocked that for us because I don't have that key."

"Did you look upstairs?" Gennaro looked doubtful.

"Yes. It all looks fine. I flushed the toilets and ran the water in the sink and the bath."

"How about the downstairs bathroom? Will she be able to manage in there?" Paula followed Claire to the nearby bathroom.

When she flipped the light on, Paula gaped. "When was a walk-in no-threshold shower put in and the handrails and all?"

"I told Aunt Jackie about two years ago that she should do this just in case."

"In case she had to live here?"

"I knew she planned to move to the mainland eventually, and I suggested she might want to get this set up a little better."

Paula slowly shook her head. "Why didn't she talk with me about it?"

"She didn't want you to feel like you had to take over the place on the island." Claire shrugged. "She knew I was working, as were you, and Jeremy was in college. And she knew you'd worry about the cottage being unoccupied when she needed to move to the mainland. So, she didn't want you to feel any pressure."

When Paula didn't respond, Claire turned to Gennaro. "And my great-aunt was right. As soon as Mom heard that Jackie was in the rehab facility, she left her job and headed up here."

Gennaro winked at Paula. "Seems my daughter, Antonia, is not the only one who worries about her parent."

Claire glanced between the two of them. "Is your daughter worried about your arthritis and gout? I mean—that's really very manageable, as are cataracts."

What was Claire talking about? *Gout? Cataracts?*

When her friend's cheeks flushed, Paula had confirmation. His issues weren't those of the youthful man she'd once thought he was.

And she couldn't help smiling, even if she was sympathetic.

A knock on the door sounded. "It's just me, Frank!"

Claire ducked out into the hallway, and Paula and Gennaro followed her.

Frank closed the door behind him. "This place looks great, eh?"

"The garden not so." Gennaro flipped his hands over.

"I wish I'd gotten my house all disability friendly." Paula rolled her lips together. She'd kept putting it off. "Sure would have made going home easier after my surgery."

"My old two-story house might be a challenge for Jackie." Frank rubbed his neck. "That became a problem for Jackie at Garden Cottage."

"Why don't you two move in here, then?" Claire made a circle with her index finger.

Paula hadn't realized she'd sucked in her breath until Frank gaped at her. She pressed her own lips closed. She couldn't imagine anyone but Uncle Victor living there with Aunt Jackie. She was being childish.

"Maybe it's not my place to say." Gennaro shrugged. "But at Garden Cottage, there are also three steps into the house—even if you have the bedroom and bath on the first floor." He gestured to the house. "Will that be safe for Jackie?"

"It's not the few steps that are the big problem." Frank shook his head. "After that fall, Jackie is scared of living on the island. It was quite an ordeal getting her to the hospital from the cottage."

"Understandable." Paula nodded.

"She'll want to go and see her friends and you and your family. But Jackie has buddies here on the mainland, too. Old friends from high school. And of course, I have all my volunteer work in the community and for the tribe and family and friends."

Frank had lived there all his life. He was a pillar of the community. Jackie would be in good hands.

"After we're married, we'll stay either in this house or in mine, eh? If I can get my own remodeled to age in place." Frank rubbed his left hand, almost as if feeling for a wedding ring. "We're ready to start our lives here on the mainland."

What about Paula? Was she ready to start over—away from Virginia?

The way Gennaro was looking at her, what was he thinking?

Chapter Sixteen

Why, oh why, had Paula let Claire talk her into that bike ride all the way around the island the previous night? Because she relished some alone time with her daughter, that was why. They'd had so much fun. But now, her muscles shrieked at her as she got out of bed. Her head began to pound. Or maybe that wasn't her head, but someone at her bedroom door.

"Someone's banging on the front door, Mom!" Jeremy called through her door. "And they're serious!"

She grabbed her robe, put it on, and then opened her bedroom door. "Who is it, son?" Was this Edna, or maybe the police, coming to speak with them again? She was in no hurry to see either.

Jeremy's hair sprang in all directions, and he still wore his sleep shorts and a white T-shirt. "I think it might be dockporters on the porch."

"Dockporters. Why would they be here?"

"I don't know." He rubbed his eyes. "Long enough to wake me up, though."

"I didn't hear them knock."

"Well, yeah." He deliberately widened his eyes. "That's why I'm here at your door, Mom."

There'd been a time she'd have corrected his behavior, but it seemed he may finally be going through his rebellious phase, which was bound to happen sometime. Jeremy headed to the front of the house, and she followed.

When her son opened the door, two guys with bikes vastly overloaded with luggage peered up at them. That looked like enough stuff for a half dozen people or more.

The one with a blond man bun and scruffy beard sported an arrogant expression. "These are for the Donatelli family."

"I don't think so. We're the Eckers." Jeremy tugged at his T-shirt.

She shook her head. "This is no longer a bed and breakfast."

The guy with short reddish hair and glasses nodded. "I told him that, but he wouldn't listen."

Scruffy guy wrinkled his long nose. "Mr. Gennaro from Parkers' Resort said you'd put them up. They lost their accommodations and there's no room anywhere."

Paula frowned.

Jeremy huffed a laugh. "Is this a joke? I know you guys can be pranksters."

It had to be. Gennaro wouldn't impose on her like that, would he?

"They were booked at LaBelle Inn, and that fire closed out an entire floor."

Oh no, this sounded true.

"Wow, yeah, I read about the fire." Jeremy nodded. "Some goof leaving their electric bike on the charger overnight."

The posh boutique hotel charged close to a thousand dollars a night.

"Yup." The redhead shifted on his bike.

"But they were already flying here from Italy to surprise Mr. Gennaro." Scruffy frowned. "That's what they said, anyway."

Panic surged through her. The place, while not messy, was lived-in, especially since Jeremy had spent the night and trashed the kitchen. Guests? No way were they up to that.

Scruffy gave her a hard look. "This is getting heavy, ma'am."

She hadn't been "ma'amed" since she'd arrived up north. His tone wasn't polite, though, like in the South.

Jeremy pulled his phone from his pocket and looked at it. "Gennaro says you're not answering your phone."

"It's turned off." Her heartbeat was hammering so loud she could hear it in her ears.

The phone rang, and Jeremy looked at it and then handed it to her. "He's calling."

She accepted the phone as he trotted down the steps to the porters. She made a face at her son as he began helping them unload the baggage, but he didn't stop.

She swiveled away and raised the phone to her ear. "Hello?"

"Oh, my friend, please mi scusi." It sounded like he expelled a big breath. "My daughters, they think it's a good idea to surprise me."

"It's a surprise to me, too! Oh my gosh." She couldn't help the edge in her voice. She'd have to send Jeremy back to the workers' lodging early, and Claire may have to come downstairs with her to Jackie's room. "How many daughters came from Italy?" Two could be easily accommodated, even if it was inconvenient. And Gennaro was her friend after all. She had to try to help.

"Three girls."

"Three?" she squeaked. No way was she ready for this. Not just the girls but everything to do with it. Were they wild twenty-somethings? But not if they were like their sister. "Is there really nothing available?"

"Believe me, I called in every favor. The Parkers would have put them up at Cardinal Cottage, that big place up on West Bluff, but it's overflowing with Gianni's kids and grandkids right now. Carter and Alyssa Parker, who live there year-round, have taken Sammy and little Kelsey and gone on a vacation to West Virginia because their place is overrun."

"Wow." The couple, only in their twenties, had married the previous year. Both brought children into the marriage.

"Yes, wow, and I'm sorry I didn't come by personally, but I'm working and we're slammed here with conference members. I only heard about this catastrophe this morning."

One of her trigger words. She instinctively raised her hand, as she did in the library. Catastrophes weren't usually catastrophes. "Hey, this is no catastrophe. We'll work this out. This is your family. And friends help friends, right?" Christian duty prevailed. No way was she going to keep them out even if they had enough luggage to clothe an army. But maybe those were bags for another family lodging nearby.

"Grazie mille. I'll be by later."

"I'll call you when they arrive."

She turned to spot Jeremy stacking the bags at the bottom of the stairway. This was obviously the dockporters' only stop right now.

Her heart sunk. What kind of divas were these young women?

Claire joined them, eyes wide as she dodged all the luggage. "There's like a dozen people trudging up this way from the corner—sounded like they were speaking Italian."

"What do you mean? He said three daughters." Paula rose.

"I saw a bunch of kids and probably their parents when I raised my window."

"Oh no." Gennaro was going to get an earful later—dear new friend or not. This was just the kind of thing her late husband pulled. He'd manspeak in abbreviated terms and leave out important details that he knew would earn him a negative response.

"We better go welcome them." Claire poked her index fingers beside her pink lips and pretended to pull her mouth into a smile.

"Fake smiley face, for sure." Her aunt never booked more than eight to ten people upstairs because of the overload on the plumbing.

When Paula stepped out onto the front porch and spied the long line of exhausted people—couples and children—all with dark rings under their eyes and yawning, her heart melted. Gennaro's poor daughters and their families. If they were anything like the other grandkids, they'd all steal her heart. She called out, "What a long trip you must have had."

The woman in front, whose dark hair was generously streaked with white and pulled into a chignon, nodded. Beside her stood a boy her height, maybe twelve or so. She couldn't help staring.

Gennaro's age was launching higher.

Behind her, a thickly muscled man with softly graying brown hair stood beside a tall slender boy of about twelve. Two more couples, one holding a toddler's hand and the other surrounded by a preschooler and two elementary-aged kids, trailed up.

Gennaro was definitely over fifty with a passel of grandkids. Was she ever gonna give him an earful.

Why had he let her think he was a young pup?

"Are they still sleeping?" It had been over fifteen hours since their guests arrived. Claire passed Mom a plastic jug of fertilizer, and she began sprinkling it with great agitation.

"Men," Mom muttered.

Claire chuckled. "At least he offered to weed for you for the rest of the month."

Mom pointed the jug at her. "I threatened him if he didn't."

"What were you gonna do if he didn't?"

"Never speak to him again."

"Ha! If Clark pulled this stunt, I'd freeze him out for a month."

Mom pushed her bangs back. "I'd rather have the weeding done."

"Fair point."

"Hey, while I water out here, would you raid your aunt's freezer and thaw enough baked goods for when they get up?" Mom directed the spray at the base of the zucchini plants.

"Sure thing."

Sunlight peeked out from the puffy cumulus clouds overhead and illuminated a new gold-and-bronze owl garden ornament that Jeremy had bought for Mom.

"I've already set up both coffee machines and the electric teapot."

"I'll run down to Doud's and get more stuff later."

"Not too much. Gennaro said he's going to make plans for them."

"When is Gennaro bringing the extra stuff from the hotel that we need upstairs?" They'd exhausted their supply of blankets, pillows and towels.

"He's probably afraid I'll yell at him in person when he shows up."

"He'd deserve it."

"He texted that he'll take them to the Pink Pony tonight. After that, they'll go to Marquette Park and let the kids run around. Tomorrow is Fort Mackinac, and they can eat in the Tea Room there."

"I love that place."

"Me, too."

"Gennaro has booked a private ferry to go around the island."

"Like a Sip n' Sail cruise?"

"Yes, same folks. And he wants the grown-ups to have a Grand Hotel dinner. You and Clark and Jeremy and, of course, Leo."

"Has he got something lined up for the kids?"

"The Parkers feel terrible that they couldn't put them up. They have got two evenings of fun planned with their big family and Gennaro's grandkids."

"Whew!" Claire pretended to swipe sweat from her brow. Her phone dinged for a text message, and she checked it. "Clark says his parents invited me to stay up at their place on West Bluff." She chewed her lower lip. She couldn't abandon her mom to Gennaro's clan.

"Can I come with you?" Mom stopped spraying and plunked down on a bench.

"Let me ask." Claire pretended to text Clark back. "He says Jeremy and you and I should run and hide up there."

Mom arched an eyebrow. "I bet he suggests Gennaro should stay here with his kids, too, right?"

"Yup. That's exactly what he said."

The garden gate squeaked open. If that was Mom's friend, she'd have to apologize to him if he heard them. But instead of Gennaro, it was their neighbor.

Mrs. Parsons, dressed in a purple and lime green caftan and leopard print slippers, pointed at them. "This place isn't a bed and breakfast anymore," she screamed. "I'm not gonna put up with all these people over here making noise like foreigners do!"

"Oh boy." Poor Mom sat staring at the disturbed woman.

Claire swiveled away, as Mrs. Parsons advanced closer. "I'm calling 9-1-1," she whispered to her mother.

Mom raised a hand. "Don't. I'll get ahold of Jackie and see if she has Edna's kids' numbers. Maybe they can help."

Claire marched over to the neighbor. "You're trespassing, and you need to go back home." She pointed to the gate.

The woman flinched. "No need to be so rude." As she shuffled away, she muttered something about "no account freeloaders." Whether she was referring to Claire or someone else, she didn't know.

"She should be glad you didn't press charges against her for Great-Grandma's antique peonies being destroyed." Claire shook her head. "Those were irreplaceable."

"I know, but Jackie didn't want to go to the police, either." Mom made a snipping motion. "I'm not sure that last attack on hollyhocks would amount to a crime."

"It sure looked like someone cut the stalks in half."

"She could have blamed the deer if we were back in Virginia. But with how few deer there are on the island, that excuse wouldn't fly." Mom made a face of disgust.

"We've got to at least lock the back gate—with something that will keep her out of your garden."

"Call John Hubel and ask him if he's got something he could suggest that would work but not look too ugly. I don't want a combination lock on there."

"I've seen some nice ones around town on garden gates. I'll ask him."

Paula couldn't believe that they had a private Sip n' Sail cruise waiting for them at the dock. The ship owner had set the whole thing up—no problem at all. Paula had always wanted to go on one of these with her husband, Terry, but since he rarely came to the island, it hadn't happened. But she and Jeremy had taken one with her friend, Linda Sorensen, for a special history cruise, it had been a blast.

Now, though, with Gennaro's daughters and their families swarming her new friend on the dock, she felt like an outsider. And Jeremy had to work.

"Mom?" Claire joined her in line. "Clark and I can both come."

Clark leaned in and pointed to the oldest of Gennaro's grandsons who were lingering very close to the edge of the dock, laughing and pointing at the water. "We thought you could use a little extra help."

When the younger boy, who was seven, took a closer step to the edge, Clark ran over and gestured them back toward their parents, who looked up from chatting with the other adults. *Crisis averted.*

"Maybe you were right." Claire rolled her eyes. "Maybe you should have stayed home."

Paula grasped Claire's slim arm. "Hey, since you're here, who is doing all that laundry?" Claire and Clark were supposed to stay behind and try to catch up on all the linens and towels that their guests had generated.

"Parker sent the mini dray to pick them up, and his laundry service is doing it at the resort. Since basically, they put us out."

"Boarding! All aboard!" Gennaro, hands cupped around his mouth, called out, "*Imbarco! Tutti a bordo!*"

His kids, their spouses, and grandkids slowly headed toward the ramp to board the ferry.

Clark rejoined them. "That was really kind of you, Mrs. Ecker, to allow Gennaro's family to stay with you."

"And it was really kind of your mom to let me stay up at your horsey house this week, too!" Claire poked Clark in the side.

She'd always called the Jeffries' home 'the horsey house' because of the huge stuffed horse toy they kept propped on the porch swing in front of their West Bluff cottage.

"Can't believe you deserted me." Paula wagged her finger at her daughter, but she didn't blame her—not one bit. "Gennaro's family reminds me of a swarm of ants at times."

"Yeah, fire ants. Raffaella's little guy tried to bite my finger when I tried to tickle him." Claire wrinkled her nose. "I hope Jeremy doesn't have a dozen kids, or I'm in trouble."

"Yeah, I'm not picturing that. First, he'd have to have a steady girlfriend."

Claire blinked at her, and Clark raised his eyebrows but said nothing.

"What? Are he and Mia a steady item now?" Paula shrugged. "I never see them together."

"Yeah, they're steady." Clark scratched at the nape of his neck.

"Well, finally."

"You like this idea?" Claire moved forward toward the ferry, and Clark and Paula did, too.

"Of course. It's time he finally got a girlfriend. Pandemic really messed him and a lot of his friends up with their social lives." It had been awful for people his age.

"He's making up for it now," Clark muttered as Claire elbowed him in the side.

Not going to react. "I'm glad he's happy dating Mia, and she's a nice girl."

"Yeah, I'd be happy to have her as a sister-in-law."

Paula stopped walking. "You already have him married off?"

Claire blushed. "Mom, those kids over there are calling you 'Nonna Paula.' Are you sure you want to discuss who else people are marrying off?" She pointed to Gennaro, who waved at them.

From nearby, a Shepler's Ferry sounded its horn.

"Yeah, Gennaro's daughters must have gotten their PhDs in gossiping because that's about all I've heard them doing." Paula made a funny face.

Claire laughed. "And Clark only knows what they're saying because he's quite fluent in Italian—but we made sure they didn't know that."

Paula raised her hands. "I don't want to know. Let's just go and have a good time."

Twenty minutes later, as they rounded the east side of the island, Claire and Clark went to get drinks. Paula, seated, gazed out the window, watching the beautiful shoreline.

"Paula?" Gennaro's daughter, Valentina moved up the aisle toward her—arms full of her two-year-old daughter, Aurora, who was arching her body toward Paula.

Paula extended her arms. As soon as her mother slipped her onto her lap, the child snuggled her silky head on Paula's chest. She'd babysat the toddler when her parents had gone to dinner at the Pink Pony earlier in the week with the whole family. The tyke had a little cold, and Paula had insisted. From then on, Aurora liked to be seated in the highchair by "Nonna Paula" at meals.

Right behind Valentina came her older sister Raffaella trailed by her two boys, who scooted from behind their mother and sat across from Paula. Raffaella, who was thirty-one, was a homemaker and had trained to be a teacher. Her sons—Leonardo, seven, and Niccolo, four—possessed boundless energy. Leonardo leaned his dark head on his hands, on the table.

The toddler shifted in her arms.

Raffaella's husband, Mattia, joined her, eyes wide. An accountant for a large firm, Mattia also did bookkeeping for all the Di Imperiali family. No one, however, had explained to Paula what all those things were. She assumed the restaurants and the vineyards. Mattia tousled the boys' hair. "I've been looking for you two outside. I was afraid one of you imps jumped over." His sharp features softened as the boys looked up at him with their big dark eyes. "I know you miss out on not having a nonna."

Paula frowned. "Neither of you have your mothers still?"

Both shook their heads.

"Cancer," Mattia said.

She blinked back tears and nodded. She kissed the top of Aurora's head. "They've got Nonna Paula now."

"I'm glad. I'm so glad." Raffaella sat across from her, nudging her boys in farther. "I've been praying for my father to meet someone special. And now he has."

Paula opened her mouth to protest but looked up to see Gennaro standing by his son-in-law, gazing at her in what looked like adoration.

"Sì, now I have met someone very special."

Her heartbeat ticked upward and surged, like the ferry did through the waves. From the back, someone cheered. His kids were clearly enjoying the ride.

"Grandpa Gennaro, we want Mrs. Paula to be our nonna." Leonardo pointed to her.

"It doesn't work like that, buddy," Gennaro said.

Mattia gave his father-in-law a little jab. "First, Mrs. Paula has to want to be Grandpa's wife."

Valentina raised her arms. "Then she inherits all this crazy bunch, including you guys."

Claire and Clark, carrying a box with three drinks, stopped at the edge of the expanding group.

"Did I just miss a proposal?" Claire made a comical face.

"Oh no. I would never ask Paula to marry me until she's met the whole family." Gennaro opened his eyes wide.

Raffaella laughed. "Right. Kids better not count on a Nonna Paula until they've met my nonna and grandpa and all the uncles and aunts and cousins."

Mattia leaned in. "If you think our bunch is loud and crazy, you just wait until you meet the whole bunch. They make us look like introverts."

Paula tried to manage a little laugh but failed.

"Um, could someone please pass this to my mom?" Claire held out a pop, and Valentina clasped it and set it in front of Paula—but far enough away that little Aurora couldn't grab it.

"Scoot over, Nonna. Boppa is sitting down now." Gennaro scooted in beside her.

Paula looked for her daughter and was relieved that Claire and Clark had sat down at a table across from the booth.

Gennaro leaned closer to her, his breath warm on her cheek. "I wouldn't blame your daughter and her boyfriend if they ran." He pointed behind her to where his other daughter, Emanuela, was marching toward them with her kids, the two oldest grandkids.

A chef, the thirty-four-year-old, raised what looked like a hot dog. "You see what my kids are trying to eat?"

"A hot dog?" Paula asked innocently.

"No." Gennaro's eldest stomped her foot. "This is carcinogenic material on a stick. Fats and icky stuff my boys *non mangiano*—don't eat."

Clark waved. "I'll take the artery-clogging greasy meat on a stick if they haven't bitten it."

Paula started to laugh, even though the chef looked indignant and appeared to be cussing under her breath in Italian.

"No!" The older boy, twelve, tried to grasp the offending piece of fast food. "I already got a good big bite and it's wonderful."

From behind her, Emanuela's husband reached and grabbed the hot dog and gave it to his son, who rewarded him with a big grin.

"Better give it up, Emanuela, they're only going to want more of it if you don't let them have it." Claire pointed toward herself. "This is coming from a nurse practitioner who knows better and yet eats a chili dog at least once a month."

"Once a week, you mean." Clark crinkled his nose.

Claire slapped at him.

"These two," Emanuela pointed between Claire and Clark. "They are not married?"

Her husband leaned in. "They sure act like they are."

Chapter Seventeen

Claire spread out her blanket at Marquette Park, grateful for the sunny day and the breeze that made it comfortable to have this picnic with Clark. Guilt had been tapping at her consciousness ever since she'd google-stalked Ivan and Tiffany the previous night. Ever since she and Mom had a heart-to-heart about what had happened with Ivan and about her job in Montana, she'd had the urge to do a social media check on her old boss and her colleague frenemy. That search had only made her self-doubts increase.

Her anger had spiked when she'd recognized the locations.

"How would you feel, Clark, if a year from now your ex showed up on the island, and she's posting pics online at all your fave secret spots you shared with her?"

"Probably not happy. That would be kinda," he held his hand out horizontally and waggled it, "weird, don'tcha think?"

"Yeah. Like a boundary mutation."

"Exactly. She'd be a boundary mutant."

They high-fived each other.

"Why do you ask?"

"Ugh." She leaned back on her elbows and rolled her eyes upward. Overhead, the startlingly blue sky and puffy marshmallow clouds taunted her that she was ridiculous. But hadn't her friend just confirmed her emotions? "Ivan is posting pics of him and Dr. Tiff at some super challenging and secluded hikes that I took him on. Ones I asked him to never share, because they were fantastically quiet and secluded."

Clark opened his can of Coke and passed one to her.

She sat up and caught the wrinkles on his forehead as he frowned. "What?"

"Has that new girl at the bookstore sent you any more mystery books?"

Claire blinked a few times. "Yeah. Just yesterday."

"Title?"

"*Down the Path to Darkness*." She cringed.

"What was the premise?"

"I didn't bother reading the blurb on the back. The title put me off. Why would I be interested in that? And no indication of who has been sending them."

Clark pulled his iPhone out and typed something. He tapped the screen. "This nonfiction masterpiece addresses five high-profile criminal cases in the past decade where the killers seemingly were pillars of their communities."

"Definitely not reading that!" Claire drank her soda. *Perfectly chilled.*

"But somebody wants you to look at them." Her pal tilted his head back. "And that's concerning."

"Let's eat. I'm concerned I'm getting so hungry that I'll gnaw at your fingers soon."

He straightened. "Seriously, I'm wondering if there's some psycho tailing you."

"Well, then, you'll just have to watch over me, won't you?" Her cheeks heated, as she realized the words that had slipped past her lips.

Clark leaned in and took her hand, warmth radiating up her arm. "I'm going to keep you as close to me as you'll let me."

Her mouth went dry. "Why, Mr. Jeffries," she affected a Southern drawl, "I do believe you plan to court me."

He scooted closer and raised her hand to his lips. "Why, Miss Ecker," he lowered his already baritone voice to bass, "I do believe you're correct."

She leaned in. "Would you like a kiss to seal the deal?"

When his hand entangled in her hair and pulled her closer, she had her answer.

"Mom! Look, those two people are kissin' in the park!" A boy, about five, raced past them. With dark hair like theirs and a face that reminded her of her father's strong features, she had the sensation of seeing her future child. *Mine and Clark's.*

When she pulled away, there was no child. No mother that he ran to.

"Did you see that?"

Clark stared at her, as if he'd kiss her again. "See what? I was kind of busy."

"Did you hear that little kid?"

"Nope. I only have eyes for you." He began to sing the old Frank Sinatra song, and she playfully swatted at him.

"You didn't see or hear him?"

"Nope. But it's all good." He squeezed her hand.

Yes, things were good between them, and she was grateful. One thing she'd not do if there was a little boy in their future—name him Clark Jeffries III. It was already confusing enough around town with Clark's dad being senior and Clark being junior. No number three. Maybe Terrance, after Dad.

"You okay?" He kissed her forehead. "Now, let's make a plan so I can keep any psychopaths on the island away from you."

"We should tell Mom and Jeremy about this latest book, too. He swore that he hadn't bought those. But since he's a psych major, maybe he has some thoughts on this trilogy of books I've received."

"I did ask Linda Borton Sorensen if she'd run into anything like this in her years working for the police—including here on the island."

"What did she say?"

"Basically, that until someone takes some kind of action, the police's hands are tied. She said if you feel you're being harassed, then they could inquire at the bookstore about those purchases."

"Yeah, I do feel harassed."

"Let's walk to the police department and talk with them about it."

When they reached Market Street, Claire spotted her brother ahead of them—but he should be at work. Sure looked like him. She stopped and gaped when he turned and wrapped his arms around a very pregnant girl. Her wavy long hair was the same coppery color as Mia's.

"Whoa, didn't see that coming." Clark stopped walking and held her hand tighter. "Did you know?"

"About which? Them or the baby?"

"Both."

"No and no. Mom is gonna freak."

Clark shook his head. "Not your place to tell her."

She exhaled a sharp breath. "Right."

Claire pulled free from Clark and strode toward the couple, praying her eyes deceived her. Nope, they didn't. When Jeremy looked up with wide eyes, Mia turned and gaped at Claire, who was working up a full head of steam.

She wagged her finger at her brother. "What's going on?"

"We're getting our marriage license." He pointed ahead to the city offices complex.

Even though this seemed awfully fast, her brother had known Mia for years. But getting married and having a baby while finishing school—sheesh.

Clark gave a curt laugh. "Dude, I understand you not knowing, but Mia—you must know you have to go to St. Ignace to the county offices for that marriage license."

Mia's fair complexion turned rosy. "I forgot. He just proposed."

"And she accepted." Jeremy kissed the top of Mia's head.

Claire resisted the urge to roll her eyes. "You better tell Mom first about all of this, or I will."

Jeremy shook his head. "Give me a few days."

"Three days, that's it." She wagged her index finger at him, like Mom used to do to them. Clark put his hand on top of her finger and gently pushed her finger and hand down.

He leaned in. "No finger pointing allowed. You ever hear that expression in the Bible about when you point the finger, you've got all the rest pointing right back at you?"

She gave him the stink eye. "That's not in the Bible, you goof, that's an internet saying."

"All right, but it's still a good one."

She huffed a sigh, still tempted to shake her pointer finger at her brother. "Listen, you two, I'm excited about becoming an auntie. But you'd better let Granny know what's about to happen first."

Jeremy crinkled his nose. "She won't go by Granny. Maybe Mee Maw."

"Mine, neither." Mia frowned.

"Not a chance that Mom will go by Mee Maw or Granny, but maybe Grandma or MiMi." Maybe Nonna, if she finally got together with Gennaro.

Mia pressed her hand against her abdomen. "My mom will be furious. I guarantee she won't even acknowledge she's a grandmother."

"That's so sad." Claire stepped toward the girl and opened her arms. "Let me give you a hug."

That belly felt like last trimester. *Yikes.*

Claire stepped back. "When are you due?"

"Not for another couple of months." Her brother's defiant expression dared her to say anything.

As a medical provider, she knew many babies came before the due date. For once, she held her tongue with her baby brother.

Clark stepped forward and shook Jeremy's hand and gave Mia a quick kiss on her cheek. "Mrs. Ecker is the best. She'll be a wonderful grandmother, no matter what she calls herself. She'll compensate for your mom."

She wanted to tell the girl that maybe her mother would come around—but she knew Mia's parents. Other than a miracle, those two would continue being the same self-centered greedy jerks they'd always been.

Still, she'd pray for a miracle.

In the meantime, she'd start gathering up baby supplies. "Have you two already stocked up on the things you'll need?"

"We'll get those when we move into our apartment." Jeremy jutted out his jaw as Mia nodded meekly.

Wow, just wow. She could feel her jaw bouncing off the ground. These two had no clue.

But Claire did. And she could help. And Mom would, too.

That's what family was supposed to do for each other—help each other. That's what she could have done for Mom if she'd only known Jeremy wouldn't be there.

Mom needed to know.

"Hey, there are rules about how long that marriage license will be valid and the wedding has to take place." Clark sounded like a bossy big brother. "I know you have to wait at least three days for a ceremony to take place."

Jeremy and Claire exchanged a long look.

She'd tell Mom about Mia and Jeremy in three days. Those two getting off the island to the Mackinac County office and back with a license should buy her a little extra time, too.

"Nonna Paula is going out with the grown-ups tonight." Gennaro pointed to his two eldest daughters and their husbands. "We've all decided."

Paula's lower lip pulled in like when she was doubtful. "And Claire got Jeremy to help them, too?"

"Yes." He wanted to tell her about the baby that Jeremy's girlfriend was expecting, but he'd promised.

Clark and Leo carried Leonardo between them, across the room.

"Here's our bonus babysitter," Leo chortled.

Leonardo scowled at his uncle.

"Fine, we'll take care of you, then." Leo patted his oldest nephew on his head.

Leonardo, who was named after his uncle, ran from the two older guys.

Paula spun around. "Where's Jeremy?"

"He needs to be here to get some practice," Clark muttered.

Claire joined them, coming in from the hallway, with a sheepish Jeremy trailing behind her. He gave a little wave.

"I hear you love children." Gennaro couldn't resist a little taunt.

Clark stepped toward Jeremy and tapped him on his shoulder. "I hear you can't wait to be a father yourself."

Gennaro began to cough. He couldn't believe Clark said that. Did he know about Mia?

To his surprise, Paula's son crossed the room and ran up the stairs—where the kids were gathered. Raffaella and her husband, Jon, an Englishman, were upstairs with little Aurora and the other kids.

This was the last night for his family to be there. In the morning, they'd have a breakfast brought in from The Chuckwagon, and then they'd have to start the task of returning to their various homes. He and Paula and Claire would drive the various families to the airports—two flying out of the Chippewa County Airport and the one from Pelston.

A mix of melancholy, pride, and love welled up in him.

Clark raised his phone. "Carriage is here."

"Taxis, you mean?" Paula grabbed her purse and a shawl.

Gennaro shook his head. "Gianni purchased one of those long tour carriages for his big family. They keep it at Cardinal Cottage. His crew just left, so he sent it for us."

Emanuela, wearing large fake eyelashes that made her look like a llama, sashayed over to him. "Must be nice to be a billionaire. But he's been a great support to the ristorantes."

Gennaro nodded and then couldn't resist. He'd been looking at those crazy eyelashes ever since she'd come downstairs with them on. He leaned in. "Take off those ridiculous eyelashes before we go. Please?"

Emmanuela placed her hands on her hips. "Do you know how old I am?"

"Of course I do."

Right there, in front of everybody, she pulled them off and handed them to him.

Her husband guffawed. "Thank you, Gennaro, I owe you one."

"Free audit of my brother's vineyards?"

Mattia adjusted his watch. "You got it."

Paula pressed her lips tight and then took the eyelashes and laid them gently on a piece of tissue on the coffee table.

His bunch headed out the front as his youngest daughter and her husband joined them.

Paula tapped Gennaro. "I can't believe you just made her do that."

He shrugged. "She chose to comply with my suggestion."

"But she's a grown woman."

"Who looked ridiculous with those things on." He glanced toward the stairs, where Jeremy was leading the kids down. "Sometimes we have to have hard conversations with our kids, you know?"

Jeremy looked terrified. Was it because of taking care of the kids or because he was about to be outed as a soon-to-be new dad?

Paula followed his gaze and smiled. "He looks like a natural, doesn't he?"

"He'd better be," he mumbled. That twenty-one-year-old was about to take on one of the hardest jobs of his life.

"What's that?"

"I said, he'd better be a natural. You know he's got all those kids tonight."

"There are all those adults helping out. But maybe I should stay."

He grabbed her elbow and directed her toward the hallway. "Let's go, Nonna Paula. It's the young people's turn to watch the bambinos."

The trip to Mary's Bistro took less time than he'd thought. Soon, the hostess, a purple-haired young woman with three rings in her nose, seated them at a large table in the center of the room. He had many creatives who'd worked at his ristorantes over the years. All manner of piercings and tattoos, but they'd been some of the most amazing people and he'd missed them.

Once seated, the waiters came around to take their drink orders. A twenty-something guy took the other end of the table while a middle-aged woman took theirs.

She stopped in front of Paula and Gennaro.

"I'll have only water, please." Paula gave the server a tight smile.

She'd been watching her sugar intake lately—said it bothered her knee when she had too much.

"What Italian red wines do you have?" He looked up at the waitress, who smiled.

Paula covered his hand with hers. "Oh no, he can't have that. He's much too young."

What in the world?

The server raised one eyebrow and tilted her head. "How about I card him, then?"

Gennaro shook his head. "I deserved that comment from cara mia, but I'm sure these patrons will tell you I am an old man." He waved toward his kids and their spouses. "And I can have a glass of wine with my meal."

The waitress laughed. "So shall I tell you the two favorite reds here?"

"Please do."

From Paula's smug expression, she'd gotten a good shot in.

But at least it wasn't a parting shot. He wouldn't let that happen. He loved having her by his side.

Chapter Eighteen

Just like Gennaro's kids, soon she'd need to head back—especially now that Aunt Jackie was being discharged from rehab. Paula wasn't part of Gennaro's family, even if the grandkids wanted that, and Frank would be Jackie's new husband soon. Claire hinted that she wanted to turn the parlor into an essential oils storage area. Paula was being pushed out—at least that's how she felt on this overcast day.

"That's quite enough," she scolded herself. Until she returned to those hot tropical days in coastal Virginia, she'd try to enjoy every cool minute she had up North.

She sat at the picnic table in the backyard, her garden flourishing. What else did she need to do before she went home? Because surely she must return home, and to work. There was nothing holding her there on Mackinac. This had been a summer trip. Something to help Jackie. But it had turned into so much more.

She started her summer list. More bike rides around the island, hopefully with her kids. Picnics at the Cannonball and at some great beauty spots along Lake Shore Drive.

Picnics. That brought to mind Carter Parker's off-hand comment about Gennaro being a chef, which his daughters had confirmed. But they wouldn't specify what exactly he'd done—not after Emanuela shushed them. Maybe she was one of those chefs who didn't want anyone else stealing her thunder.

Or maybe it was something else.

She wasn't someone to stalk or google someone, but since she'd finally learned his last name's spelling, she was tempted. On impulse, she typed 'Di Imperiali' into her phone. The thing locked up for a moment and she shook it. That's what she got for downsizing her iPhone to a smaller one. *This thing has been nothing but trouble.* She powered it off and sighed. As soon as she powered it back on, the phone pinged.

Paula opened her text message from Judy, who'd been checking on Paula's house plants and going through her mail in case there was anything important in there. She usually received mainly junk mail, and she only grew succulents which required little watering, so her friend only checked weekly.

Please call me when you get up

She called Judy's cellphone.

"Paula?"

"Hi. How're you doing?" She brushed some leaves from the tabletop.

"I'm good, but I should have called you last week about this." It sounded like she was turning on a faucet. "I thought maybe I'd dropped an ice cube or something. I wiped it up. But it happened again."

She frowned. "What do you mean?"

"You've got a leak somewhere in your kitchen." Judy sounded really stressed. "I'm sending you a pic right now."

Paula pulled the phone from her ear and looked at the screen. When the message came through, she opened the image. A small pool of water lay on her bamboo flooring, near her stacked washer and dryer. She'd had them moved up when her knee had gotten too bad to carry clothes to her laundry room in her converted garage.

She put the phone back to her ear. "I hate to ask, but can you get somebody to look at it?"

"My brother-in-law does plumbing, and I asked him to look. He found a leak and shut off the water. Paula, you should call your insurance company, too."

"I'll do it now because when our neighbors had this happen—they got in trouble for not calling it in to insurance ASAP."

"I remember that."

"Thanks so much for letting me know."

"I'm so sorry to have to tell you this. But on a happier note, your succulents are doing great!"

She gave a little laugh. "Gotta look at the bright side."

"Yes, ma'am." Judy coughed. "Ugh, we've got some wildfire smoke going here."

"Some Canadian stuff here, too."

"Do you remember that our neighbor was out of her house for three months, and it was six months for all the work to be completed on her little leak?"

Paula instinctively raised her right hand. "Don't go there, my friend. Let's hope for the best."

Would she have to go home?

"Hey, I don't mind coming over, Paula, when the insurance guy gets scheduled."

"Oh, would you? That would be great."

"Sure thing. Let me know when he's coming and give them my phone number."

"Will do." Maybe she should go home now. After all those repairs she'd had done to the house, how had this happened?

"Bye." The call ended.

"Mrs. Ecker?" A woman's voice sounded from the gate, as it opened.

Who left it unlocked?

"Yes?" Paula frowned as she got up from the picnic table.

Dressed in slim red ankle pants and a black V-neck T-shirt, the fortyish brunette looked vaguely familiar. She pressed a hand, with several large gold rings on her fingers, to her chest. "It's me, Nicole, your neighbor's daughter."

"Nicky Parsons? I haven't seen you since you were a teenager." Had she come about her mother? Jackie had said she'd call her, but Paula had never heard what Nicky had said.

"I'm grateful your aunt called me." Nicole remained by the gate. "I wanted to let you know that my mom has agreed to go get a workup to figure out what's . . . wrong." She gave a curt laugh.

"Good. She's not been herself lately, that's for sure."

"Mom's always been kinda odd, but lately she'd been doing criminal activities, and that's not like her for sure. I flew in from California when my brother and his family couldn't get up here."

"Is he still in Detroit?"

"Yeah. Maybe it is more grammatically correct to say that he wouldn't come up to help."

"Ah." Paula made a sympathetic face. "I'm sorry."

"Hopefully we can figure out if she has dementia or whatever this is. But I'd like to keep her out of jail. Did you know she dug up the tulips in the neighbors' yard on the other side?" Nicole gestured toward her mom's cottage and beyond. "And she threw her garbage onto their lawn."

"Gosh, no. I don't usually walk by there."

"She put the bulbs in a kid-sized old pool down by the street with a sign saying for people to help themselves. And she told them that the garbage was good for the soil."

"Oh, wow."

"Crazy, right?"

Paula wasn't going to say it, but she nodded. "Will you stay next door, or do you need us to keep an eye on your mom's place for you?"

"I'll stay and then commute to the hospital and go when they need me. I'm an accountant for a company based overseas, and I can work remotely."

She could live anywhere. Could Paula? "That's pretty cool. And fantastic that you could come help."

"I'd have come earlier, but I was finishing a big on-site job in Germany. I tried guilting my brother into coming, but that didn't work." She flipped her palms over. "So, here I am. But I'd better head out on the ferry—I want to travel with Mom and my kids to the hospital."

Hopefully those kids could manage Mrs. Parsons until Nicole caught up with them.

"Best wishes. Thanks for letting me know, and I'll be praying for all of you."

Nicole waved goodbye, and Paula remembered how sweet the girl had been when she'd been growing up. Time sure did fly.

Three hours later, Paula got the bad news from George, Judy's brother, that Paula's 'little leak' was from ongoing seepage that had damaged not only her bamboo flooring but her hardwoods in the dining room.

"When you talk with the insurance company," George's deep voice was emphatic, "don't let them tell you this is from some long-ago leakage. Judy said you had this floor put in, what, a decade ago?"

"Right. And we've had the house for twenty-five years."

Later, when Paula spoke with the repair specialist sent from the insurance company, she understood why George had told her that. The project manager tried to say that this may have been an existing leak. So, she pulled up her purchase documents from the flooring company that had installed the bamboo, in her email, and forwarded them to the insurance company.

The sun was lowering in the sky as Paula finished harvesting over two baskets of tomatoes and zucchini from her garden. Memories from her youth intruded. After the harvest, Paula's uncle had always manifested what he called "bipolar gardener affect"—wildly euphoric over all the vegetables he'd brought in for Granny and Jackie to can for the winter and yet in the dumps because the garden was done for the summer. No wonder harvest festivals, especially some on the mainland, were so popular. With all those mood-swinging dads and grandpas now finished with their labors of love in the garden, there had to be a celebration to lift their sagging spirits.

One of her chums from Newberry had been crowned the Potato Queen for their Fall Harvest Festival. The Pentland Township Hall had been crammed full of jams and jellies, pies and all manner of baked goods, as well as quilts and knitting and crocheted items. The place smelled like a welcoming granny's home full of comforting autumn scents.

Fall would be here soon, and her garden would be gone. Her spirits drooped at the thought of leaving and of the repair work she'd be facing at home.

Her phone rang and she answered it.

"Mrs. Ecker?"

"Yes."

"This is Nate from Hampton Roads Home Restoration Company. I just emailed you about your damaged floor and cabinets."

"Oh?"

"There's no match for either of them. The floor we can do whatever you want for replacement—get all new bamboo in another similar color or put hardwood down or whatever."

"Let's continue my wood floors into the kitchen, then."

"Sure thing. Your insurance says they'll only pay for the few damaged cabinets and not to replace all of them."

"What does that mean? I've got three walls of uppers and lowers."

"We could have the two rebuilt for you, and the faces would still match. We can send you the estimate."

"Or?"

"You could pay out of pocket for the difference between what the insurance offers for the repair of the two and the cost of total replacement."

Her friend, Linda, had the same thing happen. Their mutual insurer wouldn't pay for all the cabinets, which was kind of nuts. But the reparations company did a lousy job and overcharged on the cabinet repairs.

Maybe she should go back to Virginia and be on site for this. But then she'd be dealing with construction on her house for what could be many months. And she'd be away from her kids and Jackie again. *And Gennaro.*

"We're also checking if the insurance will have us repair more of the wood floor throughout the house."

"Why?" She frowned.

"Because water went into the dining room, and that opens to the hallway, which also connects to your living room. So we would have to refinish all those floors to match the new stuff."

The timeline just blasted through a few more months. Her friend Linda had gone through the same thing. Her contractor started in the fall and hadn't completed the job until late spring, even though they'd told her it would only be a couple of months.

"Ok, let me contact my insurance after I see your estimate. I'll get back to you today."

"Sure thing, ma'am."

The line went dead before she could say goodbye.

Claire came down the back steps, carrying two mugs outside.

"What's the matter, Mom?" Claire set the tea down in front of her.

"Thanks, daughter." Paula wrapped her hands around the toasty warm mug.

As soon as Claire sat down beside her, someone started in on yard work with a weed whacker. "That must be Mrs. Parsons."

"Not this time. Her daughter has taken her for an evaluation."

"Really?"

"Yup. Thank God she's going to get help."

The weedwhacker suddenly stopped and their neighbor on the other side sounded upset. Maybe it broke.

"Mom, you can't count on that happening. A lot of times, neurological workups for dementia can be like a revolving door."

"I hope you're wrong."

"But I'm probably right."

They sat, sipping their tea. Paula reveled in the feeling of simply being able to sit there with her daughter.

"Who were you talking with before I came out?"

"Ugh!" Paula raised her hand. "Do you remember when my friend Linda had the leak, and insurance would only replace a couple of her cabinets but there was no match?"

"The great cabinet rip-off."

"Yeah, well I've got the same deal."

"What happened?"

"There's a kitchen leak, and it went into the dining room. It damaged the cabinets, but they won't replace all of them to match."

"Time to replace with all modern cabinets. That's what your friend said she wished she'd done. And you didn't do that when you had all those repairs made on the house."

"Maybe I should go home and deal with this. Pick out the new cabinets and tie up some loose ends."

"And stay in that house while they are tromping in and out every day? Ha!"

The weedwhacker restarted, almost like a reminder of the noise there'd be at home.

Claire flexed her fingers. "They'll kick you out for at least a week once they have the floor guy scheduled."

"Right. Linda lived with that mess for months and eventually still had to leave her home for a while." That had been so stressful for her friend.

The neighbor's yard equipment petered out again, and they had only the sound of the breeze, the seagulls, and horses' hooves on the street.

"I'm staying, Mom." Claire locked eyes with her. "I'm going to start my Therapeutic Scents line."

"Really? I'm proud of you."

"I'd like it if you'd stay." Claire drank some tea. "And I could fly down to check on the house, too, if you do."

Nothing warmed a mother's heart like knowing her child wanted her with her. Paula's eyes filled with tears.

"Mom!" Claire came around and hugged her from behind. "I didn't mean to upset you."

Paula shook her head and sniffed. "I love that you want me here." What about her library job, though?

Claire sat down beside her. "You'd be closer to Aunt Jackie, Jeremy and . . ." She abruptly stopped speaking.

"Gennaro? He's going back to Italy soon, I think."

Claire blinked at her and nibbled her lower lip, like she used to do when she was a teenager.

"What?" Paula flipped her hands over. "Is it so bad that I want to be near my kids? I don't think that's being needy." Something Claire used to accuse her of and Jeremy had recently started doing.

"No. In fact, doesn't it feel weird with all of Gennaro's bunch gone now? I kinda miss those rugrats."

"Yeah, I really enjoyed getting to know them—even if it was a shock at first."

"Ha! I wonder what Gennaro would have done if you'd refused?"

"Hmm, it wasn't their fault or his about the hotel fire."

"True."

"Plus, you have to be flexible—have a little propensity for spontaneity, if you're going to get by in this world."

"I like that—propensity for spontaneity. I don't think Clark and I have that. We're planners." She tapped her fingers on her mug.

"I agree." But that had almost cost her daughter the love of her life. Clark could have ended up married to another woman because of Claire's rigidity.

“On a different topic—have you planned what you’re wearing to that big soiree at the Parkers’ that Gennaro is throwing for them?”

“I’ve got a metallic fancy two-piece pant set I’ll wear with some patent leather low sandals.” She prayed those new strappy sandals wouldn’t bother her knee.

“Thank God for Amazon and the dray drivers who deliver all that fun stuff when we can’t find it on the island.”

“Yes, I’m grateful I got everything quickly.”

“Apparently Gennaro has a few surprises up his sleeve, so we’d better be ready.”

Chapter Nineteen

If this was what a "simple family event" was supposed to look like, then Paula was hugely out of her element. She'd entered the newly expanded dining room at Parkers' Resort and discovered over fifty people there, attired in beautiful evening wear. She wasn't exactly underdressed, but she was close. Immaculate linens covered the table as well as china imprinted with a turquoise and gold "P," sparkling crystal goblets, shiny silverware, and large bouquets of mixed white roses, tiger lilies, and small blue fragrant flowers.

At the front center stood Gennaro, attired in an old-fashioned white chef's costume, including the tall, puffy, white hat. He looked . . . a little eccentric and not at all like the guy she'd run into at the fudge shop the previous year.

Paula placed her hand over her necklace—a gift from her grandmother when she'd turned eighteen. A simple blue topaz on a gold chain. And Jackie and Uncle Victor had gifted her with matching earrings. She stood at the entrance to the event, still unsure where to go.

She forced herself not to limp, even though her knee wasn't happy today, especially with the sandals, as she moved farther into the room.

Hamp Parker, now in his mid-fifties, who'd been a wild guy back in the day, had become markedly subdued since he'd married Maria. The two owners of the resort moved alongside Gennaro, flanking him.

A worker set a microphone in front of Hamp, and he leaned in. "We're blessed to have the best-kept secret on the island—"

"Except for where the HGTV stars are staying this summer!" From a nearby table, Colton Byrnes interrupted. His wife, Cassandra, swatted his arm. The two HGTV personalities owned Tandem Cottage in Hubbard's Annex. Paula loved the couple's new show, set in the Maldives. She'd known them from Virginia, where they used to live, but hadn't seen them in years—other than on their shows.

Hamp scowled at Colton. "Listen, you're only an honorary member of the Parker family tonight."

Maria took the microphone. "One more outburst and we'll take Lorelai to our resort for a week the next time we babysit her."

Cassandra's dark eyes widened. "Not my baby!" She pressed her hand over Colton's mouth, but he tilted his head and laughed.

From across the room, Claire waved Paula forward to where she and Clark sat. They, too, were all honorary members of the family this evening because Gennaro proclaimed them his close friends. A tall brunette slid into the empty spot, and Claire mouthed "sorry" at her.

So much for that plan.

"I am honored to be part of this special celebration of the Parker family. This expanded dining hall has made it possible for the resort to now offer daily meals and to host conferences. And we have a wonderful surprise." Gennaro raised a hand. "I've been overseeing the students from the culinary school in the Eastern Upper Peninsula. I am happy to announce that they have prepared you a feast tonight of local cuisine. These future chefs have left their twists, their own marks, on each selection."

The guests applauded.

Really? He'd been teaching culinary students that summer? And had never mentioned it to her? This was something like Terry would have done.

She was steamed about it, and her knee throbbed in agreement. She needed to sit down. Paula looked around. There was one open place at Alyssa and Carter Parker's table, which also included his brother, Parker and his wife, Jaycie, and an elegant red-haired beauty, whom Paula didn't recognize. *Probably holding a spot for her equally attractive and young date.*

Carter, who'd been in Paula's grief group and whom she'd known all his life on the island, caught her eye and pointed to the empty spot. "It's open," he mouthed.

At the front, Hamp patted Gennaro's shoulder, then took Maria's hand and led her to the front table.

Moving sideways around Carter's table, Paula felt like a sand crab scooting around at the Outer Banks, one of her husband's favorite mini-vacation spots. As she reached her seat, the redhead pulled it back for her and beamed up.

"Thanks."

A small spiral notepad rested on the stranger's lap. "I'm Whitney. I'm with the *Town Crier*."

Was she an intern at the local paper?

"I used to be a feature writer with the *Detroit Free Press*." She gave a furtive glance around the table. "Luckily, no one holds it against me."

"Why would they?" Paula scooched her chair in closer to the table, as a nearby server came forward and poured ice water into her tall goblet. She turned to thank him.

The young woman pointed to the front, where Gennaro gestured toward five navy-jacketed servers. They began rolling their carts to the back tables.

"Your first entrée is a whitefish pâté with arugula garnish and slivered French radishes served with made-from-scratch white cheddar crackers."

A little "ooh" went up from some of the guests, and Gennaro blushed. "Soup giardiniera will be served next. I've even included some delightful Roma tomatoes from my friend's Mackinac Island garden." He locked eyes with her. No wonder he didn't care how her tomatoes looked—he been planning to cook them down.

Sweat broke out on his forehead. She knew he hated dealing with crowds. Part of her fought the urge to run up front.

Jaycie Parker, who sat on her left, touched Paula's hand. "Is he okay? He looks kind of flushed."

"Are you two friends, then? Are you close?" The journalist clutched her pen like a weapon.

Gennaro continued, "The main course features Trout Almondine with local wild rice harvested in the Upper Peninsula with a whole grain breadbasket with both garlic and basil whipped butters." He swiped at his brow.

Paula pushed back from the table. Between his daughters' concerns about his health, and the fact that he'd told her he suffered from anxiety in crowds, she had to do something. *But what?*

She drew in a deep breath and then pushed past her knee pain to stand, exhaling hard.

Gennaro waved her forward, and she side-walked around the table again and then made her way to the front. "My dear friend, the noted author, Paula Ecker, inspired most of the selections I suggested to the students. So if you enjoy this feast, be sure to tell her!"

He smiled as she walked toward him, the tension in his shoulders visibly relaxing. He pulled her into a side hug and then surprised her with a firm kiss on her cheek. Again, the crowd clapped enthusiastically. Now her own cheeks heated.

She leaned in, wanting to make him laugh. "Are you trying for a skinny Pillsbury Dough Boy look?"

She got her reward, as a deep belly laugh emanated.

"Please don't save that outfit for Halloween, okay?"

He pulled back and wagged his index finger at her. "And no old-fashioned librarian outfits for you, either."

She frowned. "We modern librarians have purged our closets of anything frumpy." That was only partially true. She still enjoyed one oversized cardigan she'd kept since the nineties.

Again, Gennaro addressed the crowd. "A brisk citrus sorbet—not local I'm afraid—will be offered to cleanse the palate of those who wish so, between the soup and main course. Simply accept one from your server as they pass."

"Is there a big old chocolate cake at the end?" Once more, Colton Byrnes, the effusive HGTV star, called from his table, and his wife leaned in to cover his mouth.

Gennaro gestured to her. "It's fruits. Paula, you tell them."

She shook her head slowly, flummoxed.

"I'm sure you know the ones you like." The warmth of his smile shot straight through her.

"Ah, fresh local blueberries and strawberries?"

"Exactly." He turned to address the room. "Maple-syrup-coated blueberries and strawberries on a Pavlova shell, with a dark chocolate drizzle."

He couldn't have only picked the fruits because of her. She leaned in. "So you're being good and not going for a rich cake?"

He turned toward her and whispered, "Not when this is being recorded and my girls are watching."

"Ah." He had a habit of asking Claire to bring goodies back from the Mackinaw Bakery for him, in Mackinaw City, whenever she went to see Jackie. The addictive shop was in Mackinaw City, which drivers passed en route to Petoskey.

"Father Vincent will say our prayer." He gestured toward a slim silver-haired man in a priest's cassock, who joined them.

Father Vincent moved alongside them and invoked the blessing.

She was touched that not only had Gennaro done this but that he was unconcerned about his guests being offended. People today could be touchy about prayers in public, but this was, after all, a private event.

"Thank you, Father Vincent."

The man gave a slight bow and returned to his seat nearby.

She scanned the room, looking for Leo, who should have been there, but wasn't.

The first group of servers came out, and a white-coated culinary student stepped forward.

Gennaro gestured to the dark-haired man. "Juan Sanchez, who hails from Mexico City, has the first spotlight."

Guests clapped politely.

"You better take your spot, Paula. I have to mingle." Gennaro kissed her cheek.

She squeezed his hand. "This is a strange party."

"We chefs are funny about our food."

"No wonder you didn't want me to help."

"You did help. You gave me the ideas for this celebration."

"Good."

As servers slid food in front of the guests, Gennaro raised his hands. "*Mangia*, mangia, mangia!"

He kissed her cheek again. "I've got to visit with people. Go enjoy."

"Okay." She made her way back to her table. Several of the guests reached out to squeeze her hand as she passed, which surprised her.

The touch, and their admiring looks, felt almost congratulatory.

They must think she and Gennaro were a couple. A hot flash started in her neck and shot to her hairline as she scooted around her table again to her spot.

The whitefish pâté, elegantly arranged, contrasted nicely with the coral-colored crackers. "I didn't even know homemade crackers were a thing," she said as she slid into her chair.

"Me, neither," the newspaper woman said. "But they're delicious."

Paula unfolded her napkin on her lap.

Jaycie elbowed her. "I didn't realize you and Chef Gennaro were an item."

Startled, Paula flinched.

The redhead leaned closer. "I'd love to hear your story."

Paula raised her hand. "First of all, there is no Chef Gennaro—this is special for the Parkers." But even as she said it, she realized how he'd withheld from her about training the students. What else had he not told her. "Secondly, we are good friends only. Thirdly, there is no story here."

"I bet Whitney would disagree with all of that." Jaycie pointed her fork at the redhead. "Wouldn't you?"

"Mea culpa." Whitney brushed her long red fingernails against her dress's sparkling neckline.

Jaycie leaned in. "You're right. Gennaro isn't a chef. Not anymore. We were blessed to have him join us in Switzerland to help manage our hotel and add a restaurant there. But it's his daughter who is the chef now."

"I've met Emanuela." Paula eyed her appetizer but didn't reach for it.

"Emanuela took over his very first restaurant in Rome," the reporter said.

Paula was glad she'd not started to eat, or she'd be choking. His first restaurant in Rome? How many were there?

Jaycie raised her fork. "And she runs his others now, in Paris and Lucerne."

Paula stared at her food, suddenly not hungry at all. He'd lied to her. He'd misled her almost every step of their relationship—not relationship, just pals—this summer.

Whitney touched her hand. "Did you know he was called the famous dancing chef? Do you two dance like he did with his wife?"

Realizing she was gaping, Paula snapped her mouth closed. "Why don't you tell me what you have for your article so far?" She'd found the best way to deal with nosy people was to turn the tables on them.

"Well, I discovered from a guy I was dating that Michelin Star Chef Gennaro was on the island and I had to get the scoop," Whitney gushed. "I mean, he was the foremost chef in all of Europe, possibly the world, before his wife Lucia died."

"And then he quit," Paula said dumbly, making the connection. He'd told her he'd stopped working but he'd never specified what he did. That was really on her, with her habit of avoiding pushing people too hard. Problem was, she wasn't pushing them enough, at all.

Whitney adjusted her napkin. "His son said he'd been hiding out."

Paula shifted in her chair. "Leo? Are you dating him?" Was this the girl he wanted to show Rex to? The reason he'd missed an early morning visit with his sister and her family in Ontario?

"Sort of." She waggled her hand. "He's not really my type."

So she was using him for a story. Paula gave the young woman a hard look. Poor Leo. Had he finally figured out what Whitney was up to? Was that why he wasn't there?

Whitney took a bite of her appetizer. "It looks like you're his new muse for his creations."

"No." She raised her palm firmly. "That's not true."

Jaycie feigned a cough. "That's not what everyone in the kitchen says. It's Paula says this, Paula says that." She gave a little laugh.

Paula pushed her spine against the upholstered chairback. "Oh, about this menu, do you mean? He did ask for input."

Jaycie and her husband, Parker, exchanged a look.

On the other side of the round table, Carter tapped his hands alongside his empty appetizer plate. "Yeah, he told them he got his inspiration for the menu from you—just like he said." He jerked his thumb over his shoulder.

"You grew up in the UP, too, didn't you?" Alyssa scooped a little pâté onto a cracker.

"I did. And Gennaro and I discussed what would be really fresh and local." She turned toward Whitney, offering her a tight smile.

The woman quirked her eyebrows upward and scribbled something on her notepad.

"You'd better eat your appetizer before the staff takes it away." Jaycie pointed to the servers, who were removing plates from nearby tables.

Not wanting it to go to waste, Paula forked some of the whitefish pâté onto a cracker. When she took a bite, the taste shocked her. *So good. Amazing.*

"Haven't you eaten any of his cooking?" Whitney's bright green eyes held a cross between mischief and glee.

"I have. We cook together." She shouldn't have said that. "I mean, sometimes when he's free, we throw some things in the skillet. Nothing like this." Because it had usually been her cooking.

"Do you cook, or Chef Gennaro, or both of you?"

Paula took another bite of the fantastic appetizer, ignoring the woman.

At the front, kitchen staff wheeled out soup bowls.

"Our staff will be up late tonight," Jaycie commented dryly. "I'm glad I don't have to do dishes at this place."

"Me, too." Paula turned and beamed at her. Jaycie Parker finally had the child she'd waited for so long. "I imagine caring for a baby all day wouldn't leave much energy for all these dishes."

"Speaking of energy," Whitney intruded, "I heard our chef has some serious health problems and that might interfere with him opening his new restaurant in Vienna."

Vienna? New restaurant? Paula was well and surely out of her element. And Gennaro was far out of her orbit. But he'd been a good friend, and she'd cherish that.

Finally, she had recently realized she wasn't that much older than him. And she'd begun to want something more. But the way Whitney and Jaycie talked, soon he'd be back as Chef Gennaro, the dancing chef, opening his new international restaurant in Vienna. Maybe even training culinary students over there.

Paula pushed away from the table. "Please excuse me."

She headed out, trying to not attract attention to herself. Paula hurried as fast as her poor knee and her strappy sandals would allow. Exiting the atrium, she carefully crossed the entryway to the resort. Thankfully there were no carriages pulling in, but several were waiting alongside the long drive.

How had that journalist gotten into the event? Who had invited Whitney? If Leo had, then why wasn't he even there to support his father?

Her knee throbbing, Paula forced herself to walk on. There was more pain in her heart than in her knee, though. The events tonight had demolished whatever silly little hopes she'd fostered in her head. And what were they? She couldn't even be honest with herself.

You're running, that still small voice prodded her.

The message didn't resonate with her. She'd not turn around and go back.

Take some quiet time. Reflect.

What had their grief group leader, Susan Mullen, said? 'Face it head on, don't duck the wave. Stare it down, let it overflow you if necessary, and then you'll get through it.' Remembering that advice lifted her spirits a tad.

Up ahead, she spied two low cement benches. She needed to sit. One was occupied by someone bent over, dark head in hands. She was about to take the open spot, when she recognized those dark curls.

"Leo?"

Gennaro's son lifted his head, his face red and wet. He sniffed. "Mrs. Ecker."

To her surprise, he opened his arms to her and she went to him. He laid his head on her shoulder. "*Sono proprio un idiota.*"

Someone was an idiot—since he was crying, Leo must be saying that he was.

She patted his dark curls. "Tell me what's going on."

He lifted his face, eyes stricken. "I thought Whitney liked me for who I was." He coughed a sob and then put his head back on her shoulder.

This poor kid had lost his mother when he was transitioning into independence. That had to have been hard. He still needed a mom. All that acting cool was just that—an act.

Paula dug a couple of Kleenexes from her little purse and handed them to him.

"Grazie." He blew his nose.

"Weren't you supposed to be there?" Paula pointed to the building.

"Sì. But Whitney told me she'd not be seeing me anymore after tonight. And I am an idiot, but even I realized she'd just used me."

"I'm sorry. Sometimes people aren't who they seem." Like Gennaro, that was for certain.

"Jeremy always says I let girls pull things over on me. He says I'm like a lost puppy, and that scares them away. But not Whitney."

She rubbed Leo's back. "You don't act like that around my family."

He gave a curt laugh. "Jeremy and Mia are always telling me to act more confidently, but it feels bad to me—like I'm being a jerk."

Paula chewed her lower lip. "Sometimes when people are trying to be more assertive, they come across as aggressive." She stopped rubbing his back.

Leo straightened. "Sì. And I am more . . ." He made a circular motion over his heart.

"More sensitive, more emotional?" If she'd heard him say those words before this evening, she'd have laughed and thought he was trying to brag that he was that type of guy. Now, though, she believed him.

"Sì." He turned toward her on the bench.

"I think your dad is that way, too." Maybe that's why he hadn't shared about all his success.

"And he has loved being able to live his own life now and not be this big famous chef that everyone wanted something from. He can be himself with you, he always says, and I see that."

"Doesn't this party for the Parkers put him back in the spotlight, though?"

"Only because of me." He shook his head. "I knew I said too much to Whitney, and I was ashamed to go inside. Those people in there respect my father's privacy, but not her. And not me. At least I didn't tell her his biggest secret."

"Oh?" Here she was digging for it. She waved her hands in a crisscross motion. "Don't tell me, though. That's his to tell."

He bowed his head. "Did he tell you how my mother died?"

"No. Only that she'd suddenly collapsed, and she was gone very quickly."

"I was there." Leo wiped tears away. "At the end of the worst."

"Oh, Leo, I'm so sorry."

He blew his nose again. "Papà had made an anniversary dinner—I knew that much—and I'm sure he was dancing around like he usually did when cooking. But this was a private dinner. I wasn't supposed to be there, but they'd canceled my soccer match."

Paula patted his hand, and he squeezed hers. "So you got back early."

"I was embarrassed to interrupt their romantic dinner. My mother did not eat with us at night. My father was at the restaurant every night except one. She was at her art studio nearly every night."

That struck Paula as odd, but she bit her tongue.

"So when I got home, I went inside and was going to quietly sneak down to my room, but I heard my father wailing in the kitchen. He was screaming and sobbing. I heard sirens outside our villa. I ran to the kitchen and saw him on the floor, holding my mother in his arms. Limp and pale, she looked like one of her statues. And the sound my father made . . ." He shook his head and exhaled slowly. "*Non terreno.* Unearthly."

Paula gave him a hug. "I'm so sorry. That's not something anyone wants to see or hear."

"That's the day I grew up. I may act like a kid, but never after that. I opened the gate and the door when the emergency crew came. I answered their questions. I helped my father get up from the floor—and he was a really big man then, over one hundred fifty kilograms."

She wasn't sure of the conversion, but wasn't that well over three hundred pounds? That explained his daughter's comments about his appearance. "He was probably in shock."

"My father worshipped my mother in an unhealthy way. She was his everything. He would do anything for her. To have her collapse right in his arms—that broke his heart."

Paula nodded. "I imagine so. And your heart, too."

"I felt guilty, mostly. Because she was never home. Sometimes I felt like I'd never really known her." He bent again and placed his head in his hands.

Her own son had said something similar about his father.

"But you didn't share this with Whitney. That's good, because this is something very personal and not anyone else's business."

"Right. But did you leave because of her? Did she say something that upset you?" He sniffed and raised his head again.

She blinked, thinking how to put it. "She said your dad is opening another restaurant in Vienna and implied he's going back to being a chef."

"Ha!" Leo pointed at her. "I told her that right after she said we should stop seeing each other when I return to school. I decided to tell her a little fib and see what she did with that."

"No restaurant in Vienna?"

"Oh, yes, that's for Emanuela."

"But will he go back to being a chef?" And everything that meant?

"Not a chance, as Jeremy likes to say. Maybe he will do something at my grandparents' place in Italy, though."

"He may return to Italy to live?"

"I think so." Leo suddenly stood. "You should talk with him about this."

She knew she should, but right now, Paula's head was swirling.

Chapter Twenty

If ever Paula needed a little Joyce Meyer's encouragement, it was this morning, while she was preparing for the day and while her caffeine kicked in. She checked on her apps and found a podcast to download. She set her phone on the counter as she prepared some cinnamon and hazelnut coffee. The little dark circle on the downloads changed to a full white circle of light, indicating it had finished. She pushed the start button and strong-brew mode on the coffee pot and then tapped at the app's icon. But when it opened, it was for a women's conference that she couldn't attend as it was many states away.

Frustrated, knowing she needed something to lift her spirit, she opened her favorite Bible app. She'd sent the link to Leo the previous night and had encouraged him to listen. Would he? She'd had that boy so wrong, as had Claire. She listened to the verse of the day, a good one—a reminder to be gentle with others and oneself. Was that enough, though? To focus on that verse for the day? She moved to the fridge and grabbed the new mocha coffee creamer. She pulled her aunt's mug from the cabinet—the one Paula and the kids had made for Aunt Jackie that declared her their 'Honorary Grandmother' and set it by the pot.

Gennaro's grandkids had made it clear that they wanted her for their honorary nonna. Maybe she'd never get that opportunity, though.

Although only half-brewed, she pulled the coffee carafe free and poured some into the mug and then added the creamer. She set the carafe back so it could finish brewing and then went to the freezer, intending to pull out a whole-grain waffle. Instead, she spotted Jeremy's sugar bomb toaster pastries and grabbed the box. *Two left.* She put them both in the toaster. She'd save one for him.

Paula pulled an old stoneware salad plate from the cabinet. On it was a faded image of a woodlands' cottage. She smiled. She and Uncle Victor had jested that their second storage building, in the back corner of the lot, could be like that cottage. When she'd become a teenager, he'd emptied it and then made her a little getaway for when summer guests had taken over the cottage. The two of them had thoroughly cleaned the space, placed an old rug on the concrete floor, and put roller shades in the window. They'd hung an old dining room light—underneath, they'd placed one of Granny's threadbare velvet upholstered chairs from the 1920s. A small rotating bookshelf, also her grandmother's, sat alongside the chair. Uncle Victor had set another smaller chair, one from the late 1950s with faded turquoise brocade fabric, adjacent to the other, so she could invite friends inside. Paula had made several pillows, too, to personalize the space.

Why hadn't she even popped her head inside that hangout shed since she'd arrived? She sipped her coffee. She'd not looked in there since Jeremy was little. When they came to visit, he and Claire would claim it as their hangout—each taking turns but sometimes sharing. Their age difference affected their relationship.

Paula had wanted children right away, but Terry was completing his bachelor's degree in nursing. They'd had Claire once he'd received his Registered Nurse certification. Then, when he'd decided on pursuing physician assistant certification while working full-time, there was to be no child until he'd completed. By then, she was in her late thirties and Terry wasn't home, anyway, to help her—not much.

The grand gestures, though—he'd been the king of those.

She set her cup down. *That was it.* Gennaro's behavior last night reminded her of her husband's big gestures—and that sickened her. And the withholding of information—like Terry.

They'd not see Terry for what seemed like months—and then he'd announce a plan to take them all to the Rockies. Or to the Caribbean. Without ever confirming with Paula that she could get off work at that time and go. When the kids got older, she'd finally put her foot down and told him not to schedule anything like that unless she'd gotten confirmation she could take vacation time. And she'd tried to convince him that they should be more frugal. He'd left many home improvements and repairs undone, claiming they weren't necessary. Not long before he died, he'd switched to doing big trips with one or more of the kids—no Paula.

That had hurt. Her chest squeezed, remembering it. Even worse was now knowing that he'd been from a very wealthy family and had grown up expecting those kinds of vacations. It wasn't until after he'd died that she'd learned Terry had inherited several million from his parents. What a shock that had been.

Gennaro's fancy sports car. Him having been a famous chef, receiving adulation from famous people. Him being from a different world than she'd known. All those things firmly placed her new friend in the 'summer pal' zone.

Which he'd been from the beginning.

So why was she so sad? Was it her knee pain speaking? Her discomfort the previous evening?

And why was she disappointed in last night's events?

Because you're not being honest with yourself.

If anything, she should be relieved that Leo had been able to share with her some truths and some of his struggles. Poor kid. Should she believe him about Gennaro being happier since being around her?

Paula clutched her mug and headed outside to the second shed. She was a little afraid to go in there. Part of her wanted it to look exactly as she'd left it, and another part of her wanted it to have been transformed, in at least some way, by her kids.

Wasn't that what her life was like this summer?

She'd wanted the comfort of the cottage, the sameness, yet when the kids ended up being on Mackinac with her and then meeting Gennaro, she'd longed for something more.

A transformation.

And now fear kept her from moving forward, in at least speaking with Gennaro about how she really felt. This wasn't what she'd planned.

The back door opened, and Rex trotted down the steps. Claire must be up. Paula clapped and Rex crossed the lawn to her. She turned and opened the door to the hangout shed. When she flipped the switch, light illuminated the same old furniture but covered with crocheted afghans that Jackie had made for the kids. A round hooked pastel rug replaced the previous old carpet. The scattered stuffed toys were some she'd given the kids over the years as 'summertime friends.'

Claire's apothecary jars for her scent experimentations lined a newer table. Paula went to the utility table and opened one of the small glass jars. A heavenly scent filled her nostrils. *Wow.* This was amazing. No wonder her daughter thought her concoctions could help people. It was like getting a garden's worth of flowers in a single sniff.

Rex flopped down on the floor, looking bored.

She flipped over a new pillow. Embroidered on the front was 'Jeremy Ecker, Ph.D., Best Psychologist in the World.' She laughed. Jackie must have done that one. Or had Claire? She'd given embroidery a go as a hobby when she'd been in high school. Had she known even then where Jeremy's educational pursuits would lead?

Paula sat down, mug in hand, and smiled.

God was good. He'd blessed her with two amazing kids and a wonderful aunt and uncle. Her husband, despite his faults, had done his best.

She'd sit there in the shed and let gratitude wash over her—and take care of her soul.

And then she needed to make her plans to get back home. The library expected her back in three weeks. And that would get there fast.

"Mom?" Claire's voice carried across the yard and through the open shed door. Rex ran out to his owner.

In a minute, Claire and Rex joined her in the shed. "Gee, I never thought I'd find you in here—this is our little hideaway place."

"Ha, and this was mine before it was yours!"

"Yeah, I figured. Anyway, can I leave my pup with you while I'm gone to lunch with Clark?"

"No. I can't stand that dog." She crossed her arms and tried to look grumpy. "No way could I watch him." Rex barked, and she petted his silky fur.

"Um, yeah, I can see that." Claire bent and kissed Paula on top of her head, just like Paula used to do to her. "I'm thinking Rex is your good buddy."

"You're right. And where are you and your good buddy going for lunch?"

"Pink Pony."

"Have fun."

Paula's phone rang. She didn't recognize the number but took a chance and answered. "Hello?"

"Paula? This is Nicole Woods. Nicky Parsons. My married name is Woods."

"Oh, yes, we haven't seen you next door."

"We stayed down with mom because they ran a bunch of tests. They believe she had a psychotic break or may have a psychotic disorder. No indication of dementia."

"That's good—no Alzheimer's or dementia."

"Right. But next she'll go to a psych hospital for a week or more. I wanted to update you. We'll come to the island for that time. I've really got to get some work done, so I imagine my son and daughter will explore the island while I get stuff accomplished."

"How old are your kids?"

"Zach is sixteen, and Perri just turned eighteen."

"Perfect ages for being able to be on their own on the island."

"And a great place for not getting into trouble."

Paula laughed. "At least not too much."

"If I get a break, I'll try to run over to catch you up with any updates on Mom."

"Thanks."

There was a pause. "My husband left us a year ago. It's almost like that triggered my mom's setback. She wanted me to move back here, but I couldn't see that happening."

Nicole could use some support, no doubt. "You come over whenever you want, Nicky, and I'll crack out some of Aunt Jackie's goodies from the freezer."

"That would be great. See you soon."

"Bye."

She called Jackie's cellphone to give her the latest news. She'd be relieved to hear her friend and neighbor was finally getting help.

Clark pointed to the large screen television over the bar at the Pink Pony lounge. "Isn't that near where you lived in Montana?"

Claire looked up from her menu. The newscaster spoke as the camera scanned her favorite hiking spot. "This is where it happened, folks," the suited man said.

"What happened?" She frowned.

Her buddy leaned closer. "They said someone got killed or someone tried to kill someone."

"Dr. Tiffany Morton, a renowned neurosurgeon in Bozeman, was airlifted out this afternoon, and her husband Ivan Zudika of only several months is under arrest."

"What?!" her loud cry caused several other patrons to look in her direction. Claire pushed her chair back from the table.

Clark laid a hand across hers.

The reporter continued, "In a case reminiscent of one several years back, Dr. Morton's husband, a physician assistant at the Boeman Hospital, brought her hiking to this very remote area. Zudika allegedly took her phone before pushing her over the ledge."

Pressing her hands to her mouth, Claire covered her gasp.

"Dr. Morton fell about fifteen feet to a grassy ledge, which she believes saved her life unbeknownst to her husband, who drove off. Police said they received a call for help from Zudika, claiming his wife fell. Dr. Morton had a second phone, an Iridium satellite model, which she used to call 911 for help, and she informed them Zudika pushed her. The emergency dispatcher advised her to remain quiet until help arrived."

Claire shook her head in wonder. "Thank God she had that phone."

"We'll have more on this breaking story on the ten o'clock news." The announcer looked stoically at the camera before the scene switched to something else.

"Oh my gosh, Clark. That's crazy."

"That coulda been you."

"What?"

"If you'd ended up with that psychopath, he might have killed you and dumped your body."

"The books." Claire tapped the table, having a hard time finding her words. "The paperbacks from the Island Bookstore."

The waitress came to their table and slid the beverages they'd ordered in front of them. It was the bookstore clerk who maybe wasn't really a worker.

"It's you," Claire pushed back in her chair.

The young woman pointed at her. "It's you, too."

Her dear friend scowled at the waitress. "Why did you send Claire those books?"

"My boss sent those, not me." She flicked her long blonde hair over her shoulder.

"Tamara or Mary Jane?"

The woman gave an enigmatic smile as she pushed an orangey drink with cherry on the bottom in front of Claire. "We call this mocktail the 'Dodged a Bullet' so enjoy."

That wasn't the name of what Claire had ordered. But before she could protest, the server slid Clark his customary Arnold Palmer. "Here's your 'Aren't I the Lucky One for Second Chances.'"

Then the waitress gave them a cheeky grin and bowed at the waist. "Until you need me again."

"What the heck?" Clark scowled at the woman's retreating form.

"This night is getting stranger by the moment."

Their original waitress stopped at the table. "Sorry it took me a moment. That new girl, Angela, brought your drinks out, right?"

So, the strange blonde had been a new hire there, too, at the popular restaurant.

"Had you ever seen her here before at the Pink Pony?" Clark asked as he removed the paper from his plastic straw.

"Can't say that I have." The server shrugged. "But she sure had a sparkling new uniform on, didn't she? I've never seen one look so immaculate."

"Hmmm." Claire tapped the menu. "I could order now if you're ready."

"Same as usual?"

"Yup."

He folded the menu. "Smoked whitefish dip. Two house salads with balsamic dressing. Perch for me and trout for her. Fries for me and coleslaw for her."

"Sure thing."

When their waitress walked away, Claire clapped her hands. "I'm gonna watch for that other new waitress and give her a piece of my mind. No way did Tam or Mary Jane send those creepy books."

"I think her boss might be higher up than those two." Clark raised his hand and pointed his index finger upward.

"Wait, wait, oh my gosh," Claire was flooded with a recollection. "She's the same gal from the vet's practice in Montana. The one who wore a scarf around her head and had oversized glasses."

"Pretty sure this one is an angel."

"The vet's assistant told me I should put myself down as Pup's owner." Claire remembered how Ivan had only bought the dog when he'd learned that Claire missed having one. "At the vet's office, she encouraged me using my name for Rex's care."

"Sounds like she understood Ivan wasn't going to be bringing him."

"And he didn't." Claire raised her eyebrows. "And then the last visit when I took him, the assistant said I should see if he liked going for long rides—that some dogs found them very soothing. I'm sure it was her—that same woman but dressed differently."

"Listen, regardless, you did dodge a bullet with that guy."

"Yeah, maybe so."

He reached for her hand. "I'm glad you're safe here with me."

"Me, too." She sipped her mocktail, which had the effect of making her feel hopeful—but maybe that was from being safe with Clark.

"Can you imagine how Jeremy and your Mom would have felt if something had happened to you?"

"Oh!" She set her drink down. "I forgot to tell Mom about Mia and the baby. It's been so crazy busy. I was wishing he'd do it, but I'm pretty sure Jeremy hasn't."

Near sunset, Garden Cottage's backyard transformed into a verdant, but fading, oasis—if Paula ever needed peace, it was now. Rex lay crashed on the lawn, oblivious to her angst. She'd ignored Gennaro's texts that day, reminding herself that they both were leaving soon. Plus, he had a lot of Terry's bad habits that she didn't want repeated in a relationship.

What relationship?

She commenced watering the last of her plants, which soothed her. This garden and its wonderful vegetable plants had so far yielded a good produce. Wasn't that kind of like parenting? You put in all that time, tried to help your kids, but then you had to leave it to God. So many of her pals with adult kids had told her that even though grown-up, they don't really leave. She'd been so afraid they were dead wrong.

Now Claire was here, seeing Clark again. Jeremy had finally begun dating his longtime friend, Mia. Who knew where life would take them? Her son had to return to school soon. Who were his new roommates? He'd never mentioned them.

"Hello?" a female voice carried from the gate.

Paula released the nozzle sprayer and turned as Rex lifted his head and then barked.

A trembling Mia stood there, holding a large backpack in front of her, as Rex bounded toward her.

"Rex, stop!" For once, he listened. Paula cocked her head. "Hi, Mia. I haven't seen you in a long while."

To her amazement, the girl burst out in tears and dropped her bag—revealing a pregnant belly.

Stunned, Paula hesitated only a moment. She went to the young islander and took her hands. "Mia, what's going on?"

When she started to sob, Paula led her to the cushioned outdoor chairs, the dog trailing behind them.

"We hoped . . ." Mia took a shuddering breath and dug a tissue out of her pocket, "that we could make it through the summer."

Paula nodded, not sure what to say. Was this baby Jeremy's? If so, why wouldn't he have said something to her?

"But my parents kicked me out today when they realized." She pointed to her abdomen.

"Oh. Oh my." If Jeremy was the baby daddy then he'd, they'd, need to help—regardless, really, because she was his friend.

"And we don't have our rental house until next month."

"Rental house?" Paula repeatedly dumbly.

"Yes, in Ann Arbor."

She closed her eyes. Jeremy's new roommates—Mia and her baby. Except they weren't roomies. They would be his family.

Family. Hers was growing.

"You can stay here until then."

"Thank you, Mrs. Ecker." Mia sniffed. "Jeremy said I should come to you if something happened."

Paula raised her eyebrows. *It would have been nice if he'd told me.* "Come sit down, Mia."

A pair of seagulls swooped down into the garden and squawked at them as they headed toward the lawn chairs and sat. Paula could swear they were some kind of couple and the same ones she kept seeing all summer, but she was no bird expert. She did know the pair never stole food from them, nor were they destructive.

Mia laughed and swiped at her tear-streaked face. "We're naming our little girl after your mom. Eileen."

Now tears swelled in Paula's own eyes. A grandchild. A granddaughter. Named Eileen, after the woman she'd loved so much and lost so early. She patted Mia's hand. "Thank you."

"She's not supposed to arrive for a couple more months." She patted her belly. "Lately she's getting quite active and something feels different."

"Have you been getting prenatal care?"

Mia rolled her pink lips together. "Not like I should. I've been working so much."

"Oh my, we'll need to get you caught up. But you're on prenatal vitamins, right?"

"Yes."

"But you shouldn't be sitting out at that bike stand for long hours."

Mia gave a curt laugh. "My dad fired me, so no problem with that."

"He'll come around." Paula hoped so.

"Not if you could've heard all the awful things he said." Her pretty face turned an even deeper shade of red.

The gate squeaked open, and Jeremy jogged across the yard. She wanted to fuss at her son, but seeing his concern, Paula resisted.

He ran to Mia, knelt, and wrapped his arms around her.

Rex barked and then chased his own tail.

"Mia is going to be staying with us." Paula rose, patted her son's shoulder, and left the couple to talk. "I'll bring some refreshments out. We can't have Mommy getting dehydrated." Mia a mommy—who would have thought it?

A baby. A granddaughter. Paula couldn't stop that amazing feeling of excitement that kept rushing through her.

Gennaro paced his apartment within Parkers' Resort. What had been a welcoming minimalist aesthetic temporary home—no, an escape—for him, had become a sterile prison.

Nothing within reflected his home in Italy, his years as a world-renowned chef, no photos of his extended family and beloved wife. And now, since the party, his soul longed for all of that. For the grape and olive scents of his parents' and uncles' groves. For the feel of marble underfoot in his family's spacious apartment in Rome, with marinara, garlic, and seafood happily co-mingling. For the feel of welcome arms around him. Hundreds of family members. To the tension in his muscles after standing at a stove, stirring, mixing in ingredients, smelling, tasting and then sharing his creations.

It was as though part of him had reawakened.

But he couldn't imagine having a life without Paula beside him. He knew he'd upset her at the party. Gennaro knew he was what his kids had called "a lot" or "too much," and he'd never wanted to be that way with Paula. This woman had saved him with her words. And while Lucia may have been the love of his life, wasn't Paula his soulmate? He loved her with a different kind of love. Something more complete and mature. There wasn't time enough left on this earth to be spending it doing things that didn't involve her, didn't benefit her, or didn't interest them both.

If he was too much or a lot, then Paula would need to know who he was, what he had been, and where he hoped to go next.

He rubbed at the tension in his scalp.

He'd share with Paula. He'd ask her to consider joining him in the next part of his life.

If she'd come visit the villa, then he'd make decisions from there.

He had a lot of explaining to do and some groveling. But he was half-Italian, and he could do it—with God's help. And that little Holy Spirit nudge had him rethinking asking her to come to Italy.

First apologies—later requests.

Sending up a little prayer, he headed out. She wasn't responding to his texts, but surely she'd not run when he showed up at Garden Cottage.

When Claire and Clark arrived at the cottage, Rex raced from the back out to them in the front. "Whoa." Claire grabbed her dog's collar. "Someone's gonna get yelled at for leaving that gate open."

Clark closed the gate behind them and latched it as they entered the backyard. "Your mom's garden did great this year."

"It did. And I helped, too."

"Yeah, I know. And I brought you extra manure, so there." He actually stuck his tongue out at her like he used to do when they were little.

She laughed. "Cover your ears now because I'm going on fuss mode about this gate being open."

"As long as it's not me."

When she spied Jeremy, she pointed at him. "There's the miscreant who almost cost me my beloved pet."

Her brother turned, revealing Mia seated there. Claire's jaw dropped, and she stopped walking. She and Clark both turned and stared as the back door opened and Mom carried out a pitcher of lemonade atop a tray of glasses with ice.

"Let me take that." Clark jogged over to Mom.

"Thanks, Clark."

He carried the tray to the table and set it down. "Would you like me to pour, Mrs. Ecker?"

"Sure. Let's start with my granddaughter's mommy first."

Clark's dark eyebrows rose, but he complied with Mom's request and filled a glass and handed it to Mia. "Congratulations."

Next, Clark poured lemonade for Mom, as all of them took a place in the many cushioned chairs. Finally, he offered her a drink.

"If you're lucky, you'll get to be our baby's uncle." Jeremy grabbed an ice-filled glass and extended it for Clark to fill.

Clark did Jeremy's bidding and then got his own lemonade. "I'd be fortunate if one day I got to be her uncle." Clark smiled at Claire, and warmth flowed through her.

That sweet feeling was swept away when Leo hollered from behind the gate, "Please let us in!"

She thought she heard Leo's dad muttering something as her brother hurried over to unlatch and open the gate. The rest of them turned to watch.

"I got your text." Leo hugged Jeremy and pounded his back. For once, Leo didn't have that cocky look on his face. He genuinely looked pleased for his buddies.

His father trailed in behind him. *Definite whipped-dog look going on there.*

Leo jogged over to Mia and took her hand and kissed it. Then he danced over to Claire and placed a firm hand on her shoulder. "Congratulations on becoming an auntie."

"I'm not one yet." She swatted his hand away.

"Mi scusi." He sounded almost humble.

Guilt skittered through her conscience. "No, I'm sorry for being rude. Thanks."

He gave her a quick nod.

Gennaro, head bent, walked slowly to her mother.

"You can earn yourself a seat out here by getting us a couple more glasses of ice." Mom's tone suggested she was still ticked off about last night. But Gennaro must have thought he heard hope, because he hurried toward the house.

Leo sat near Mom, his hands in his lap. "My dad is here to apologize, Mrs. Ecker. I told him that I was sorry about Whitney."

Clark gave a curt laugh. "Did you hear that he had her thrown out?"

"No!" Mom looked shocked.

"I wasn't sure if I should mention that." Claire set her lemonade on the rattan table nearest her. "I felt a little guilty."

Her mother tilted her head. "Why?"

Two glasses held aloft, Gennaro ambled toward them.

She leaned toward her mom. "When I realized you had bailed. I found Gennaro and asked if you were okay. Then he went to Whitney's table."

Gennaro crossed his arms. "When I found out this paparazzi woman weaseled her way in, and that my Paula had been seated next to her, I figured this intruder had done something bad. So I had Parker's security guards escort her out."

My Paula? Had he just called Mom his Paula?

Things were heating up between those two, just as autumn's chill approached.

Could their friendship survive the different paths that lay before them?

Chapter Twenty-One

Paula eyed her wedding and engagement rings in the pink crystal jewelry dish on her bedroom bureau. She always wore them to church and to work. But this summer, with working in the garden so much, she'd only donned them on Sundays. Today, though, waiting for Gennaro, she hesitated to wear them for the church service.

"You almost ready, *bella*?" Gennaro's deep voice carried down the hallway and did something to her heart, forcing it to beat faster.

She left her rings in the dish and departed her bedroom. "Coming!"

Claire, who'd been strangely somber since the previous day, stood in the kitchen, clutching her phone. "Clark is almost here. Said there'd been a bicycle accident by the marina that held him up." She chewed her lower lip.

Gennaro grinned at her. He wore that same well-fitting suit he'd had on when she'd first met him—only now she realized he wasn't some late-thirties guy but a grandpa of seven who, like herself, had a few health issues.

"I'm looking forward to the 'preachers in the park' thing today." Paula moved alongside her sweetheart, and he bent to kiss her.

"I hope you have your sunscreen on." He quirked his dark eyebrows.

She turned and grabbed her 90 SPF umbrella. "I've got this."

"Great."

"I'm lathered up." Claire gestured to her bare arms. "And Clark has a good tan, and Gennaro is half Italian—so we all should be good." That was the most that Claire had said in the past twenty-four hours.

Paula wasn't pushing it. When her adult daughter wanted to share with her—she would.

Claire's phone buzzed. "He's here."

Rex rose from his bed and wagged his tail.

"Sorry buddy, but Mommy has to go to church now," Claire cooed to her dog. She petted him some more and as Paula passed, she spied tears in her daughter's eyes.

Paula opened her mouth to finally say something, but Gennaro grasped her elbow and propelled her toward the door.

In the street, Clark's carriage had a driver up front today.

When she got to the carriage, Paula carefully climbed in, with an assist from Gennaro. She sat across from Clark. "Thanks for the ride."

"You're welcome. I thought today was perfect for the new driver."

"Oh, yeah?" Claire scooted in beside Clark.

Gennaro climbed in and closed the door behind him.

Clark pushed back in his seat. "This driver is fully vetted by Gianni."

"*Certamente.* Gianni Franchetti always makes sure his family is safe."

"Yup. He's getting some practice in, for driving Gianni's big clan around. They'll come soon for an autumn visit."

Gennaro shook his head. "That guy has more kids and grandkids than I do."

Paula nudged him. "Stop boasting. I'm about to claim my own bragging rights soon to the best little granddaughter in the world."

"You and all the other nonnas out there," Gennaro murmured.

She couldn't wait to be a bona fide nonna.

Two weddings in Garden Cottage today? The kids wanted their ceremony before they returned to Ann Arbor that week. Everything had been pulled together quickly when Aunt Jackie and Frank asked to join Mia and Jeremy for a double wedding—and they'd happily agreed. Paula's nerves buzzed with excitement—or maybe it was because Edna Parsons had returned home from the hospital. Nicky had said her mom was on medication that had helped clear her thinking. Paula sure hoped so. And she prayed Edna didn't disrupt the ceremonies.

Gennaro had prepared heavy hors d'oeuvres for the outdoor event. Claire had obtained a wedding cake from St. Ignace as well as two bridal bouquets the previous day. Both Mia and Jackie wanted things kept simple. Too bad Mia's parents refused to attend, but Paula would keep praying for their hearts to soften.

When Paula had offered her wedding ring set to Mia, it hadn't fit—but then Jackie found Grandma's and Mia loved the ornate set, which fit her perfectly. Frank had a wedding ring custom-made for Jackie, inlaid with sapphires and diamonds, swirled to represent the Straits of Mackinac.

Paula knocked on the bedroom door where the two brides were changing. "Can I come in?"

The door opened. Beautiful, in a floor-length loose ivory lace gown, Mia waved her inside.

"You look gorgeous." Paula took her hands. This young lady was joining her family and would soon give her a granddaughter. Her heart swelled.

"Thank you."

She turned toward her aunt. In a turquoise and navy knee-length sheath dress, with a matching cane, Jackie looked amazing. Claire, a bridesmaid in a periwinkle midi-length dress, struggled to pin a little navy cap with a veil to Jackie's hair, but her aunt waved her away. "I've changed my mind. It's too fussy."

Paula crinkled her nose. "I agree. It's not your look. And all Frank will see is that you're there for him—to be his wife."

Her aunt blushed. "I can't wait."

Mia patted her belly. "Someone is beating on the drums this morning in there."

Paula pointed to the water bottle imprinted with 'Bride-to-be.'. "Maybe drink some water."

"That would help baby." Claire handed Mia the tumbler.

"Oh, let me put my necklace on you." Paula pointed to the pearls, with a diamond studded clasp, that Terry had given her for their tenth anniversary. One day maybe her granddaughter, and his, would wear that necklace, too.

"Thank you." Mia turned and lifted her long hair, which had been curled into spirals for the wedding.

Paula attached the heavy clasp and patted Mia's back. "These are yours now. For you to enjoy and later for your daughter to have."

Mia swiveled around and hugged her hard. "Thank you."

"Oh! I think baby Eileen just kicked me!" Her eyes widened as Mia took her hand and placed it on her abdomen. A little foot or hand pushed against Paula's palm. *The wonder of life.* "She stopped."

Jackie moved closer, her eyes sparkling with unshed tears. "My turn next time, eh?"

Paula leaned in and kissed Mia. "I'm so glad we're adding to the family. I'm very glad to have you for my daughter-in-law and look forward to meeting my granddaughter this fall."

Claire moved forward as Paula stepped back. "Sister-in-law and niece—spectacular." She gave Mia a big hug. "No kisses—I don't want to smear my lipstick on you."

Mia swiped at her eyes and opened her arms to Jackie. "I'm thrilled to get one of the most wonderful ladies on the island for my new grandma."

"I'm proud to be your grandma, your aunt, or whatever you want to call me." Jackie patted Mia's back.

"Jeremy and I don't want to confuse the baby, so we're gonna call you Grandma Jackie, and she'll call you Great-Grandma."

Aunt by marriage, mother figure to Paula, grandma, or great-grandma, it didn't matter—family was family.

And Paula's was expanding. How could it be that only a few months earlier she'd sat in her empty house accepting that she'd be alone?

God was good, and she was truly blessed.

Ann Arbor, Michigan

Not exactly in a good mood after hearing that morning about Ivan being charged and jailed, Claire honked at the idiot who'd just cut them off. "I'm glad I put in a prayer request for travel safety yesterday, because this is nuts." Even nuttier was that Ivan's lawyer tried to get him bond. *As if.* When she saw Tiffany in court, her arms and hands bandaged and the reporter saying the neurosurgeon would likely never perform surgery again, Claire felt genuine sympathy. *There go I, except by the grace of God.* She shivered.

"Everyone's trying to get back to school," Mia stated the obvious, but it didn't ease Claire's tension.

"I've got precious cargo on board." Claire cast a quick look in the rearview mirror.

Jeremy leaned forward. "Me?"

"No, your spawn." She gave a curt laugh.

"My spawn?"

"Isn't that what you always called the little alien offspring in all your crazy video games?"

"Yeah, but—"

Mia leaned in. "Yup, you did and so did I, since that's what cemented our nerdy love story."

"At least she owns it," Claire called over her shoulder.

Clark tapped the seat divider. "Hey, that sounds like an oblique reference to someone else in this oversized testosterone-fueled vehicle. Remind me to never buy one of these."

She gritted her teeth. "Check out that miles per gallon. Under twenty in this thing."

Jeremy did a fake drum roll with his hands on the back of her headrest. "Hey, I'm just glad the Parkers let us use this to haul our stuff."

"Do that again on my headrest and you'll be glad I didn't throw you from a moving vehicle." She glared at him in the rearview mirror.

"Sorry."

Of course he wasn't sorry. *Brothers, ugh.* And she was possibly getting another even more annoying one. "I bet you're even more grateful that Leo drove your car back for you."

"He said he wished it was his dad's Lamborghini, but he's happy to be driving at all again, off the island. And he's wondering if his grandmother's car at their farm where he's moving will be running okay. The property caretakers start it up once a week, but it's almost twenty years old."

"We'll find out soon." Clark and Claire were driving Leo over to his great-grandmother's home, about ten miles outside of Ann Arbor.

"I think he might be lonely there." Mia sounded concerned.

"Especially since he'd originally come to school here to be near his great-grandmother, and then she died his second semester."

"That was an awful time." Mia sighed. "That's when Jeremy adopted him."

"I didn't adopt him. We were already friends, we just got . . ."

"When you become a psychologist you can't just befriend all of your clients, though." Mia's firm voice left no room for argument.

"He wasn't a client. He was the best student in my agricultural science class, and I learned a lot from him."

"Until he flipped out after his grandma died." No sympathy there in Mia's voice.

"Let's stop talking bad about poor Leo." Claire couldn't believe she'd uttered those words after all the complaints she'd had about him. "He's bailing you two out today." Just like she and Clark were.

"We ordered a pull-out sofa at our place for him," Jeremy shared.

"Ha! Buddy, once you have a baby, do you really think Leo's gonna want to come crash on your sofa with the baby screaming in the nursery?"

"He's the uncle to seven kids." Mia leaned in and placed a hand on Clark's headrest. "Plus, Leo ordered furniture for a nursery at the farmhouse."

"No way." Clark huffed a laugh.

"Way. He said we can come out there any time. Said if your mom and his dad don't come back from Italy, then—"

Claire flinched. "What do you mean if they don't come back?"

"Yeah, Mrs. Ecker, I mean Paula, can't stay indefinitely."

"You can call her Mom if you want. Right, Sis?"

"You're right, Jeremy."

"But the Italian government must have rules about your mom staying that long." Clark always analyzed situations. "Like we have here."

Claire sure hoped so.

As traffic bunched up, she slowed, ready for the exit to U of M. Her heartbeat ticked upward.

"Anyway," Mia continued, "Leo set up the house so we can come out any time we want."

"And stay as long as we want." Her brother hadn't mentioned any of this previously. Why?

An SUV cut her off. She had to stay focused.

Clark turned toward the back. "Does Leo intend to live at the farm permanently?"

"He's got a lot of plans to get the farm back up and running, so maybe. And he'd said if Mia and I and the baby want to live there for a while after graduation, he's cool with that."

That kid had sure changed his tune. "And no Italian supermodel involved in his plans?" Claire muttered. Then she bit her tongue as she had to slam on her brakes to avoid an overpacked compact car.

When they reached the campus area, she couldn't believe how many students were there. The place swarmed with college students. It had been years since she'd finished her program, but it seemed a million years ago in one way, and just an instant in another. "This big truck is going to be a bear to maneuver through all this traffic. I forgot how crazy move-in days are."

"I think Montana's lack of traffic messed with your head, Sis."

"Maybe." She pushed her hair behind her ear. "Can you believe it's your last year, little bro?"

"Uh, no, not if I'm gonna get my doctorate, it isn't."

"Well, yeah, there's that. But I meant here in Ann Arbor."

"Claire, you'll need to turn at that next light to get to our place." Mia sounded excited. "I've started the GPS."

Soon the computerized voice announced the turns. Mia and Jeremy helped when the GPS faltered.

She recognized Jeremy's car when she pulled into the apartment complex. As she parked in the lot, Leo emerged from a first-floor apartment, carrying an empty box. He ran up to them. "Hi, Claire. At least you got to drive the Parkers' huge truck."

She made a face of disgust as she closed the driver's door. "Oh, yeah, just what I want to be driving."

"You won't have to carry anything heavy," Leo asserted, pointing to Jeremy and Clark.

"Yup. That's why I'm here." Clark shoved his T-shirt sleeve up. "For the muscle."

"Pregnant lady coming through." Mia hurried toward the open apartment door and hurried inside, presumably to the bathroom.

Leo marched to the back of the truck and opened it. "When you said ugly furniture, you really meant it."

"This is stuff my Aunt Jackie and my soon-to-be new uncle Frank didn't want."

"At least those two boxed memory-foam mattresses look new." Leo jumped inside the back of the truck.

"They are." Clark grabbed them both. "From me and Claire."

"Thanks, dude." Jeremy patted Clark's back and waved at Claire. "Thanks, Sis. Mia will love this mattress."

"You've got our biological grandparents' trunk for a coffee table. Aunt Jackie said they'd also used it at college after they got married."

Clark jumped up, joining Leo in the back.

"That makes me a little sad." Jeremy took the trunk Clark pushed forward. "It's heavier than it looks."

Clark jumped down from the truck. "Will hold stuff, too, man."

Leo pushed two metal bed frames to the edge of the open truck bed.

They'd also packed a large folding table for the dining area and folding chairs for the living room. Frank sent two small older pine chest-of-drawers and two matching ugly bedside tables. Jackie found several 1970s mustard-yellow ceramic lamps at the St. Ignace house, that still worked well, so she also sent those. Mrs. Parsons, who seemed more like her old self, sent a beautiful quilt that she no longer used and a box full of dishes that looked in great shape. Her daughter, Nicole, confirmed that they were Mrs. Parsons' belongings and that it was fine for them to take them.

Even though Jeremy could have purchased or rented all new furnishings, Claire was proud of her frugal little brother. They may have inherited a lot from their dad, but Mom had brought them up to not squander their resources. She didn't want to be like Dad, who'd had some messed-up ideas about money—like hiding what he had inherited and making separate life insurance policies for her and Jeremy without telling Mom.

Clark stacked the two bedside tables on a dolly. "These are not getting brought back up North, so don't even think about asking."

"You don't think your folks would want them?"

"They're moving off island."

"What? For sure?"

"It's been decided. Mom wants to sell and move closer to my grandma and to where they both grew up."

"What about you? Where will you live?" Was he hoping they'd marry and live at Garden Cottage?

"Candlelight Cottage is up for sale." He kissed her.

"Candlelight Cottage?" Could that make a good location for her business, too? Was it zoned for that? Maybe the inheritance from the Connecticut family she'd never known could be put to good use.

"Yup, it's on the market." He poked her arm. "Ha, and it's on Market Street—a pun."

"A bad one." She poked him back. "No worries. I'm sure Mom will let you sleep in our little hangout shed behind Garden Cottage if needed."

"There's no heat in there."

"Correct."

"You could keep me warm." He leaned in for another kiss, but she swatted at him.

"Behave yourself. Let's get this stuff in and get going."

When she got back, she'd investigate Candlelight Cottage—and its possibilities.

Chapter Twenty-Two

Late August

Gennaro reviewed his mental checklist as he strolled to the Eckers' cottage. Installed back at her St. Ignace home, Jackie was doing well with her new husband, Frank. Jeremy and Mia and Leo had made it safely back to school. Claire and Clark offered to handle the fading garden's cleanup and put it to rest. Meanwhile, Paula's Virginia home was still a construction zone, and she'd extended her work absence.

Although he'd rehearsed his question several times, it still didn't seem right. But how hard could it be to ask this beautiful woman, "Paula, do you want to come to Italy with me?"

Two seagulls swooped down nearby and squawked loudly at him, as if mocking his plans. He made a shooing motion. "Go away." The gulls squawked again and then flew off.

He walked up the street toward the charming cottage. Like his Italian birthplace, Garden Cottage was over a hundred and fifty years old. And like his family, generations had lived there and called this place home. He admired the two lovely large topiary trees, trimmed into spirals, that grew alongside the front porch. They reminded him of some he had near his villa in Italy. Maybe Paula would see some commonalities if she visited with him. His aristocratic ancestors might never have accepted her, but since his father had met his mother, an American, and married her, there should be no complaints about her roots.

How had it happened that he'd gone from being so very touched by Paula's book, to the point of feeling that she had saved him from his grief over Lucia, to now growing to love Paula more each day? It wasn't wrong to have a love of one's life and then to find a new, different, special love for someone else. This was different. This was the kind of relationship he'd hoped he and Lucia would have in their later years—but for them, that was not to be. He'd imagined them moving back to the family farm, helping his brothers with the gardens, and having the kids and grandkids visit them. Lucia had laughed at that notion. "I'm an artist," she'd said. "Artists don't stop creating. If we did, we'd stop breathing." She'd explained that she intended to remain in a large city near all the galleries and museums when he retired from running his restaurants. They'd walk the boulevards, sample other chefs' cuisine, and she'd continue to have showings and sell her work. That conversation had made him a little sad. He'd have done anything for her, though. But would it have cost him a part of himself to have remained in Rome or Paris or Lucerne instead of never returning to the villa? No matter now. And he would not feel guilty about imagining that kind of future with Paula. First, though, he wanted her to see his home and meet the rest of his family.

Paula's front door opened, and Clark bounded out with Rex. The dog barked playfully at Gennaro and tugged at the leash, but the younger man held tight. Claire stepped out onto the porch and waved at him.

He waved back. Thank God Paula's kids liked him. And his children loved Paula. All his daughters could keep asking was when they'd be married and who could help plan the ceremony. At least his son was staying out of it. If it was up to him, he'd do like the two couples who had just wed there—keep it simple and quick. *And soon.*

"Buongiorno, you two." He grinned at them. "I'm here with a special request."

Claire slacked her hip. "Mom says she isn't volunteering for anything."

He laughed. "No volunteering! I'm here to pitch a wonderful Italian holiday—in a beautiful rural setting."

"I think she might do it." Clark held tight to Rex, who was pulling.

"Do what?" Paula peered out the screen door and then stepped onto the porch.

Impulsively, Gennaro dropped down on one knee, right there on the front lawn. "Oh, dear lady, would you honor me by—"

Paula motioned with her hands for him to stop, eyes wide. "Oh, no, no, no—too early for those kinds of thoughts."

"Mom, he just wants you to go to Italy with him." Claire sighed dramatically.

"A vacation to travel Italy and meet his other family members." Clark bent and grabbed Rex's collar because the pup was trying to wind the leash around his legs.

"Yeah, Mom, he's got even more family over there who want to meet you. Leo texted me that if his dad doesn't bring you soon, they'll all fly over here and try to stay at the farmhouse with him."

Leo was texting Claire? Like brother and sister. *Fantastico.*

Gennaro got to his feet slowly, his back and knees complaining. "We need to get the trip scheduled so they will stop harassing me, too."

"Oh." Paula's face glowed a strong pink color. "Sorry. I'm so embarrassed. I just thought . . ." She raised her hands to her cheeks. "With those two weddings . . ."

He waved that away. "No worries, dear lady. One day soon I'm very likely to ask that other question."

Again, her eyes widened. Her daughter turned and squeezed Paula's arm.

"But I won't be dropping on that knee again. I am getting too old for those dramatic gestures."

Paula made a sympathetic face. "Do you need an ice pack?"

"No. But for the trip, I'll need them when we get there after all that flying."

"Me, too. My knee is acting up, and I need one right now." She beckoned him toward the porch.

Clark gestured between the two of them. "Is this what old-people romance looks like?"

Gennaro chuckled as he headed toward his sweetheart. "Go away and do your own thing. *Capisci*?"

Scowling at the young couple, Paula shook her head. "Leave us senior citizens alone."

Clark saluted her and then passed the leash to Claire, who took off in a fast jog with her boyfriend following her.

"Kids!" he said, as he mounted the porch stairs. He leaned in and kissed her soft cheeks, smelling roses and strong coffee.

She pulled away. "You've got enough kids to understand them, don't you? Plus, all those grandkids."

"And I've got my parents, my brothers, my sisters-in-law and all those nieces and nephews and grand-nieces and grand-nephews." He took her hands. "Will you come meet them and see where I grew up?"

When she nodded, he wrapped his arms around her and pulled her close. She fit exactly in his embrace. He ran his hand over her silky hair. When she stepped away, he released her.

"But right now, I really do need to ice this knee, Gennaro."

He laughed again. "You are always full of so many romantic ideas."

"I'm not twenty, thirty or even forty."

"Come on. You can put your legs up on my lap, and we'll put that cold pack on your bad knee."

"That actually does sound nice."

"I can sit like that for about an hour, but then I'll have to get up and walk around." He put his hand on his lower back. "Or I seize up like a statue sometimes."

She shook her head. "And I thought you were a young pup."

"No, *amore*, but I am loyal and devoted. But I never drool, bark, or beg for treats." He stuck out his tongue and pretended to pant. "No panting, either."

"Rex has you beat on all of those." She patted his jawline. "I do want some kisses before I put my leg up."

"Happy to oblige." And he kissed her beautiful face until she made him stop.

"Let's put a pause on that and have some hot cider while we do our icing, okay?" Paula headed to the counter and poured two mugs full of apple cider for them. Maybe what she needed was ice-cold cider, with the way Gennaro had heated her up.

She put the mugs in the microwave and set the timer. When the chime sounded, she removed the two ciders and handed them to him.

She motioned toward the freezer. "I'll grab the ice packs and bring those with us to the parlor."

"Grazie." He carried the mugs to the living area and set them on the coffee table in front of the sofa recliner. "Nice to have the modern convenience of this couch."

"Aunt Jackie had that shipped over last year, especially for me, when my knee was really acting up. Thank God it's doing so much better. I used to wear a brace and was in excruciating pain."

"Yes, God is good. So good." Gennaro scooted in and sat down. "He's so good in fact, that if you could ask him to allow you to do anything, what would it be?"

Paula sat down, placing the ice packs beside her, and grabbed her cider. "First things first." She cupped her hands around the mug and stared down through the steam. "You wouldn't believe it, but I've wondered about that same thing. But I don't think this cider is going to show me any answers."

Her sweetie set his mug down and pointed at her. "I've also considered where God was moving me—when I lost my wife."

"Same—after my husband died and during the pandemic."

He pushed his hand back through his thick dark locks. "Pandemic was like a whorl—like a swirling tunnel in the water that I disappeared into—and your book was like a life raft that I grabbed onto."

She reached and squeezed his hand. "I'm so glad my story helped you."

"Because Lucia had just died before all the shutdowns in Italy, and because of my grief, I felt . . ." He shook his head. "Like I was in one of those old *Twilight Zone* shows that my mom used to sneak and watch when we were here in America. Like my reality wasn't real."

"I think a lot of us felt that way. But to lose our spouses and go through it—that was another level of surrealness."

"Is that a word? Surrealness?" He cocked his head.

"Yes. And even if it wasn't, the whole COVID-19 epidemic would've made it a new word."

They each sipped their cider. Sunlight streamed through the far window. The season was winding down.

Paula wanted him to know her secret. "I told them no, Gennaro."

Creases formed around his dark eyes as he grinned. "No more library lady?"

She leaned and patted the side of her hair. "I told the paparazzi that no, I can't be a senior citizen model for Vogue's bathing suit issue."

Gennaro ducked in his chin and straightened. "I see. That's good because I don't think that's what you want to do."

"Exactly." She made a funny face and laughed. "You're right. I did tell the library that I won't be coming back. No return for me."

"You're retiring, but you're not going to become a volunteeraholic again?"

She sipped the delicious cider. "This tastes amazing. You're right, but that's not a real word either. I don't think I was an addict. I was trying to keep busy and be helpful, but you know what?"

"What?"

"I wasn't helping myself. God loves me, and He wants to help me. He wouldn't want me to stay in my self-inflicted pattern of meeting everyone else's needs but my own!"

"I agree. That's part of the reason I had to stop being a chef. It was not good for my health, but I didn't want to disappoint anyone. It took my wife's death for me to realize—and for my kids to point out—that I had to change things."

"And you feel so much better on that healthy regimen, don't you?"

"Absolutely. And even more so since I met you."

"You are so sweet. I didn't realize how much I'd missed out on until I met you."

"Ah, but you threw yourself into your gardening and simply tolerated that youthful man," he grinned and patted his chest, "who'd stop by your cottage."

"Yes. I had loved gardening with my uncle. I wanted to feel that connection again." She pulled her lips to the side. "Um, but I didn't realize I'd forgotten almost everything he taught me, which is pretty sad."

"You had a decent harvest given the size of the garden and some of the weird weather we've had."

"But back to what you asked, I guess if I could imagine what I'd love to do, if I could do anything at all, I would keep trying to improve my gardening skills. But very honestly, I think it's the gardens themselves that appeal to me, not the work involved in getting them that way." She drank from her mug.

A strange look passed over his handsome face. "So, if this beautiful big garden is just . . . there, then this would make you happy? Like a magical garden that takes care of itself?"

"Well, if we're going to make believe, then I'd also add all kinds of animals." She raised her hands for emphasis. "I'm lousy with anything but a dog. But I love lambs, horses, goats, cows, bunnies, chickens, and all those—I just don't want to have to take care of them." She chuckled. "I'd like them to keep alive and that wouldn't happen if I was their caretaker."

Gennaro's expression grew more serious. "And you don't mind all those animal noises? And all the people who'd have to come to take care of them? All the workers?"

She waved his comment away. "As long as they aren't expecting me to go milk a cow or shovel out manure."

"That's very interesting." The way he quickly drank the rest of his cider, covering his mouth, made her feel like he was hiding something.

"What about you? If you could do anything, what would you do?"

"This job, I took this when I'd gone to Switzerland, after Lucia's death." A cloud passed over his face. "I was helping my daughter with starting the restaurant there and then it got shut down for a while. The Parkers were there. They had long-term guests at their new inn and needed to feed them properly, but with limited kitchen staff."

"So Parker and Jaycie had just started, had bookings, but didn't normally feed their guests?"

"Just a simple breakfast—like your aunt did for her tourists."

"And you, a famous chef, came in and cooked for them?"

He shrugged. "Honestly, I felt more like I was on automatic pilot. My daughter helped me. This also allowed her to keep the Lucerne restaurant going and keep her staff." He rubbed the side of his face. "I could do the kind of cooking I did for them in my sleep—mostly family-style Italian cooking like I was raised with at home by my nonna."

"Did you like that?"

"I liked being able to make whatever I wanted—I remember that. Guests didn't get to choose. They either ate what I prepared or they went hungry."

"I'm guessing no one turned up their nose at your cooking."

"I don't think so. It was like I was there in body, but my mind wasn't."

She nodded. "When I went back to work, it was like that. But would you like to do some cooking for groups of people if you weren't required to make specific things?"

"Maybe." He shrugged. "Or maybe I'll just lie around on your sofa all the time. This place is cozy."

She laughed and gestured around the parlor. "Yes. I love cozy and comfortable."

"For me—no more of that minimalist and modern sleek stuff my wife loved and like I have at the Parkers." His face flushed. "And it's okay that I feel that way."

"It sure is! We don't have to have loved everything about our spouses. I sure didn't love Terry being a workaholic."

Gennaro took her hand. "I know I was too immersed in my work, and I regret that very much. But it's funny how only recently I've realized that Lucia was a workaholic and obsessed with her art. I'm embarrassed now to say that my wife had her own apartment right near her studio."

"Really?" Unease worked through her. But maybe European artists needed that space.

"Yes, I feel like that was not right, and I'm embarrassed I said nothing."

"No," she squeezed his hand. "I mean, she had a separate apartment near her art studio where she stayed, alone, sometimes?"

"Sometimes I worked so late that by the time I fell into bed, I'd not even have known if she was there." He leaned in and kissed her forehead. "I'm not making that mistake again, not when I marry again."

Warmth coursed through her. What would it be like married to this man? "Do you think that's what made the marriage work for you two, though?"

"Maybe so. But my kids were affected not just by me being gone, but by my wife being at her studio. Only recently have they begun making the comments like Emanuela shared with you."

"I was a little surprised." She leaned against him. "You made it sound like your wife was perfect."

His heart hurt thinking about what the reality had been in their marriage. "Oh, an amazing woman. Absolutely. Wonderful artist. Gorgeous. A charmer. Fantastic dancer." He could still feel the warmth draining from her, in his arms, after she'd collapsed during their last dance. Now, though, that warmth was replaced by the sweet woman leaning against his chest.

Paula looked up. "I hear a 'but' don't I?"

"Yes. She wasn't a good mother to the kids. I certainly wasn't the best father, either. But something inside me believes that she'd have continued to have put her art first before me and the kids even as we headed into our senior years. My mother tried to compensate for Lucia being gone so much and taking so little interest in the kids."

"But she went through those pregnancies. She must have wanted children." Paula patted his chest.

"Yes, she wanted to make me happy. I wanted many kids. And she enjoyed them when they were babies and even in the wild toddler years—but always on her own terms. She was a highly gifted artist, world-renowned, and there's something about those creative geniuses that is different from the rest of us."

"But isn't your creativity as a chef the same?"

He patted her silky hair. "Oh no. Not with me—maybe with others. I am not that temperamental gourmet chef. I created experiences for my customers."

"Ah, like the dancing chef thing?"

"Exactly."

"I love it when you do that." She looked up at him.

He bent and kissed her, enjoying the warmth of her sweet lips on his. "Do you love that, too?"

She narrowed her eyes. "I am filling out a requisition for a bunch more of those."

"Very good."

"But back to your 'chefness,' and then we'd better get icing our knees."

"Again, no such word as chefness. But, I wanted a celebration of family, so there was always a family-style entrée at my place. And I wanted there to be fun." He pushed a button and the couch legs elevated as the backs reclined.

"Oh!" She grabbed his arm. "Hey, give me warning next time."

"I like a little unexpectedness." He kissed her again, more soundly and she rewarded him with a smile.

"I don't think you were talking about kissing."

"I wanted experimentation with local cuisine and vegetables, so at my Rome ristorante we harvested from our own gardens on-site—"

"Really? That's pretty cool."

Would she think it was great to live where his family was, in Italy? He studied her beautiful face—one he could look at forever. "We had lots of vegetables and fruits brought in from my family's farms."

"You did?" She made an adorable 'O' with her pink lips. "Do they grow a lot of things?"

He'd leave out about the vineyards, the dairy, and the sheer vastness of their acreage. "Sì, yes, they do."

"That's great." Her eyes did that funny thing she did when she wanted to say something but wouldn't.

If he got his wish, she'd see his family's land very soon. "Hey, how much do you trust me?"

"A lot. And that's saying something coming from the mean old librarian." She grinned, not looking mean at all.

"Is your passport up to date?"

"Yup."

"And you're not going back to your job?"

"Nope."

"Then I'm going to make a plan for us in Italy, but I want you to trust me with the details."

"As long as I get the first ice pack on my knee right now, that's fine." She crinkled her nose and he tweaked it.

Then he leaned in for one last kiss before the icing commenced. "You know, amore, if we keep kissing then that ice pack will melt very fast."

"I'm willing to risk it."

Chapter Twenty-Three

Tuscany, Italy, September

Tires rumbling on an uneven road startled Paula awake. Where was she? Definitely not in bed on Mackinac Island. In the fog of jet-lag fatigue, she vaguely recalled landing at the airport, Gennaro waking her there, and then picking up their luggage and getting into Gennaro's Maserati GranTurismo, which a pal of his had brought to the airport. Then she'd promptly fallen back to sleep. Shockingly, now, full sun burst through the clouds. How had she slept through that? She'd felt so safe and secure with Gennaro, despite being in a plane flying across the ocean, that she'd zonked out.

"You awake now that I'm done driving?" Gennaro teased.

She grasped the luxury car's arm rest. She sat up and blinked as she took in vast fields. "Wow! That's a lot of grapes!"

"For sure. Lots to harvest." Gennaro pushed up the bridge of his sunglasses. "I hope and pray you are ready for this. My family can be as Leo says, 'extra, extra.' Haha."

"As ready as I'll ever be."

If she didn't stop gaping, her jaw might get stuck permanently open. "What's that fort doing there?" The tall stone circular building rose up commandingly at the end of a wide swath of land.

"The Di Imperiali family home."

"That's a villa?"

"It's actually more than a villa."

"A *palazzo*?" She'd been reviewing her weak Italian skills, but right now, this fatigued, she was lucky she remembered her own name.

"Technically, it's a *castello*."

"Like a castle?"

"Sort of. More a *fattoria* now, though. A farm."

"Doesn't look like any farm I've ever seen."

She sat straighter, gawking at the imposing structure as they drove closer. It looked like the kind of place where armed guards would be standing out front.

Soon, Gennaro pulled the car into a cobblestone courtyard. The interior courtyard was bigger than even the Parkers' carriage entrance—

about half as big as a football field. At one side stood a low building that may have once been for carriages but now had a dozen bays for a multitude of vehicles.

Gennaro parked the car in the center of the courtyard. "Let's go in, and then I'll ask where I should park."

The castello's back, in contrast to the front, featured large windows and was softened by gorgeous landscaping, potted plants, and some massive hanging plants. The air was redolent with floral perfumes intermingling beautifully. Paula closed her eyes. If this was the scent of Tuscany, then someone should bottle it and sell it. Maybe someone already had.

"Gennaro!" A woman about Jackie's age with longish blonde wavy hair, dressed in jeans and a University of Michigan T-shirt, ran toward them, arms open.

Paula had to do a double take. For a moment, she thought she was back in Michigan.

His mom gave him a bear hug, and Gennaro kissed her on both cheeks. "Mom, I'm so glad to see you."

"Now introduce me to Paula. All the girls have been talking about her and so has Leo."

Paula stiffened. "Hopefully nice things."

"All very nice things." Mrs. Di Imperiali pulled her into a surprisingly strong hug.

"Good."

Mrs. Di Imperiali gestured around the courtyard and beyond to the fields. "What do you think of our little place?"

Paula laughed. "A castle? Really?" She gave Gennaro a little punch on the shoulder. "I wish your son had told me."

"Ow, she hurt me, Mama." Gennaro rubbed his shoulder and bent over.

His mom waved him away. "He's one for keeping too much to himself. I heard he never told you he'd been a famous chef."

"Nope." Paula shook her head. "And he wouldn't tell me anything about this place other than that I would be surprised. And boy, am I ever! This is amazing."

Gennaro's mother wrapped an arm around her. "When I first came here, I thought I had died and gone to heaven." Her cheeks flushed, and she turned and squeezed her son's hand. "Sorry, son. That was insensitive."

He shrugged. "I think heaven for Lucia was full of Michaelangelo and all kinds of paintings and sculptures—definitely not gardens in the countryside. And not an old castle that we've spent decades remodeling."

"It's all right. Lucia blessed us with five grandchildren, and now we've got seven great-grandchildren." Mrs. Di Imperiali clapped her hands together.

Gennaro kissed Paula's cheek. "Come inside and let's get you settled in one of the guest rooms. Mama, where did you put her?"

Given the size of the place, there must be a dozen or more rooms upstairs.

"There are twenty-five to choose from. But how about that one you most recently had remodeled with the new-style bathroom?"

On the flight there, Gennaro had shared how he'd financially assisted his parents with the great expense of the property—especially when there were crop failures. Now seeing this place, she was astonished by what that must mean. What a good son he was. And he explained that he intended to continue helping but was considering what his next steps might be. Definitely hinting at marriage to her. And maybe living here?

"Will you take Paula to see Uncle Carlo's dairy tomorrow?"

"The vineyards first—she could see a little of them on our drive."

A massive farm, vineyards, animals, a gorgeous house—and she didn't have to weed or fertilize, unless she wanted to do so. This was quickly becoming what she'd imagined she'd love to do with her life.

No wonder Gennaro had asked her what she'd like to do if she could choose anything.

The first few days in Italy had passed like a massive country festival, the culmination of which had been her sweetheart's fifty-fifth birthday party. Gennaro had taken her to each of his three uncles' homes, and she'd been fed amazing local Tuscan cuisine and met all the uncles' wives and Gennaro's nieces and nephews. Each uncle had a different type of farm, so she'd been given walking tours through olive groves, vineyards, and vegetable fields. The vast plots were amazing and made her cottage's garden seem like a mouse's version in comparison. The tomatoes here were massive and so sweet and juicy. But more important was the love and support all the family members gave each other—and his siblings' joy in celebrating their beloved oldest brother's birthday. What a shocking thing to realize that one year earlier, she'd first set eyes on Gennaro, who in actuality turned out to be only five years younger than her.

Today, they'd stayed the morning at the Di Imperiali's *castello*. After a European-style breakfast of strong coffee with assorted fruit pastries, Gennaro's mom, who'd asked Paula to call her Brenda, was showing her some of the rooms in the place. They started at the top floor and worked their way down.

At the second floor, Brenda led her into a dark room and turned on the lights, which unlike the other rooms, were recessed can lights. "This one was my middle son's room. My granddaughter Antonia was named after her Uncle Anthony."

"That's sweet." Paula entered the second-floor room, which faced the front and had no windows.

"Why he chose this depressing room, I don't know. We're going to leave it as is. He and his wife and kids stay up on the third floor in that suite I showed you with the three bedrooms. He's president of a bank in Milan, and he had that all repaired and restored and remodeled about ten years ago."

On one of her bike rides, Gennaro had described that brother as very serious and driven, and he'd not seen him much.

Brenda turned to Paula with mischief in her eyes. "Don't tell my son, but Anthony and his family will be coming tomorrow to surprise Gennaro and meet you."

"That will be a wonderful surprise." At least he told his folks, unlike Gennaro's daughters had done. Was he coming to meet Paula or vet her for approval?

"Come see my baby's room." Brenda waved Paula on. They crossed the hall to a room with three tall windows, no shades or curtains on them.

"What a contrast." The bright yellow walls and deep green mid-century modern furniture was cheerful and compact. The bed, however, was ornate, with four intricately carved posts and a headboard covered in what looked like a hunting expedition.

"That's the Di Imperiali bed from the sixteenth century."

Paula coughed. "The fifteen hundreds?"

"Yup. Not something we saw in the mid-Michigan farmlands." Brenda grinned. "But my son chose that bed for his own. He and his wife still sleep in this room, and the kids are up in that Hansel-and-Gretel-themed playroom for now. I imagine they'll soon age out of it once they're teens."

"There are so many pretty rooms to choose from. That salmon-colored one with the golden marble bathroom would make any teen girl swoon."

"I know. That was my idea, and Riccardo is the one who paid for that, so it would be fitting for her to move to that room. He's a terrific exporter of agricultural produce to the States, including Michigan."

"That sounds like a tough job, with the changes in the tariffs and then Europe trying to change the agricultural import-export jobs."

Brenda feigned wiping sweat from her brow. "Good thing I don't have to sweat it because Riccardo handles all our farm exports."

"Gennaro said you often called him Richard, because he was named after your father, his grandfather."

"Ha, I did. I do sometimes, but my husband said it would be easier to name him Riccardo. So I did." She pressed her hand to her chest. "But he'll always be Richard in my heart. My dad was a wonderful man and so is my son. All my sons."

"I can't wait to meet them."

"Richard," she faux-whispered the name, as if someone might hear, "is coming up from Rome the day before you leave. And he hopes to bring his family to America for Leo's graduation in May."

Pleasure flowed through Paula. "Oh, that will be wonderful."

"I don't know how we'll all fit in the American farmhouse, but Leo is hoping we can."

"My daughter said it is very pretty. Four bedrooms, though?" And small, she'd said.

"Gennaro already reserved an entire floor at a nice hotel near the university. He's not telling my grandson until we get closer to the date. Leo can come stay there, too." She made a funny face. "It's not like he has livestock he has to take care of like we do here."

One of the house servants, a young man of about twenty, knocked on the open door. "*Signora* Di Imperiali, the stables are ready for inspection."

Brenda chuckled. "That sounds so formal. We're just looking at them."

He nodded. "Sì, signora." He swiftly and quietly left the room.

The stable stalls were made of beautiful wood, some gates carved with the family crest.

Gennaro called out to them as he and his dad entered the spacious building. "Ready for a ride?"

She pointed to her leg. "I asked my knee and it said not today."

Brenda kissed her husband on the cheek. "Don't ride too long. Cecilia has a nice *pranzo al fresco* planned for us."

"Lunch outside sounds good to me." Paula accepted a kiss from Gennaro.

"Your Italian is improving. Maybe we stay longer so you can be fluent."

She gave him her best look of incredulity and he laughed.

"I'm taking Paula through the flower gardens now. She's going to tell her daughter all about them. Maybe she can come sometime and see if any would work for her botanical line."

Gennaro held his hands wide apart. “I can see it now—Di Imperiali Neuro Botanicals.”

“I think Claire would want to name her company herself.”

“Ha, talk to my other sons about that. We’ve had to rename product lines in different countries dependent upon what appeals to them.”

“I guess that makes sense.”

Brenda linked her arms through hers as two stable hands assisted Gennaro and his dad in preparing the two horses for a ride.

Paula opened the far stable gate, and they exited out to sunny skies.

“We start with the rose garden. The poppies, of course, are long gone but we have wonderful ones earlier in the summer.” They walked through rows of roses in many different colors.

“Are those mums I see?” Paula pointed to the left field.

“Yes. Chrysanthemums and some dahlias mixed with some cyclamen.”

“The pinks look so pretty with the whites and oranges.”

“I like color, as you could tell from the castello.”

“Signora!” A gardener waved to them as they moved toward the end of the rose garden. His basket held a bushel of trimmed stems and deadheaded flowers. As they neared him, he spoke in Italian so rapid that Paula couldn’t catch a single word. So much for her improving skills.

Brenda gestured to Paula. “Did you enjoy the bouquets in your room this week?”

“*Molto bello*.” She was pretty sure that wasn’t quite right. “Grazie.”

“His wife did the arrangements.” Her hostess nodded toward him. “*Fiori molto belli*.”

Again, the rapid-fire Italian from the gardener.

“He’ll tell her.”

The worker touched his hand to the brim of his work hat, and Brenda led Paula to the late summer flower patch. Faded sunflowers filled a back acre, forming a gentle brown-and-green backdrop for the pink, coral, white, and orange flowers.

Now, after lunch in the courtyard, they’d all transitioned to the family room. Seated on the soft coral-colored couch that could seat sixteen, Paula pulled out her phone and looked at the video her friend, Judy, had sent her. She flinched as a noise roared in the video of her backyard.

“What is that sound?” Gennaro’s mom marched out to the patio, carrying a tray of almond biscotti their cook had prepared, followed by her husband, who hoisted a large coffee pot aloft. They set them on the five-foot-long coffee table that centered the sectional.

Paula laughed and tapped at her phone to stop the sounds of home—or what had been her previous home. "This was a video from my house in Virginia."

"Play it again so we can hear what that is." Gennaro's dad was so cute—he did a little dance as he poured coffee into the mugs that Paula had set on the table earlier with a creamer and a sugar bowl. She could see where Gennaro got his dancing moves.

"Are you sure you want to hear this?"

"Sì!"

She turned the volume fully up and tapped the screen. An airplane thundered overhead. "That's one of the many military aircraft that fly over my neighborhood."

Brenda cringed as dogs barked and a lawn mower blasted on the phone. "What is that thing—a supersonic lawn mower?"

Paula shook her head as a weed whacker revved up to join the noise. The jet's sounds disappeared but then cars from the nearby highway joined in, immediately followed by a small propjet's whirling noise. Finally, all quieted for a moment, and the sounds of dozens of different birds filled the air—crows, bluebirds, and cardinals. Then another lawnmower, louder if possible than the last one, chimed in and drowned out all the sounds of nature.

"This is why you don't go back there, Paula." Gennaro leaned over her shoulder and kissed her cheek as he held a tray with sugar, cream, napkins and spoons in front of her. "Doesn't sound like Mackinac Island."

"Not too many seagulls and ferries and horses there," she agreed. "Every time I used to come back from up North, I'd have to readjust to all the noise. It was stressful."

Gennaro walked around and slid the tray onto the coffee table. "It's pretty quiet here."

"Most of the time."

"It's peaceful here. You stay here with us." Mr. Di Imperiali sat further down on the sectional and extended his legs.

Brenda slipped in beside him. "You two should come live here. We've got room." She laughed.

"You know I can't live here just yet."

"You just retired, though, Paula?" Brenda held her mug balanced on her hand.

"I guess so. Sort of."

"We want you to marry Gennaro and either move here or come visit often until you can," Mr. Di Imperiali announced.

Surprised, she blinked as she turned toward Gennaro, who'd just fixed her coffee and his. "I think your dad may have just proposed for you."

"I'm not getting down on my knee. It hurts from riding my beautiful mare today. It's been too long."

Her face heated. "I was just teasing."

"We're not." Brenda pulled a small box from her maxi dress's pocket. "Here, son, give that to Paula."

Gennaro popped the box open. "Where did you find this, *Madre*?" His voice was stern, and he shook his head.

Uh oh, she'd started something in his family, and their week there wasn't even up yet.

Brenda shrugged. "I cleaned your room up a little, that's all."

Gennaro leaned forward to look at his father. "Did you know about this?"

"No. I was going to offer my grandmother's ring." Mr. Di Imperiali pulled a small, faded gray leather box from his shirt pocket.

Paula closed her eyes.

"Let Paula choose which one she wants, Son." Brenda pointed to both boxes.

This was getting more embarrassing by the moment. Obviously, Gennaro wasn't quite ready.

"Am I ever glad I don't have to drop down on one knee." Gennaro caught the box his father threw in their direction. "I can propose in the comfort of the Di Imperiali home."

He opened each box and held them out to Paula. "Which one do you like best?"

The new solitaire he'd picked was well over three carats. The chandelier overhead made light from the diamond flicker onto the pale stone walls.

He must have read her reaction because he murmured, "Too much. That's what Leo said, too."

She nodded as he opened the other small box, it's leather flaking off. Inside lay a gorgeous Belle Époque ring, with a center diamond surrounded in a swirl by smaller diamonds and sapphires. It reminded her of a fancier version of Jackie's that Frank had designed for her. "It's beautiful."

"It's eighteen-karat gold with platinum beneath the diamonds." Mr. Di Imperiali rose and came closer. "My grandmother loved that ring. It will look *maravigliosa* on you."

"You like my dad's *wonderful* choice better?"

His father raised his hands. "I pick her for you. Didn't I do a good job telling you that's the right one? So I think I can find the right ring, too."

Paula couldn't help laughing. Although he looked serious, she could tell Gennaro's father was holding back a chuckle.

"My father is not going to ask for me." Gennaro removed his great-grandmother's ring from its case and held it in his palm. "I know it's too soon, but I'm not some young fellow anymore. Will you spend the rest of your days with this old grandpa?"

"Say yes and kiss him!" Gennaro's father raised his hands.

"Yes." And she happily obeyed Mr. Di Imperiali's command.

"Congratulations, Mom!" Claire turned to Clark. "They're engaged. It must be the Tuscan air."

He raised his eyebrows at her, then lifted his Lucky Bean Love Potion #9 to his lips and sipped.

Claire took a quick drink of her own frappe and slid into one of the café's outdoor chairs at a small bistro table. "That's awfully fast." Hadn't Mom just been kind of freaked out when Gennaro had dropped down on one knee at the cottage?

"When you know, you know."

Claire looked at her longtime friend, her sweetheart, and sent him an air kiss. "You're right, Mom."

"I did have a favor to ask Clark if he's there."

"We just got our coffees at Lucky Bean and are sitting down outside. Want to hear the horses?" A carriage rolled by with the clip-clop of horse's hooves, and she held the phone out on speaker mode. She turned off the speaker and put the phone back by her ear. "We miss you."

And she really did. When she'd gone off to Montana, she'd delighted in becoming independent and setting up her own place. Funny how you didn't know what you were missing until you lost it. She even missed goofy Jeremy and sweet Mia now, too.

"I miss you, too, honey, but can I please ask Clark a computer thing?"

"Oh, yeah, sure." She handed the cellphone to Clark, who gave her a questioning look.

"Hello, Mrs. Ecker and congratulations." He nodded, sipping his coffee, listening. "So Gennaro's family could use help in setting up a proper website for the farms?"

Clark tapped his fingers on the tabletop like he did when he was thinking about something. “If my colleague, Alyssa Parker, wasn’t pregnant I know she’d want to jump on that, Mrs. Ecker. She did an amazing job for her grandmother, the Evangelist Romelda.”

“Alyssa is pregnant?” Claire squeaked. “When were you gonna tell me?”

His eyebrows lowered, and he shook his head. “I’m thinking I’d have to bring your beautiful daughter over there to help me, though. Maybe take her to check out the botanicals in the countryside? Something for her neuroscience therapeutic oils line.”

She nodded enthusiastically.

“So you’ve already found some things for Claire? Great, I’ll tell her.”

Claire gave him a thumbs up.

“All right then, you speak with the Di Imperialis and see when they’d like to chat with me.”

When Clark handed her the phone, the connection was lost. “Did you hang up on my mom?”

“No. She said she and Gennaro were headed out to watch some of the olive oil being pressed and bottled. She said a quick goodbye and hung up.”

“Without saying goodbye to me?” She pouted. “Who is that woman, and what happened to my mother?”

“Um, I think she has a life besides being your mom. As do my folks, which is why they’re making their move to the mainland. At least it’s not to Italy.”

“She’s not moving to Italy.” Or was she?

Chapter Twenty-Four

Detroit

Paula jammed her spine into the seatback as the jet made a bumpy landing on the tarmac, and she grasped her sweetheart's hand.

"It will be okay." Gennaro assured her, but the luggage rattling in the overhead storage sounded like the contents wanted out.

Soon, though, the plane slowed, and the noises and rumbles dissipated to little wobbles. When the plane fully stopped, she released Gennaro's hand and unfastened her airplane seatbelt. "I can't believe our time in Italy is already over."

"We're back in Michigan. Better turn on our phones."

She removed her iPhone from her pocket and changed it from airplane mode to regular and turned the ringer on. The phone began dinging repeatedly as messages came in. Gennaro's did the same.

"Uh oh," they said simultaneously.

They remained seated as all around them passengers grabbed their belongings and queued up to exit.

"Leo texted the address of the hospital where our new granddaughter will be born." Gennaro punched the air.

Ours. They weren't married yet, but he was already claiming this little baby as his family.

She blinked back tears as she read Claire's message. "Claire says Jeremy is beside himself and isn't communicating with her, but she and Clark are . . . Let me see, she sent this several hours ago, they were near Gaylord, so they should be there in Ann Arbor by now."

"We should scan all the texts and see if anything jumps out."

People looked at them while they removed their luggage from the overhead bins, but Paula stayed focused. Jeremy had texted her that the baby was coming early. That was it from him. Aunt Jackie texted that since the baby was coming early, they'd come down to see her once it was safe. Claire texted that her little niece would be four to five weeks early, but usually infants delivered at that time didn't require intensive care.

"Intensive care? Yikes!" Paula blurted out.

Gennaro's dark eyes widened. "Is she in the neonatal intensive care? Is she okay?"

Paula pressed a hand to her chest. "No, but my daughter gave me a heart attack suggesting she might need that."

"I sent a prayer request to all my family, and Leo sent one earlier, so let us hope for the best."

"Yes." Passengers continued to move forward in the aisles.

"I texted Leo that we will drive over once we get our baggage and pick up our car."

"Thank God we flew out of here and not from up North. I know our plan was to check on Jeremy and Mia before we drove up, but the hospital wasn't in the plans."

"It is now, and it will be okay." Gennaro leaned in and kissed her forehead. "Come on, let us get our things and you call Jeremy, Claire, and Leo while I am driving over there."

"Surely one of them will answer." Her fatigue from the international travel vanished like she'd inhaled five shots of espresso.

They exited the plane and the terminal and picked up their luggage—the last ones circulating on the baggage carousel.

Her phone rang as they were heading for the garage. Jeremy's name flashed on the screen on the incoming call, and she answered. "Hello!"

"Mom! I'm a dad! We have a beautiful little girl."

"Oh my gosh, congratulations!" She grabbed Gennaro's arm and squeezed.

"You're a grandma!"

A surge of joy made her want to jump up and down. "How's Mia? How's baby?"

"She's good. Emergency C-section. The cord was wrapped around the baby's neck, and Mia's blood pressure was up."

"Oh, wow. I'm sorry she had to go through that. But little Eileen is okay too?"

"Yes, good Apgar scores."

An older couple walking by arm-in-arm glanced at them and then exchanged a look, followed by a kiss. *Probably grandparents, too.*

"Hey, let me talk to Mom," Claire said in the background.

"Okay."

"Mom, can you believe Pipsqueak is a daddy now?" Claire sounded as over the moon as Paula felt.

"I'm sure his daughter won't call him Pipsqueak. And at over six feet tall, neither should you."

"Eileen is so cute. She reminds me of Jeremy when he was a baby."

"Send me a picture, please." She stepped aside as a young man pulling an oversized black suitcase steamrolled past.

"Sure."

"Give me my phone back, Sis. Call her on your own phone later." Same old brother-and-sister feuds still going. So much for that.

"Whatever. Talk with you later, Mom."

"When will you and Gennaro be coming to see my little angel?" Jeremy sounded like he'd just finished first in a contest. "She's amazing."

"I'm sure Eileen is the best baby in the world. We're heading outside to the garage now and should be there in—"

Gennaro gently took the phone. "Congratulations, Daddy! I will have us there as quick as I can, under an hour."

Gennaro nodded as Jeremy said something. "Oh, and Jeremy, you tell them I am the grandpa when we come or else they might not let us in, okay?"

When her fiancé handed her the phone, her son had hung up. But then the text message sounded. An image file was attached, and she opened it. Her heart clutched in her chest. She showed the picture of Eileen to Gennaro, and he pulled her into a bear hug.

They got to their vehicle and hurriedly put everything inside. Traffic wasn't bad, and soon they arrived at the hospital. As Gennaro parked, she shook her head. "If I am this excited now, then how am I going to be when I actually see that little girl?"

He turned off the ignition and took her hand. "You will fall in love with her in a way like nothing else—not like our love, not even your kids. It's this kind of love, a generational love that connects you to all those who came before you. A new appreciation for them."

"Wow, I don't know if my little librarian's heart can take all that."

"Your huge Paula heart has lots of room." He leaned in and kissed her. "*Ti amo*. I love you, Grandma Paula."

She kissed him back. "Love you, too, Grandpa Gennaro."

Soon they'd checked through hospital security and were taken to Mia's room. As she entered, Paula spotted the rolling bassinette and sighed in relief that Eileen was not in an incubator. Her son raised his index finger to his lips. Poor exhausted Mia, hair still drenched from labor, lay asleep in the hospital bed, while Jeremy sat beside her.

"Congratulations, son," she whispered.

She stood there, mouth agape, staring at the perfect baby sleeping peacefully in the bassinette.

"You can go see her," Jeremy softly encouraged.

Gennaro waved her forward and accompanied her, holding her elbow as they both peered down at Eileen. She had no eyebrows. Paula tucked her lip in. "Her little ears haven't unfolded yet."

Gennaro pressed a tissue into her hand and she wiped at tears she'd not realized were falling.

"She's early, Mom, but she's got all her toes and fingers and her lungs and heart are doing great."

"She's so beautiful." Claire's picture didn't do her justice. More tears rolled down Paula's cheeks. "Where are Claire and Clark?"

"I told them you were almost here, and there's a limit on who can be in the room. So they went for coffee. They'll see you before they run over to Leo's place."

"Leo is with them, too, right?" Gennaro turned toward the door.

"He left. He said he'll see you all at the farm, and he's getting extra groceries on his way home."

Gennaro squeezed her hand. "We should all have room there. Not like in Italy, but we will have space for everyone."

"If it's a problem, you can go crash at our apartment."

"Thanks, but we will go to the farm—right, Paula?"

Transfixed, she stood by the baby's bassinette. "I don't know if I can ever leave."

"Mom! That's *my* baby."

She looked up to see Gennaro rubbing his face to cover laughter. "I know she's yours but right now I can't get enough of her."

"Grandma Paula, we will get plenty of chances to babysit her later."

Jeremy yawned. "I'm not leaving Mia alone in here tonight. But at some point they will come and put Eileen in the nursery. Claire said she'd stay in here with Mia if I need to leave."

"Gosh, when did labor start? How long have you been here?" Her son had been on an emotional roller coaster today, no doubt.

Her fingers longed to reach out and take the baby from the bassinette and cuddle her. But with her being premature, she wasn't sure if she should or even could.

"Hello folks. This must be Grandma and Grandpa." A slim man, attired in a hospital coat and matching white pants, entered the room, clipboard in hand.

"That is us." Gennaro placed a hand on the bassinette as if protecting Eileen.

"I'm Dr. Joshua Barbish, your granddaughter's first pediatrician." His soft Southern accent placed him as from Virginia or someplace near there.

"Room calls, that's pretty cool." Paula smiled up at the tall young doctor.

"Daddy?" Dr. Barbish took two steps closer to Mia's bed and narrowed his eyes as he looked at Jeremy.

Her son's eyes were fluttering. *Oh my goodness, he's falling asleep.*

The doctor turned toward her. "Ma'am?"

"Yes?"

"I need permission for the exam from Eileen's father—I'm definitely not waking Mommy—she had a rough time earlier."

Gennaro eased his way toward Jeremy and gently touched his shoulder. Her son startled awake, eyes wide.

Dr. Barbish waved at him from the foot of the bed. "Permission to examine my patient?"

Jeremy looked at Mia and shook his head. "She's got to rest. The nurse said you'd be in tomorrow morning."

"Here for Baby, not Mommy." The pediatrician pointed to Eileen, who'd begun to stir, making adorable little squeals.

"Oh," Paula leaned closer. "She's waking up."

"Yes, go ahead." Jeremy leaned closer to Mia and kissed her forehead. She must be somewhat awake, because she smiled.

The doctor went to the bassinette and began his exam. Eileen's eyes popped open just like Jeremy's had and she fussed, this time a little louder than before. The doctor, with one hand on the baby's chest, turned and pointed to a stack of tiny diapers. "You want to do the honors of the first diaper change, Grandma?"

Paula quickly grabbed the itty-bitty disposable diaper and brought it over. The doctor had removed the side tabs, and Paula lifted Eileen's tiny legs and set the diaper aside. She took the new one and diapered the tiny baby. "She's so little."

"Over six pounds, so we're proud of Mommy and Baby for that good weight, even though she's a month early." Dr. Barbish grinned.

Paula pulled the green infant gown so it covered Eileen's small pink feet. She was already in love with this little cutie.

"You want to hold her, Grandma?" The doctor cocked his head at her.

"Oh, I'm afraid to lift her."

He pointed to a nearby chair. "I'll bring her to you."

"It's okay, Mom. We got to hold her earlier, and I didn't drop her. Not even once."

Gennaro chuckled. "At least not on her head."

The doctor shook his head. "No dropping on head or any other body part." He passed Eileen to Paula, and she cradled her warm body in her arms. "She's so absolutely beautiful."

"Just like her mom." Jeremy stretched.

Gennaro kissed her and placed his hand on the baby's head. "Beautiful like Nonna Paula, too."

"Nonna Paula, that's going to be easier for everyone, than Grandma." Jeremy had given her this new grandchild, and Gennaro was sharing his seven wonderful grandkids with her, too. She was blessed beyond imagining.

Paula pulled Eileen closer and rocked her. She kissed her tiny forehead. The baby opened her eyes and began to fuss, her little mouth forming a rosebud shape. "Oh, I know what that means."

As soon as the infant wailed in hunger, her mom woke.

Dr. Barbish waved at Mia. "Hello there, Mommy, your baby is doing great. And now she wants to nurse."

To her surprise, the young man lifted Eileen from her. Gennaro backed away as the pediatrician presented the baby to her mother. He made waving motions to her and Gennaro. "Time to give Mommy and Baby some privacy."

Something about seeing Mia getting ready to do what mothers had done since the beginning of time made Paula love her daughter-in-law even more.

Thank God they'd gotten back in time for these precious early moments. More family, more love, new beginnings.

Six months earlier she'd faced the fact that she'd be alone—widowed and her children gone. She'd hardened her heart to accept the reality of her life situation.

Now, God had filled her empty nest to overflowing, and she'd thank Him every day. With Gennaro by her side, they'd share family on two continents, blessed beyond measure.

THE END

Acknowledgements

I thank God for His provision for me to write this story, and all of my other stories! Much appreciation to my son, Clark J. Pagels, who in particular helped with elements about Italy. Clark traveled to Italy and we also researched and watched specific shows set there. He's a great brainstorming partner. Much thanks, too, to my husband, Jeffrey D. Pagels, for his support. I am grateful for my critique partner, Melissa Main, who is also a professional editor and author. Shelia Stovall, a wonderful author, did a fantastic job critiquing this story, too. Much appreciation to Ivy Sterling Lasley, copy editor.

Garden Cottage Promo and Review Team:
A big "thank you" to Beta Reader: Robin Auten. Kudos to Early Advance Readers: Rory Lemond, Angela Maynard, Eileen H. Byron, Sharon Robarts Kirby and Elaine Sapp.

Advance Readers: Much thanks to Gail Mundy who made some great catches. Thank you to early ARC readers Diana L. Flowers, Susan Johnson, Angie Ford, Melissa Henderson, Linda Thomas, Julia Wilson, Connie Saunders, Paula Ecker Shreckhise, Revée Kraszewski, Sarah Lynne Dupree, and Andrea Selaty. I'm grateful to Jennifer Devon Hibdon, Sherry Moe, Terry Dean Felix, and Betti Mace for reading a final manuscript copy. Much appreciation to Mary Winzenburg for feedback about early knee replacement and to Sonja Hoeke Nishimoto, who caught an important error! Thank you to Angie Ford, Joy Ellis and Teresa Mathews who were also on the team.

Appreciation to Early paperback reader, Brenda Murphree and Audio early reader, Tania Plunkett.

Thank you to my Pagels Pals group members for your support. Much appreciation also to Avid Christian Fiction Readers Facebook group and co-administrator Martha Artyomenko Hurley who have been so helpful on this journey! The Addicted to Mackinac Island Facebook group is a great source of information about visiting the island and has been a wonderful help to me.

Names borrowed: Paula Ecker's name is from Paula Ecker Shreckhise and Jeremy is her real-life son's name. Dr. Joshua Barbish is the future name of my friend's pal, who will be entering medical school in the near future. Debbie Nabozny really does own a beautiful rental house in St. Ignace and is a friend of mine. Linda Borton Sorensen is one of the co-administrators of the "Addicted to Mackinac Island" Facebook group, formerly worked on the island with the police for years. John Hubel is also a co-administrator and is a locksmith and assists in island ministries.

Tamara Tomac, manager, and Mary Jane Barnwell, owner, of Island Bookstore really can be found there in the summer. Much thanks to these delightful ladies for hosting me for book signings and for keeping my books on their shelves!

That cover! Wow, what a blessing to have multi-award-winning watercolorist Lorna Bricco, of Bricco Designs, create the cover artwork! Thank you to Small Point Bed & Breakfast owners, Christina and Brian Findley, for usage of this beautiful cottage for our cover inspiration! Small Point, which is white not yellow, is located on Main Street on the east side of Mackinac Island.

Author's Notes

Inspiration Songs: "Fear Is Not My Future" by Brandon Lake and Chandler Moore and "Goodbye Yesterday" by Elevation Rhythm.

I am certainly no great gardener, although I enjoy it. I was brought up with a family garden providing our vegetables. That same massive plot where we grew our own potatoes (and many other vegetables) is now used to produce potatoes at a corporate level for Frito Lay. It makes me smile to eat a potato chip and wonder if any of the potatoes may have been grown on my Williams' great-grandparents' farm in the Eastern Upper Peninsula of Michigan!

The microclimate on Mackinac Island, nestled between two large land masses and surrounded by water, combined with the long summer days, makes for good growing conditions. Since it sits atop limestone bedrock, however, the soil needs frequent amendment. Mackinac Island's beautiful horses contribute to a thriving manure market.

Mental illness in the elderly is often overlooked. Mrs. Parsons, in this story, doesn't have dementia—she's having psychotic episodes. I was a psychologist for twenty-seven years. Our country is failing our American people who suffer from emotional and mental illness. Unlike most people, who may never get help, Edna in this story gets (and accepts) appropriate treatment. Sadly, many do not, and there are terrible consequences.

When Gennaro and his wife started their family the average child born per Italian woman had dropped significantly to almost only one child per mother. I was quite shocked to learn this. My son told me about that and of course I had to google-check him! And he was correct.

The inspiration for the Gennaro character came from a chance meeting, after a book signing, with an intriguing very well-dressed dark-haired youngish man who was very kind when I slopped my ice cream cone all over my dress. My friend, Sherry, was with me and got to witness the whole thing. It's funny the people or experiences that will inspire a character or a story!

Clark Jeffries' name was originally borrowed from my son, Clark Jeffrey Pagels, when I needed a replacement name in a previous book. Also, in the Mackinac Straits' Lumberjacks Series, I have Tom Jeffries as a hero, his name inspired by my husband, Jeffrey. So the Clark Jeffries, Jr., in this story is a fictional descendant of that character.

Every season on Mackinac Island the opening schedules change somewhat. I took some fictional license with Lucky Bean being open for Claire at the end of April. Carolyn-May Fairbanks and her husband run this wonderful coffee shop on Market Street. When planning a trip to the island and wondering what is opening, a good source of info is the Mackinac Island Tourism Bureau website to check season updates.

Editor's Note

By Ivy Lasley

As the editor of this novel and one of Carrie's longtime readers, I was delighted to see my last name woven into the story in the character of Aunt Jackie (widow of Victor Lasley). My husband, Corey Lasley, descends from one of Mackinac Island's early settlers, Samuel C. Lasley, who arrived at Fort Michilimackinac in 1796 with a battalion of American troops aiming to take the island from the British. He and his wife, Rachel, soon settled on the island where they raised a large family and later established the island's first boarding house, known as the Lasley House.

The Lasley sons all married Native American women, primarily from the Ojibwa (Chippewa) and Odawa tribes, and were involved in the fur trade and pioneering endeavors of the region. Members of the family also held notable roles in the community, including the island's first postmaster and U.S. marshal. Samuel and many of his descendants are buried on the island today.

Although the Lasley House no longer stands, the inclusion of a Lasley bed-and-breakfast passed down through generations is especially meaningful to us.

Mackinac Cottages Series – Book 1

Selah Awards 2nd Place Winner in Women's Fiction

Three generations of women unexpectedly head out to the family's cottage at the Straits of Mackinac for a small-town Michigan summer together. Jaycie begins an Archeology internship on Mackinac Island. Her mother, Tamara, takes a break from teaching kindergarteners. And her grandmother, Dawn, struggles with a decision to sell her successful travel agency and possibly retire.

Each has her own journey to pursue during this short respite time from "normal" life. One of them has a secret that will change all of their lives. Can she make this one special summer to remember or will all be devastated? Faith for family and friends will be tested, with some finally able to put the past behind them and begin anew. (Set in 2018, pre-Pandemic.)

Mackinac Cottages Series – Book 2

Selah Award Second Place Winner in Women's Fiction!

Out of options, Rachel Dunmara "camps out" at her deceased Grandmother's cottage on Mackinac Island. Next door, her childhood nemesis, Jack Welling, is overseeing his family's remodeling of their home on the West Bluff. When Rachel's new boss, at a local coffee shop, pushes her to work as Jack's assistant, for her second job, can they mend their rift?

Kareen Parker, widowed in the past year, returns to the island to share long-held information with her son and to transition ownership of her resort to her son. Her grandson befriends Rachel, who was banned by her family from associating with the Parkers. In a summer full of secrets that are finally revealed, can three families be healed?

Mackinac Cottages Series – Book 3

Newly minted computer science graduate, Alyssa, has plans to obtain work and finally live independently with her son. Summer programming for Alyssa's son, who has Aspergers, is tossed when his biological father and new wife, an attorney, insist on summer visitation. With her plans completely upended, Alyssa pursues a job on Mackinac Island with the hopes of acquiring an internship. Young widower, Carter, who has suffered the tragic loss of his wife, is working remotely on Mackinac Island as a computer programmer and hires Alyssa as nanny for his baby girl.

Susan, a social worker with unknown links to Alyssa, is also Carter's former group therapist. Susan consults at a Mackinac Island summer-long retreat as she mulls retirement options. With Alyssa's estranged grandmother a famous television evangelist, Susan's mother the senior-most congressional representative, and a mysterious artist all adding their dramatic flair to the Mackinac Island mix—what could go wrong?

Associated Story

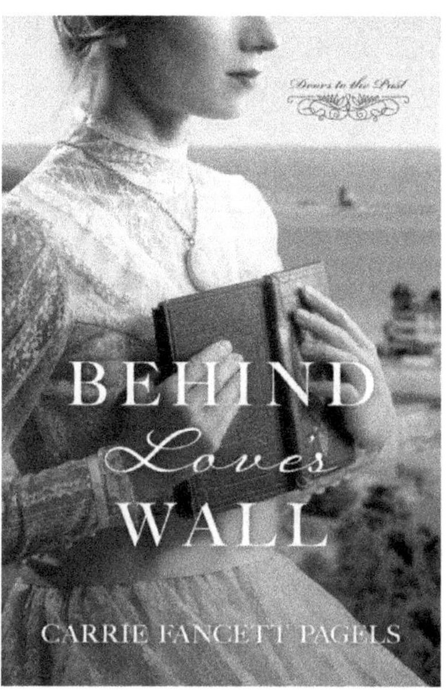

Behind Love's Wall novel (Barbour, November 2021)

Two successful women, a hundred and twenty years apart, build walls to protect their hearts. Modern-day Willa, a successful interior decorator, is chosen to consult for the Grand Hotel's possible redesign. She discovers a journal detailing the struggles of a young woman, Lily—which reveals dark secrets. The renowned singer wasn't who she pretended to be. As Willa reaches out to Lily's descendant, a charismatic and prominent landscape artist, she lets down her guard. Should she share the journal with him, or once again erect a wall as she struggles to redesign both the Grand and her life?

In the 2020 part of the novel, modern-day characters include some from the Mackinac Cottages Series Book 1 - *Butterfly Cottage* and Book 2 - *Lilac Cottage.*

Biographies

CARRIE FANCETT PAGELS, Ph.D., served twenty-seven-year career as a school and clinical psychologist. Although Carrie misses being a psychologist, she brings her expertise, as well as her faith, into each story she writes. She is now the multi-award-winning and bestselling author of over twenty-five Christian fiction books. She has two series set on Mackinac Island—a historical series and a contemporary—and a third series set at the Straits of Mackinac. Her novel *My Heart Belongs on Mackinac Island* won the Maggie Award and was chosen as a Romantic Times Top Pick. Her book *The Fruitcake Challenge* was a Selah Award finalist and was chosen by Women's World Magazine as a recommended Michigan Christmas Read selection.

Carrie grew up in Michigan's beautiful Eastern Upper Peninsula. Although she now resides with her family in Virginia, she vacations most summers at the Straits of Mackinac—where many of her stories are set. She has a new granddaughter to spend time with and spoil! She's a tea addict with an overflowing tea cart. The family dog, an Aussie Kelpie, tries to walk his granny daily and often succeeds.

Social Media:
You can find Carrie on her author page on Facebook, on Instagram, goodreads, BookBub, Pinterest, LinkedIn, and don't forget to 'Like' her Amazon author page!

LORNA BRICCO is a high energy artist with a love of vintage, decorating, painting and family! Bricco's Art & Design became her favorite job after retiring from the State of Michigan in 2021. Lorna's watercolors are all originals. Lorna also creates cards, ornaments, jewelry, mugs & tumblers and more using her original artwork! Lorna's heart goes into all her artwork. She's a multi-award-winning artist and a popular artist at events across the Mid-West. She's on multiple social media outlets. Please visit her Bricco's Design page on Facebook!

Thank you for being a reader!!!

If you enjoyed this novel,

a review is very much appreciated!

www.ingramcontent.com/pod-product-compliance
Lightning Source LLC
LaVergne TN
LVHW010651110826
845149LV00014B/3024

* 9 7 9 8 9 9 2 8 2 6 7 5 3 *